The One, the Many

The One, the Many

A Novel of Constantine the Great,
Athanasius of Alexandria,
and the Battle to Unify the Roman Empire
and the Christian Church

Tim J. Young

SunWard Books, Sugar Land

THE ONE, THE MANY

SunWard Books, Sugar Land, TX 77479
www.sunwardbooks.com

Cover illustration: Detail from *The Battle of Milvian Bridge*, by Giulio Romano, from the collection of the Apostolic Palace of the Vatican City. (Source: Wikimedia Commons)

ISBN 978-0-61-594687-0

This book was published in the United States of America.

SunWard Books is a division of EuZōn Media
www.euzonmedia.com

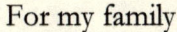
For my family

Contents

Letter of Theophilus

THEOPHILUS, MONK POSTULANT, new to the rigors of monastic life

To Abba Pachomius, true athlete of the Christ, founder of Tabennisi and surrounding monasteries, where men strive to know the one God and grow in virtue

Venerable Father, I rest in good faith.

I have finally completed the work you requested nearly a year ago, shortly after Arnobius of Carthage came to the monastery seeking respite and new life. What follows, however poorly crafted, is the fruit of your commission.

In those days, you asked me to meet with Arnobius in order to learn about what had transpired between Athanasius, the bishop of Alexandria, and Constantine, the late emperor of Rome.

At the time of our conversation, nearly one year had passed since the Lenten Disturbance in Alexandria, which Athanasius wrote about in his encyclical letter to the bishops of Egypt, Libya, and the Thebaid, as well as to other men of rank in all the major cities of the world. Abba, you are familiar with these more recent events. You know how the usurper Gregory of Cappadocia now rules the ancient See of Alexandria with the backing of the emperor Constantius and his army.

How different the present emperor is from his father, Constantine! Whereas the father heroically fought to liberate the Empire from tyranny and the Church from disunity, the son despotically fetters the Empire with violence and Christ's body with heresy and ongoing persecution.

Abba, you know how the fight first began among those in the Church. Arius suddenly appeared with Eusebius of Nicomedia and many other bishops taking aim at the saving message of our faith. I am afraid these same men have acted with more consideration for personal gain and victory than the noble aspiration to advance the light and life of the Word made flesh. Fortunately, men such as Athanasius of Alexandria have carried on the battle to defend the true nature of the Christ. I can only hope that justice and truth will ultimately conquer every injustice and lie.

As for the following account, I have gathered most of its material from the narrative recollection of Arnobius, intimate of both Constantine and Athanasius, and from discussions we had arising from one issue or another. I have rounded it out, however, with several other sources. Among them are valuable manuscripts of the late bishop of Caesarea, the other Eusebius, who famously wrote a history of the Church up to our time, and more recently, a life of Constantine. I also made use of a tract delineating the decline and fall of the persecuting emperors written by that fiery man Lactantius, the tutor of Crispus, the first son of Constantine and Minervina.

As for its form, I have taken the liberty to organize my work in a manner more consistent with the rules governing the telling of a tale. As a whole, I trust I have composed it in a style more desirable to the heart and mind. I leave that for you, however, to judge.

I began this history shortly after I had interviewed Arnobius in the spring of 340. But as you must know, Abba, research and writing demands time. Furthermore, I had to travel to Alexandria in order to consult the above-mentioned sources, among others, and to inquire into the well-being of the Church there as you asked me to do. I hope you are pleased with how long I have taken and pardon me for any delay.

I trust I shall see you soon. Until then, I pray that you will be content with perusing Arnobius' story and the brief report added to the end.

In closing, I ask that you intercede for me, dear Abba. May the grace of the God of our Lord Jesus Christ be with you and the others at the monastery.

Written from Alexandria, just before the holy season of Lent, on the last day of Mechir, the sixth day prior to the Calends of March, in the consulships of Constantius and Constans, during the prefecture of Longinus of Nicaea, prefect of Egypt

Prologue

Arnobius of Carthage

340 A.D.

The Cell in Tabennisi

The Dawning of Day

Theophilus: WHEN I FIRST SAT DOWN with Arnobius, I sensed he was afraid of speaking with me about what had occurred. I saw fear lurking in his eyes.

Grayish-blue light, shifting to pink, orange, and a pale yellow, and throughout the morning to a luminescent brilliance absent all color, shone through the one opening of my cell. We shared an earthenware pitcher of water drawn from the well and a brown loaf of coarse bread. I sat on a stack of reed mats, my work from the days and weeks gone by that supplied the needs of the brothers inside the monastery and assisted the poor outside. My back rested against the dusty mud and stubble wall. Arnobius sat opposite me, hunched upon a simple wooden stool—mine when alone. I sat before him a young man; he, by contrast, was old. His hair was salty white, though a sprinkling of black remained. His face betrayed the lines of years gone by, his eyes a fullness secured by endurance. Soon, I thought, I would be as he is.

What was Arnobius' fear? It certainly wasn't that of a small boy who is afraid of the dark or a loud clap of thunder or the creepy fellow who lives at the end of a long row of crowded apartments—though I suppose these fears in a boy are the lengthy foreshadows of greater fears to come. Rather, it was as though our proceedings might cause Arnobius to lose the peace he had recently come to possess. Therefore, he hesitated, as I did.

Arnobius' life had not been free of turmoil. As with most mortals liable to change, he had suffered considerably, though not so much in his body as in his soul. Although his hope as a young man had been to remain aloof, tranquilly pursuing the steady way of philosophy, Arnobius had found himself plunged over the course of time into the world of change, of the many, of that flux which Heraclitus of Ephesus describes as a madly flowing river, always rushing, never the same from day to day. *A man cannot step into the same river twice. We are and we are not.* How true.

And what was Arnobius' river? It was life and death; it was finding love and losing it; it was the nature of the world and the nature of his own soul; it was he himself and all men—emperors and bishops, philosophers and priests, and the mob of ordinary men as well, always surging, always swirling, always crowding, pressing, flooding!

Sitting before me, Arnobius had finally found the shore of this madly flowing river. It was Tabennisi, the monastery. Now his one determination was to keep to it. God in heaven you know as much! He desired nothing more than stability, peace. Yet this is the problem, Abba. The river forever threatens the shore with flooding waters. Even so, I dutifully plunged in.

"Arnobius," I began, "what was it that first brought on Athanasius' exile?"

Briefly, he told me about Tyre. Indeed, it was in all too brief a manner. The answer was quite to the point, as if I had posed a question requiring a simple affirmation or negation with little explanation.

"Arnobius," I said, "I understand that Athanasius was called to Tyre by command of the emperor. But why?"

Again, sparing words, he replied, "There were bishops who wanted to depose him."

This was not quite the intended point of my question, which I meant to elicit more information regarding the emperor and why he, rather than the bishops, had insisted upon the council at Tyre in the first place. Nevertheless, hoping he might open up, I encouraged Arnobius to proceed.

"Did the bishops succeed?" I asked.

"No."

Ah yes, I sighed. My role would be that of a surgeon extracting some tinyish object from the taut skin of a soldier. A few grunts. Little blood. The whole procedure done with before I could call down a blessing—or curse! I needed more.

"Why, then, was there the urgent desire for a conference with the emperor?"

Arnobius didn't immediately respond with words. Instead, the features of his face tightened, expressing, I gathered, something of the past.

"What?" I begged.

After a moment's hesitation, he finally opened up. "We encountered Emperor Constantine along the main road leading into *Nova Roma*, the New Rome."

"Go on," I urged.

"We were tired, dead tired, having just arrived from a long and dangerous journey by sea. Our destination lay just beyond the Forum of Constantine, and sorely we walked on toward the newly constructed Imperial Palace where Athanasius hoped to speak with the emperor."

He paused.

"What happened?" I prodded.

"It seems we were favored by God that day, Theophilus."

"How so?"

At first, he didn't answer, and for my part, I worried. I watched him as he shifted position on the stool and adjusted his *lebiton*, the linen garment worn by all the monks.

Then he said, "Just before passing through the gates of the wall Constantine had built west of the city, we heard a tremendous rumbling from behind. All of us turned to look. There was a massive cloud of dust rising from some distance away."

"What was it?"

"At first we didn't know," he explained, "but soon it became clear."

"It's the emperor!" shouted a gruff looking man, who was also making his way into the city with an old, wooden cart rolling along after an old, brown mule.

"The emperor?" asked Athanasius, hoping for confirmation.

The man, however, didn't answer. He was calming his mule, which had become unnerved at the sound of the emperor's entourage.

By then I recognized that it was in fact the emperor. I had often seen him in similar circumstances and had been privy to such a party. It was clear they'd been hunting. There was his standard, the *labarum*, and there were his advisors, mostly churchmen, and his personal bodyguard, the *candidati*, riding high upon their horses, the company of handpicked men chosen from the *scholae palatinae*. Scores more followed.

Athanasius asked me if it was indeed Constantine. I said yes. Just as soon as I confirmed it, he turned back toward the crowd of men moving our way, his gaze fixed in stubborn determination.

As the emperor approached, the roadway grew all but empty. Someone called out, "Make way for Emperor Constantine!"

For a moment, there was a group of small boys playing with a weathered, goatskin ball, but soon they moved along with the gruff man who was just beyond, enticing his mule to pull the old, wooden cart off to the side of the road. Aside from these few, all passersby shifted to the edge in order to give way to Constantine—all but for us.

This fact became evident to the emperor's guard as they approached. "Clear the way!" they commanded.

But Athanasius, short and stout like a typical Copt, would not do it. Rather than move aside, he boldly stepped toward the middle of the road.

In response, a few of the guard drew *spathae*, long swords, in order to demand our removal. I grew afraid for Athanasius. He was bold, yes, a man of great courage, yes, but against the emperor of Rome and his guard it was madness.

Now Constantine drew ahead riding a great, white Libyan steed. I could see him speaking with his men.

"Who's that man?" he demanded.

"Whoever it is," one said, "he's not where he belongs, Lord!"

A few rode forward suggesting they put him in his place, knock him down, introduce his insolent face to the dust of the paving stones. Constantine, however, ordered them to draw back. Reluctantly, they did.

Soon Constantine rode up to us inspecting each one of us in turn. When he reached me, our eyes locked. It was then that he recognized me. I felt it. He stopped the sauntering of his horse for a moment and studied me closely, expressing neither pleasure nor displeasure.

Moments later the guard advanced not willing to leave Constantine alone. They drew nearer to Athanasius who was now stationed dead center in the road, shouting.

"What's the bugger want," barked one of the candidati, "intimacy with the tip of my sword?" They all laughed and surrounded the bishop.

Meanwhile, Constantine stared at me wondering, I imagined, what had become of me. It had been years since we'd last seen each other—nearly a decade.

Finally, Athanasius' strong voice beckoned his gaze away from me. Loudly, the bishop called out, "I request an audience with the emperor!"

Again, the soldiers sniggered, preparing to act.

"I demand judgment!" he shouted, ignoring their mockery.

Constantine rode forward dispersing his men. He was not one to ignore a plea for justice.

"Who's asking?" he demanded.

Bravely, Athanasius offered, "It is I, Athanasius, the bishop of Alexandria!"

At last, there was a moment of recognition as Constantine and his men halted just shy of the bishop.

There I stopped Arnobius. Foolishly, perhaps, but it's what I did, Abba.

I was bothered—simultaneously disturbed and fascinated—by why a bishop of the Church would beg judgment on ecclesial affairs from the emperor of Rome, that same office both pagan and Christian that had all too often persecuted the Church. In the recent past emperors had driven her shepherds and holy liturgy underground. When that wasn't enough, they had put the faithful to death. My own uncle had been a *martyr*, a witness, in Palestine because he refused to offer the small token of sacrifice to the demons of old Rome. Now, the Arian Constantius harries the Church in Alexandria and elsewhere, imposing counterfeit bishops and foreign doctrines. True, his father Constantine was positively different—vastly so!—but why would he, the emperor of Rome, be in the place to judge a bishop in a matter having to do with the discipline or doctrine of the Church? I put the question to Arnobius.

For a moment, he resumed his former silence, and I was concerned that his speech would end. Thankfully, I was wrong.

"To explain," he said, "I have to go back many years."

Eagerly, I conceded.

Book One

Constantine the Tribune

November 297 to March 302 A.D.

One: Along the Road

November 297 A.D.

I REMEMBER THE FIRST TIME I saw Constantine. I trembled.

Following him was an army, steadily marching, thousands of men dressed for battle with packs on backs and *caligae* on feet, hobnailed sandals, drumming the ground metrically. *Clip-clop, clip-clop.* The ground shook. They were on to the hunt, chanting, moving along as they did nearly every day in parade drill. With them was a crowd of supply wagons and hangers-on and far more animals. Beside Constantine rode the emperor Diocletian clad in bone white and Tyrean purple, his cape fastened with a golden brooch just above his right shoulder. He'd been fighting his whole life, was weathered, and once again, he smelled the scent of blood.

There, next to my father, I stood watching. I felt afraid. I felt exhilarated. Before me were Constantine and Diocletian riding through the immortal city of Alexandria, fame of Egypt, and indeed glory of the whole world.

My pedagogue, a Greek slave called Tyrannio, first told me of Alexandria when I was a small boy in grammar school, back when I had a big heart and a mind composed mostly of imagination. Perhaps I was then nine or ten.

"Alexandria," he said, "was founded by Alexander of Macedon some six-hundred years ago."

I smile. Alexander had been a hero to me—a Hercules, a Ulysses, an Aeneas, or better yet, he was like Hannibal of Carthage, who drove thirty-seven elephants over the snowy Alps in order to wreak havoc on Rome. His *daemon*—a personal spirit—drove Alexander to adventure and conquest. He claimed so himself. Later, my admiration for the Conqueror waned. As I came to desire a settled life devoid of adventure, I came to suspect Alexander just as I suspected other men.

"Then," Tyrannio explained, "hundreds and hundreds of years ago, inspired by a vision of a venerable old man with very white hair—Alexander claimed it was Homer—the Conqueror fixed the boundaries of Alexandria along the sea to the fore, with the island called Pharos just offshore, and the immensity of Lake Mareotis some distance behind. Afterwards, Alexander reeled off marching once more to conquer the whole world, never to see his beloved city again."

Ptolemy, Alexander's successor, gave shape to Alexandria. Then, from a small Egyptian fishing village and sometimes home to pirates, it became a *cosmopolis*, a world-city. He and his chief architect Dinocrates of Rhodes conceived of a rational city, a *metropolis*, built from scratch on measured grid, reflecting divine wisdom on high as well as making space for the inevitability of human sprawl below—Egyptian Copts, Greek Macedonians, Persians, Arabians, Indians, Jews, and eventually Romans from every province. In time, blessed by the god Osarapis, the city would surpass Nicomedia in Bithynia, Antioch in Syria, Carthage in Africa, and I daresay it would grow as large and become as great as Rome.

I'm sure you know, Theophilus, how Alexandria is a center of trade. It has two magnificent harbors separated by a causeway leading from the mainland to Pharos Island. Sailors and merchants from every nation make voyage to Alexandria guided by its towering lighthouse, some four hundred feet high, attracted like moths to a fire by opportunity. You can make millions in every quarter of the city—the Rhacotis Quarter in the westernmost reaches, the Brucheum and Royal Quarters midway, and the Jewish Quarter to the east, where the light of the sun first falls on Alexandria every day. Each quarter has its own markets, each its own character, and each is a mine for those searching for wealth.

"There's far more!" exclaimed my pedagogue, full of enthusiasm. Ever since Ptolemy established Alexandria's renowned library replete with thousands of manuscripts from around the world, it has been home to men seeking the wisdom of philosophy and has served as inspiration to great feats of learning both profane and divine. Tyrannio had me memorize the greatest achievements of all. Early on there was Euclid who measured squares and circles and cubes and spheres. He gave us the rules and tools to measure things on earth and things among the stars—geometry and astronomy. Sometime later Eratosthenes measured the circumference of our globe with just the sun and a stick. Later Ptolemy mapped the heavens above and the world below, arguing that the celestial spheres and wandering planets travel about the earth in perfect Euclidean circles. By contrast, Aristarchus saw the same in opposite manner as did the Pythagoreans of old. He envisioned the earth, the planets, and the stars whirling around the fiery sun. But this is Alexandria—argument and counter-argument paving the way, let's hope, to better understanding.

Tyrannio also informed me that Alexandria was home to the Ptolemaic pharaohs down to the very last one before Rome came to rule. The last was the most tragic. She was Cleopatra who, rather than allowing Octavian to parade her in humiliating triumph, took her own life by means of the poison of an asp. After her death, Rome ruled Egypt. Consequently, on and off again Alexandria has been home to political discontent fueled by the love of freedom and greed.

And so, Theophilus, there was the march of a Roman army before me and my father, and the resolved determination of the emperor and Constantine set upon restoring the breadbasket of the Nile to Roman rule.

That day, when I first laid eyes upon him, I saw Constantine thundering through Alexandria with Diocletian and his well-disciplined army in order to subdue the rebellious usurper Lucius Domitius Domitianus.

Domitius had rebelled nearly a half year before during the heat of summer. Taking advantage of the news of imperial defeat by the Persians and using the pretext of heavy Roman taxation, Domitius had himself proclaimed emperor by will of all the people of Alexandria and Egypt. In truth, it had been more the wealthy few who had declared for him. Affluent Greeks and other wealthy Egyptians had never cared much for Roman rule.

When Rome finally showed up hunting for Domitius, the latter was hiding somewhere beyond Alexandria in the dry Egyptian countryside with his own personally funded band of men. Poor man! Now that the emperor had come, he scurried off like a frightened weasel upon seeing a pack of wild dogs.

"We must retreat!" he bawled upon leaving the city. "But we'll return!"

It was all bluster. Domitius and his men fled Alexandria with the wind, flying toward the Nitrian Desert deep into *Aegyptus Iovia*.

Of note, the wild dogs in pursuit were two. The first was Diocletian, emperor of the East, who had securely ruled the Roman Empire for fifteen years after violently dispatching his own predecessor Aper in order to end fifty years of bloody civil war and assassination. The other was the tribune Constantine, *my* Constantine, son of Constantius Chlorus, caesar of the West and second in command to Maximian, the western emperor.

Behind him, the weasel Domitius had left an even poorer specimen to defend Alexandria. This was the man called Aurelius Achilleus, the Golden Achilles, a man who lived without pity for others—a glutton, a drunk, a lecher, and a leach. Presently, he was hiding in the palace complex just north of the Brucheum. No matter. Diocletian figured he would leave him cowering for the moment, guarded by a small contingent of men in order to ensure he wouldn't imitate Domitius in flight. He'd be back, and Aurelius Achilleus knew it and trembled.

As for me, I was in Alexandria with my father, Buteo. He was there tending to established business and hoping as always to find more. That's how he had earned his nickname Buteo, the Buzzard. Like a bird of prey or a scavenger, he was always looking for profit.

The olive groves and vineyards of our estate near Carthage are the source of our family business, Theophilus, which is in wine and olive oil, though we mostly deal in the latter. At the time, when I stood in Alexandria watching Constantine and Diocletian pass by, we had business in every corner of the Empire, north and south, east and west. We were wealthy. Yet Buteo never quite saw it that way. Nor did Mother. There was always some gain to make somewhere and accordingly something to do. There were contacts to establish, plans to make, trade to direct, or records to write. The business we had was never enough. Therefore, when Buteo caught wind in Carthage of the rebellion in Alexandria and Diocletian's plans to reconquer Egypt, my father immediately sailed from Carthage armed with profit-yielding plans and me, his son.

I am my father's eldest son. My father always said that I would bring a lot of wealth and prestige to our family. Early on, I promised him I would. Then I was hesitant. In the end, I suppose I have.

Buteo claimed I was named after the Arnus River in Italy that flows down from the Apennines through the province of Tuscia et Umbria. We had business there in Florentia and Pisae and in Luca just a hair to the north. We also had distant relatives, he claimed, though I've never met one.

"Why the Arnus?" I asked him once when I was a little boy.

He beamed with pleasure, saying, "Arnobius, tell me about the Arnus River."

I told him I knew nothing about it. "Is it in Africa?" I guessed.

"Pah!" he exclaimed. "We have only a few driveling streams in our province. And besides, the Arnus is superior to all of ours put together."

"Why then?"

"It's self-evident," he boasted. "Someday you'll match the river's bountiful magnificence."

Whatever the case, Buteo took me to Alexandria because my Greek was as good as my native Latin, and because the interpreter he usually hired had suddenly died. "He'll come," he explained to Mother, half-asking, half-declaring, "because he's intelligent, and so he can interpret for me." She nodded. "He's a smart one, but it's possible he's *too* smart. He always has his nose in a book. He hasn't shown interest in love since his infatuation with that young slave girl." My father agreed. "That's why he should go. Alexandria will wake him up to living once more. It'll attach his mind to the pleasures of real life instead of useless theories."

Despite the rhetoric, my father was proud of my learning up to a point. I was educated in Carthage in the manner usual among those with means. Early on, I mastered reading, writing, and arithmetic, and memorized all the myths and tales. From the age of fourteen, after a thorough training in grammar and logic, I studied with the *rhetor* Proteus, learning to speak publicly and mastering Roman law. The goal was public life. That, of course, is not to say that I myself was personally interested in politics. Nevertheless, my father was, and so I was too, I suppose. I was then fifteen nearing sixteen.

"Arnobius, you'll bring much wealth and prestige to the family," my father declared to me when we first landed in Alexandria.

"Yes," I responded dutifully.

At the time, however, I wasn't interested in wealth and prestige. I had been some years before, but not then. Then, I yearned *to know*. I wanted to pursue philosophy, the most recent field of study with Proteus the rhetor.

At the early age of fifteen I had already had enough of money and rank-climbing in Carthage, shuttling back and forth between our townhouse in the city and our ample estate just outside, the latter replete with a large villa, green vineyards, dusty olive groves, grazing cattle, bleating sheep, and more than enough slaves to keep me idle. I stuffed my life with social engagements and the finest clothing derived from the latest fashion. There were food and wine enough to last several lifetimes. As for entertainment, I went to the races that no one ever definitively won, cheered on the gladiators who always had one more man to conquer, and attended the most recent theatrical productions that dragged on and on, one after the other, festival after festival.

Beyond all this, there was my doting mother who always fretted about the allegedly insecure future. "You must work hard to secure your life, Arnobius!"

"Yes, Mother," I promised.

Therefore, I would pursue education to acquire a position; I would use the position to earn more money and prestige; and I'd leverage them to … what?

That's what I wanted to know, Theophilus. What was the goal, the *telos*, of this mad cycle of earning to live and living to earn? Mine—ours—was a frivolous life. I could see that. I felt it. Consequently, more than anything, I desired to throw myself upon the steady way of philosophy aimed at the Absolute, the One. I wished not only to study wisdom but also *to be* a philosopher, to both know what is and to act wisely.

For this reason, I was excited to be in Alexandria. Although I didn't let my father know, as it had nothing to do with profit making, I hoped to visit one or two of the famous schools of philosophy near the Museum and even, if I could slip away, attend a lecture. As it happened, though, it was a hope dashed upon the rocks of reality, a one that would have to await fulfillment.

"If we are lucky," Buteo went on, "and the gods grant us favor, then we'll land an appointment in the imperial administration."

By "we," he quite simply meant *me*. Politics. Connections. Money. I knew this simple equation before I could divide a penny into a hundred parts. I would find a position in the Empire's vast bureaucracy as rhetorician, speechmaker, panegyrist, or lawyer. Then I would climb as if to the heights of Mount Olympus. I wasn't exactly sure how it would happen, and I don't know if my father was either, but *he* was Buteo, and this meant he was nevertheless positive, an optimist. We would somehow find a way to climb. At the very least, we would make contacts, and contacts lead to—

Forgive me, Theophilus, enough!

"But what if they don't come?" I asked Buteo, referring to Diocletian and the army.

"Oh, they will. I can assure you of that. Where there's the fire of rebellion, there's sure to be one of the emperors and his army." He grinned, explaining that where the army is there's always business. "And that means money, my son! And,"—he popped his mouth in the expressive way he had when positively excited—"you'll eventually find yourself employed by the most powerful man in the world!"

I suppose I smiled.

There they were. I could see them right in front of me. Constantine. Diocletian. The flies around their horses' muzzles. The stubble upon their own chins. The midday sun gleamed off the metallic brooches holding their brilliantly colored riding capes in place. If I had had a stone, I could have easily hit one of them as they marched by. But I didn't. And truth be told, I was never a very good throw. Anyways, if I had thrown a stone, I would have been dead in a moment. The earth shook.

When Constantine rode through Alexandria with Diocletian and the army, thousands of men and women quietly lined the road stretching from outside the Canopic Gate on the eastern wall all the way to the other side of the city. Buteo and I stood just inside the gate. From our position, we could see some distance outside Alexandria along the dusty, gravelly road that leads into the city. Turning in opposite direction, we could gaze down the long, spacious stretch of the Canopic Way, paved with dark granite, past the Street of the Soma and on towards the Mausoleum where Alexander and Ptolemy have rested for half a millennium.

"Why don't we cheer?" I asked, whispering.

For a moment, Buteo said nothing in reply. There was the steady, rhythmic sound of the army chanting and marching, the horses trotting along, and the supply wagons grinding against the dust and rocks of the road. Aside from that, it was relatively quiet except for a few hushed words spoken here and there. It was strange to experience a city as large as Alexandria hushed and still, a quiet that defied the numbers standing alongside the road.

Finally, my father answered my question. "It's a game, son. They wait to see who will win. If Diocletian crushes Domitius, which is expected,"—he chuckled and popped his mouth—"then they'll throng the roads and cheer loudly the next time he comes through as victor. If not," he went on, shrugging, "their allegiance must be with Domitius and his goons. They're a fickle lot. But don't forget, Arnobius, it's the opportunity for profit we're after, and fickleness is just as fertile a field as any."

I guess I already knew this—that the people of Alexandria must remain aloof until the end of the contest. Aurelius Achilleus had already put too many to death. You could still see a few corpses hanging outside the western walls near the Necropolis.

I looked up. As Constantine sauntered by, he appeared as a vision of courage upon his coal-colored mount. Brave. Strong. Physical. He was just then at the peak of life, if not a little beyond. He must have been twenty-five or twenty-six, Theophilus. I could see he was proud. I could see it in his determined eyes. Even so, there was a detachment to his pride—or perhaps I'm reading into the past what I have since learned. His pride was not like that of Achilles, ringing in the ears, originating in and oriented toward his own good and honor; rather, it was aimed like an arrow seeking the good of others. I would say humility tempered his pride, but I fear anachronism.

Constantine had just returned from fighting the Persians in the East. Prior to this, Diocletian had appointed him a tribune of the First Order, and Constantine had lived up to the charge, leading the men under his command with heart and intelligence.

The latter—his successful command—irked Galerius, Diocletian's caesar and second-hand man who hoped to succeed Diocletian as the leading emperor once he retired or died. Moreover, it caused a budding hatred for Constantine to grow and fester and eventually turned his thoughts toward murder.

Galerius' hatred for Constantine had grown over the years ever since Constantine had come to the East as a hostage in order to keep his father Constantius Chlorus in check in the West. Most significant was the bitter humiliation Galerius had suffered at the hands of Diocletian after the Persian campaign. During the victory parade, the emperor forced Galerius to march on foot, dragging his toga in the dust, while Diocletian and Constantine rode above him in a spectacular chariot. Galerius was supposed to learn a lesson because he had failed against our longtime enemy along the eastern border. I'll explain.

The fight against the Persians was a cleanup maneuver. It was the first in decades given the fact that we Romans had been successful against them ever since Shapur had died, the wicked Persian king who had captured the emperor Valerian, flayed him alive, and left his shriveled, vermillion-dyed skin as a sacrifice to the Persian god of fire. This ongoing success had ended when Shapur's son Narseh came to rule some twenty years after his father had died. He hit Rome hard, first attacking our Armenian allies before penetrating all the way into Mesopotamia, bringing with him a mortal threat to Galerius and his army by successfully invading the province of Syria and beyond. In the end, Galerius failed against Narseh. And so, having botched the defense of the eastern Empire, he shamefacedly called upon Diocletian for help.

The latter rushed from Antioch along with the newly appointed tribune Constantine to rectify matters. Still, even he had problems. Unconquered up to then, Diocletian also failed. On a field between the Euphrates and Tigris rivers and between the cities Callinicum and Carrhae, the Romans lost thousands to a swarm of Persian soldiers and a herd of bellicose, stampeding elephants. Yet in a way, Theophilus, Diocletian won. For just as with Pyrrhus of Epirus' victory at Asculum centuries before against an expanding Roman Republic, the Persians' won their victory at far too high a price. Consequently, despite their triumph, Narseh and his men retreated, and Diocletian, ever a man for appearance over reality, loudly proclaimed a Roman victory.

After the battle, Diocletian made sure Galerius learned his lesson by humiliating him. And so, following the logic of an impassioned, disgraced heart, Galerius came to despise Constantine instead of Diocletian because he walked afoot while Constantine rode elevated next to the so-called victor. In time, Galerius vowed revenge. Someday Constantine would pay—and preferably with his life.

On that day in Alexandria, however, riding next to Diocletian at the head of five legions, I imagine Constantine didn't think about the Persians, imperial politics or Galerius' hatred. Rather, like any other young soldier, he eagerly looked forward to hunting down Lucius Domitius Domitianus.

That day, standing next to my father and watching Constantine, I wondered what it was like to be a soldier. I wondered if I had the strength to carry a sixty-pound pack. Could I endure long marches, tolerate camp food, or sleep in a hot and odorous leather tent with a crowd of dirty men? I also imagined what it would be like to do the grisly work of war, the task Mars commands, to kill a man, to see the light of life extinguish in his eyes. Considering Constantine, I wondered how many he had killed and thought about what it must be like to stride in his sandals. He was the son of a caesar. He was a future ruler. Perhaps he would be emperor someday. He seemed so much older than I was. He was—by nearly ten years. But then, at fifteen going on sixteen that was a lifetime.

Constantine and Diocletian eventually passed out of sight. Making their way through Alexandria, they marched out the other end of the city through the Necropic Gate into the City of the Dead.

Once the dust settled, I was unsure that I'd ever see them again.

I told my father and he disagreed. "They'll be back," Buteo assured me, grinning and popping his mouth. "Then we'll get rich!"

Two: Conquest

WEEKS LATER, toward the end of the year, we heard the news that everyone in Alexandria heard—Lucius Domitius Domitianus was dead. Having learned about Diocletian's imminent attack, which he correctly interpreted as his own imminent defeat, Domitius had opened his veins with a razor-sharp knife, draining his own dark blood into the sands of the desert. Afterwards, his men scattered, vanishing into the emptiness of Egypt to await the next uprising.

This made my father very happy. He figured Diocletian and the army would now turn back to Alexandria and winter in the great city. Then Buteo would have his opportunity. Somehow, through this or that contact, he would insinuate himself into the emperor's affairs and become a supplier of the eastern army of Rome. That one stroke of luck would earn him a small fortune.

Others doubtlessly were not so happy—the Greeks foremost among them. Well, some, and a small number of Jews and a few Copts. Many of these had gambled—with their lives at it happened—to support Domitius and his co-usurper. Now their ends drew near, as did the end of Aurelius Achilleus.

The latter, needless to say, was despondent upon hearing the news. In fact, in the days following the reports of Diocletian's success, city gossip had Aurelius Achilleus conducting himself with abnormally erratic behavior. I say abnormal because even before the news had arrived, he had been a man of exaggerated tastes and habits, indulging in perverse pleasures of every kind. Now that he knew Diocletian was turning back to mop up the city he had been charged with guarding, he despaired, retreating even more to the comforting numbness of pleasure—as if passing bodily gratification would make his death any easier! Had he not read the philosophers? Nevertheless, such were the rumors.

Sometime later, I believe it was toward the Ides of February, my father received word that Maximian, the emperor of the West, was wintering in Carthage. A merchant associate who had ties to the requisitions officer in Africa relayed to him by post that Maximian was looking for procurers to supply his army. Among other items, he required olive oil. "Ah-ha!" exclaimed Buteo, recognizing the opportunity.

Still, he faced a dilemma. He could turn and brave the sea, speeding as rapidly as possible to this seemingly certain prospect in Carthage, or he could wait for Diocletian who had already begun to rebuild military supply structures in Upper Egypt, as at the enormous bakery in Panapolis along the Nile. He was sure to do the same in Lower Egypt, and Buteo imagined Diocletian would direct operations from Alexandria.

In the end, my father gambled for both, a move based not so much on his gut as it was on calculation. For one, Buteo assumed Maximian might be gone by the time he arrived in Carthage; therefore, it would be pointless to go—for now. The western emperor would be off battling the confederation of Mauritanian tribes he had come to fight in the first place. What he did not know was whether Maximian would return to Carthage the following winter. This was the gamble. Either way, he figured he had a relatively secure deal in waiting for Diocletian and the eastern army in Alexandria. Domitius was dead; Aurelius Achilleus was next. So he stayed.

In the end, it all unfolded just as my father had foreseen. I saw Constantine atop his coal-colored mount once more in early March. Again, he rode next to Diocletian, who led an army of thousands marching behind. This time I didn't tremble. I was elated. Aside me, thousands thronged the road in Dionysian frenzy.

I'm sure Aurelius Achilleus, feasting and pleasuring himself in the palace, trembled in the few ominous moments remaining to him. As news of Diocletian's march came to Alexandria, he barricaded himself in the Royal Palace along the royal quay. Men situated atop the lighthouse were supposed to signal him when the emperor arrived. Then he would end his life on his own terms just as Domitius had done.

As the emperor entered the city, the men in the lighthouse did their job. In the palace, however, Aurelius Achilleus' nerve failed when the moment came to enclose the blade into the folds of his blubbery flesh. Consequently, in addition to winning the titles rebel, usurper, and tyrant, titles inimical to any true Roman, he also earned that of coward.

Diocletian's men found him trembling behind a set of magnificently embroidered curtains, just as Claudius had done centuries before to escape certain death at the hands of the German guard searching for Caligulan allies. Aurelius Achilleus wasn't as lucky as he was, of course. Whereas the guard proclaimed Claudius fourth emperor of Rome, the usurper was tried, his memory damned, and he was put to death without ceremony in the public market. One moment Aurelius Achilleus gazed through beaten, swollen eyes that dimly gathered images of the market surrounding the executioner's block; the next moment the light went out and there was darkness as his head tumbled to the ground.

In the days to come, others were dispatched as well—though far fewer than could have been. Diocletian, after all, had sworn an oath of vengeance that rebel blood would flow to his horse's knees. In the end, though, to cause fulfillment, he had his horse genuflect as it were in the blood of several Greek noblemen. And so, Theophilus, there was clemency for the many. In just a few weeks, the rebellion was all but forgotten aside from a collection of coins that remained in circulation declaring Domitius *Imperator* and *Augustus*, alongside the image of Nike, goddess of victory.

Sometime later, Diocletian departed from Alexandria in order to make another tour up the Nile before Hapi, god of the river, brought flooding early on in summer, and before returning to Syria where Galerius, now self-redeemed, was stationed with his newly triumphant army, the recent victor over Narseh and his Persians. Constantine stayed behind in charge of imperial affairs in Alexandria. It was then that my father pounced.

Through the machinations of this contact and that, and a merchant he knew who was acquainted with Evander of II Triana, and promises due in Carthage upon our return, Buteo insinuated himself into meeting Constantine's chief officer of supplies. He was a man called Denis, as I remember, whose calculating mind was as accurate and as fast as an abacus in skillful hands.

When my father and I went to see Denis, Constantine happened to be sitting on a stool opposite him across a large, wooden table. He was laughing and turned when we made our entrance. I was there, doubtlessly, on the off chance of making a connection. *Lucky me*. Denis stood and Buteo introduced himself.

"Ah yes, you're the oil man," observed Denis.

"That's fair to say," my father happily agreed.

As for me, I was studying Constantine. He sat there evaluating the short, crafty man who stood there hoping to make a good deal of profit. In the end, Denis agreed to Buteo's proposal, and so my father secured his coveted contract with the army. Beyond this agreement, Denis assured him he would write to Feodore, his counterpart in Maximian's army, recommending Buteo's business to the western emperor. My father thanked him. So far, the gamble was working.

Then the conversation took a sudden turn. Constantine, who had been quiet up to that point, stood from the stool and clapped his large hands. "Magnificent!" he exclaimed, facing my father. "Now, Rome has its oil. But tell me, good man, who is this striking young fellow to your side?"

My father beamed with instant hope as I quickly realized Constantine meant *me*. "This is my son, Arnobius," he announced, gesturing toward me, "the wonder of Carthage!"

I blushed.

Constantine, however, smiled indulgently.

Buteo assumed the expression was an invitation to go on, which he did, and which caused my eyes to fall down to the floor with embarrassment as an anchor drops to the bottom of a heaving sea.

"Arnobius is very well educated," he boasted. "He gained high honors in Carthage, studying privately with Proteus the rhetor, who, on any account, is the best in our city."

My face grew redder, my sight fastened ever more securely upon the tile of the floor. Then to my surprise, after mentioning my studies in rhetoric and the law, my father mentioned my keen interest in philosophy, though with some hesitation as if only to cover all possible ground.

I next heard Constantine's voice. He turned to me and called out my name. I looked up and my eyes met his. "What do you think," he asked, "the One or the many?"

Flustered, I didn't know what to say, and so once again, my head fell.

I understood the question, Theophilus, but now in the presence of such a great man I couldn't form a coherent thought let alone marshal a single sentence from the end of my dead tongue. Instead, I assumed what must have been a blank expression.

Then, with two determined words, Constantine answered for me. "The One!" he boomed.

With that, my father sniggered, embarrassed, faintly remembering, yet not quite, the point of reference. Quickly, the businessman took over. "Yes, yes," he affirmed, "of course, *the one*."

I'm sure Buteo had in mind the one contract he had just worked so hard to secure and how he should leave with it still in hand.

As for me, I held my downward pose, madly reflecting. The One. Yes, of course. But what about the many? Unsure, I couldn't decide. In any case, whether the One or the many, I didn't have the courage to glance up to confirm or deny Constantine's assertion. That would have to wait for another time.

The Cell in Tabennisi

Theophilus: I MUST CONFESS, Abba, that I straightened up when I heard Arnobius speak of the One and the many. It's *the* metaphysical puzzle that has confounded the Greeks and others for nearly a thousand years.

"Arnobius," I said, "I'm surprised."

"By what, Theophilus?"

"By Constantine—his interest in philosophy."

"That, a surprise—why?"

I guess I didn't exactly know. It's just that I had never imagined someone like him thinking about anything but politics and power.

"He truly posed that question to you?"

"I assure you, he did."

"I can't think of a more foundational question," I declared. Then foolishly, as if Arnobius didn't already understand, I went on to explain. "It's the first question philosophers ask about what actually is—whether there is one, simple, unchanging reality, or whether all is many and in flux, constantly moving and changing. It's been the hound of philosophy ever since Parmenides of Elea claimed that the world we experience is an illusion and that all which is—truly, actually, really—forms a radical unity of being, the One."

Arnobius nodded, taking a drink from his earthenware cup of water.

"And so Constantine sided with Parmenides?" I asked.

He set the cup down. "Not exactly."

"Then what did he mean?"

"I'm not quite sure."

"He never explained his position?"

"Yes, but I can assure you that it wasn't the same as Parmenides. Constantine was answering an altogether different question. His was more political or moral or—"

Thinking that Arnobius had perhaps forgotten the finer subtleties of Parmenides' argument, I decided to lay it out before us.

"Parmenides asserted that all is Being itself," I explained, interrupting him. "While one can say Caesar is strong and Caesar is a conqueror, in the end, Caesar is dead—and buried, Caesar is dirt. So, what is Caesar?"

"What?" he asked, but it was more to humor me.

I went on. "What remains is not his strength or the conquering, his death or the dirt. Caesar himself doesn't even remain. What remains is Being itself, the *is* that couples one vanishing reality to another. Consequently, Being itself is the one, underlying Reality. The many is an illusion."

Arnobius smiled. Then, as if he couldn't help but say something, he asked me if I remembered Parmenides' student Zeno whose paradoxes likewise demonstrated that all change or motion is an illusion.

"Yes," I replied, thinking, *he does remember*, and I felt a fool.

Arnobius carried on now apparently pleased by the discussion. "My favorite," he announced, "is the Achilles who can't pass by the tortoise in a race."

"Mine too," I agreed, "but I think I prefer Aesop's version."

"So do I. At least with him you have a moral dimension. With Zeno, all is suspended in a kind of unfrozen-freeze, as if the river of life flows without flowing."

I brought up the paradox that had always given me the most difficulty, the one about the century of men that couldn't march from one end of a field to the other because it could never reach the halfway point.

We discussed this one and both laughed when we realized we had had the same experience as a boy upon first hearing it.

"I remember my professor," I said, "a man we called Pluribus due to the size of his girth. He stood before us, say fifteen boys, asserting with utter conviction that change or motion, that is, change from one point to another or from one state into another, is impossible—in fact contrary to reason."

Arnobius grinned as if he had had the very same professor.

"We all objected vociferously, you know, like only boys can do. Our professor—having stirred us up—boldly went on to assert that the boy toward the back couldn't reach the front of the lecture hall. The latter, of course, boasted he could."

"Let me guess," said Arnobius, "while issuing the challenge, he simultaneously forbade him."

I nodded. "He explained it was only an exercise—a thought experiment. Still, riled up by the ridiculous claim, the boy did it anyway. Up he went, off the bench, and a moment later he proudly stood next to him having disproved both Zeno of Elea and, more sweetly, our professor. 'See, sir,' he said, 'motion *is* possible.'"

"Did your professor beat the boy?"

"No," I responded, "not that day anyway. But red-faced, he howled, 'Sit down! Sit down!' And once the boy was sitting, he went on to prove that what had just happened was impossible."

"In thought, anyways."

"Exactly—and that's just what our professor declared."

"Of course he did."

" 'It's simple mathematics, boys,' he claimed. 'In order to pass across the whole distance of a field, or in our case, the lecture hall, you must first pass through the halfway point. And so on with that distance.'"

"You mean the distance between the back of the lecture hall and its midpoint," Arnobius clarified.

"Yes. To arrive at the first halfway point, you must pass through a second, that is, the halfway point between your start and the first mid-point. And so on with that distance. But half of a half is a quarter, and half of a quarter is an eighth, and half of an eighth is a sixteenth, and half of that is one thirty-second, and on and on and on all the way to infinity, the end of which one cannot reach as that would require an infinite amount of time."

"It's beautiful," Arnobius judged. "Every time I hear it, I can't help but admire the paradox."

"Nor can I," I admitted.

"But it's as good as bunk as Aristotle demonstrated. It's the difference between reality and an imaginary line of numbers."

"Apparently my professor didn't know this."

Arnobius laughed. "Or, as you said, he just wanted to stir you up. Isn't that what they all do?"

"Possibly," I agreed. "Either way, he lectured us, arguing that reason forbids the crossing of an infinite distance. Motion is consequently impossible, as is all change. He finished by telling us that the apparent world of the many is an illusion."

"Were you all satisfied with his argument?"

"Not at all!—and certainly not the boy who had moved across the lecture hall. For his part, he protested vigorously as we all did! 'Didn't I return to my seat?' he demanded.

"Meanwhile, our professor had exchanged his very serious expression for an odd grin, and for a moment we all thought we had entered the bizarre *Thinkery* of Aristophanes' Socrates, where the untrue is true, and what is right is the wrong."

We both laughed.

Finally, getting back to the original point of the discussion, I suggested that the ancients had never quite solved the puzzle relating the One to the many, Being itself to non-being. Instead, they had left an infinite gap separating the two.

Arnobius sighed.

"What's wrong?" I asked.

He waited a moment before saying, "Parmenides threw everyone off—the Greeks, the Romans, and now, some in the Church."

I was surprised at the turn of conversation. "What do you mean?"

"Everything that's gone wrong in the Church in the last few decades is related to this one question and indirectly to Parmenides."

"Do you mean what's happened with the Eusebians?" I offered, thinking he meant those who adhere to Arius' doctrines and all the trouble that has followed.

"Yes—but the *homoousians* too, the allies of Athanasius who believe the Son is one in being with God."

"How did he throw everyone off?" I asked.

Rather than directly explaining, he quoted Parmenides. "What is known *is*, what is sensed *is not*."

"I don't follow," I admitted.

"I'm sorry," he said. "The question is this—how is Being itself related to non-being?"

I said that I didn't know, repeating that philosophy has never been able to answer the question.

He shook his head. "The answer is that they're *not* related."

"But they must be," I countered.

"Not if we go along with the argument. Didn't we just say that things don't actually move or change because doing so would require an infinite amount of time?"

"If we admit the claims of Zeno and Parmenides, we did."

"That's what I mean. So, doesn't it follow that things which appear to move and appear to change are really not?"

"Do you mean they don't *actually* move and change?"

"Right."

"Okay, it follows."

"And if you accept that, then you have to further accept this: these things as we sense them—moving and changing—don't actually exist as they appear."

"Except as an illusion," I added, "like a mirage."

Arnobius nodded. "And so there's a gap between what is and what is not, between what is truly known and what is merely sensed. As Parmenides wrote in his poem, 'What is known *is*, what is sensed *is not*.'"

Now it was my turn to nod. "Of course—it's the gap between Being itself and non-being." It seemed we were back to where we had begun.

"But there's more," said Arnobius. "The gap between Being itself and non-being implies a similar gap between what is Perfect and what is imperfect, between Eternity and time."

"Okay."

"This means that for us, all that remains is this liminal reality called *becoming* found somewhere between the two, between Being and non-being."

"And according to the argument, becoming itself leans toward what is not," I observed, "if one can say it is at all."

Arnobius shook his head. "It's all so depressing. If true, then our lives are utterly meaningless, without substance, no better than ghosts are fading at the light of day. Fortunately, it's not true. It's flawed. Our own thinking has indicated the contrary."

"Do you mean the thought of the Church?"

He didn't exactly answer. Rather, Arnobius said, "Even so, this way of approaching reality has given many in the Church so much grief. It's not so much that anyone follows Parmenides anymore. The real problem is philosophers such as Socrates and Plato who came after Parmenides and developed his belief about what is and what is not. They're the origin of the difficulty for many in the Church who think of God as the ever-distant One. Socrates' One—the Good or the Beautiful—is very similar to Parmenides' One, Being itself. Do you remember what Parmenides said of the One?"

"I don't recall his exact words," I admitted.

"I do, and I'll never forget them. He compares Being itself to a flawlessly round ball. The ball is perfect, lacking nothing. It's a radically simple unity, a whole without parts, entirely complete in itself. Consequently, it is unchanging, incorruptible, and eternal."

"Does it bounce?" I asked, foolishly.

"Not at all!" he countered, smiling. "The perfect ball doesn't rise or fall."

"Of course not!" I interjected, laughing. Then, reigning myself in, I observed, "That would make it contingent upon or relative to the up and down, whereas the One is absolute and necessary being."

Arnobius nodded before adding, "Here's the point—the One is Being itself, not the countless qualities or quantities that come and go. It's not the strength, conquering, dying, or dirt of your Caesar. Alone and simple is the One."

"But what of the many?" I asked. I thought of the void that must necessarily surround the One.

"Try to think of the opposite of the One."

"Okay," I consented.

"The many is desire. It is lacking. It is need itself. As such, the many is always frantically seeking what is—though blindly, impossibly, changing from this to that. The many, then, is the world of change, of motion, of imperfection and suffering."

"Suffering?" I asked, not immediately getting the connection.

"Yes, suffering as change—for instance, from whole to partial, living to dead, healthy to diseased, and happy to wretched. Think of it. It's when a green leaf fades to brown for lack of water, or a man dies on the battlefield due to a loss of blood, or a woman loses a child to sickness. Nothing is permanent, Theophilus."

"No," I agreed, "it is not."

"And so," he continued, "having discovered the impassible perfection of the One, the One that cannot suffer change in any way, Parmenides posited that the many, or the way the One seems to manifest itself, is just that—a seeming, an appearance, a mirage. The passible many, the things of change, of corruption, of suffering impermanence, are always fading toward non-being. The One is real; the many is an illusion."

"And so the many doesn't exist?"

"Well," Arnobius clarified, "not exactly. The many is like a moving mirror around this perfect ball. Does the image exist in its polished metal surface?

Does it remain? It's more a shadow reality, appearing somewhere between what is and what is not, like shadows cast by a fire."

"So there's the connection to Socrates and Plato," I observed, "the same two who inspire many in the Church."

"That's right," he confirmed. "Like me, Theophilus, you must know Socrates' allegory of the cave and the shadows there flickering on the wall deep down in its depths, caused by a fire above. Prisoners are there below, you and I, chained to a small wall so they can't look back and up to see the fire above or the puppet-objects in front of the fire casting the shadows. Pathetically, the prisoners stare ahead toward the dark wall of the cave and have contests over who can best identify the shadows. They call it knowledge, but it's not. It's sensing; it's mere opinion. The cave is meant to be our world, an image of our own shadow reality, that of the many. The shadow world dancing upon the wall before them is a dim reflection of the ledge above, where the fire burns and the puppet-objects move. In a similar way, that same fire and those same puppet-objects are but an image of the life-revealing sun outside the dark cave, and the men, women, and other real things found beneath its light."

"And so the gap," I remarked. "The dark world of the many, our shadow world, is as far in being from the brightness of the One as those shadows on the wall are from the sun and people outside."

He agreed. Then, on further reflection, he added, "But perhaps it's not as far as all that."

"What do you mean?"

To my surprise, Arnobius didn't explain. Instead, he commented on the apparent breadth of my education.

I told him I had studied long and hard as an auditor in the Catechetical School in the years before Athanasius was first exiled. I was then seventeen. I confessed I'd later pissed away my learning for other things that vanished like the wind. He knew what I meant and told me he understood.

Then, wishing to know what Arnobius had intended by his previous claim, I offered, "It seems our own philosophy has finally solved the mystery of the relation between the One and the many."

Arnobius gently corrected me. "It hasn't exactly been solved, Theophilus. I doubt it ever will be. That would be to reduce the mystery to a few pat words, the Infinite to the finite. Even so, there's still much work to be done in knowing how to best express it."

I told him I accepted that.

"More importantly," he went on, "we men are alienated from one another, and so our hearts remain divided, Theophilus. That sad fact, I'm afraid, is an even greater gap to mend. Remember, our religion is not merely a theory but a way of life."

"The way of love," I added, and he agreed.

We both grew quiet, our words dissolving into the silence of my cell and the desert beyond.

After a while, Arnobius returned to my initial comment some time before. Reminiscing, he declared, "Constantine was a thoughtful man. He always was. Though a man of the world, his mind and heart were often elsewhere. Whenever he could—times which seemed to grow rarer and rarer with responsibility—he mulled over all the great questions. In fact, that's how we next met."

"Oh?" I asked. "How'd that happen?"

Pleased to remember, Arnobius told me.

Three: Carthage

Late 298 to 301 A.D.

CONSTANTINE TRAVELLED NORTH to Antioch and then on to Nicomedia early that fall, sometime around the end of September or the beginning of October. This was my father's prompt to return to Carthage. Having secured a contract with the eastern army, he now desired to do the same in the West. A few weeks later, we embarked on a grain ship in order to make our way home.

My father soon discovered his gamble had paid off handsomely. News had it that Maximian was making his way to Carthage, marching from the Atlas Mountains where he had fought the confederation of Mauretanian tribes. He planned to spend one more winter in Africa before returning to Italy.

As for me, I continued my legal studies and dutifully shifted around seeking contacts while helping my father manage business and other family affairs. Occasionally, I tutored my two younger brothers, twins, who were just then embarking upon a serious study of grammar. They were then eleven. One, I'm sad to recall, died midway through the next year as a summer fever swept through Carthage. The other died of sorrow. Not truly, but his heart shriveled up as if part of him had passed away. His twin had been his life.

My two sisters who were then thirteen and fourteen were in Mother's domain. I cannot describe what they did with any precision, but of one thing, I'm certain. They were less like the virtuous Lucretia who spun nightly by candlelight and more like Tarquinius Sextus' wife spending all their time preparing for and attending parties. Mother approved for one simple reason. Like my father, she was always on the lookout for opportunities. Suitable men. Profitable husbands. With conviction and clear purpose, then, and older escorts of course, my sisters went nearly every week to a dance, a get-together, or a feast in celebration of this god or that goddess. Without fail, they attended as devotees of Tanit, the Carthaginian patroness of love.

"Why don't you go?" Mother asked me one evening before a party, just a few weeks after we had returned from Alexandria.

I failed to look up. "I'm reading tonight, Mother."

"Your law again, Arnobius? You *must* have a break."

"No," I said, ignoring the latter. "The lectures of Plotinus."

"You're sure to see some of your old chums," she promised. "And possibly—"

"Oh?" I said to forestall her.

I wasn't interested. I felt I had changed since being in Alexandria where I'd seen the emperor and Constantine, and where I had witnessed the end of a rebellion and Aurelius Achilleus lose his head.

"How will you ever meet someone?" she begged. Mother wanted me—like my sisters—to circulate among the girls, who circulated like open flowers among the young men.

I finally looked up. With an expression of bewilderment accompanied by filial love, I offered, "I'll leave that to you, Mother."

Yet there was more to my attitude than a simple lack of interest, Theophilus. I cannot honestly suggest that I was then uninterested in girls. How could I have been? I was sixteen. But let me explain.

Two years before, just as I was beginning to desire girls, something happened that changed the course of my life. I was strolling through a grove of olive trees on our estate when I came to a small oil press. Not far away was a mud brick structure used to shelter the slaves in the heat of day when the press was operating in late summer.

I stepped over to the press and looked down into the pit. Standing there, I thought about all the olives it would crush with its large stone wheels revolving round and round, and about all the oil it would hold in another half-year or so. I could see it. It was green and gold, the color of olives mixed with honey. I smiled. It was the gold my father loved, and at the time, the gold that secured for me everything I wished to have.

In the midst of these ruminations, an old friend startled me when she appeared in the dark but open doorway that led into the slave's shelter. She was weeping.

Her name was Stella, or that's what we had called her thanks to her bright blue eyes. She came to us when she was seven or eight, an orphan of one campaign or another, sold into slavery and sent south into the slave markets of Massilia in southern Gaul. There, one of my father's agents had purchased her to work on our estate. That's when I met her.

At the time, I was just eight, and as is often the case with young children—whether slave or free—we became friends. When she wasn't performing one chore or another, we would play together. Mostly, we ran around outside following the goatherds far away in the rolling hills or picking olives and grapes in the groves and vineyards. She was fast—as fast as me, which is perhaps not to say much, but as a boy, I appreciated this. She also had a strong and accurate arm.

Our play lasted for many years, until one day, when I was eleven or twelve, she disappeared.

"Where's Stella gone?" I asked Mother.

"She hasn't gone anywhere," she replied, evasively.

The truth is Mother had grown tired of my running around with a slave girl. I was getting on in age and she believed it was time I separate myself from her.

"But she's not working in the house anymore," I observed to the contrary.

Mother waved me off. "Then she's away in the fields."

By fields, Mother meant that Stella was gathering olives with the other slaves, as it was late summer.

Immediately I went to look for her. When I found her in a distant grove and called her name, however, it didn't matter. She turned away from me without a word, moving on with the rest of the slaves in their work. Mother had said something to her. I knew it.

I lost Stella that summer, and I wept, Theophilus. I wept like a small boy because I had come to love her.

Now, a few years later, there she was. From the darkness of the doorway, she stepped out toward me, weeping.

I walked to her, my heart beating furiously. "What is it?" I asked as if we had never been apart.

Stella said nothing.

"Come here," I said. I put my hands on her shoulders. "Why are you crying?"

She didn't say. She only nudged closer to me and finally burrowed into my chest. I felt her, and I knew the difference of those years. She was now a young woman.

Embracing her, my body changed. I felt a heat course through me, the burning heat of desire, and I yearned above all to hold her as close as was physically possible.

"What's wrong?" I whispered.

She was sobbing, her body convulsing into mine. I held her and gently stroked her and silently thanked Tanit for returning her to me.

Later, we sat with our backs against the stones of the olive press and talked. By then Stella had calmed some. It was then that I noticed the bruises on her face and arms.

"What happened?" I asked.

She turned away.

I turned her back toward me. "Who did this to you?" I demanded.

She didn't say. Her trembling eyes, begging for compassion, for affection, stared into mine before she looked away again.

I knew better than to pursue the answer. I knew that someone had beaten her, that her heart, always full of courage and spirit, had been broken.

Stella stared at the dusty track surrounding the olive press. "I've missed you," she said. "I never meant to reject you. Your mother—"

"I know," I said.

"I loved you," she revealed.

I loved her too, Theophilus. She turned to me and I told her so. Then I kissed her.

That day, we spent hours in each other's embrace before Stella suggested she had to return to her people and work. Before saying goodbye, we agreed to meet again on the same day a week later at the same oil press.

The following days brimmed with fate. Every hour my desire grew for her until it was nearly unbearable. By the time we met again, we barely said hello before entering the dark shelter and joining as one.

We did it then and the next week and for the many months that followed. We would meet up and lie in each other's bare arms, expressing profound feelings of desire, of love.

Eventually Stella grew with child. When it happened, we were both afraid. I told her not to worry, though. I promised I would care for her, that I'd free her, that she would be my wife. She was happy when I told her this.

Despite my good intentions, however, it never happened.

Some five or six months after she discovered the pregnancy, Stella once again disappeared. When I searched for her, I learned that something was dreadfully amiss.

"What's wrong with her?" I asked, after locating her in a distant hut. She was lying on a blanket spread out on the dirt floor. Her eyes were closed.

An old slave woman, stained with the sun and wrinkled with work, shook her head. "She's given birth."

"She has?" I asked, surprised. It was early.

"It's dead," she replied.

"The baby?"

"Yes."

"And Stella?"

"Not so well. She'll follow the child soon enough."

I gasped.

Later, when I insisted upon bringing Stella to our house, Mother acted put out and asked, "Why would you want to do that?"

I said nothing.

"Was it *you*?" she asked.

In the end, she permitted me to bring her home. Mother had her ways, but she was not cruel.

I was there when Stella died a few days later. Lying on a cot in the slave's quarters, she grew pale due to the loss of blood. She had ruptured when giving birth, and slowly, her life leaked away.

"Stella …" I called when she stopped breathing.

"She's dead," judged the slave woman tending her.

I knew it and closed her blue eyes, and quietly, I cried. I laid my head on her chest attempting to smell her one last time. But she was gone. "I'm sorry," I whispered.

The slave woman stroked my back. "It's not your fault," she said, trying to comfort me. "It's the will of the gods. We all have the same fate."

I knew better. It *was* my fault, and so I lamented the past. I'd do anything to bring her back.

When Stella's body was cremated a few days later after the rites were performed, I fell into a dark stupor. Where had she gone? From something to what? To nothing? How, I wondered, does something become nothing?

It was then, Theophilus, and in the following months, that I began to withdraw as the horror of impermanence filled my mind like a poisonous fog.

Nothing, I judged, is permanent. Not me, not Stella, not anything I desired or had, or anything I could desire or have. It's not that my thoughts were coherent, but they haunted me. It was then, I suppose, that I first ached for the Permanent, for something that would never pass away.

One day, a few months before going to Alexandria with my father, I mentioned this desire to the rhetor Proteus when he noticed I was especially glum. In response, he revealed knowing just what I meant and explained that it was a common feeling among men. Few, however, feel it so intensely, he said. For most, it's a dull ache amid the flurry of life's activities, or at worst, an intellectual abstraction, if they think of impermanence at all. I was different, he declared. Proteus suggested that my desire for permanence, deep as it was, was one that deserved satisfaction. Stella's death had spoiled the world for me, revealing life for what it actually is beneath the merciless dictates of fate. "What can I do?" I begged. "What you need is a remedy," he assured me. Like a doctor, therefore, Proteus prescribed one. He told me to read a part of Plato's *Phaedrus* that he'd never before let me read.

Later that night, reading alone in my sleeping chamber, I happily thanked the gods. It was there in the *Phaedrus*, Theophilus, that I first soared up to the realm of the One, circling around the throne of Being itself, the Permanent and truly Real. Darkness faded and I bathed in light. I saw, I knew, and consequently, all was well.

Needless to say, I could have stayed there forever, my desires fully satisfied. The *Phaedrus*, however, also taught me the true nature of my soul and why remaining there forever would be very hard. I learned of the two winged horses pulling the chariot of my soul. There's one that is noble and good and another that is not. The first horse gallops toward the light-filled throne of Being itself, while the other pulls away toward shadows and darkness.

As the weeks passed by, I felt the tug of the latter horse, as if learning about it had somehow enlivened it. Although I tried to rein it in, I couldn't. The passions flared. However much I wished to remain circling around the delightful beauty and glory of Being itself, I faltered. As a result, I plunged toward our world once again, sad, wondering if I'd ever permanently know the One.

That is why I sat earnestly reading Plotinus' lectures when Mother invited me to join my sisters that evening so long ago, a few weeks after I'd returned from Alexandria with my father and his imperial contract. The more I read about the One, the more I yearned to know. Mother, of course, had other plans.

"Fine," she said, once I had rebuffed her attempts to garnish my well-being with the opportunity of meeting other young girls. "But at least do something useful."

By useful she meant something having to do with increase. I should make money, chase prestige. Stella had never been more than a slave girl to her and a nuisance at that. She had never understood my great sorrow when she died or my subsequent need for permanence. Nevertheless, being a good son, or wishing to be one, I promised Mother I would be useful.

Oftentimes, therefore, I would tag along with my father whenever he was out seeking profit. One day early in December, Maximian finally arrived with his field army. As soon as he did, Buteo, ever the buzzard, flew into action like a scavenger swooping down to eat carrion lying in the field.

His associate, a rotund man called Leonardus, the one who had first alerted Buteo to Maximian's presence a year before, contacted a merchant friend who put him directly in touch with Maximian's chief officer of supplies. Feodore had been waiting.

"Quintus Fabius Buteo!" he greeted him when my father met him a few days later. "I hold here a letter from Denis, my counterpart in the East."

Buteo grinned. His eyes narrowed. Negotiations followed.

A half hour later, he stepped aboard his gold trimmed litter a happy man. I sat next to him. Once again, his plan had worked, and now he had a contract with the West. Off went the litter carried by a handful of slaves into Carthage's bustling city center.

Buteo's happiness lasted until Diocletian promulgated price reforms a few years later, which drove all prices down and consequently profits fell. The point was to keep costs low for the armies of Rome. What was good for Rome, however, was not good for us. My father took a hit, though nothing fatal. Even so, to continue the simile, like a feasting buzzard seeing the approach of a rumbling wagon, Buteo eventually flew out of the army supply business altogether. There would be better deals elsewhere. There *must* be, he assured me.

As Buteo searched for those deals, a few years passed by. All the while, he was impatient to find me a job connected to the Empire. Money was not enough. Our family required greater honor and prestige.

For my part, I was less than enthusiastic. In fact, during that time, aside from halfheartedly obliging my father in glancing about for contacts, I thought little about prestige or the Empire and its never ending politics and wars. I continued to long for a different kind of life altogether, a philosophical life, one that would lead to unity with the One and the possession of a wise soul, what Socrates had called a monarchy, where the soul is directed by the wise rule of the intellect. Having this would make me happy, I thought— not all the other things.

At the time, Plotinus' description of the sage captivated my imagination. "Adverse fortune does not shake his felicity." That's what I wanted—to be an unwavering sage.

Yet to become wise and unshakeable, I had to study philosophy with other wise men. Accordingly, I felt I had to go to Alexandria. You can imagine, Theophilus, that my father was firmly opposed to the latter.

"What's the value in it?" he challenged me one day after I had revealed my true desire.

He wasn't upset. On the contrary, Buteo was calm. It was a practical question asked for practical reasons by a practical man. He wasn't against the divine or any higher reality. No, like many a man, Buteo was religious. He fulfilled his duty to the gods, as did the rest. Reduced to what it was, though, his piety was simply one more way of earning greater profits. Like contacts on a grand scale, the gods were useful. But philosophy?

"It's empty speculation," he judged, as if definitive.

"Empty?" I asked, feeling threatened.

"Materially," he answered. "It'll never produce olive oil or bread, or secure bricks to build up a villa, or labor, or honor, or an increase for your family as is demanded by the law for each and every *paterfamilias*."

"Yes, I know," I replied, as if bored with the law. I could cite it sleeping. "A dutiful father must protect and increase the family property," I quoted.

"So the goal of life is to get rich, my son!"

Buteo smiled and popped his mouth. I did not.

Instead, I countered using Aristotle who argued that the goal of human life is contemplation. "To think," I said forcefully, "to know!" My father sniggered while I advanced the argument. "It's to contemplate the good, moving toward it both practically and theoretically!"

"Theoretically!" he balked. "Don't be ridiculous, Arnobius! Life's point is practical activity alone—*agere*, to act and to do! Don't ever forget that acting and doing are proper Roman virtues. Be a Roman! Forget this Greek speculation. If you want the latter, then remember what Hesiod wisely said, 'Work is no disgrace, but idleness is.' The gods worked hard to make what we have and so should you. Forget the other!"

"Forget it?" I said, horrified. "Philosophical speculation is not idleness! I'll *never* forget it!"

"But you must!" he directed me, forcefully.

I said nothing to counter, stewing silently instead.

Buteo lowered his voice. "What you need is to live, son, and to live well."

I laughed at the irony of it all. Although a citizen, my father's soul was anything but Roman. Romans have timocratic souls, ones that yearn for glory and honor above all else. Think of Cicero who said that the greatest misfortune is disgrace, or Caesar who conquered for his own glory, or Caesar's enemies Cato and Brutus who murdered the dictator for getting rid of their place of honor in ruling Rome. These are real Roman virtues—acting for the sake of dignity, glory, and honor. By contrast, Carthaginian souls are plutocratic. We hunger after trade and the wealth that comes from trade. While we want honor, what we really desire is the money that buys honor.

But what about the wise soul? I wondered. *Where does the philosopher naturally reside?* Although I was from Carthage, I had not yet become a merchant like my father, a plutophile. In my mind, I was a philosopher or one in the making. Thus, I had to study philosophy, whether my father wanted me to or not.

Seeing me madly thinking, Buteo grinned, patting me on the back.

"What?" I asked, letting my guard down.

My father changed tack, a strategic move I should have recognized in his narrow eyes. He said I could go.

"Go?" I asked, surprised.

"Yes, go speculate to your heart's content. We'll call it the capital stone to your education—pure decoration, worthless, like the top of a Corinthian column!" He chuckled.

Ignoring the latter jibe, I said, "You'll let me go to Alexandria?"

He agreed that I could study philosophy for one year, that I could give my undivided attention to *these theories*, he said, as long as I consented to a few stipulations.

"What?" I asked, willing at this desperate point to concede just about anything. If possible, I wished to go with his blessing.

"First, wherever you are, you'll have to keep an eye on family affairs." This would keep me anchored to the practical, he said.

"Fine," I shrugged. I could do that asleep, just as I had been for years.

"Second, you must be on the lookout for—"

"Contacts?" I interjected.

"Yes," he smiled.

"What else?"

"Lastly, you must forget these theories once you return. Or at least stuff them in some backside fold of your tunic."

"Okay," I lied, not happy with the last demand. My demeanor must have betrayed a slight deflation at his insistence.

"Chin up!" he commanded.

I looked at him.

"You're going to Alexandria again! And this time, you'll be on your own!"

I was then nineteen.

"Did you hear me, Arnobius? Alexandria!"

I did, but I was furiously thinking. Now, the reality of what my father had offered began to seep into my skull. I grew excited and my mind began to race. What I'd do, Theophilus! I had heard that Iamblichus, an associate of Porphyry, was then lecturing in Alexandria. Porphyry had been taught by Plotinus, the distant follower of Plato, the student of Socrates. Plotinus had mystically experienced the One four times. Porphyry had done so once, but he had also gone off to Sicily suicidally depressed. I was unsure about Iamblichus. Nevertheless, I was going to Alexandria to find out! The schools! The men! The wisdom! My heart thumped with eager anticipation.

Meanwhile, my father snuck away. He had things to do. As he left, he grinned once again. Years later he let me know that it was all a ruse. He knew that after a year in Alexandria, after I'd seen what bastards men are and after I had more experience with women, I'd wake up to the reality of the world and so, to family business.

My father was right. My time in Alexandria shifted the course of my life. But the flow of time, Theophilus, has a way of doing that. Rather than becoming a wise man as I had hoped to do, I encountered Constantine once again, and that turned me more and more toward my father's way of life.

Four: The Lecture Hall

Late 301 A.D.

SOMETIMES I WONDER if I saw Athanasius that year in Alexandria. Did I see, without knowing it, the future advocate the Homoousion? If so, he would have been a small three to four year old boy hanging on the side of his mother in the marketplace. What was her name? I can't say, Theophilus, because I never met her. She fell asleep before I encountered her son, the bishop. Nevertheless, I wonder what he was like even then as a small child. Did he have the same powers of mind, the same charisma and intensity?

It's possible I saw him that year but unlikely. I didn't spend much time in the Coptic part of town, the Rhacotis Quarter. Instead, I favored the Brucheum and the Great Library and Museum. I liked spending my time where the Street of the Soma intersects the Canopic Way. There, men sat around imbibing cheap wine and arguing over metaphysical positions as if they meant everything in the world. Oftentimes they would come to blows. Beyond the barbaric rumbling, I preferred the schools and the intimate halls found therein where I could listen to lecture after lecture. I would try to divine that one drop of philosophical nectar or one morsel of true ambrosia that would release me from this world of impermanence and usher me into the everlasting world of the One.

I encountered him once again at one of those lectures. I mean Constantine, not Athanasius—though what a contrast the latter child would have made to the former man who was then nearing the fourth decade of his life.

I saw him a few months after I had been in Alexandria. I believe it was October. Once again, Constantine was in the immortal city with Diocletian tending to matters of state and, as it turned out, matters of soul. We were both attending the same lecture in a polished marble hall off the Museum. Like all the other auditors, Constantine sat on one of the lacquered wooden benches listening attentively. Because I had arrived slightly before him, I spotted his entrance along with his guard.

As soon as the instructor for the day recognized the tribune, he made his way over to Constantine in order to greet him.

"Hello, hello!" he hailed him, effusive in manner.

Constantine stood and embraced him.

Iamblichus, the instructor, claimed to be a proficient, an expert philosopher you might say, a mystic who has attained unity with the One. More accurately, Iamblichus had others make the claim on his behalf. This is not to say that he was deceitful per se. He was not. It's just that there was something sour about him—or so I subsequently discovered.

I later learned about his dubious qualities from a man who had once known him while residing in Antioch where Iamblichus usually lived and taught. This man said that Iamblichus had chosen Antioch as his residence for two reasons. The first was to be nearer to his hometown, Chalcis, in Syria. He was superstitious and felt he should be nearby his family's house in order to propitiate the gods and goddesses of home and hearth, family and clan. The other reason had to do with being closer to the wealth of imperial patronage without which his life might be very poor indeed. As you may know, Theophilus, the emperors oftentimes use Antioch as a base of operations. Galerius did. He stationed himself there in order to keep an eye on the Persians.

Galerius was a great admirer of Iamblichus. He appreciated the philosopher's drive to propitiate the One by all the customary means, by methods utilized since the ritual institutions of Rome's second king, Numa Pompilius—sacrifice, the spilling of blood, and all the other rites Roman priests have performed for ages. These Iamblichus carried out faithfully in addition to various occult methods of mediation he had purportedly perfected called *theurgy*, the work of God. More exactly, it was the work of the gods, plural—the many.

Iamblichus believed the way to cross the gap between the many and the divine Unity was by means of multiplicity. This is how he resolved Zeno's paradox. Accordingly, he emphasized the many gods, reveling and luxuriating in their intermediary existence. Between the One and the manifold visible world, there stood a plethora of divine beings. These were not only the traditional Greek or Roman gods. He recognized all intermediary beings, any he could find—heroes deified, angels ranging from seraphim to cherubim, daemons of varying rank, and gods and goddesses from every mountain and river, tribe and nation. In short, theurgy involved the vast plenitude of spirits reflecting the infinite nature of the divine Mind.

That afternoon, the one shared with Constantine at the lecture in the hall off the Museum, Iamblichus spoke of the method of purification, of how one could rise up by means of the many in order to cross the great divide and tie oneself mystically to the One.

"It is within you," he declared, soberly, "that impulse to the divine, to the One, and to the One beyond the One. All that's required is knowledge of the proper rites. You must understand how the gods work and how each work corresponds to different layers of reality.

"First," he explained, "there are sacrifices of the inorganic and organic, stones and plant-life. Then, moving upwards we find oblations of creatures that move, of sentient beings, of animal blood releasing life unto Life. Highest of all, in the realm of pure understanding, though most difficult to achieve, there are sacrifices of intellect, of thought itself. The latter are immolations of nouns and verbs, adjectives and adverbs, all words which bind, tie, and falsely delimit."

The hall was silent. The hall *was* the realm of pure understanding. At least it was the attempt. But what did it *mean*? Was Iamblichus being literal? Or did he mean it all metaphorically or symbolically, or all three somehow?

I glanced over to Constantine to see if I could make out what he was thinking. I couldn't—except to suspect a look of mild frustration. Perhaps, however, I was merely projecting my own. While I agreed with the goal, with the soul's movement toward unity with the One, I was unsure about the means. The whole business of finding wisdom and growing wise had become so puzzling since I'd arrived in Alexandria. Rather than gaining clarity, I'd grown confused. Iamblichus wasn't making it any easier. His way seemed too messy, too archaic, *too ridiculous*, I judged. In my mind, whether literal, metaphorical, or symbolical, it mistakenly held to all the old myths and multiplicity of gods and consequently to all the violence, perversion, and absurdity that philosophy has tried to overcome ever since Socrates gave witness against the gods of Homer and Hesiod in the *Republic* and elsewhere.

However I felt and whatever I thought, Iamblichus quite headily explained how these divine works, these works performed through and by means of the many gods, somehow led to a kind of union with the One where the human is subsumed into the divine reality beyond all name and quality. He went on.

Gliding back and forth along the marble floor, his hand alternating between the smooth and oiled curve of his chin and the back of his head where downy hair fell upon a neck free from the sun's stain, he spoke of this complex method known only to the few.

I faded.

What was he saying? Ah, right. The One by means of the many. I glanced at Constantine again. For a moment, I followed my own thinking. How strange, I thought. If the One is beyond the many—which I firmly held despite my uncertainty regarding how to reach it—then why the need for propitiation of any kind? Why the sacrifices? Why the gods? If the One is beyond the realm of everything that moves and changes, and if the One is perfect as the Greeks and all wise men have always had it, then what could the One possibly require? Iamblichus was wrong, I judged.

Returning now to the lecture hall and the lecturer who was going on and on, pacing back and forth, I nearly expressed this hostile sentiment aloud— for as you know, Theophilus, instructors oftentimes invite dialogue in this way. For a moment, I raised my hand to ask a question. There it was, my hostile hand, like a lone soldier in the middle of a battlefield. That's how I felt. I was nervous. Would he listen or would he simply ignore me?

Look my way, I silently implored.

Iamblichus, however, didn't turn to look. Instead, gazing at Constantine or beyond—I couldn't tell—he proudly forged ahead with his teaching about the One. Finally, I lowered my hand as the initial passion to confront him surrendered to my ongoing nerves.

Meanwhile, Iamblichus was confidently explaining the nature of the One. "The One is beyond the Good," he asserted. "It is absolute Unity, a oneness to the bone you might say, about which nothing more can be said. It's pure abstraction, *the* Abstract."

I glanced at Constantine who stirred at Iamblichus' claim. As he later told me, this idea bothered him along with Iamblichus' proud demeanor. Now the irritation came to a boil. I could see it. Right before Iamblichus and without first gesturing for attention, Constantine boldly stood to say so.

"Iamblichus!" he called.

The instructor's eyes turned toward Constantine, a bit startled at his rising. "Yes?"

Constantine lobbed a simple question. "Does the One beyond the Good have a name, a specific identity?"

The lecture hall fell silent for a moment, after which came a collective gasp from the many. Clearly, they judged, it was an impossible question. Hadn't the instructor just explained that nothing more could be said?

"I mean to say," Constantine confidently went on, "cannot the One be known or identified in any other way than as pure abstraction?"

Iamblichus began to respond, but before he could, Constantine finished by asking, "Is the One a *who*, or just a what or that?"

I smiled—for several reasons. This is when I first saw Constantine's true character. While he was many things, Theophilus, he was not a man of abstractions. Although he would converse about abstractions, with abstractions, toward abstract conclusions, and to an extent, he'd enjoy doing so, he was ultimately a man of concrete thought and concrete action—though not for lack of intellect. Rather, a sense of concrete destiny always drove him forward. He intended his question to yield useful knowledge in place of mere abstractions.

In the meantime, Iamblichus turned a whiter shade of white the longer Constantine carried on. As for me, I thought that his question made sense. If in fact there are concrete, singular, ritual works corresponding to the many concrete, singular gods and different layers of reality, then there must be further correspondence to the One itself. Therefore, if the former had names, so too must the latter.

I must stop and explain.

This is why I did not favor Iamblichus' cosmic construction and his work of gods, his theurgy. The One is entirely alone. The gap is unbridgeable between the One and the many. I knew that either this is correct and the One is truly distinct from the many, or there is no separation at all and a man must accept the radical unity of both. To do that, however, is to do away with the One, I concluded, and so with perfection and perfectibility. And that, Theophilus, was unacceptable to me.

No, to me, Iamblichus' theurgy seemed a cheap manipulation, a trick. What did it do for philosophy? While accurately declaring the gap and so a distinction between the perfect One and the imperfect many, his system nonetheless professed some kind of ambiguous relationship between them by means of both earthly and ethereal correspondences. Yet *what in Jupiter's world was that?* I wondered. Confusion—*that's what*. Consequently, his system seemed similar to the various magical rites that have always been with us such as we find in the mystery religions and Gnostic cults. Theurgy seemed a way to gain power over the One and so manipulate the One by means of the many—the many intermediary gods and immolations of stone and stick, animal and adjective. Absurd, I thought. *That* is no way to the One—not, of course, that I knew any other way.

Nevertheless, I saw that many of the auditors were becoming impatient with Constantine. As he continued his line of questioning, many doubtlessly thought that if he were not the son of a caesar and a financial supporter and close to the emperor Diocletian, then Iamblichus would have shut his mouth with the magisterial wave of his hand. Contrary to what he should have done, however, Iamblichus was patient. Here was a prestigious student and, yes, a patron who required affirmation more than explanation. If nothing else, Iamblichus had to maintain his reputation for wisdom.

Therefore, wisely—though it was little more than sophistry, Theophilus— and posing once again as the authority rather than the one challenged, Iamblichus rhetorically asked, "What is the name of the One?"

Ah, the art of oration. Wrongly used, it is the art of composing one clever word after another to make the wrong seem right, and what is not seem to be. Still, I was genuinely interested. If in nothing else, I was curious to see how Iamblichus would maneuver to answer Constantine.

After an appropriate stretch of silence, Iamblichus ingeniously proclaimed, "The One's name is No-name or No-one—*Nemo.*"

There was a collective sigh and nodding all around as if *that* were the answer to it all.

Grinning, Iamblichus went on. "We can't say. It is like the reply Odysseus gave to the blind one-eyed Cyclops, Polyphemus. *Do you understand?* It was only after *not* seeing that Polyphemus came to know Odysseus' real identity. Just so, we too must be satisfied with blindness, for in blindness we see, and in nothingness we know. The One is beyond naming, beyond name, indeed beyond all knowing and seeing.

"This, my good man," he finished, "is precisely why I hold to our vision, our philosophy, and our religious rites. Because the One is beyond, there is a corresponding need for the many traditional gods to serve as mediation between the One and us. There is consequently the need for the traditional religion where both the old and the new, what Rome was and what Rome is, encounter the Always, taking us to that divine abode for which and to which we all possess a natural impulse and consequent movement."

Iamblichus stopped for a moment. He took a breath, having arrived at the conclusion of his—what?—argument? description? assertion? Then, looking at Constantine, he asked, "What do you think, dear man?"

I couldn't ascertain what Constantine the tribune thought, but as if inspired by the gods and suddenly fearless, I sprang to my feet to supply my own considerations.

Emphatically, though begging his pardon, I objected. "But Iamblichus," I said, "the traditional gods are full of so many contradictions!"

Iamblichus turned to me; then he swiveled upon his delicate feet shorn of hair back to Constantine who had now also come to look at me; then he turned back to me.

"Young man—" he began, no doubt having fashioned a high-minded retort, or more likely, given my status, a heavy-handed rebuke.

I didn't wait for him. Boldly I explained, "It was Socrates' judgment of Homer and Hesiod. Zeus and all the Olympians are beings replete with violence and every impurity." I glanced around the room before tacking on, "They're adulterers, murderers, vicious, lustful, and brimming with petty jealousies."

Iamblichus gasped.

An auditor sitting near to Constantine clamored, "Come on fellow, be quiet for a moment and let the instructor speak!"

Another spoke harshly to the same effect, telling me to shut my mouth. "We came to hear Iamblichus, not your worthless speculations!"

I turned red and slunk back onto the bench.

Another intervened. "No! No! Let him speak!"

It was Constantine himself.

The problem was I had nothing more to say. I'd finished my one point.

Constantine said to me, "By Jupiter man, how then is the One known if not by agency of the gods and the traditional ritual means?"

For Constantine, this was a genuine puzzle as I later learned. Although he was then devoted to Apollo the Unconquered Sun, he sensed something beyond.

"I don't know," I peeped, cornered.

I had nothing to give him—nothing to say at his insistence, nothing to satisfy the sincerity betrayed in his voice, nothing to better his faith in the One. The truth is I hadn't a clue myself. I simply believed Iamblichus was wrong.

Whatever the case, Iamblichus finally escaped scrutiny. The color returned to the round of his cheeks as he glided across the hall toward the door. "That's all for today!" he announced abruptly, dismissing the thirty or forty-some auditors that had come to hear him. It was his way of avoiding shame.

Many of the auditors clamored in disappointment, and many more cursed at me in the name of every Greek, Roman, and Egyptian god, not to mention others. Jupiter! Zeus! Amon-Re! I was to blame for his departure, they claimed.

I was, and so I suffered a nearly intolerable embarrassment.

But not Constantine.

As we all stood to go, he waded through the unsettled crowd moving toward the foyer and ended up standing above me. Two of his guard stood behind him, their faces that of stone. Sheepishly, I glanced up not quite sure what to say. His look was severe. No, I realized on second thought, it evinced a searching intellect deep in thought.

Thinking it best now to make my escape, I stood to go, concluding I would never see him again, just as I would never come to hear Iamblichus teach.

As I stood, Constantine grinned at me, leaving me to wonder with some trepidation why he was standing there.

"That's it!" he declared with evident joy.

I imagined he had made a speculative breakthrough. Happy for him, and pleased he was not upset with me, I smiled at him politely before moving to go.

But he didn't let me go. As Polemarchus had done when Socrates and Glaucon tried to make their way up from the Piraeus, he barred my way.

"Three years ago!" he boomed.

"Three years?" I asked, feigning ignorance.

"Of course," he said. "That's where it was! I met you here in Alexandria three years ago!"

Now I let go a note of dim recognition before Constantine went on to recount our original meeting. "Don't you remember? You were here with your father who was doing business with Denis, the chief officer of supplies." He remarked on how much I had changed since then. Now I was a man, he said. "You've transformed from a timid mouse to a roaring lion."

"Not quite," I demurred.

Perhaps not, he agreed; nevertheless, he complimented me on my learning and increased eloquence since that day.

Increased eloquence! I thought. *I'd hope so!* That day I had been so much younger and had played the role of a tongue-tied mute.

Then to my great surprise, Constantine suggested we dine together.

"Eat?" I repeated stupidly, my voice betraying a certain hesitation. Did I want to dine with *this* man—the son of Constantius Chlorus, caesar of the West?

He insisted. "You *do* eat, don't you?"

"I do," I dryly confirmed.

So finally, with my father in mind and thoughts of family obligation and, yes, curious to know the man himself, I agreed to join Constantine for a meal.

Five: Friendship

Late 301 to 302 A.D.

I'M SURE THAT MY FATHER sensed something that afternoon. He had a sixth sense like that, one for good opportunity, for profit. I'm sure that sitting back in Carthage in our country villa Buteo felt something and was quite pleased.

"Something's happened to Arnobius," he would say to Mother, popping his mouth.

She'd doubt it. "In Alexandria? How do you know?"

He'd throw up his hands, half-jesting, half-serious. "Always wanting, woman, never believing. How do I know? You should know, *you* of all women, that when I know, *I know*."

"Did you receive a post?"

"No, I did not."

"Then what?"

"I just know."

"Something good?"

"Something good! Would I tell you if it were not so?—you the queen of worrywarts. It's good. But what, I wonder. I'll have to write him to ask."

I returned his correspondence telling him that indeed something good had happened, that his sense, whatever power *that* was, was right on the mark. It was good for him and good for me. Later on that afternoon, after the lecture given by Iamblichus and its ignominious end, Constantine and I had become quick friends.

"I knew it!" my father cried when he first read my letter.

"What, this time?" Mother returned, drearily rolling her painted eyes.

Buteo bounced up and down like a happy schoolboy. "He's done it! He's done it!"

Mother glanced away from her mirror and demanded an answer. "Buteo," she commanded, "quit acting the fool!"

"Oh, you'll leap with me as soon as you hear what Arnobius has done in Alexandria!"

"Let me guess. He's made you a grandfather. Just remember, whatever it is, it's a bastard—he's not yet properly betrothed."

"No woman! He's met Flavius Constantinus, the son of—"

"I know who he is, Buteo! He's the son of Constantius Chlorus, caesar of the West. You've told me about him a thousand times. A million! How you met him in Alexandria when you made that deal with … *what* was his name?"

"Never mind! Did you hear what I said? He's met him and they've become acquaintances. No, more!"

"Oh gods!" Mother cursed. "Not—!"

"For the god's sake, no!" cried Buteo. "Here, let me read a snippet of what he wrote." My father found the spot and began reading from my letter.

I've attached myself just as you would have wanted, Father, to Constantine and the imperial household. My attachment to him, however, is far more than that of a contact or a business associate—as you always say. It's more a partnership, a friendship of the highest order, an affiliation ordered toward excellence of life. For months, we have been inseparable. When he's not tending to matters of imperial business—with which I oftentimes assist him, as an accountant or lawyer or translator—we're together attending lectures, thinking, and debating. You see, Father, he's a man of both practicality and speculation. I thought you'd like that—at least the former.

"What *does* he mean?" asked Mother.

My father grinned. "I don't know," he lied. He didn't want to get into it.

Mother went back to her mirror and thought of me and my success. Maybe I'd turn out well after all.

Over the months that stretched from that afternoon and the lecture to March the following year, Constantine and I were inseparable. I oftentimes worked with him during the day at one piece of imperial business or another, and in the afternoons, we'd sit in on a lecture given by a number of resident or visiting philosophers. Afterwards, we'd drink Falernian, and alone or with company, we'd debate long into the night imitating the course of the moon in its reflection of light.

During those evenings, Constantine oftentimes burned with metaphysical speculation. I know that sounds abstract, Theophilus, but it wasn't. Rather, his burning desire had a very concrete purpose. He yearned to know who the One was. The hubris, you might say! The pride! Perhaps you're right to object. But not in his case. For him it was more a simple trust, a faith that aspired to know the full nature of its object. It wasn't enough for Constantine to know *that* the One was; he wanted to know *who*.

As for me, I was doubtful about the whole project. I told him we couldn't possibly know. And, I said, whether a *that* or a *who* or a *whatever it was*, it didn't really matter. The permanent One was behind the changing many, and that, I urged, was all we had need of knowing. From the One we came and to the One we would return. I accepted Plotinus' basic formula, "*Exitus et reditus*, exit and return."

"You're really not curious?" he asked.

"Well, a little, sure," I allowed, feeling sophisticated, "but why be curious about something you can't know?"

I had grown more skeptical during the months I had been in Alexandria. As I've said, although I still yearned for certain knowledge and that life which would follow therefrom, I doubted the possibility of it more and more. Sad to say, but it was a trend in my life that developed over time like a chronic illness.

"But what if we *can* know?" he insisted.

"We can't," I said with reason.

I felt I had been over it a thousand times. I had explained that the One is beyond the Dyad, and the Dyad beyond the Nous, the divine Mind, both Thinking and Thought. The Mind, I said, transcends the World Soul and the Demiurge that fashioned us and every other living thing. Why the hierarchy of transcendence? Simple. It is so the perfect One will have nothing to do with the imperfect many.

Despite my better moments of explanation, Constantine persisted in his demand to know who the One was. It was this I came to admire and love in him—his dogged persistence in the face of impossibility. He would know, period; he would conquer, period; impossibility could rot in Hades with the dead.

Later on, I understood why. Some power, a divine madness, drove him to understand and do what he did. It was something with personality, something like Socrates' famous *daemon* from the god, which drove him in his mission to make all men wise. Something akin to that, Theophilus, drove Constantine to know the One and caused him to lead a life that was different from what one might expect from the son of a caesar.

That's not to say that he hadn't lived it up, as they say, when he was younger, drinking and whoring like any other young soldier. He had. That all changed, however, after he had met Minervina. She was the daughter of an innkeeper, and he had a son by her, the boy Crispus. He had loved her; he told me so. Tragically, though, she had died giving birth to Crispus, the son he loved. Afterwards, Constantine had changed as I did after Stella's passing. He had grown more serious, sober. Now, above all, he yearned to know the nature of the Absolute and to serve the One wholeheartedly.

Meanwhile, Constantine continued his practice of solar devotion. He had been initiated years before under the direction of his father, Constantius Chlorus. For Constantine, the god Apollo, driving his golden, blazing chariot across the sky, was the best image he had of the One. Then, when we were in Alexandria together, I couldn't disagree with the image, though neither could I bring myself to offer worship to the Solar Disc—or as devotees call him, *Sol Invictus*, the Unconquered Sun.

"How can you not?" he asked during one of our many intense discussions late at night.

"Because it is *fire* Constantine, mere fire, as the Pythagoreans postulate of the sun. What should I do, give praise to every fire I see?"

"Not *every* fire," he corrected, "only the one fire that gives every other fire its fiery properties."

"I don't think so."

"And consider," he went on, "what better image is there? Have you ever seen the divine Sun?"

"Not directly."

"Exactly my point!" he said with fiery excitement in his voice. "It's just like the One. We can only get a glimpse—and hardly that. The divine Sun is an icon, I tell you, a perfect image of the One."

"Just so," I allowed. "You're right that it is a beautiful image. As Socrates said, the sun is an offspring of the Good. By its light we see, just as by the brilliant truth of the Good we know. But to give the sun worship, to adore an image?"

"Well?" he asked, thinking it plausible.

"Well, no. I don't worship a handwritten script or any other word just because it's a worthy image of the *Logos*, the divine Mind's thought."

Constantine considered this and laughed aloud before drawing up quite serious again, pondering what I had said. Sitting next to him, I assessed the argument as well, and we talked some more.

That's what we did nearly every evening before everything changed. I say everything, because our happy life of diurnal work and nocturnal contemplation came to a sudden end around the middle of March.

One day I woke up to Constantine bursting through my door. "Diocletian's said we have to go!"

I struggled to focus, my mind awakening, attempting to grasp as if clutching at a fog the nature of this obnoxious man. The dark hair pulled neatly forward. The high cheekbones flanking that imperial nose. The muscular chin. The thick neck enveloped by a simple tunic. Strange, I haven't even known him for half a year. Who in all of the cosmos would have burst like this into my sleeping chamber at home? Nobody—*that's who*. The steward would have never allowed it. Then again, Constantine was different.

"Did you hear me, Arnobius? We've got to go!"

"I did," I said, groggily. I leaned up on my elbow. "But I don't understand. What do you mean by saying you have to go? And where?"

"Antioch," he answered, "where we'll keep an eye on the eastern frontier just in case those damn Persians get restless again. Then it's on to Nicomedia and the Imperial Palace."

"When do you leave?" I asked, growing sorrowful. I had known this day was on the horizon and had to come, but I had always hoped he would postpone it indefinitely, that Constantine would stay in Alexandria for another year, that we would go on studying together and—

Suddenly, I realized that I'd be saying farewell today or the next.

Then—

"*You*?" he said. "Don't you mean *we* … didn't you hear me say we—*we* have to go?"

"What?" I replied. "*I'm* not going with you. I can't. I'm here to finish my education. Philosophy, remember? Those useless theories! Then I have to find a post. Don't you remember Buteo, my father, the profit hawk? I made a promise. He'd have a heart attack if I just up and left to Nicomedia with no better purpose than I wanted to see the world with a friend."

"You're usually right, but not this time. If you want purpose then you have it. I'm telling you, I want you to come with me—*and* I've got a job for you."

"What could that be Constantine? You know I'm hardly interested in politics or imperial affairs, at least not for any length of time. And Diocletian frightens me."

I laughed. Constantine did not.

"I know," he admitted. "But you *are* interested in me. And you've helped me a great deal many times before."

"True," I acknowledged.

"And think of your duty to the Empire."

"True again," I allowed, thinking of Cicero's dictum that to serve the commonweal is to do the highest good.

"And so," he proclaimed, "I hereby install you as my chief advisor and chief philosopher."

I fell back to my pillow. "Come on," I said, "quit joking. It's too early. And," I went on, "it doesn't befit you. You're a man of far too many responsibilities and I'm hardly yet a man."

"I'm not joking. I could use you, Arnobius. Look, you can see it as an apprenticeship of sorts. Your father would appreciate that, right, for you to work with the son of Constantius Chlorus, caesar of the West?"

I sat up, intrigued. "By the gods he would! But doing what?" I asked.

"What you've *been* doing. You can do just about anything. You're smart, Arnobius."

"Not really," I demurred.

"You are. Thanks to your father, you know about business, the law, and speech making, and your Greek is superb whereas mine is functional at best. I'm telling you, though young, you'll be my advisor."

I nodded, attempting due measure of modesty. He said nothing more about the *philosopher* part, and I didn't ask.

"And no more about being young. That's such an old line that you've used far too many times. Wisdom has little to do with one's number of years. You of all men should know that. Simple age does not confer wisdom. Remember Alypius?"

I did. He was an old man whose body had never been satiated. He was a Gnostic of one kind or another who claimed unity with the Cosmos by means of carnal activity—sexual orgies, Theophilus. I'm sure you've heard of these fools. He was a drunk and a glutton.

Constantine went on. "Unlike many who have attained a superior number of years, *you* are truly a man, Arnobius. If not yet a man of responsibilities, you're a responsible man."

"I don't know."

"I do. Now come on!"

"I suppose," I agreed, betraying far less excitement than I felt.

Then I threw my legs over the side of the bed so that my feet touched the concrete and tile of the floor.

"Suppose not! It's done!"

And so it was. And so my life altered course, Theophilus. My year in Alexandria was up early, and now, as if fulfilling the promise I'd made to my father or the words he'd spoken like the prophecy of some god, I moved toward becoming a practical man in contrast to the philosopher I had hoped to become.

We departed for Pelusium later that day. Diocletian had business there as well as in Caesarea, Tyre, Berytus, Tripolis, and every city, it seemed, but for Jerusalem, what the Romans call Aelia Capitolina. It was the last time I was in Alexandria for a very long time. But that day, I had no idea. If I had, I would have watched and marveled at the life of the city passing by—the people, the markets, the schools, the Sabaean wise men selling forecasts of the future. Instead, I argued with Constantine about some inconsequential matter and wished to the gods that I had spent more time riding a horse. My rear, Theophilus, ached in a way neither Constantine nor Diocletian riding nearby would ever understand.

Before we went, I sat down to write my father. I'm sure he felt elated when he received the letter many weeks later. In fact, as Mother told it, he bounced up and down again like a schoolboy.

"Arnobius has hit it big!" he cried.

"A grandson?" she asked, smiling.

"No, woman! He's now in Constantine's personal service! An advisor, he says. His title is Chief Advisor—capital C capital A. I can't believe our lucky stars! I just knew he'd come to be interested in real life and work and making money instead of all his books and empty speculation!"

"That's good," she approved, content with my accomplishment. It was another thing done toward the goal of security. "Still," she went on, "he needs a wife and family."

Buteo tossed up his hands. "Oh, leave him alone! There are plenty of young girls to keep him occupied for now. Let him focus on a career. The wife and family will come along with the blessing of the goddess."

"May Tanit grant it then," she finished, returning to her mirror and her own thoughts.

Secretly, Mother hoped there wasn't something *Greek* about our friendship. Later I assured her there was not. Indeed, our relationship became far more Roman once we reached Antioch and even more so once we moved to the Imperial Palace in Nicomedia where we focused more on Roman practicalities and doing than on Greek speculation and thinking.

Living in the imperial city, Constantine and others in the imperial administration kept me busy. I practiced law in the courts, wrote speeches for Constantine, advised him on imperial matters, made orations before a variety of gatherings, accounted for grain and other shipments, and interpreted for a whole range of officials. Although I kept up with new trends, I felt I hardly had time for philosophy amid the swarm of activity. Consequently, the nature of my life shifted considerably, Theophilus, from what I had hoped. But then again, given the kind of men and interests that surrounded me, it would have been impossible for me to forge ahead on any other course.

Caesar Galerius comes to mind. Aside from Constantine, he was the man most responsible for shifting the direction of my life.

Book Two

Constantine the Hostage

303 to July 306 A.D.

Six: Galerius

Early 303 A.D.

I FIRST ENCOUNTERED Caesar Galerius in the Imperial Palace, though on many prior occasions Constantine had told me much about him.

He's the kind of man, Theophilus, that no other man should ever have to know. Yet Fate has deemed it necessary that such men exist. On the one hand, Galerius was a great man. He was a formidable general regardless of his one failure against Narseh. On the other hand, he was pathetic. As he grew older, it seems his gut—both his stomach and groin—progressively held captive his mind, resulting in corpulence, sexual decadence, and a general state of irritation. His passions knew no bounds. Immoderation defined Galerius, his desires given licentious reign for whatever he happened to want. When he didn't obtain his wish, Galerius would fly in rage battling against the man or thing that stood in his way.

There was a particular trait, however, that seemed to temper his vicious nature somewhat by causing an inordinate fear of what might happen when his soul passed on from its fleshly abode to the dark regions below. I speak of his overbearing religious beliefs. Galerius was a superstitious man given over to a constant dread of the gods, of ghosts and demons, and of all spirits that rule the air. Eventually, this trait was one cause among many that led Galerius to hate Constantine as I have mentioned. I'll explain.

Although imperial affairs were moving along favorably, Galerius convinced Diocletian that they were less than satisfactory. This occurred over the course of some months in conferences that were sometimes private and sometimes not. I attended many of these with Constantine who was alarmed by what he heard. I was less so, but then, those many years ago, I was blind.

"Can't you see!" raged Galerius at one of these meetings. He'd drunk far too much wine and was nearly drunk. "The gods are unhappy!" he belched with conviction.

He had arrived at this conclusion for many reasons. As I have explained, Galerius was a partisan of Iamblichus—who, incidentally, was in Nicomedia lecturing and attending to the rites of old Rome. But more, Galerius was strongly influenced by his mother who was a priestess of certain Moesian deities, Tages his chief haruspex, and Malichus his personal priest and an ogre of a man. People said that the latter two had terrifically dark powers by the aid of the hollow spirits of Middle Air. I feared them, as did most.

Galerius spouted his drunken pessimism. "The gods rage, I say! Rome has lost its way! It's failing! Our borders are insecure! Our money system is in shambles! Our population is in decline! Our women are having fewer children! And the men—!"

"Yes, the men," Diocletian interjected, yawning. "Women have no offspring because men like you refuse them the fruit of their wombs."

Galerius turned white with rage. "Are you blind? Our Roman character, I tell you, it's slipping away, draining like the blood of a man slain on the battlefield. We must return to the traditional rites! Everyone must! No excuses and no one excused! Not the followers of that hoodwinking Persian called Mani and certainly not the devotees of the miracle worker, the one we crucified for foolishly proclaiming himself king—the Galilean, that pernicious little Jew they call the Christ. Let the gods hurl curses upon them all!"

"I understand your concern," returned Diocletian evenly, used to Galerius' histrionic fits. Nevertheless, he remained cautiously unsure. He granted there were problems. Hadn't there always been in an empire as vast as Rome's? Even so, he was unsure of how to make a proper diagnosis. Were the problems spiritual in nature? Were the gods truly unhappy? Were these to blame, the beliefs and practices of a few poor men and women on the fringe?

Constantine thought Galerius' fits were all balderdash, and he said so.

Privately, away from Galerius, Diocletian, and the equestrian knights who sat on the Council, I revealed I didn't know. "That's not to say I think the gods are to blame," I clarified. "What a ridiculous idea. And Galerius," I whispered, "*is* a ridiculous man. For all I know, the gods are off playing lawn games in the sun, drinking stiff nectar, and eating dainty morsels of ambrosia without a care."

"Don't be so cheeky, Arnobius."

Although Constantine thought Galerius' analysis was wrong, this was far too serious a matter for him.

"I'm sorry," I offered. "But despite his idiocy, Galerius *does* have a point."

"What's that?" he asked.

"Whether or not the gods are behind our problems, religion is necessary for the Empire."

"Of course it is. But what's that got to do with his demands?"

"Everything. We need a common cult. That's why Numa Pompilius instituted all the rites in the first place. Don't tell me you actually believe the story that's told of how he used to meet up with the goddess Egeria by night."

"Well no, not exactly."

"One would have to be a moron. Livy's very straight about it in his histories. The king did it to keep a hold on the people. They were rough and ignorant, he says, and so Numa intended his legislation to inspire them with a fear of the gods. As I said, for a people to cohere, there's need of a common cult. If some are exempt, then—"

"I don't buy it!" exclaimed Constantine. "Romans are anything but coherent when it comes to religion. Think of it. Every man and every woman in every village from Gaul to Mesopotamia worship their own gods."

"You're right," I conceded. "You're right on that. But ..." I proceeded to mumble something again about the need for an official religion.

Constantine ignored the latter or didn't hear and proclaimed victory. "Of course I'm right. Religion is important. No doubt the god's have always led Rome to her destiny—and so the need for an official cult. Nevertheless, Rome's strong point has always been toleration. One set of gods, yes, and one imperial religion, but many private practices and beliefs. That's what's required now. What do you say to that?"

What did I say? I'm afraid I said nothing.

By contrast, Galerius declared the reverse of Constantine. Rome couldn't afford toleration. Instead, Rome should persecute those who denied the official cult in any manner whatsoever.

Because of this difference, Galerius had one more reason to despise Constantine who tenaciously and defiantly held to the more traditional idea of toleration, the one of Minucius Felix who boasted that Roman syncretism resulting in open-mindedness and forbearance was part of the great edifice of Roman strength.

"The fool!" judged Galerius, glowering at Constantine. "We must drive the foreign, offending religions to extinction! Those who have the temerity to practice them should be burned!"

Diocletian shrugged.

"Not at all," argued Constantine, calmly. "Rome must be tolerant, like the divine Sun that gives light to all."

Galerius scowled.

On and on they argued in the presence of the emperor. Over time, however, given his rank, Galerius eventually won the day, finally persuading Diocletian to support his own view.

I told you, Theophilus, that there were many reasons for his insistent, intolerant position, but Galerius' mother was chiefly to blame. If Galerius was a beast of a man, then she was a monster, the source of his savage character. She herself possessed a nature so horrible as to merit the rumors that circulated about her—that she was a daughter of Hades, ruler of the Living Dead. Even so, she had a tenderness for her son, it was said, a one that brought Galerius to his knees causing him to desire and command her every wish.

His mother was a devotee of the many deities that dwell in the mountains of Moesia. They are fierce gods all and demand sacrifice at every turn of the day. Faithful to them, she gave as desired. In the morning in misty grove, she poured libations upon dewy grass over darkened soil. At evening time when the sun faded beneath the earth, she offered barley grain and fruit. Late at night under the dark sky and the pale face of the moon, she sacrificed bleating goats and screeching hares as the gods preferred, sprinkling their blood on trees and soil, lintel and hearth, and somberly making their sign upon her forehead.

Afterwards, she took the flesh of those poor beasts and gave it to her servants—for she wished her whole family to participate in her service. Yet not all would partake. The religion of some forbade it. More to the point, the Christians in her family refused. They not only declined to worship and make sacrifice, but they also refused to eat the flesh she offered. While the rest of the household feasted, they huddled in a corner praying and fasting for her soul and for the conversion of her whole family.

"You ungrateful dolts!" she yelled. She called down all manner of curses upon their thrice-blessed heads and abused them in many other ways as well. But more. She wrote to Galerius telling him of their hatred for the gods and demanded that he do something. She desired the obliteration of all offensive foreign beliefs and practices.

Her written request corresponded well with the rumor that was prevalent among those who wished to preserve the old ways. They were chiefly philosophers like Iamblichus and certain statesmen. Among them was Hierocles the governor of Bithynia a man who styled himself a freethinker. The rumor? "Christians are atheists," they asserted. "They don't believe in the traditional gods. They follow a mortal man, a rebellious Jew."

"All too mortal!" screeched Galerius angrily at yet another conference intended to persuade Diocletian of his point of view.

"Perhaps," allowed Diocletian.

At present, though, the emperor saw no need to move until he gained political support. He didn't want people to blame him for such an atrocious policy if it wasn't popular and failed to work. Consequently, rather than immediately issuing an edict, he consulted his advisors, civil magistrates, and military commanders in order to ascertain what course of action he should take.

The response was clear. Christians and Manicheans deserve punishment, they advised, because they hate the gods and therefore the foundations of Rome. Some suggested that the Empire should confiscate their property. Many called for torture and death. Tages the haruspex and Malichus the priest called for their evisceration.

A few disagreed. One, of course, was Constantine who was convinced that Rome should respond tolerantly to both. Once again, he bravely stated his position to the emperor in contrast to the view of the majority of his counselors.

Aside from his own reasons, Constantine argued based upon what his father had written to him in a letter some time before. His strong advice was for forbearance. Constantius Chlorus pointed to the legal precedence of the emperor Gallienus who had ended the persecutions of Decius some fifty years before.

Constantine also had in mind discussions he had had with Lactantius who held the chair in Latin rhetoric in Nicomedia. Diocletian had appointed him despite the fact that he was unapologetically a Christian. Embarrassingly so. Still, he was a brilliant man. Lactantius himself firmly advocated tolerance based upon the idea that in matters of religion and philosophy, rational discourse and persuasive dialogue should always prevail over coercion. He argued that a forced belief is no belief at all. Constantine agreed.

"You're right in one respect," Diocletian allowed him. "The Empire has always been tolerant—though perhaps to a fault."

"Indeed to a fault," Galerius sneered.

Whatever the case, high-ranking men began to assert that the Christian religion was inherently treasonous. These men declared that as far as Christianity was concerned, loyalty was a simple either-or. A man could either be loyal to the Christ, their Lord, or loyal to the emperor, the ruler of the Romans. The same was true for the Manicheans and their leader, Mani. Given the opportunity, Christians would rebel just as the Jews had done so many times and the Manicheans had prepared to do in Coptos not ten years before.

This frightened Diocletian. Still, the emperor was hesitant to act. In recent months, he had become old and indecisive. Mentally, he went back and forth. If Galerius was right, he should take action in order to mollify the gods of Rome. Yet what if he upset other gods, such as the Christian god?

In the end, to settle the question he sent off a delegation down the Sacred Way along the coast of Asia to the oracle of Apollo at Didyma. The reply came back some weeks later.

The chief haruspex of the oracle, a frail man with silver hair and one blind eye, made his way up to the Imperial Palace in Nicomedia in order to give report. When he did so, Diocletian hovered over him menacingly, sitting high upon his Persian inspired, golden throne. Regally he commanded, "Tell me, how did Lord Apollo judge?"

After having raised himself from a lengthy prostration, the haruspex reported the god's revelation word for word. "The pious are a disease. They harm the empire. The emperor must do something."

"That's all?" demanded Diocletian.

The haruspex nodded, afraid to say anything more.

The emperor thought for a moment before asking, "What did Lord Apollo mean by *the pious*?"

The haruspex hesitated.

"Tell me!" insisted Diocletian, raising his voice.

"The followers of the Galilean, Lord."

"Ah," said Diocletian, "I see."

Galerius was elated when he heard the news. And drunk. But his elation soon turned to irritation and that to rage when he discovered Diocletian's restraint in persecuting the religion he so despised. It was mid-February.

"The edict does nothing to exterminate these rodents!" he shouted. "Not a damn thing!"

"Nothing?" asked Diocletian, sober and therefore unperturbed.

Actually, Theophilus, the edict did more than nothing. It made provision for the destruction of Christian churches, literature, other ritual paraphernalia, and eventually Christian life. The first to go was the church that stood on a hill next to the Imperial Palace. It had been there for decades. On the day after the emperor promulgated the Edict against Christians and Other Sects, however, it was torn down brick by brick, by a mob of rollicking soldiers.

Galerius was still unhappy. "Why didn't you burn it?" he demanded, storming into the great hall where Constantine and I were speaking with the emperor about another matter.

Diocletian said nothing.

Constantine turned to Galerius and remarked, "Consider it—a large fire in the middle of the city might have led to a conflagration throughout the whole."

Galerius glowered at Constantine before turning back to Diocletian. "Why does he think anyone wants to hear him speak his mind?"

"I do," said Diocletian, ending his silence. "And we did use fire. We burned their filthy books, the togas used by their priests, and whatever else it is they use to celebrate their rites."

Galerius wasn't pleased. Still, he got his all-consuming fire the following day.

There was a man, a Christian, who lost his mind when he saw the *scutarii* posting the edict around town. Seeing one freshly hung, posted on the brick wall along the palace, he tore it down, ripped it to pieces, and cursed the madmen who had unrighteously declared against Christian practice. Immediately, the palace guard snatched up the poor man and brought him to the imperial prison. There he was judged and found guilty of high treason. Galerius himself pronounced the sentence with pleasure. He'd be burned alive on the ruins of the church that had been demolished the day before.

I was there, Theophilus, when it happened. I witnessed the man struggle for his god, the Christ, remaining brave and faithful to the end. The guard tied him to a large bundle of sticks doused with pitch fuel for more efficient burning. Then they set everything afire. I could see his eyes glancing heavenward, calling on his god. I felt for him, horrified, as his skin and flesh began to burn and melt and pull away from his bones.

"It's a fool's errand," declared Constantine standing next to me, less horrified than full of dismay. "It'll never work if unity is what Diocletian desires. There must be toleration—like the divine Sun, the one Sun that gives light to all."

Nevertheless, there was little Constantine could do. Even so, he didn't give in; he continued to make his case against intolerance and persecution.

His persistence, however, merely served to attract the hatred of Galerius and others who wished to take even harsher measures. In fact, the more outspoken he was, the more Galerius thought about how to eliminate Constantine. He had been a source of irritation and embarrassment for far too long.

Seven: A Change of Power

Late 303 to 305 A.D.

LATER THAT SAME YEAR, satisfied that the Empire was moving along in the right direction and confident the gods and Galerius were satisfied as well, Diocletian celebrated his *vicennalia* in Rome, his first twenty years as emperor. He did so accompanied by the western emperor Maximian and Constantius Chlorus, his caesar. As Diocletian's own caesar, Galerius attended as well, as did Constantine, who met and spoke at length with his father about Rome, religion, and the true philosophy. I did not go for the simple reason that Galerius forbade me to go in order to irritate Constantine. His intention was to demonstrate who had the real power.

Consequently, I don't have much to say about the vicennalia celebration itself, except for that which formed the usual buzz of court life in Nicomedia. My chief source of gossip at this time was a small, round man called Pila, his name signifying a bouncy ball. He was son to one or another of the higher court officials, he was just about my age, and from all appearances, he moved in every last one of every court circle. It seemed he had nothing better to do than to laze around all day and night drinking wine, eating dainty foods, and hearing and spreading court gossip. Like a pretty fly, he'd buzz from one pile of refuse to another. Therefore, whenever I wished to know what was going on within the imperial court or in any part of the Empire, or indeed anywhere with anyone, I'd dine with him.

According to Pila the following occurred. Diocletian, Galerius, Maximian, Constantius Chlorus, and Constantine met in Mediolanum in northern Italy. From there they traveled together in one vast and glorious entourage down to the ancient city of Rome where "magnificent, Arnobius, perfectly magnificent" celebrations were held among the ancient structures of the Old City just beyond the Palatine Hill and below the Capitoline Hill. Pila, powdered and plump, his little fly legs and fly tongue twitching, sat across from me in my private dining room. A Sarmatian slave served us wine and sweet meats.

"Have you been there?" I asked Pila.

"No," he answered—as if *that* mattered.

"Nor have I," I admitted.

For him it was of little significance. He went on to describe what had happened as if he *had* been there by means of the ancient art of gossip. Hands fluttering, Pila said, "On the day set for the chief celebration, the imperial party processed down the Via Sacra, the wide roadway leading westward into Trajan's Forum. Try to see it, dear man."

I did—though fighting a sense of too much wine drunk far too early in the day.

Pila leaned toward me, and breathing wine, he continued. "A million Romans turned out lining the Sacred Way down past the point where it branches into the Clivus Palatinus and the Sacra Via Summus. The majestic Temple of Jupiter is on your left and the Temple of the Lares, right."

Pila paused and swallowed from his goblet, washing down a marinated oyster he'd been gnawing on, before going on.

"Senators were attired in traditional white togas shimmering beneath the sun, carried forward, dear man, by hundreds of slaves in open gold-trimmed litters. They looked proud. Some were young and handsome; most were older and hardened with dignity. Behind them rode the four eminent ones astride white horses in full battle regalia, all draped in capes dyed purple. I love white horses, do you, Arnobius?"

I had never thought about it.

"In any case, there was Diocletian, subjugator and peacemaker, Maximian, conqueror of Britain and barbarian tribes north of the Rhine, and Galerius and Constantius Chlorus, their strong right arms!"

I wondered where Constantine was and asked him.

"He'd already passed by long before. Rank is everything, dear man."

"True," I said.

"Finally," Pila effused, "sacrifice was made to Jove that day in his magnificent house held erect by a plethora of white marble columns crowned with Corinthian capitals—my favorite. It was in the Temple of Jupiter Optimus Maximus, or, as the magistry would have it, Jupiter Stator, the divine Attendant to Rome."

I nodded. I knew these landmarks from a map of Rome my pedagogue Tyrannio had made me master when I was a young boy in Carthage.

Pila grew quiet for a moment, closing his eyes. Then, as though he too had arrived along with the imperial procession, he spoke in the present tense.

"The imperial procession arrives at the base of the temple stairs. The goal, dear man? Rome as Earth will wed Jupiter as Heaven."

"Right," I nodded, eating a sweet meat.

Pila sniffed at his wine before continuing. "Diocletian begins to ascend in order to honorably perform the duty of *Pontifex Maximus*—the Supreme Bridge-builder to the gods. He plays a role that leading men of Rome have always played. Do you see him, Arnobius?"

"I do," I responded, growing somewhat weary of his antics but liking them all the same.

Pila's voice grew louder. I smiled. He was self-absorbed but entertaining. I trailed his voice, which followed the emperor up the stairs to what he must do in service of Rome's gods.

"Now, Diocletian makes the sacrifice. He ascends the stairs one at a time to the great white marble altar perched at the top where it has stood immovable forever. There, other priests await him assembled to assist him and share his glory. This day, the sacred day of celebration, an immaculate, great white bull is given to the Father of the whole world—Zeus to the Greeks, Jupiter to the Romans, Sky-Father to all. Its nostrils flare in anticipation as the men crowd around it."

I lowered my cup not wanting to associate the wine, red as it was, with the blood of the bull. Pila, in contrast, drank deeply.

"The bull shudders when the cold blade severs its life-chord. At last, its eyes fall dark in the hollowness of death. Do you see its life ascending to the Father?"

I saw it. By then I had closed my eyes to better follow him.

"Bright red blood drains from its mouth and from its underside when slashed open for inspection. The bull's entrails gush out and men rush forward to read them for the divine sign. Diocletian, with the help of a small horde of *haruspicis*, finally declares the god's eternal communication. 'It's good!' he proclaims. The auspices are good! Rome will prosper in the years to come and so too will the people of Rome! Once the message of future fortune is relayed among the millions, the people are ecstatic!"

Pila stopped. Now he fell back into the past tense puckering his mouth. "And that," he declared, "was when everything soured."

"How?" I begged, opening my eyes.

"Well," he delivered, "at first, everything was positively cheery. After the great white bull was dragged away and the emperor changed his blood-soaked rags, the crowd was given wine, bread, and entertainments—fulfillment, Arnobius, of Jupiter's sacred testimony regarding the future. The festivities lasted all night, my friend, and like a drunken man, they spilled into the following day."

"Typical, no?" I remarked, for it was.

"Yes, Arnobius, but it seems the merriment rapidly went awry. There were orgies in the streets, debaucheries, violence. Not all half bad, but ..."

But it *was* bad.

It seems, Theophilus, that like a hangover following a binge, the celebrations devolved to tragedy. Whatever the truth of it, Diocletian dejectedly thought as much—*that* is without question. Consequently, or perhaps just coincidentally, he became ill. Very ill. In fact, news had it that he was on the verge of death.

"Near death?" I asked Pila sometime later, sitting across from him once more over cups of wine.

"Indeed. But there *is* a bright side, dear man," he assured me. "At least his death will be natural."

How true, I thought—at least compared to those emperors who'd come before. Still, I was shocked. It was as though a great mountain were finally crumbling apart and tumbling down.

The imperial city was also shocked. Nicomedia quaked with anxiety over what would transpire if he did die—naturally or not.

Despite his very poor condition, Diocletian and his train slowly crept back toward Nicomedia over the next few months. From Ravenna, they passed to Aquileia and to Mursa in Pannonia along the Danube. There he hoped to rest awhile before moving on. But his fever lingered frightfully before growing worse. His end was near.

It was then that Galerius made his decisive move. Finding the emperor near death and out of his usual mind, he took advantage of the situation to force his interests in two matters, among others, that had choked his ever shrinking and lust filled heart for ages.

One, the lesser, and more for his mother, was simple. Galerius convinced Diocletian to pass further legislation making Christianity an illegal religion, prohibited outright, not merely in terms of ritual houses or implements or as a matter of harassing Christian officials, but entirely illicit for everyone in every place. This, the emperor did with a simple nod of his fevered head.

His second interest was also quite straightforward, though more complex than the first in execution. Galerius maneuvered to gain absolute power. Driven by greed, he forced a dreadfully weakened Diocletian to carry through with an idea the emperor himself had already bandied about in Rome—though perhaps Galerius had been behind it all along. Diocletian had spoken of it quite seriously to Maximian—to his great displeasure—and to Constantius Chlorus. The idea? Retirement. Now that the Empire was in order and now that he had reigned successfully for twenty years, Diocletian and Maximian would give up the imperial purple so that the next in line, the two caesars, could replace them.

Somehow, Pila heard how the whole conversation transpired. He had it from a servant, who had it from another, and he from another. Thus—

"*Peacefully,*" he shared with me, winking. "It's the word Galerius used when he asked Diocletian to step down."

"Peacefully?" I said.

He nodded.

"Ah," I said, knowingly. I took a drink.

What, after all, could Diocletian do? Whatever he did, he could not let someone assassinate him after twenty years of peace. No, that end had come to far too many emperors before him—Aurelian murdered by his secretary; Florian and Probus lynched by a mob of angry soldiers; Numerian killed by his father-in-law Aper; and Aper put to death by Diocletian himself, then called Diocles, by a sword thrust into his gut before the gaping eyes of his own army. No, he was in no position to disagree. Galerius, it seemed, now held power de facto if not yet de iuris.

Diocletian conceded.

Nevertheless, he stalled, hoping to retire on his own terms. Complaining to Galerius, he said the timing was all wrong. If he stepped down now, his name would fall in disgrace. "The emperor was forced out," he thought people would say.

Wonder of wonders, Galerius agreed. Taking pity on the old man, the small bit of pity found in his shriveled heart, he agreed to give him a few months.

Miraculously, given a new chance at life and the aid of Asclepius' priests, Diocletian willed himself better.

Meanwhile, Galerius pondered the *imperium* he had won, the power he would soon wield thanks to Diocletian's retirement. He thanked the gods because it would allow him to achieve several ends, among others.

First, in time he would use his power to conquer the whole of the Empire. He wasn't satisfied with being the leading man of the East. No, Galerius had to have it all. He wished to be the sole emperor of Rome, the only power, the only man glorified and honored along with Jupiter and the other gods. It was something he had long coveted and something he would soon achieve. Eventually he would use his status to project himself into the position of the one and only ruler of the Empire.

Otherwise, Galerius pathetically still wished to get rid of Constantine, his old rival. Constantine was the one who had championed toleration to the detriment of the gods. He was the one who had been wrongly paraded with Diocletian after his so-called victory against the Persians. And, as Galerius frequently recalled to anyone who would listen, including Pila who happily passed it along, he was the bastard son of Constantius Chlorus and his whore Helena, the daughter of a mere innkeeper. Once he had the power, Galerius would quickly sideline Constantine, and if the opportunity presented itself, he would murder him.

This made Galerius happy. He'd like that, to see the strong man, the young hero, the man favored by Diocletian, dead. He'd like to see him stabbed to death by his own guard or snuffed out by Rome for treason.

Still, Galerius would have to move carefully. He'd have to proceed with patience. He couldn't get ahead of himself. First, Diocletian must retire. Even then, he must move cautiously. He would have to share power with others, including Constantine's own father, which implied at least the appearance of a certain respect for his son. This would be true until he could arrange something.

Unfortunately, patience was a commodity that did not come easily to Galerius. Nevertheless, at it happened, events didn't quite occur in the way he envisioned.

I was surprised when Diocletian finally returned to Nicomedia. We had all expected his death—or so had the rumors. In fact, Pila had proclaimed it's inevitability with certainty. Yet it was not so.

"He looks like he's aged a thousand years," reckoned Constantine in private, shortly after we had reunited.

Having not yet seen him up close, I tried to imagine Diocletian old. Sick. Even dead. But how? Ever since I had first seen him in Alexandria when I had stood beside my father nearly ten years before, he had always seemed so strong to me. Invincible. He was a man whose strength had frightened me.

Constantine was more realistic and matter of fact. "It's the way we'll all go," he said, "strong or not."

It is, I thought.

Constantine finished the last of his cup of wine, and after a moment, he queried, "What's the latest on the street?" By latest, he meant the most recent of ideas in the East.

"I wish I could say differently," I reported, "but Iamblichus and his band continue their ideological rule and Hierocles continues to give them his support. He wrote a long epistle rambling on about the gods and how offered blood is the surest doorway to the One. Limits break down when it spills from an animal's body. Then the soul's able to—"

Constantine cut short my report. "So, nothing new?"

"No," I laughed, "though I must say that contrary to every prohibition, a few Christian philosophers have drawn a strong following. There's one fellow called Lucian. He's gathered a group around him in Antioch. They're a brilliant lot if you listen to what some say."

"Was he here?"

"No. I heard about it from Jason of Ankara. Do you remember him? The load of it is they make Iamblichus sick."

Constantine smiled.

"Iamblichus is terribly jealous," I observed. "Imagine that! Yet his rivals are outlaws! Quite a few have given their life, though many have scurried off to do their duty to the emperor."

"Their duty?"

"Surely you've heard?"

"I imagine, Arnobius, but you speak cryptically. Are they employed by Rome?"

"No, I speak of the duty to let drop a pinch of incense into the emperor's altar fire. It's really just a sign of loyalty, nothing more." I chuckled and sniffed at the wine held high in my hand.

Constantine, however, did not. I could see the persecutions continued to bother him.

Now that he was back in the East, the Empire's policy of intolerance confronted him once again. He'd escaped it for a while in the West where Maximian and his own father were unenthusiastic to carry out its demands. But in Nicomedia men died every day. It made Constantine sick.

Despite my laughter—more nervous and a matter of fashion than malicious—I too grew tired of the daily reports of those dying and those soon to be put to death. I recall the members of the imperial household, Dorotheus and Gorgonius, or the aged bishop of the city, Anthimos, among others. Along with Constantine, I earnestly began to hope for change. The persecution seemed barbaric, below Rome's dignity and traditional forbearance.

Still, all hope vanished in early May. It was then that Diocletian retired. Finally healthy, or relatively so, he offered Galerius the imperial purple as if of his own volition, and the latter modestly accepted it. Maximian behaved in like manner in the West.

What did all this mean?

For one, it meant that Galerius was now emperor of the East. As such, he was the leading man in all of the Empire and so he could mostly do as he willed. In the West, Constantius Chlorus rose as his counterpart. The rest was a scandalous joke.

Contrary to the expectations of everyone—that Constantine and Maxentius, the sons of Constantius Chlorus and Maximian, respectively, would be chosen as seconds-in-command—Galerius elevated two men who were entirely unconnected to the prior ruling structure. The two would be the new caesars of Rome. One was Severus, an old soldier friend. He took the West—Italy, Africa and Pannonia—and was nominally under Constantius Chlorus. The other was Maximinus Daza, Galerius' nephew. He took the Oriens.

"You see what he's doing, don't you?" Constantine asked me later on.

"Of course I do," I answered. "It's good old-fashioned nepotism as well as a move to satisfy his hatred for you."

Constantine shook his head. "That's only the beginning," he explained. "At bottom, Galerius needs allies. He's got his eyes set on being the sole power, the one emperor of a united Rome instead of one divided East and West."

I listened.

"Maxentius and I will not do. If he had chosen me, I would have allied with my father against him. For similar reasons he didn't elect Maxentius. No, with his friend Severus in the West and his nephew Maximinus Daza next door, Galerius is secure all around. They'll be his puppets. Now all he has to worry about is my father."

"What about you?" I asked.

"Me!" he scoffed. "I'm actually his strength. With me here, he's got my father trapped in the West doing his duty in Britain and Gaul until the day he dies."

"So what'll you do?"

"I don't know," he replied.

In the end, it all became a waiting game.

When Galerius moved his court from Thessalonica to Nicomedia, Diocletian transferred his, as was the agreement, to the coast of Dalmatia near Salona, where he had been building a palace for just this occasion.

It was then that Galerius' undying hatred for Constantine became immediately evident. With it, danger grew as Galerius began a whispering campaign among the servants and all levels of officials that Constantine was a man who had fallen from the good graces of the emperor, and perhaps, or so the rumor went, he was a potential traitor to the interests of Rome.

Constantine and I spoke about it one afternoon deep into summer.

"I was safer," he said, "when Diocletian was emperor. He was always faithful to my father, just as my father was loyal to him."

"But won't your father march with the army of the West if Galerius harms you?"

"I'm not sure he can. Severus stands in the way. Still," Constantine declared upon further reflection, "Galerius must know that my father will never back down."

I considered this, imagining Constantius Chlorus' one army in a contest with Severus, Galerius, and Maximinus Daza. It wasn't hopeful.

Constantine went on gravely. "To some extent, sacred bonds still hold. Although I'm kept here against my own will as a hostage, even as I was with Diocletian, I'm nonetheless a protected guest, safeguarded by the gods."

"Oh, I feel reassured," I offered, sarcastically.

"You're right," he frowned. "Galerius will only respect the traditional hostage-host relationship if he needs to, if it satisfies his own interests. Ultimately, I'm just a pawn in an empire-wide game, and he's just like any other man who lusts for power. He'll take what he can get, and if he can, he'll take me out despite my divinely protected status."

How true, I judged.

Constantine grinned before saying, "And then you'll be left all alone with him."

I made a sound intoning my displeasure. I'd sooner return home than stay in the service of the Empire under Galerius.

Constantine grew serious again. "Look, he's already moved to put me aside. I haven't had any real responsibility for the past two months. No one approaches me—he's made sure of that. Moreover there are the rumors that I've colluded with the Persians and the followers of Mani."

Foolishly, perhaps, I asked, "Do you think there's any chance he'll let you go west to your father?"

"No chance," he answered, before changing his mind upon further consideration. "There's a small chance, but it's unlikely."

By this small chance, he meant the letter he had received a week before. Galerius had received a duplicate along with other officials to ensure it was widely read. The letter was from Constantius Chlorus asking permission for his son to join him in the West where he was preparing an offensive maneuver against the Picts in northern Britannia.

Constantine continued, "Galerius, whatever other defects he may have, is smart. He must know that if he lets me go he'll have no real way to counter my father. On the other hand, if Galerius receives another missive, one more insistent in tone in contrast to the more diplomatic request of the previous letter, then I suspect he'll have no choice. His position may be forced."

Hopeful, but only by degrees, I said, "Your father *will* send one, won't he?"

"I can only hope. Even then, there's no telling what Galerius will do. However smart, he's a man controlled by the passions and engorged with his own power."

Another letter came in late September. This time Constantine's father insisted with hinted threat upon his son's return, and so Galerius had to give in.

Still, the latter waited, stalling, hoping he could delay Constantine's departure for as long as possible. We first heard it from Pila.

"Galerius is beside himself," he reported, glancing around to make sure no one else heard him. Pila's nails, well-filed and well-shaped, tapped nervously beside him.

"What's he thinking?" asked Constantine.

"Delay, my friend. Ever to delay."

Constantine and I glanced at each other. We knew something must be done. But what? Sure his father had demanded his return, but if Galerius barred the way, then what could be done?

That question plagued us over the next few weeks through October and into early November.

About that time, Constantine told me of an intuition he had had, one that had haunted him for many years. The intuition was of a divine plan, of divine providence.

I admit I was intrigued. Still, given my views regarding the One and the many, I was skeptical. I had fundamental doubts about anything as simple as divine providence. I asked him what he meant, but his response was vague. So wisely, I thought, I conceded his general position before countering the specifics that usually followed from such a view.

"Possibly," I allowed, "there is a kind of providence for the cosmos as a whole, in some grandiose manner. But not for us, not for you and me or for any other individual souls."

In my mind, there was far too great a gap for that—or so I believed, Theophilus. I persisted in my conviction that there was a great divide separating the One from the many.

Constantine, however, disagreed with what I had allowed. His claim of providence was far more personal.

"How?" I asked, nearly smirking. "How *exactly* is the divine involved? Is it as we read in Homer? Apollo shows up, strengthens the hand of Hector, son of Priam, and Patroclus dies?"

"No," he responded, straight-faced.

"How, then?" I pressed. "Isn't it all a bit absurd?"

"I can't really say," he answered sharply. Then tempering himself, he explained, "I don't know exactly. I just do, Arnobius. I would say it's a feeling, but it's more than that. It sustains me; it strengthens my will. I know it in a way that surpasses reason."

"Perhaps," I gave in, backtracking some.

I felt I had offended him.

To conciliate, I suggested, "It might be that you feel the movement of the World Soul. It is possible this movement stimulates and motivates great souls, men of import like you, Constantine. But I can't see it for all souls."

I certainly didn't understand it that way for me.

Constantine smiled. He *knew*.

After a moment of silence, he steered us away from the abstract and declared, "We must plan our escape."

"Escape?" I repeated, taken aback at the sudden shift in conversation.

"I've thought about it long and hard and have concluded that Galerius will never let us go. He can't. Even if he releases me by some intervention of the gods—and he won't—he'll prevent you from leaving just to irritate me. Do you wish for that?"

I didn't.

"Then we have no other choice. We must act."

Possibly, I thought. Yet I had no such wish to leave. Consequently, I harbored the belief that events would unfold in another way. Yet as it happened, he was right.

Eight: Escape

Late November 305 A.D.

ON THE IDES OF NOVEMBER, Galerius announced a great feast. As soon as I heard word of it, a servant knocked at my door asking me to come to Constantine's apartment. I begged Pila's pardon and walked there.

"What's going on?" I asked him as soon as I passed through the door to his private rooms.

The servant closed the door behind me.

Constantine said nothing for a time as if giving the servant a moment to walk away. Then whispering, he asked, "Have you heard about the feast Galerius plans to hold?"

"I have," I said. "I was just with Pila."

Constantine grinned, as he knew what *that* meant. Pila had probably known for weeks. Then he asked, "Do you recall what we discussed the other day, the need to escape Galerius and go west to my father?"

I nodded that I did remember.

"So that's when we'll go," he declared. "We'll leave the night of the feast. Galerius will be drunk along with all his henchmen. He'll not notice and—"

"Leave?" I asked, interrupting. I hadn't taken him seriously—at least as far as my own role was concerned.

"Escape," he replied, perfectly serious.

I stood blank faced. Did I really *want* to leave? Not particularly. I had grown used to court life, and to all the gossip, and to Pila, among other friends and associates, and had even come to take an interest in imperial business. Further, I had come to appreciate the intellectual life of Nicomedia, where there was always one philosopher or another lecturing. It was certainly better than it would be in Gaul where we'd go. What was in Gaul? Forests? Wild animals? Barbarians?

Thinking about it, however, reason to go piled upon reason. I had no desire to go home and lose Constantine's friendship. Moreover, Father would never forgive me for voluntarily giving up such a huge and intimate contact. In addition, life at home would be boring compared to what I had in Nicomedia. But if I stayed in the imperial city, it would be with Galerius, and that, I didn't want.

Hence, I nodded my understanding that we must go, and Constantine told me how to prepare—how to pack lightly and how to dress.

"How will we travel?" I queried.

"Leave that to me," he ordered.

So trusting, since such an operation was beyond my own expertise, I did. We'd leave in three days.

Two days later, I was eating with Constantine when a dark servant from India came into the dining room bidding us to follow him, saying the emperor Galerius wished to see us.

When we arrived, Galerius Augustus, half nude, was sprawled out on a brightly colored silk couch, partially draped with yet still more silk and drinking Falernian from a golden cup. Fires roared nearby. A beautiful young woman, painted and diaphanously clad, ministered to his body and particularly his feet.

"You called, Lord?" Constantine inquired after kneeling.

"Yes," laughed Galerius. "You may rise. You too, my dear man, Arnobius."

Turning to Constantine, Galerius announced, "I hear you wish to leave."

A chill traveled up my spine, gooseflesh spreading over the whole of me, while Constantine shifted feet.

Then peering into the emperor's hollow, diseased eyes, with his own eyes unmoved, Constantine boldly ventured, "It's true. My father wants me to join him. You know that—you've also received his correspondence."

"Yes I have, and yes I do know it. However, Constantine,"—he said it sweetly, or as sweetly as a man could who was full of hatred for the one addressed—"up to now, contrary to your father's aspirations, I haven't wanted you to leave."

Galerius let his words have their effect. As for me, I began to sweat a cold sweat.

Then there was a duplicitous smile as Galerius shifted. "But now, things have changed, dear man. I'm granting permission—you may go."

Calmly, as if it were ordinary news, Constantine confirmed, "I have the emperor's consent? I'm free to go?"

"That's correct. And soon I'll write your father to that end."

I grinned, but quickly I contained it.

Galerius continued. "Even so, you must wait to leave until the days following the feast I'm giving on tomorrow's eve. Then take your time—there's no rush. After all, you may not return to Nicomedia for a long while. Enjoy the city and the palace while you have it, for Gaul is nothing more than a pisshole."

"Fine," replied Constantine. "I'll do that. Perhaps after a week or so?"

The emperor nodded. He looked at the young woman sitting by him and visually stroked her curves before looking at me and saying, "Oh, and one other thing."

"What's that, my Lord?" Constantine asked.

Galerius swung his legs, chicken legs shorn of hair, over the silk covered couch and placed his bald feet upon the cold marble floor. The young woman meekly backed away. Finally, he stated, "Arnobius must remain here in Nicomedia with me. I have important business for him to accomplish."

There was a brief moment of silence as Galerius feasted upon our apparent consternation. My own, I'm sure, was palpable.

He frowned, however, when with seeming indifference Constantine agreed. "I understand, Lord. I don't imagine Arnobius would want to go anyway. He's no partisan to cold climates and has grown fond of court life and imperial business."

I flushed white wondering why Constantine was betraying me. Even so, I remained quiet, as the emperor had not spoken to me.

In response, Galerius said, "Perfect, then. I'll see you tomorrow night." Then shifting his glance to me, he added, "And you too, Arnobius."

I forced a smile.

Turning back to Constantine, he politely said, "Do come with an empty stomach for once. There's bound to be *everything*, and even *you* might find it nice to indulge yourself for once in the great variety of tastes given by the gods!"

Galerius cackled before abruptly dismissing us.

+ + +

Minutes later: "You understand?" I demanded of Constantine, severely irked, once we were well away from Galerius and anyone who might be interested in reporting our conversation.

"Quiet!" he sternly commanded.

I was.

An hour later, we were walking along the Sea of Marmara whose waters lap gently along the walls of Nicomedia. Locals call it the Propontis. We were alone.

"I'm sorry I hushed you like that, but we weren't safe."

"Safe?" I asked, incredulous. I stopped walking. "We were near your apartments."

"Exactly—where I fear there's a spy."

"How do you know?"

"Why do you think Galerius freed me to go? Why did he call us to him just a few days after we made our decision to leave? I may be wrong, but I believe it's because he had heard from his spy that I was going to simply up and leave on my own without his consent. *And* with you. Don't forget, Galerius has ears everywhere, including among my own servants."

"But why the permission to go?"

"A feint to stop me. In order to frustrate my plans he's given me leave to go."

"That's odd."

"Not really," he explained. "It's a common strategy in battle. You go in one direction to make way for another."

I conceded the point. "So what's the plan now? Are you leaving me alone?"

We began walking again. Small waves crashed upon the pebbly shore.

"No," said Constantine, "I'm not leaving you."

"Of course not," I declared as if I'd never believed it.

"And we won't wait until the days after the feast."

"Why not?"

"Because that's his plan. If we wait, Galerius will contrive something. He intends his permission to delay me. Once I'm relaxed and thinking I can leave whenever I wish, he'll beg my presence for another week or month, or more likely he'll find a reason to arrest me or—"

"He'll arrest you for treason and put you to death."

"Naturally."

"What then?" I begged.

Constantine stopped walking and faced me.

"We'll stick with our plan," he declared.

"But we can't," I protested. "Galerius already knows about it and he'll have men posted everywhere. A flea won't be able to get away!"

Constantine disagreed. "No, he won't. Now he thinks I'm quite secure to him—at least through the night of the feast. He believes I've taken his offer to heart—and that's what I'll feed to his spy, this servant of mine. He won't have to worry about me until the following day or so. After that, he'll watch me closely and plot. The time to go, therefore, is toward the end of the feast, when he will have quite literally lost his guard."

"Then he'll be drunk," I said, my heart thumping.

The following night, we attended the feast as planned.

Earlier that day, we individually prepared to go packing the few things we'd take with us. Later, Constantine gave me careful direction about how to behave—how to be brave, standing up to fear. That may sound odd, but up to that point, Theophilus, my life had never been in danger, at least not like his. Now, since we were directly contravening the emperor's command, we would be in mortal danger, and so, being a good friend, Constantine spoke to calm me as he might a new recruit under his command. At the end of his speech of encouragement, he commended me to the divine One in which he had fostered confidence, to the Unconquered Sun, and, as he said, to divine providence.

As he muttered the prayers of commendation, I sheepishly wondered how he was so sure that I, Arnobius of Carthage, was part of that plan. I imagined myself caught, tortured, and dispatched by the razor-sharp edge of a knife wielded by some goon addicted to blood and giving pain. I admit I was afraid. I didn't believe in his providence. Still, I believed in him, my friend. I placed my trust in Constantine, son of Constantius Chlorus, emperor of the West.

We arrived late to the feast, as was the custom. It must have been the third or fourth hour. By that time, many of the lower members of the court were already eating and getting drunk.

+ + +

Some hours later, well after Galerius had arrived with his entourage of partygoers, the sodden emperor approached Constantine, and drunk and stumbling over his own tongue, he queried, "Where's your l-lover?"

"Lover?" asked Constantine, shrugging his shoulders. It had been one of the rumors fostered by Galerius about him.

"Oh," retorted Galerius, "D-don't pretend. You're little jewel, Arnobius?"

Constantine said he didn't know. "I trust, though, he's enjoying himself."

We had intentionally separated before the feast. Constantine figured it would appear less suspicious if we sat apart, though in the end, it probably didn't matter. Indeed, when Galerius was searching for me, I was in another room sitting and speaking with an old associate. Presently, we were discussing imperial business and praising the year's grain shipments from Alexandria, and—as bureaucrats are used to doing—dreading the next.

"Well," said Galerius, "I shall have to d-discover where he is later."

Time dragged on, the hours and minutes distended by fear. I tried to maintain courage and a steady disposition but found it difficult going. At one point, the associate noticed and asked me if there was anything wrong.

"I think it's the wine," I prevaricated. "Cheap Greek," I said, forcing a smile, "not Falernian."

He laughed. "For our table, not for theirs," he remarked, pointing in the emperor's direction.

I joined him in laughing—anxiously.

The anxiety grew when Pila briefly stood over me before moving on to another group sitting in a dark corner.

"Who will I talk to?" he asked, cryptically.

"What do you mean?" I shrugged.

Then, bending over to whisper into my ear, he declared, "I will miss you."

I pulled away from him in wonder. *Does he know?*

His expression answered the question.

Then he was off.

Goodbye, I thought. Trembling some, I wondered who else knew.

Finally, deep into night, I saw Constantine pass by. My heart leapt. It was the signal to leave, and I must have lurched, for the associate again asked me if I was all right.

"I'm fine," I replied, thanking him.

Then after some time, just enough to avoid suspicion, I took the opportunity to beg off. Citing a long day and consequent sleepiness exaggerated by the wine as my excuse, I politely dismissed myself.

"I must have fallen asleep for a moment," I said.

"Am I *that* dull?" he asked, laughing, though knowing the sad truth.

"Not at all," I lied.

Then nervously, I got up to go.

It was a moment later.

"Ar-Arnobius!"

I turned.

There was Galerius just behind me leaning up against two rather sober looking eunuchs, both tall. Several guardsmen stood behind.

"Are you l-leaving so soon?" he demanded.

My voice collapsed, and simultaneously my heart and stomach rose to fill my mouth.

"And so soon after C-Constantine?"

I barely managed to say, "Did he?"

Galerius squealed with drunken laughter. I nodded, my eyes wide.

"Well," he said, "I s-suppose you must be off then."

Finally, mastering my tongue, I answered, "I must be. I'm tired and have a long day ahead of me tomorrow."

"I imagine you do," he responded. "Not to mention a long night …"

I nearly fainted. *Does he know?*

I turned and walked out into the palace grounds beneath a sky that was dark except for a slivered moon. Briskly, I began to cross the distance to where Constantine had asked me to meet him. I walked along a stone paved path with a colonnade to my right and a mostly open space to my left. Behind me voices from the feast faded. Ahead I walked toward silence.

As I moved, emptiness settled in my gut and a knot tied itself around my throat. Fear. I felt like a child. Every sound startled me. A cat meowing. A dog barking. A woman and a man whispering love some distance away. Servants, drunk, banging up against the empty wine jugs. Still, I plodded on to our rendezvous point some distance beyond.

Then a man!

A man sprang out from behind a column and grabbed me by the shoulders! I nearly shrieked aloud, but his large hand flew over my mouth to prevent it.

Next, the man roughly yanked me into the dark colonnade to my right. Oh gods! I panicked, squirming. *This is it!* I'd be beaten and dead by morning. I'd never live to see the rising of another sun or Constantine or my father, Buteo, or Mother or …

I faded.

I heard a voice.

It was my father's voice. "Arnobius!" he whispered forcefully. "Be quiet! You'll ruin the deal!" I was.

Then—"Come over here!"

I couldn't, though. I was crippled. I was in the dark, that darkness I feared so much as a small boy when the moon was but a sliver and darkness covered the whole world.

Then another voice. I wrenched open my eyes.

"Arnobius!" it whispered urgently.

"Constantine?" I ventured.

"Quiet!" he ordered.

"What?" I said in hushed tones, finally realizing where I was.

"It's Tages," he announced gravely, "and Malichus!"

My heart froze, for there they were less than a stone's throw away, robed in dark cassocks and whispering to one another.

As I've said, Theophilus, Tages was Galerius' chief haruspex and Malichus his chief priest. I feared them, as did many. They saw the future in the entrails of sacrificed animals, and saw everything, near and far, visible and invisible, by astral projection and by aid of the dark spirits of Middle Air. More, they emanated evil.

We huddled there silently, hoping they wouldn't sense our presence.

As if to comfort me, Constantine quietly assured, "If we're still, they'll just move on."

I wasn't so sure. In broad daylight I would have been. But not in the dark. And not, as I imagined myself to be, a fugitive running from Galerius.

They moved on. Suddenly and with seeming purpose, Tages and Malichus walked off in the direction of the feast.

Shortly thereafter, we crept away, one by one, to where we had originally agreed to meet.

Having arrived, Constantine grasped me by the shoulders and smiled. Still, he said nothing. I knew what he was thinking, though. *We're not safe yet, Arnobius, not yet.*

We quickly changed our clothes, grabbed several small leather bags we'd prepared, and stealthily made our way out of the remaining palace complex to a house where we had horses waiting. Then we mounted and trotted off so as not to draw attention to ourselves.

That changed just outside the city gates and once the Propontis was in view, a small, partial moon reflecting yellowish-white off its placid surface. Then we cantered and finally galloped at full speed toward the Bosporus some fifty miles away, knowing that behind us Galerius might discover our absence at any moment. It was unlikely, yes, as he was drunk, but that sense of probability did nothing to calm my heart. Doubtlessly, I thought, my imagination racing, Tages and Malichus had already spoken with him. My only desire was to keep up with Constantine and make it away as far and as quickly as our mounts could ride.

At the fifteenth mile marker, I fell behind.

It's not that I was tired per se. It was more that I was shaking with fright and both warm and cold at the same time and my thighs began to ache and spasm from the constant tension of grasping the horse's body with my short legs. Already I wondered if I'd be able to make it. Constantine was a soldier. And me? I laugh.

At that point, we had more than a thousand miles to ride until we'd be safe. Then there was half that again across Gaul. In the dark of night and the chill of near winter, the distance seemed impossible. For a moment, I thought I might let Constantine go on by himself, and so I slowed down considerably. I imagined he was already miles ahead of me speeding toward freedom. Perhaps if I turned around, Galerius wouldn't have noticed yet.

Just then, Constantine rode out of the dark, lurching, until his horse's muzzle was next to mine.

"We've got to go!" he shouted. "We haven't time to linger!"

"Linger!" I yelled, indignant. If he only knew the truth!

He turned his horse around next to mine.

"I'm sorry," he offered. "I know you're not used to this. But we *must* move as hard as we can, at least for now—for the next few days. Galerius will send men after us!"

"What will we do?" I asked, frightened. "How will we stop them?"

He still hadn't informed me of his plan.

"Leave it to me," he said. "We'll be okay. But for now, we must ride!"

I shook my head.

Then, "Yah!" and off he ran again at a full gallop, bidding me to follow him closely.

Forgetting my desire to turn around, I thrust my legs into the horse's side, and off I went following Constantine at some distance, though striving to remain close to him even while falling more and more behind.

A half hour later, I saw the torchlights of a *mutatio*, a posting station, in the distance. I was not surprised as these exist every twenty or thirty miles along every Roman road in the Empire as part of the *cursus publicus*, the imperial transport and communications system. Some are for exchanging animals, as was this one. I could tell because of its small size. Others, larger *mansiones*, serve as inns for official couriers and others.

As I rode nearer to this mutatio, I saw Constantine afoot prowling around outside as if attempting to see what was happening inside. When he saw me, he ran to me.

"Quiet, Arnobius!"

I hadn't said a thing.

"Where's your horse?" I asked, whispering.

"Dead."

I was tempted to ask how and why, but I stayed my tongue.

"Dismount," he commanded.

I did.

And shock! Constantine killed *my* horse! Just like that, he forcefully grasped its muzzle with his left arm, and with his right, he cut up deeply into the animal's throatlatch. Horror flooded the horse's deep brown eyes. I could see it in the dim moonlight, and I saw its black blood gurgling down from the wound, and with it, life. Not ten counts passed before the animal fainted; in thirty, it was dead.

"Let's go," he ordered. "I think this should be simple."

Simple? I wondered. I'd be able to agree—or not—if I knew the plan! Nevertheless, faithfully, or rather, petrified out of my mind, I followed.

Constantine knocked loudly at the door of the mutatio. The sudden sound unnerved me even more. A minute later, an older man answered. He had been sleeping and had a coarse woolen blanket wrapped around him. It was gray with blue threads.

"What is it you want?" he demanded, gruffly. He held a small oil lamp. "We weren't expecting anyone."

I could smell he'd been drinking.

"It's your job to expect," Constantine countered. Then he explained who he was—Constantine, son of Constantius Chlorus, tribune of the First Order.

"I'm sorry, sir," the older man explained, now standing more erect. "What can I do for you?"

"First," Constantine said, "we need fresh tunics and riding capes and two large pitchers of water."

The man eyed the bloody mess under Constantine's arms and understood that something was amiss. He didn't want trouble, though. He'd been a soldier all his life and was now retired, a veteran, working a sleepy post in the middle of nowhere. Slightly trembling, he promised, "You'll have it, sir."

Then Constantine asked him how many horses were stationed at the mutatio.

Nervously, stuttering or still inebriated, the man began by giving him more of a report as if to a commanding officer—how many horses were usually housed there, how it changed from season to season, and—

"*Now*, man! I mean how many now?"

"Ten," he said, firmly.

"Good," remarked Constantine. "We'll be back in a moment for the clothes and water."

"Aye, sir. I'll have them ready."

Constantine sped off toward the stables not forty yards away. When he was more than halfway, he turned and shouted, "Come on, Arnobius!"

I ran after him.

When I reached the stables and the horses therein, he had already dispatched a few.

Panting, he glanced up as I entered. "We'll take these two." He pointed to two black horses. "Help me kill the rest."

For a moment, my whole world stood as still as the frozen Rhine does in the middle of winter. *Kill the rest?* Yet quickly I realized what was happening. If Galerius sent his thugs to retrieve us, they'd soon have nothing to ride. I swung into action, making quick work of—well, I killed one animal while Constantine took care of the rest.

Five minutes later, we led the remaining two, for now the lucky ones, up to the mutatio where the old man awaited our return with fresh riding wear and water and an expression that begged us not to harm him. We quickly rinsed ourselves of the slaughter and changed clothing. Then, bidding a sorry farewell to the old man, we dashed off once more. Our next stop was Byzantium some twenty-five miles on.

As we sped away, a smile enveloped my face. I have little doubt it had to do with the surprise of the men who would come in pursuit of us. I saw their shocked faces as they discovered the bloody mess we had left behind. Ten dead horses—eight in the stables and two outdoors—all cleanly butchered, except my one, perhaps. I heard them hurl curses at us and at the stars and at their own fortune for what Galerius was likely to do. I laughed for a moment. Then I shivered with fright. They could still gather mounts from farms in the surrounding countryside.

My mind raced in anxious consideration. They were after us! And they'd reach *me* first, lagging behind, as Constantine was already well ahead.

We made it to the Thracian Bosporus just as the sun, blood red, was breaching the horizon from behind. Not usually given over to omens, I took it badly as dooming us to failure or worse—a violent death. Constantine, however, was thankful. For him, the sun was a symbol of new life.

"Wait," he said, just as we reached the ferryman who would take us from the eastern shore to the west. He pulled out a flagon of wine and quickly made an oblation. He was thankful that the gray waters were calm. Not many months before, he had crossed with Diocletian and his men when they had returned from Rome. Then the sea had raged and many had been lost to the foamy white spirits of the water. Not today, he thought, chanting aloud to the Sea and to the Unconquered Sun rising higher now and oranger into the sky.

Trusting the Divinity, we boarded a midsized ferry and drifted away, feeling better to have even more distance between Nicomedia and us.

Two hours passed and now the sun was well overhead. Having landed on the other side of the Bosporus, we passed through Byzantium and eagerly awaited the next way station where we could exchange horses. If Fortune were with us, we'd quickly be off again on fresh mounts, speeding on our way to the next station some thirty miles away. If not? I tried not to think of it.

Nor did I think of the cold, or my back or thighs, or the fact that Constantine could leave me behind.

"Go horse, go!" I yelled.

Some twenty miles outside Byzantium, we encountered the next mutatio. This time we rode straight up to the station, dismounting.

"Come on," bade Constantine. "I know several of the guards here."

"Thank the gods," I said.

We knocked.

True to his word, Constantine greeted the guard as if he knew him. He was an older man, just as the one before had been, but this time awake and sober.

"Justin!" bellowed Constantine.

"Flavius Constantine!" he said in response.

They embraced.

"Are you here with the emperor again?" asked Justin.

"No," answered Constantine, "private business."

"Ah, of what kind?"

"I can't say. But we *are* in a hurry."

Justin dropped his hands from Constantine's arms. "In that case you'd better be on your way. But first a drop of wine?"

"No, we don't have the time."

"No time for an old friend?" remarked Justin, a bit put off.

Constantine apologized. "We can't, our lives depend on our moving rapidly."

Justin's eyes opened wide beckoning explanation.

Constantine delivered. "Justin, I must ask you to cooperate with me."

The guard stepped back. "What is it?"

Constantine explained what had happened since Galerius' succession—the need to escape, their flight west to his father, and the need to slaughter all the horses *now.*

Nervously, Justin snorted, "I can't do that, old fellow."

"Sure you can. You *must.*"

"But I can't!"

Constantine went to grab Justin by the shoulders in order to plead, but Justin, taking his move as a threat, threw his hands away, and with one quick sweep he drew his sword, a spatha just over two feet long.

"Away, friend!"

I began to perspire—or rather, I continued.

Constantine stepped back. I wondered if he would draw his sword, and for a moment, the matter remained uncertain. He just stood there eying Justin. Planning his move. I thought he might have to kill him.

Justin stood opposite him, staunchly, his eyes on Constantine's hands, eyes, and mouth, awaiting a twitch, a blink or any move that would indicate Constantine's mind.

Then Constantine grinned, his mouth pregnant with prevarication. "Say, Justin. Let me be honest with you. Put away your sword."

Justin didn't move.

"Come on, now."

"I can't. You know that. I have my duty."

"I understand," allowed Constantine, "but you're in danger and perhaps on the wrong side of a fight."

The guard tilted his head obliquely as if confused.

"You see, I'm racing to my father in Pannonia."

Justin protested. "That's Severus' territory. And I know your father's camped at Gesoriacum along the straits. A man rode through not a month ago. Said he's preparing for war."

"You're right," admitted Constantine, calmly. "He was. But now he's in Pannonia preparing for war against Galerius. Severus is dead."

"Impossible!"

"It's true."

"But it …" he hesitated, "it can't be!"

"It is," averred Constantine. "And you don't want trouble! Now be a good friend and allow us to do what we need to do!"

"I can't!" he shouted.

"If not …"

I stepped back. And with that, with my few distracting steps and his few words, Constantine jumped at Justin and overpowered him.

Five minutes later, Justin was knocked out and bound, his back resting against the wall, and we were already outside bloodying our hands. I killed three this time, Constantine slaughtered ten, and we kept our usual two. Then, after washing, changing, and appropriating several loaves of old, crusty bread, we rushed westward.

+ + +

We did this repeatedly until we reached Serdica. Our race was nonstop—aside from the hour or two Constantine allowed for sleep. I lost count of the number of posting stations after Hadrianopolis, nearly two hundred miles and two days from our beginning point in Nicomedia. Thereafter, past Serdica and some three hundred sixty-five miles out, Constantine believed it would be enough simply to take new mounts without all the slaughter.

"But don't rest too easy in your saddle," he wryly advised.

As if. I couldn't think of resting, my feet dangling, my thighs squeezing to hang on. My rear, Theophilus, and my crotch I'm loath to admit, hurt more than any pain I'd ever known. At first it was dull, then pointed and intense, then dull again shooting up my spine and uncomfortably lodging at the base of my skull.

"I won't," I said, dryly.

"Good. We've got nearly two weeks before we reach Gaul."

"But what about Severus' territory—Italy and Pannonia? Isn't it safe? He's under your father's command."

Constantine raised the left of his thick eyebrows. "He is, is he?"

No, I thought, of course not.

From Serdica we rode toward Sirmium. On the way, we passed through Naissus, a small military town near the Danube where Constantine grew pensive. For a while, I let him be. Then, curiosity getting the better of me, I asked him what he was thinking about.

"My birth," he revealed.

"And why is that?"

"Because this town, Arnobius, what used to be a mere military outpost, is the town of my birth."

"You never told me."

"You never asked."

Of course I hadn't. It hadn't occurred to me. Constantine, the son of a caesar and now emperor, came from, well, from powerful loins! That's how I'd thought about it, if at all.

"My mother was the daughter of an innkeeper."

"Oh?" I said without further inquiry. I had known that thanks to Galerius and Pila, and I knew what it meant. Everyone knew she had been a whore.

"My father brought her here, and so I was born along the river."

I didn't ask where his mother was now. That I also knew. Constantius Chlorus had sent Helena away for political reasons. His father had long since married Theodora, Maximian's stepdaughter.

"What's your father like?" I asked.

A great, muscular smile stretched across Constantine's face. "You'll like him, Arnobius. At the very least, you'll respect him. But like me, I think you'll come to love him."

I imagined so.

"But enough talk, we must ride!"

We rode along the Danube for days and days, close to its very end—or its beginning more accurately stated. From Sirmium we rode north to Aquincum, then westward to Carnuntum. Finally, we crossed the Great River at Castra Regina.

"We're near to Gaul," Constantine declared.

The landscape was a spotty alpine all around. Great rocky crags surrounded us on either side. Below were snow-covered hills.

"Thank the gods," I rejoined.

Four days later, we crossed the Rhine, which meant we were finally in Gaul. I fell to the ground exhausted and kissed the dark soil.

Constantine looked at me from atop his mount and laughed.

"What?" I asked. I was too happy to care.

"You, Arnobius."

"I know," I said. "I should have been a soldier."

"Perhaps you'll be one yet."

I grinned.

That night we slept in a cozy inn for five hours straight after supping heartily by a warm fire. The inn was owned by a gnarled looking man who I supposed must have been as Constantine's grandfather had been. We were safe, and I for one was happy and content.

Still, we had the whole of Gaul to cross. About this, I wasn't very happy. I would have been pleased to stay in that inn for a week or more if Fate had so deigned. Alas, Theophilus, Fate is rarely so kind.

Nine: Gaul

Late December 305 A.D.

IN GAUL, WE SLOWED after pressing hard for over two weeks.

By that point, I could hardly stay erect on my horse. Before I had hurt and I had cursed the gods and I had even wished that I had never stepped foot in Alexandria or met Constantine or gone to Nicomedia with him. Now the suffering was different. The trotting—the constant, droning, never-ending clipitty-clop of horse hooves against moss-covered paving stones, or the silence when we rode upon bare earth—and the lack of fear now, the lack of blood pumping, ever-present concern, drove me to drowsiness. I was weary and grew wearier.

I'd stare ahead of me and fade. Then, hunched over I'd wake up dragging my eyes open. There was Constantine some distance ahead, blurry through two burnt umber equine ears, topped with small tufts of silken sable hair. The horse was my latest mount, the last. I'd come to call him *Felix Servator*—Lucky Savior.

Constantine, in contrast to me, seemed delirious with joy. I saw it in his eyes when he sauntered next to me and mine were open long enough to see and take notice. It was as though he were in a state of exaltation, the sort I'd heard about before with soldiers—exaltation in action, in victory. This was a new Constantine for me. Although I had imagined him in such a state, picturing what he was like battling in Persia or fighting the Sarmatians above the Danube, I'd never seen the expression. Now, I knew it. Here was Constantine the conqueror, the victor. He had vanquished Galerius and now he was on his way to help his father conquer another enemy.

As we rode through the countryside of Gaul, passing out of the mountains and into the foothills and toward the coast where rivers drain and where we hoped to meet up with his father, I thought of another conqueror, one who had shaped Gaul so many centuries before, Gaul of the Longhairs as it was then called. I thought of Gaius Julius Caesar—conqueror, first man of Rome, dictator, and finally, dead, murdered on the Senate floor.

One day, I shared my thoughts aloud when Constantine slowed enough to ride next to me. For an hour or more that day, while the sun shone in a mostly blue sky on an otherwise bitterly cold afternoon, we considered the good and ill that had come from his brilliant conquest of Gaul and Britannia and how Rome had both changed and remained the same once he famously crossed the Rubicon. As you must know, Theophilus, by then Rome had passed from being a Republic run by the Senate and tribunes and various committees of men, to something else. It became an empire, say some, *the* Empire. And yes, doubtlessly it was. But we had been that since—well, since the Romans had destroyed Carthage some hundred years before.

"Perhaps," I said to him, "it would have been better if it had never happened."

Constantine laughed. "You only say that because you're from Carthage."

"No," I rejoined, "not so. It seems the republicans were right."

"How so?"

"The rule of law has suffered."

"How can you say that?" asked Constantine. "We now have the greatest system of law ever created by mankind. Roman law is famous worldwide. Our courts. Our justice. We're not like the German barbarians who rely on trial by ordeal, leaving justice to the whims of the gods. And," he grinned, "we've more lawyers than salt in the sea."

"Right. But that's just a veneer, don't you think? I mean, what about Galerius? How is it that he can hound you as he's done without legal cause, chasing you all the way to Gaul? You're innocent!"

"Yes—but he didn't get very far!"

I laughed, before countering, "You know what I mean. The rule of law has suffered and so the rule of reason. Emperors are beasts—and force has won out. Might rules rather than what is fair."

"Watch it!" said Constantine with a smile.

"Excepting your father, of course!" I exclaimed.

"Of course!"

"But seriously, I wonder for what? For what did Caesar conquer in the first place? Why did he care for Gaul or Rome? Was it for power? Was it to satisfy his appetites, his desires?"

If so, I thought, without saying so aloud, then this was the true meaning of the change—from Republic to Empire. It was about one man's power and the rule of one versus the authority of the law and a rule shared by the many in different capacities. Wasn't this, after all, the critique Cicero had made—that in having himself declared dictator for life, Caesar had obviated the traditional need for the senators and others who had always helped to guide the state like the various crewmen of a ship? It was. And that's why Cicero had retired to his villa at Tusculum just south of Rome. He'd had enough.

Constantine strongly disagreed with my former sentiment though not with my major premise. "You're right, Arnobius, on one point at least. Rulers are not always just, just as men as individuals mostly fail to seek wisdom and the good. However, with Rome there's something different—and that despite Galerius and his ilk. Don't confuse one man and the ill he causes with the Empire and the good it brings. Have you never reflected on the peace of Rome?"

"Peace!" I challenged. "You've got to be joking. We're constantly at war!"

"True—but always in defense."

I'd heard this argument many times, and so quietly, I scoffed. According to this line of reasoning, the Roman Empire had never fought an offensive war. From the beginning, even when it was Rome against the Sabines or Rome battling the men of Alba Longa, as when the three Horatii brothers heroically fought the three Curatii, it was a matter of defense. Advancing forward in time, Rome never meant to take Italy. Furthermore, after three long wars against Carthage, the great colony of the Phoenicians, Rome never intended to become the one solitary power around Our Sea. And perhaps not. Once her borders stretched so far, they were bound to grind against others—Carthage, Macedon, Parthia, Persia, India, and now the Germanic tribes north of the Rhine and Danube.

Still, whatever my own conviction, Constantine persisted. *He* believed. The Empire was a power for good; Rome was a peacemaker.

"We only fight against the barbarian tribes," he explained, "because they press in upon us. What are we supposed to do, Arnobius? The rest, even the occasional civil war and imperial court mayhem, is an aberration and not what Rome is truly all about. I believe this is where you are wrong. Our Empire and the unity found within is the will, somehow, of the Divinity. It is a matter of divine providence. It's a good we should fight for and cherish."

"Divine providence?" I asked, doubting it.

"Yes. I believe Caesar was acting upon the impulse of the One toward unity, a unity of peoples under Rome. It's like the earth beneath the divine Sun. The foundation he lay—with his own blood no less—has grown now into this more or less irenic land we ride through today. It's the prosperity we know, the culture we possess, the philosophy we practice, and the peace we enjoy."

As we rode along, I thought about his argument, still uncertain.

Constantine, however, was not—of *that*, I was certain. He possessed an inkling of something I would only later come to grasp. Yet of what, I could not yet fathom.

As we continued our journey through Gaul, I had the chance to observe the people and the countryside: the farms and farmhouses under a thin veil of snow, smoke rising out of stone flews, or, if it was as with the majority of dwellings I observed made of mud and thatch, out of a hole cut in the top. Occasionally I saw men out tending animals with small boys in tow keeping them company. The women and their girls, I guessed, were inside preparing modest meals, making ready for their return.

I thought about them as they would be several months on in spring—the many happily at work, men and women, boys and girls sowing seed, expecting an ample harvest in the fall, tending small vegetable gardens, and fattening the few animals they possessed for an occasional feast. Then they would collect eggs and hunt for berries by wild briar thickets and hunt in the woods. I thought about what it all required, how their lives required peace. I reflected on how this peace was won by the suffering of others—a glorious suffering no doubt as won in battle, but suffering nonetheless. Thousands and thousands of soldiers line the *limes*, the borders of the Empire, in defense of Rome. They make their stand along the cold Rhine and Danube to the north, and east aside the Euphrates in Mesopotamia under a glaring, unrelenting sun, and south in the deserts of Africa where one rarely sees green, water is rare, and camel flesh is considered a stroke of luck.

Perhaps Constantine was right, I permitted.

Then one day, I reached a conclusion. Up ahead I saw a family walking. There were the father and mother laughing. The children bundled in coarse woolen cloaks to keep warm were hopping and skipping around as children do. I thought about them as we sauntered by.

Soon after, I grinned and declared to Constantine, "You know you're right."

"Rarely," he said, "but what about this time?"

"Rome."

"And what?"

"About the peace of Rome."

"Yes," he proclaimed, "it's divine."

But I had said nothing about the divine.

Moreover, honestly, Theophilus, although I had conceded the fact of peace, I still couldn't see how our Roman peace, a human peace which seemed so obviously imperfect, could be a reflection of the divine life. How, I thought, can the finite ever reflect the infinite? It was the old gap, that stubborn distance between the One and the many. It seems my mind and its own abstraction had trapped me.

Even so, Constantine could grasp the relation. He did. He knew it. Rome's was a divine unity and sacred peace meant for the whole world.

Presently he smiled, believing me enlightened. We trotted onwards towards Gesoriacum on the coast. We were now just days away.

The Cell in Tabennisi

Midmorning

Theophilus: ARNOBIUS SLOWED FOR A MOMENT in the telling of his tale as if something—certainly in his own life, but I suspected something more—hinged upon this one idea, the preordained, divine unity and peace of Rome.

Indeed, my own heart fluttered. If true, I thought, I knew what I had to do. If not, then what? It's the refrain of the emperor Marcus Aurelius in his reflections—chaos or cosmos; atoms haphazardly falling in the void or nature advancing with purpose; chance or providence. But more, Abba, even more.

"Arnobius, do you now believe?" I queried.

He said nothing in reply. Instead, he placed his face in cupped hands and sat there for a moment as if tired, undecided.

Outside, I heard a brother call us for midmorning prayers, and through the opening in my cell, I saw many monks moving toward our usual meeting place. There you, Abba, would greet us with the grace of God and bless us with that thrice-holy name. Then we would pray, standing erect, arms outstretched:

> *O God, yours is the world and all therein,*
> *the sun, the moon, the stars, and the sky.*
> *O God, yours is the world and all therein,*
> *the birds and the fish, all creatures alive.*
> *O God, yours is the world and all therein,*
> *the peoples praise you, O God on high.*

I nudged Arnobius. "We have to go."

He looked up.

"Theophilus?" he said, but hardly audible.

"Yes?" I responded.

"I *do* believe."

I was silent, though my expression, I trust, invited him to tell more.

"Polybius the historian was wrong," he explained. "Rome is not like the other empires which have risen only to fall. It will last forever."

I listened as he went on.

"Though Caesar fell away and thousands upon thousands have died to make purchase, Rome's was meant to be a preparation. The peace is eternal, the unity divine. Constantine was right."

"A preparation?" I asked, hoping for clarification. What he said was something of an enigma to me.

"Yes," he confirmed.

But he said nothing more. And since it was time to go, we stood to pray with all the other brothers.

Sometime later, we returned to the cell, and Arnobius continued with the story. Now he seemed eager to go as if he'd come to some kind of resolution about where things had gone and where things would go. He had admitted to direction, a direction to events and to the great sweep of time. Perhaps he did not then believe, that is, those thirty-some years before when he rode with Constantine to go meet the emperor Constantius Chlorus in Gesoriacum. Yet now he did—or so I suspected.

Even so, I didn't press, not then. Rather, I asked Arnobius about Constantine's father. "What was he like?"

"Oh," Arnobius said in cheery reply, "if only you could have known him. But then you were hardly alive."

"Not even," I admitted.

"No, I suppose not. But if you had been, and if you had known him, you would have never forgotten him. I know I haven't."

Ten: Gesoriacum

Late December 305 A.D.

WE ARRIVED IN GESORIACUM toward the end of December. Perhaps the greatest wonder of our arrival was the Great Western Ocean, comprising the end of the world and stretching far wider than our own sea around which the Roman world thrives.

It's not that the Great Western Ocean appears differently from Our Sea; instead, it strikes more at the mind as metaphor. It's the great unknown versus the known. Yet it is that in a way which surrounds our—dare I say— little world. Still, there we were, we Romans, expanding our known world further, or in opposite manner we were defending our world against forces which threatened to disrupt our peace, that peace which Constantine had argued for and which I had come to see and believe in as a matter of plausible interpretation.

When we first approached Gesoriacum, Constantius Chlorus rode astride his horse in the distance through fields covered with hoarfrost.

"There he is," announced Constantine. "Look!"

I peered downwards far away from where we were riding, down a small frost covered hill, and saw nothing but a mass of cavalry to one side and foot soldiers to the other. Both were drilling. For the life of me, I could not spot anything that resembled an emperor.

"Where?" I asked, amazed at Constantine's apparent power of vision.

"Just wait," he replied. "You'll see him soon enough."

We trotted towards them for a while longer. In that time I noted the waves, small, falling against the shore and receding again into the Great Western Ocean and the dark-gray waters beyond. There, far away, I hoped to see the shores of Britannia. I had heard that there were tall and majestic white cliffs there, and that sometimes, if the air were just right, one could see them glimmer in the sunlight as if the body of some divine being. At first I could not see them and I wondered if it were really so. Then—

"There, do you see him now?" asked Constantine.

I glanced toward where the emperor should be, but I didn't see him. Then I looked back in order to see the cliffs.

"Constantine!" I said, full of excitement.

"Do you see him?" he asked.

"No," I countered, "but I *do* see the cliffs across the straits. Do you?"

Constantine glanced in their direction. "No," he answered. Then dousing my enthusiasm, he went on, "It's probably just a low-lying bank of clouds."

I *did* see the cliffs, however, and I knew it but cared not to argue.

"At any rate, we'll travel to that land soon enough. That's where we're heading after we meet up with my father."

By then three men on horseback had ridden out to us. "Stop!" commanded one of the men. Obeying, we slowed our mounts to a halt. The man was one of the emperor's personal guards. Sitting on his horse, he glanced back and forth between Constantine and me.

"Don't you recognize me?" asked Constantine. "Crassus!" he bellowed—a name that fit the large man quite well—"it is I, Constantine, son of Constantius Augustus."

"Constantine?" he asked skeptically.

It was evident Crassus didn't recognize him.

I must admit, Theophilus, that this was understandable given the way he looked at present—unkempt, a longish beard creeping along his jowls and chin, and stubble elsewhere. It was all quite the opposite of his usual, fashionably trimmed *barbula*, something he shed once and for all shortly thereafter. Then there were the grubby looking clothes and a non-descript cape. It goes without saying that the guard didn't recognize me. We had never seen nor met each other before. As for Constantine, he had briefly met him a few years before in Rome when he had consulted with his father during the celebration of Diocletian's vicennalia.

Crassus searched all the harder before there was finally a glimmer of recognition. "Ah, yes!" he proclaimed. "Of course—Constantine!"

"We're here from the East," the latter explained. "Galerius Augustus granted us permission to join the emperor and the rest of you in your struggle against the Picts."

"We didn't receive word of your coming," Crassus countered.

"No," said Constantine, "you wouldn't have."

He glanced at me and winked, before Crassus directed, "Well, let's be off to the emperor!"

We rode along with two other guards, Philipus and Gnaeus.

"There he is," Constantine announced to me, pointing as we drew nearer.

This time there was no need for him to show me his father; now there was no mistaking who he was. Immediately, I recognized him for the fact that he was an exact duplicate of Constantine—or reversed, the son was the image of his father. The emperor was taller than average, I judged, possessing a strong, broad build, Constantine's aquiline nose, and that thick neck for which the son was often called bullnecked. It was clear. There was Flavius Valerius Constantius mounted upon a bluish-gray steed directing his men in the field.

"That's it!" he called out. "Bring her around! Now jab!"

Before him his men jabbed in concert as others opposite them, their wicker shields giving way, fell in practiced droves, now laying upon the ground as though dead.

When the din quieted a few minutes later, Constantius Chlorus shouted, "Excellent, men! Well done! Now get up! Get up and reform!"

They did.

As this transpired, I gazed upon our emperor in awe, impressed he was out training his men as any two-bit centurion would usually do. There he was without regalia. No wonder I had not recognized him. Galerius would have never done as much. It's possible he did long before I knew him when he had yet to gain final glory over the Persians and secure his place against Diocletian. But not now. He had grown far too fat for that. I imagine he hardly rode a horse any longer let alone commanded his men in the field in martial exercise. By contrast, Constantius Chlorus was a vision of manly fitness. And at what age? I guess he then fell somewhere in the fifties.

"Augustus!"

It was Crassus. We had finally come near enough to the emperor for introductions.

"It's your son, Augustus!"

Constantius Chlorus spun on his horse, and with one rapid glance, he both studied Constantine's appearance and recognized his son so that he was able to proclaim, as if obvious, his recognition without the passing of another heartbeat.

"Constantine! *Filius meus*—my son!"

He rode nearer to us. It was then I noticed with a sense of verification the paleness of his skin, the cause for his cognomen, *Chlorus,* Pale Skin. But I was hardly surprised. The clouds are never absent for long in that part of the world.

"Father!" Constantine called in greeting.

They dismounted, embraced, and then stood studying each other for a moment before Constantius Chlorus admitted, "I'm surprised you've come."

"As well you should be," his son replied. "If only you knew how difficult it has been."

Forestalling any discussion of the matter, the emperor raised his weathered and muscular hand and said, "Let's not speak of it now. First, we must look to your comfort and well-being; you must clean up and eat. Then, we'll speak at length. And later tonight"—he paused and turned to one of his stewards—"tonight we'll celebrate your coming with the whole army."

Implicitly commanded, the steward rode off to make preparations.

After Constantine briefly embraced his father and introduced me, we too sauntered off to a fresh bath and a full table.

Some hours later, we sat with the emperor in a large stone house located in the outskirts of Gesoriacum. We drank a nondescript Gallic wine tempered with water, and Constantine explained what had happened and how we had come to be in Gaul. Behind us and to our side, two fires burned driving away the cold. Outside, the sun had disappeared behind a blanket of thick, gray clouds, and sleet mixed with rain had begun to fall. Presently, Constantine was speaking of Galerius and his refusal to let him go.

"Galerius," observed his father, "I never much cared for the man—just as I do not now care for Severus. Nevertheless, we must put up with him just as we did with Maximian for so many years. They're men who don't always have the good of the Empire in mind. Still, in some measure they do seem to pursue the good, though with more an eye on their own wealth, fame, and glory, than Rome's."

Constantius Chlorus had spent the better portion of his adult life fighting for the good of the Empire. Yearly he battled against a great number of barbarian tribes that continuously rush against the Empire as waves rush the shore. Even now, he had this good in mind in preparing for conflict against the Picts in northern Britannia.

"But," he went on, "Galerius was bound to let you go."

Constantine and I eyed each other. We both knew that wasn't quite true.

"Galerius used to be a rock of a man. Even then, however, I could sense that under that hard rock surface, where you might expect the warmth of flesh, there was nothing more than a cold heart of stone."

I wanted to say that with Galerius, there was now plenty of flesh, but Constantine beat me to it, even though I should have refrained anyways.

Constantius Chlorus laughed aloud at this remark. Then, drawing up sober again, he observed, "So, you've come to join me."

"Yes, Father."

"Good. I've desired your presence for many months now—ever since Galerius and I became the leading men of the Empire in May."

"When do we sail?" asked Constantine.

"Soon. We're nearly done with training and should be ready and well supplied in a few weeks."

Then, to my surprise, the emperor turned to me and asked, "Arnobius, are you a man of arms?"

I glanced at Constantine and then back to his father. "I'm afraid not," I admitted, grinning slightly with shame.

Constantine came to my rescue. "He's a man of letters, Father. Still, recently he's become skilled at riding a horse."

He said the latter with a smile curving his mouth.

I blushed, shifting upon the couch.

"No matter," declared Constantius Chlorus to me. "You'll come with us and do your share, though undeniably yours is the truest battlefield—the mind."

Constantine and I nodded.

"Well," the emperor said, rising, "let's meet again this evening. For now, go and rest. You've had a hard journey, and at the very least, you deserve a few hours to yourselves. Afterwards, I'm afraid it'll be all business. The Empire first, ourselves last. We've got the Picts to conquer."

We stood.

"Thank you, Emperor," I offered.

He bowed, and I to him—a gesture I genuinely meant in contrast to all the insincere genuflecting and groveling before Galerius. Then father and son embraced once more, and finally Constantine and I walked away to rest, enthusiastically discussing the merits of his father, the army of Rome, and the evils and peculiarities of the Picts.

Ah, yes, the Picts. I had heard of them before, a truly nasty bunch of men. They live somewhere north of *Britannia Secunda* in a stretch of green, hilly land called the Highlands, the land of the Caledonii, well above the Bodotria River. Like most barbarians, the Picts are a vicious lot. Although they possess farms and homes, as do many tribes of men, their own labor fails to provide all they desire. Nor does trade acquire for them enough to satisfy their lusts. Consequently, as Thucydides reports of the ancient Greeks, the Picts resort to piracy and raiding.

At the time, this caused great consternation among those Romans who lived along the coast of Britannia. They never quite knew when the next invasion would come—and this despite Roman garrisons dotting the coastline and northern limes. Earlier that year, the Picts had swept down to raid the Roman town of Maia some one hundred miles from their homeland and nearly the same from Eburacum, capital of Britannia Secunda. The Picts had slaughtered many and carried off a great deal of wealth. Additionally, they had raped half the women, and now Pictish boys and girls were growing within Roman wombs, though many of the women had chosen to abort rather than carry such progeny. When word of the disaster in Maia had finally reached Constantius Chlorus in Gaul, he resolved to lead his army against the Picts later that year.

Now the time had arrived to face these barbarians. Many soldiers said the Picts were ferocious in battle, though contrary rumors had them vanishing instead of standing their ground to fight. Whatever the case, when on a raid or when battling, they would paint themselves with the most dreadful looking tattoos—ghoulish swirls daubed of woad-blue and bone-white representing death and destruction for the assaulted and wealth and glory for them.

Later that evening, as his father had promised, we feasted outdoors around a great bonfire celebrating Constantine's coming.

It was a night I will never forget, Theophilus. For even while there was the usual gluttony and drunkenness among the ranks, from centurions down to the lowest legionary, there was evidently something more, something having to do with Constantine's father. With him at the helm, there was appropriate order. He was the sober, self-restrained symposium captain of Plato's *Laws*.

As time passed near to the fourth hour of night, Constantius Chlorus stood before his men in order to advise them. "Your life is not your own," he declared. "Think, men, who has created his own life? Was it you?"

As he asked the last, he pointed to a young, ruddy looking soldier sitting nearby, gnawing on a bone. The fire's light lit his face. When the emperor lobbed his question, the man suddenly had the look of a stag moments before the whistling impact of a well thrown javelin.

The emperor chuckled. "It wasn't you! Nor was it I! Therefore, it follows that we aren't here for ourselves! Think of it! We are here for one reason, men. It's quite simple, really. It's to do the will of the One which has made us all, the universal Mind as expressed in the ordered nature of all things."

He stopped and paused for a moment, glancing here and there among the men. As he did so, Constantine leaned over to me and whispered, "Do you hear the Stoic philosophy in what he says?"

I did. But as I later learned, the emperor was more than a Stoic, Theophilus. Like many a man in the Empire, he mixed his philosophical doctrines well—a bit of this, a bit of that. Yet he didn't mix them to squirm away from the truth and the responsibility to fall in line with it; rather, he did so in order to follow the truth more closely.

The emperor went on. "Do you know what that is, men, do you know the will of the One?"

"More wine!" cried an already drunken soldier from some distance.

The emperor laughed. "At times, yes, more wine is necessary for relaxation, restoration, and recreation. But that's not our goal, our purpose. We re-create in order to work. And our work, men, is to battle for the Empire, for the glory of Rome!"

Everyone erupted, cheering, since that glory merited a hearty cheer—not to mention, of course, that most were beyond the point of happy inebriation.

"But more, I say! It must have substance! Glory cannot be a mere shimmering on the surface alone. Though such is fine, it is the substance of what shines that has true value. For us, that's Rome's state of being, its mode of existence. This, men, is the reason for our own warring. We don't fight because we love to kill and maim—though some of you, perhaps …"

There was another round of roaring voices, low and high, sober and drunk.

"No! We fight to secure the borders! We fight for peace! Let it be known that we sweat and struggle and give our life's blood that all may be one and in harmony within the arms of the Empire!"

The men shouted their enthusiastic approval while I looked at Constantine, recognizing that along with his physical appearance, his mind was the same as his father's was.

Finally, the great martial sea grew quiet. Above, dim clouds softly illumined by the moon drifted along the coast. Occasionally, I saw patches of a night sky where millions of eternal stars speckled the roof of the cosmos.

Once the men were quiet, the emperor acknowledged the presence of his son. "I want to introduce to you someone you will come to admire over the next few months."

I glanced at Constantine who focused on his father like the rest.

"Tonight, men, I present you my son. He has come to us from the East where he has lived and fought for well over a decade. There he has become a true man, a courageous soldier, and a strategic leader, fighting bravely alongside Diocletian Augustus of eternal fame and glory!"

Constantine stood.

Meanwhile, his father finished the introduction by proudly shouting, "He struggled for Rome along the Danube, in Mesopotamia against the Persians, and in Egypt against the cowardly usurpers Lucius Domitius Domitianus and Aurelius Achilleus!"

Now, the men began to chant Constantine's name. They had heard of his military prowess, his physical ability, and the powers of his mind, and so their voices rose with well-rounded zeal. "Constantine! Constantine!"

As if in polyphonic response, his father declared, "Tonight he's yours— my son, the man who will fearlessly aid us in our fight against the Picts!"

After Constantine resumed his seat next to me, the emperor directed his speech toward what was to come.

"I say the Picts, men. You know about them. You've heard. We've trained hard for the past several months in anticipation of this fight."

A few grunted and a few even booed recalling the many grueling days out on the field. Many more, however, cheered with pride for what they had accomplished.

The emperor smiled. "Yes—it's been hard, men, as it always has been since we Romans have carried the burden of our empire. Who, after all, enjoys the blunt end of a stick when it brings nothing more than black and blue and very little of real glory or immediate practical consequence?"

He paused. Then his smile grew even larger. "However that may be, soon you will be paid in hard-earned honor! I have no doubt that after we have crossed the straits we will march along the hinterland of Britannia and finally send the Picts to everlasting destruction!"

Now every man cheered, and I could hear many of them chant, "To hell with the Picts!"

As they calmed some, the emperor was once again matter-of-fact. "In a few weeks' time, we sail to make peace. Britannia Secunda will never again have to know the fear of those barbarian men falling on them like ghosts in the night. By summer, what's left of them will be above the Old Antonine Wall. And that, men, to your glory, to your everlasting honor and fame! For now, however, we must remain focused and give our all to training and making final preparations. Then we'll sail."

"Let's go now!" I heard one man yell.

The men were ready to go—*then*, that very night. The sooner the better. Anything was preferable to remaining stationary another cold, winter's day.

Constantius Chlorus agreed, he admitted, but he assured the men they required another few weeks.

Accordingly, he commanded, "Men, hold still! Have patience! Do what needs doing! Soon you'll board a ship and be well on your way. Then, we'll go to the walls and push the barbarian Picts beyond!"

Spontaneously, many responded by shouting, "To the walls, to the walls!"

Silently, I thought the same. *To the walls*, I intoned. And I must admit, Theophilus, that in the excitement of it all, I meant it.

Eleven: Battling the Picts

January to February 306 A.D.

OVER THE NEXT FEW WEEKS, the men continued training and making preparations. Although I practiced some maneuvers with the horsemen, I mostly observed, watching the many work together as one. Moving. Charging. Stabbing. Falling. Standing. Withdrawing. Reforming. Charging again. For his part, Constantine took charge as co-commander of the cavalry, alongside the *magister equitum*, the master of horse. Then, just as the emperor had promised, we departed for Britannia.

Early the morning of our departure, I walked down to the harbor with thousands of other men who were busy carting loads of supplies to the docks. Along the shore was anchored a small fleet of ships, transports mostly. Among them, I spotted several fivers and a larger one that would serve as flagship. When I counted the rest, I found there were too many before my mind wandered amid the great variety of sights and sounds. I saw carved monsters, animals, and gods meant to identify each ship and frighten potential aggressors. I heard horses braying onboard, sheep bleating while being led below deck, and men singing, happy to be leaving. There were Roman and Gaulish children chasing around amid the excitement, wives and mothers bidding farewell, and large wooden cranes webbed with ropes and pulleys hoisting up sacks of grain before placing them below in cargo holds.

Later, I boarded the flagship along with Constantine, his father, and his personal guard, Crassus, Philipus, and Gnaeus. Onboard, the trierarch greeted us. "Good to see you, Lord," he offered to the emperor. The latter bowed. Then warmly, he returned, "It's good to finally go!"

Standing on deck, I told Crassus that I'd never sailed on the Great Western Ocean before. "Our Sea many times," I expounded, "but not these waters." He smiled at me before walking off to do something for someone leaving me all alone.

Constantine was elsewhere giving orders no doubt. So were his father and everyone else it seemed, except for those, of course, who took the orders— the *velarii* preparing the sails, the scullers who had drawn the lot of rowing first, and the *proreta* who took his place upon the prow, readying to relay the orders of the *gubernator* on the poop to the steersman aft.

Later, just as we drew anchor, Crassus stood next to me once again. We were both looking out over the *Fretum Gallium*—the straights between Gaul and Britannia—when he said, "You've never sailed on the Great Western Ocean, huh?"

"No," I responded.

"You'll enjoy it," he said, amused.

"Why?" I asked.

But he wouldn't say.

Soon, when after the scullers had rowed us beyond the shore and out into the straits, and after the great ship began to rock up and down, pitching slowly up and falling quickly down, I knew exactly what Crassus meant. By then, the gubernator had loudly ordered the velarii to drop the sails, and we were speeding along. We hoped to arrive six or seven hours from then, perhaps five with all luck. Either way it was far too long. If you've never sailed on the Great Western Ocean, Theophilus, do not. The swells are far larger than those of Our Sea. And with them comes sickness. Your blood drains and everything else swells. I spent the next few hours leaning overboard and the rest of the twenty-some miles below deck in a hammock, swaying with the waves. My only care was to reach port as rapidly as possible.

Once landed, our army met up with II Augustus, a legion led by Gallinicus Duces, a bear of a man. Greeting us were ten ground-shaking tubas and just as many horns, birdlike, blowing us a fine welcome. We were all thrilled to disembark, and when the order was given to pitch camp, I don't think one man complained. We camped for the night alongside II Augustus' permanent camp, a fortress built up in wood and stone between the shore and Dubris.

The following day, after meeting with several local commanders early in the morning, we marched northward on a walk that would span some four hundred miles and a month, meaning we would arrive shortly before the middle of February. I traveled with the emperor, Constantine, and the rest of the commanding tier of men, riding my old mount Felix Servator, the one I'd grown used to riding through Gaul.

During the march, as we rode along the hills and valleys of Britannia, mostly brown and barren but for patches of frost and snow, Constantine would often speak with his father of matters both profane and divine. Several times, I took part. One morning, halfway into our long trek north, Constantius Chlorus revealed that he had come to consider the Divinity in a new way.

"Consider," Constantine asked, "or have you come to believe?"

"Consider, I say."

I wondered how, but before the emperor could tell us, Crassus called our attention away. "Chief of the Britons!" he announced.

And so it was. Amicably we camped and ate with him and his men that night. "The gods bless you," he offered to the emperor at night's end. "You and your men as well," returned the latter.

The next day, just as the sun neared its zenith, Constantine turned to his father and queried, "How so?"

"How what?"

"Yesterday you proclaimed you have come to consider the Divinity in a new way. All last night I thought about this. As the chief made his speech, and when he blessed us at end, I wondered how. Aside from the light of the sacred Sun, I wonder what more can be known of the One."

The emperor shrugged his shoulders. "Known? That, I don't know. Even so, one can consider matters anew without leaving behind what we already believe."

For a moment, he gazed forward as if he were deciding whether to share his considerations or not. Afterwards, given my impudent response, I'm sure he wished he had not. Nevertheless, he asked, "What do you know of the Christians?"

"The Christians or their god?" Constantine clarified.

"Either."

Constantine shrugged his shoulders. "Well, for starters, they're not very fortunate. It seems their god is not very powerful; therefore, he is not a god, as logic would have us conclude. Reason suggests that any true god must at least have some power."

"That's fair," said his father, "but have you ever heard their teaching about God?"

"*I* have," I interrupted, urging my horse forward.

Constantius Chlorus politely turned to me. "And what do you know, Arnobius?"

"I know what they claim, that a god took on the form of a man—Jesus, the Galilean. They call him *Christos*, the anointed. This same man was crucified during the reign of the emperor Tiberius. He was a rebel and called himself the king of the Jews."

As if to correct me somewhat, the emperor responded, "They say he was the One—the one God in flesh."

Constantine added, "They believe he was a son of God."

"Precisely," I affirmed, ignoring the emperor's point. "This is why I find their idea so simplistic and revolting. It's similar to all the stories told forever by old women about the various gods taking on any manner of flesh and lustfully siring sons and daughters and wild beasts."

I went on to explain my position, moving from my sentiments about the traditional gods of myth to the immense gulf found between God, the One, and creation, the many. Finishing my brief monologue, I asserted, "If you have that kind of God then you have no God at all. If God takes on flesh, then flesh becomes God and the many becomes the One. It's impossible! No, logic demands that the One is far removed from the flux of our world!"

"Yes, yes," said the emperor, patiently. "So we need the demiurge which creates on behalf of the One, while insulating the One from the many. You are right Arnobius. I understand. But what if it were possible? What if somehow—*somehow*, I say—it was different?"

"Different?" asked Constantine, curious and willing to listen.

Not I. Full of stubborn confidence, I asserted, "It's *not*."

Both father and son grew quiet, glancing at each other. Later Constantine explained he felt embarrassed for me.

But I was not yet finished. "What about Christian vice?" I challenged. "Isn't that an indication of anything? What about their treason to the Empire and the rumors of incest and cannibalism? Doesn't this indicate their stories are lies told to deceive the poor and old?"

"Possibly," allowed the emperor. "But what do you have to substantiate such rumors, Arnobius? My experience of their behavior is quite the opposite. Christian men are wise, just, and moderate, and when harassed, they endure with courage and fortitude. Doesn't virtue require divine inspiration? Can good fruit grow from an unhealthy tree?"

While he was speaking, I foolishly thought of something Pila had told me once. It made me wince. I began to share it with them.

Constantine, however, cut me off, chastising me. "Be serious, Arnobius. *Pila?* The man was delightful and useful at times but not exactly trustworthy. He was a gossip monger!"

True, I judged. I fell quiet, and on this sour note, we ambled along in silence with thousands of soldiers marching up ahead, the cavalry behind, and a train of pack animals at the rear. I must keep my thoughts to myself, I admonished.

In time, in nearly as many days as it took the moon to pass through all its phases, we arrived at Hadrian's Wall. There we rested for three days, planning, training, and hobnobbing with the soldiers who lived along the wall in small forts that dotted its length from Maia in the west to Segedunum in the east.

The wall itself is nothing terribly impressive, Theophilus. Certainly, it is no architectural wonder. There is little of theoretical beauty and design. Instead, it is pure practicality at some fifteen to twenty feet high and a fraction of that for its width. In its westernmost parts where we spent most of our time, the wall is mostly wood and turf. This is due to the scarcity of other materials in the west as compared to their availability in the east where the wall is stone. Some distance behind it, on the Roman side, a long ditch about ten feet deep called the *vallum* runs its length. It serves as a boundary line for Roman civilians and quite literally as a last-ditch defense.

The emperor's hope was to draw the Picts down from Caledonia beyond the Old Wall—that is the Antonine Wall, which cuts across a narrow isthmus some thirty-five miles wide, where at the eastern end the Bodotria River flows into the frigid and gray German Ocean. The Antonine Wall is termed "old" not because it's older than Hadrian's Wall, but because it used to be the farthest extent of our line of defense until we fell back to Hadrian's Wall.

Despite Constantius Chlorus' hope to draw the Picts southwards, in the actual event, just five days after we had first seen Hadrian's Wall rise above the horizon and two days after we set off in search for them, the majority of the barbarians didn't show.

Still, I didn't know that the morning of the day we expected to encounter them in a fight. Rather, as the army prepared itself, I feared for what the day would bring. I had heard so much about Pictish men—horrible tales from our own soldiers who were themselves seasoned with the blood of war.

Constantine, in contrast to my own misgivings, was elated that morning. As he prepared to ride and fight, I could see it.

He noticed me staring at him. "What is it, Arnobius?"

"Nothing," I lied.

I was already set. I had fastened my armor with the help of a servant and sat waiting.

"Are you worried?"

Again, I lied.

Knowing the truth, he said, "You'll be fine. These Picts are all bluster."

Bluster or not, contrary to the intelligence we had obtained of countless Picts riding south of the Old Wall, they were nowhere in sight. As a result, we marched all day long without seeing one blue and white painted Pict.

Eventually, the emperor ordered the army to pitch camp, so the *groma*, the surveyor, laid out our camp along the rolling hills, and the men set to work constructing temporary earthen fortifications and raising hundreds of *papiliones*, leather tents, which accommodate eight to ten soldiers. I shared one with Constantine.

We kept north the third day, and still there was no band of Pictish warriors. Just before sunset, we did take an old man who had been conspicuously riding alongside our men all day and demanded of him what he knew of the Pict's whereabouts. At first, he denied knowing anything at all. But when Crassus flexed his muscles, he broke. It was sad, Theophilus. Here a man as old as my grandfather was breaking down like a young boy facing a thrashing. When he did break, he said that although he was a Pict, he no longer lived among his people. His wife had died and so had all his children at one time or another. Crassus just waited until the man waded through all his muddle. Then the sudden revelation. It turns out he *had* seen a large body of Pictish men a few days before, five hundred or so, all riding on Gaulish mounts and heading north toward the Old Wall.

"We'll march to the Old Wall," the emperor declared later on, after we dug in for a third night. We stood in his large field tent atop a hill in the middle of the camp.

"Do you believe they'll hold there at the wall?" Constantine asked.

"I can't say for sure," his father responded. Then with a smile, he quipped, "I just hope those bastards hold long enough for a solid beating."

We encountered the Picts at the end of our fourth day marching north. It was the end of the day, perhaps three hours before sun fall. It was then that three Roman scouts came galloping toward Constantius Chlorus.

"They're here!" shouted one, the captain presently in charge of reconnaissance. "They're coming toward us, just ahead of us a mile or so."

"How many?" the emperor shouted. He was already off, trotting toward the van of our column of men. We followed behind.

"Seventy-five—up to a hundred, but no more," the other returned.

"So a lure," he said.

We galloped away to the fore until finally we could see a large body of Pictish men charging our way on horseback. They were now five hundred yards away and appeared as giants even from that distance. Quickly, the emperor called a wedge of horse forward and ordered half a division of footmen to stand behind.

"This won't be long!" he cried. "They're not full force!" Then he dropped back as the master of horse and Constantine took the lead. "Surround them if you can!" he ordered.

But it was no use. As soon as the Picts reached within a hundred yards of our men, they turned and galloped away, disappearing over a hill three hundred yards distant and somewhat west of where they had originally appeared.

"Hey!" Constantine bellowed.

His men behind him yelled the same in disappointment.

Then, turning to the soldiers afoot and horse, Constantine commanded, "Steady, now! Don't break up! They'll be back!"

He expected them to emerge full force over the hill, as was their common maneuver, to lure and surprise.

We waited. And waited.

Eventually, however, not a Pict in sight, we marched toward the hill ahead and the Old Wall beyond.

"Those damn barbarians can rot in hell!" the emperor cursed. Crassus grumbled from behind. No one was happy.

After another two hours one of the forward scouts reported that the Old Wall was in sight.

"Good," observed the emperor. "We'll camp a few hundred yards beyond the vallum, and tomorrow, we'll slaughter them."

Constantine tacked on, "May the divine Sun grant it!"

Quietly, I agreed.

That night, we saw the Picts moving up along the Wall. Occasionally they fired small missiles burning with fire at us. The night sky was black when suddenly, whistling across the darkness, a line blazed yellowish-orange. None came close—or very. But each time an arrow flew, our men roared with anger and anticipation. If the order had been given then, they would have rushed the wall, casting consequence aside to hell.

Late into night, the emperor met with Constantine and his other generals for several hours in his field tent. They devised a plan for the following day in which several divisions would breach the wall miles away and march back in order to crush the Picts in a two-sided attack on the northern side. The rest of us would attack straight on. In the event, it hardly worked as planned. But that's war, Theophilus. Uncertainty. Thucydides observed this truth seven hundred years ago, and it still holds true today.

Early the next morning, I awoke to the sound of men readying themselves for battle. Emerging from the tent, I saw some grooming horses, some sharpening weapons, and some cleaning their armor. Others ate and stood around joking nervously. As for Constantine, I discovered him next to the tent pouring a small libation to the sun as it climbed higher into the early morning sky. Earnestly, he prayed for success in the coming battle.

His activity, Theophilus, led me to wonder. As I looked at him practicing his devotion, I wondered if the sun cared. Odd question, I know, but I mean the divine Unconquered Sun. Think of it. Its rays shine everywhere, on everyone; its light is given to all. On that day, the light shone on us Romans and on the barbarian Picts alike. Given the omnipresence of its light, I wondered what it meant. I mean, if one takes the sun as a metaphor of some more profound and ultimate reality, does it signify a kind of universal toleration, a tacit approval of all? I didn't like this conclusion. If ultimate reality is such, then light is indifference and ultimately a kind of darkness. But how can light be darkness? And how can the One remain silent in the face of evil? Where is justice?

This was my problem. I had oftentimes thought of the One as absolute Silence. At times, the thought comforted me, as if the many were a clamorous scream that would at last die out and fade into that ultimate Silence. Yet now, as I watched Constantine pray, and as we prepared to fight the Picts who had murdered innocents, raped, and pillaged, it was offensive. It was an empty, impersonal silence that favored neither good nor evil. Indeed, it favored nothing at all. The sun's illumination seemed a terrible illusion.

I desperately wanted to stop Constantine and talk with him about this, but he was busy preparing for battle—as I should have been—and I could tell he wanted to do nothing more.

Consequently, I readied myself and thought of the fight to come and of the one sun that would silently shed its light upon the battle carnage, uninterested, I judged, in whether or not justice prevailed.

The sun was a full quarter into its daily run when commanders down the line gave the order to advance against the wall. Slow at first, then speeding up, we marched forward to the sound of high-pitched whistles which kept us in line and the deep chanting of men singing marching songs, armor fastened, boots thumping, and helmets gleaming in the light of day. The march, of course, was short, as we had camped and formed our lines a mere three or four hundred yards distant. With each step, the wall drew closer, growing from a narrow line on the horizon until finally it was the height of a midsized tree.

As we advanced, we expected missiles—arrows, stones, and whatever else the Picts could get their hands on to hurl. But nothing flew. And aside from our own racket, all was quiet. It seemed the Picts had vanished altogether.

"It's a ruse," judged Crassus. "They're biding their time atop the wall. Just wait. As soon as we're near enough, they'll rain hell down upon us."

Constantius Chlorus agreed.

Nevertheless, as we neared the wall, there was nothing.

Finally, scouts galloped up to the emperor, reporting, "They've gone!"

The emperor cursed the Picts, declaring, "They've disappeared again!"

Constantine suggested an immediate pursuit across the wall. The suggestion, however, was unnecessary, for his father and the rest of his men had already begun to speed forward toward the large gate that had been heaved wide open by the scouts. The rest of us followed as rapidly as we could. As I called Felix Servator forward with all my might, I heard the footmen behind me ordered ahead at a brisk walk. In unison, they all cried, "Aye, sir!"

Soon we on horseback were through the wooden gates and the sound of the marching infantry fell behind. Rushing forward, I wondered how wise our sudden sense of urgency was. What if the Picts hoped to trap us? Still, what did I know?

A half hour passed. We rode on, hooves thudding on the frozen earth.

"The Picts!" yelled a man in front of me.

It was only part of them, though, two or three hundred at most. They were speeding upon horseback away from us.

"Go!" commanded the emperor.

Around me, I heard everyone shout, "Yah!" urging their mounts forward, rushing ahead and shouting insults.

After a few minutes of riding hard, it became clear the Picts had no intention to turn and fight. They dashed up and over the hills and disappeared.

Shortly thereafter, the emperor commanded, "Slow up, men!" After pulling rein, he turned to the master of horse and Constantine and explained, "We must preserve our horses' strength."

They both agreed.

"Still," the emperor ordered, "we'll keep riding in the direction they've gone. They can't go on forever."

Yet forever they seemed to go. By midday it was clear they were gone and had no immediate intention to fight.

"What'll we do?" asked a low-ranking captain to my left.

"We'll retreat some and march in the morning once we've met up again with the footmen."

In the end, after assigning the Picts to a very profound cave in the depths of Hades, we declared a tepid victory for the day and turned to retreat in order to rejoin with the footmen and make camp.

Sometime later, once we had encountered them, the emperor conferred with the master of foot explaining to him what had happened and what we would do. After the brief consultation, we marched on to make camp.

Then—

Then deep into a valley, I nearly died.

I was speaking with Constantine and praising my brave horse for having done so well in the chase and thinking about something inconsequential, when a yard long wooden arrow topped with barbed iron came whizzing by my chest at ten times the speed of a racing horse. It flew so hard and so quickly that a moment later and thirty feet away, it knocked another man off his horse after piercing his armor and punching deeply into his flesh.

The emperor ordered us to a halt. After commanding men to help the fallen man, he advised us to watch our sides. Eagerly, we turned left and right searching for the men who'd shot this and a few other sporadic arrows.

But there was no one. The hills above were empty.

Then we heard it, the noise we all expected, a terrifying cry announcing the arrival of the Picts. They appeared over the hills and trotted toward us slowly. I swallowed hard and shivered. Due to the numbers, I could see it would be no feint, and so I commended myself to our leaders, to our men, and, I must confess, Theophilus, to the care of the One even though I didn't know whether the One actually cared.

The Picts were now some five hundred yards distant. Quickly, Constantius Chlorus gave orders, and just as quickly, captains and centurions repeated his command all the way down the line.

"Draw up in formation, men, draw up!" commanded the master of horse.

We did. Meanwhile the footmen maneuvered into position ahead of us. They were supposed to hold the center so we could flank and surround the Picts.

Then, as rapidly as we gained our place, there sounded the order for the infantry to march forward. "Slowly, now! All together!"

The Picts were now just two hundred yards away and moving closer. They'd probably charge at a hundred yards or perhaps fifty. Our footmen steadily walked toward them, shields and helmets ahead, right foot in time with right and left with left. As for those of us mounted, we waited knowing the infantry must do their work before we could launch into ours.

Then a surprise! Some hundred yards ahead the Picts abruptly stopped. In response, the master of horse ordered us to amble forward at a slow walk so we wouldn't overtake the footmen. Ahead I heard the master of foot shout out, "Time to run, boys. Draw them in! You know the drill!" The men afoot jogged out far ahead of us, hundreds of men wielding long pikes above their shields.

Seeing this, the Picts screamed frenziedly, hollering curses in a bastardized Latin evidently learned from captured Romans, which our own men returned word for blustery word. Then, as if wild beasts unable to resist, the Picts kicked their horses forward, aiming themselves at our trotting infantry, their swords raised high, their spears pointed tip down, Romanward.

At fifty yards, just as the Picts neared our infantry, our men squatted over, readying themselves as one body for impact, shields interlocked in order to form a wall of protection.

"Steady! Keep on!" cried the master centurion in the lead.

Now, as the Picts neared—forty, twenty, ten yards away—our men chugged forward confidently.

Finally, there was a loud crash, as if simultaneously hundreds of trees had fallen at the hands of just as many woodsmen.

Their horse slammed into our footmen head-on: shields angled upwards; horses reared; long pikes entered equine flesh; men slashed and jabbed angrily; spattered blood fell to the earth.

Through all of this and during what must have been far less than a hundred counts, our footmen resolutely held as a unit while the Picts broke apart, unsuccessfully attempting to wade over them in order to cut a path through our middle.

Finally, the master of horse ordered the cavalry into action.

"Lances ready!"

"Ready!" the reply.

"Go!"

This meant charging speed. We galloped toward our men and the Picts.

Seeing us, the enemy lost any semblance of order it still had. As soon as they saw our cavalry riding at breakneck speed, they began to scatter, hoping to make it up and over the hills.

But it was far too late for that.

We slammed into them, pressing from the right and the left and circling around to prevent their escape. Our footmen now stood up from their hunched over and more defensive position and fell back somewhat in order to draw them inwards. Finally, we surrounded them.

Nevertheless, their will to fight had not expired. Just as a cornered beast lashes out in wild desperation, so too they cut at us with careless abandon.

It was then I witnessed that which has wormed its way into our existence by some dark power, Theophilus. I saw men hacked asunder, the beauty of wholeness forsaken as an arm, leg or head fell beneath thundering hooves and stomping feet. Ahead of me, Constantine made sport of the Picts. He slaughtered them like the poor horses we had killed during our harried escape westward. I saw his lance plunge into one unlucky fellow's throat. The Pict, a giant man with bright red hair and muddied and tattooed skin, raised his brawny hands in order to pluck the wood and iron out of his windpipe. But nothing helped. He gurgled and cursed the best he could and held onto the wood as blood and bile filled his throat. Then, as his life drained, he fell from his horse. One of Constantine's squires had to pull the lance loose by holding his neck steady with his boot and heaving up with both arms. As he did so, the barbarian stared up at him with open yet lifeless eyes.

Suddenly I had to defend myself. A large Pictish man made it past Constantine and swung his long sword at me. Fortunately, the angle of his swing was oblique. If it had been head-on, I might have suffered the same bloody fate that many of their men had suffered that day. By some miracle, I blocked it. A half moment later, one of our men stabbed him from behind, and in horror, I saw the light of life pass from his speckled green eyes as blood spurted from the hole where the sword had passed through his chest.

Thereafter, I retreated in order to avoid the fighting. I should add, Theophilus, that I had already positioned myself in the middle of the ranks, a position from which I could follow the action in relative safety without pretending to be a soldier. Yet after this stray Pict attacked me, I moved off behind the lines.

There, in relative safety and dripping with sweat, I laughed nervously, thankful to be alive.

Soon the battle was over. In fact, not long after it had begun, the fight ended, as our circle tightened and we slaughtered nearly all the Picts.

At one point, a captain of horse trotted up to the emperor and asked, "Should we take men?"

"No," he ordered. "Let's make it damn certain they understand we don't want any more trouble."

At battle's end, however, the emperor allowed a few to live for practical reasons. He spoke to them by means of an interpreter. "You must ride and tell your people that you may not trespass beyond the wall. If you do, we'll march against you again. Next time, however, will mark the end of your days. We won't leave anyone alive. Do you understand?"

The few, bloodied and humiliated, sullenly nodded.

Later, I sat atop a hill adjacent the action of the day. I looked out and saw our men below pitching camp some distance away and the five hundred or so Picts all stiffly laying there aside their horses, likewise dead, in the field of battle. Then I saw Constantine making his way up to me.

He greeted me with a smile across his grungy face. His tunic was bespattered with blood and only the gods know what else. "Quite a fight—no?"

"Quite," I allowed.

I wished I could tell him it wasn't so bad, but it wasn't true. Instead, we just sat there for some time in silence.

Eventually we ventured down to camp where we stayed for a few days before returning to the Old Antonine Wall and finally south to tragedy.

Twelve: Eburacum

Late May to July 306 A.D.

THE END OF MAY ushered in the beginning of June and the emperor judged it was time to begin heading south. His desire was to travel eastward toward Segedunum inspecting the installations along Hadrian's Wall before turning to Eburacum where we'd celebrate our victory against the Picts. From there, we would make our way to Petuaria along the coast of the German Ocean where the emperor hoped to gain the benefit of the sea's moist air blowing in from the east. Illness had dogged him for some time, and his physician, a Greek man called Philemon, explained he would never grow well until breathing healthier air. The final destination would be Arelate in southern Gaul.

As it happened, however, the emperor never made it. Instead, we spent several dreary weeks in Eburacum, the chief city of Britannia Secunda, but really more an outpost, Theophilus, a town of wood and thatch and soggy lanes beneath oppressive gray skies. It was there that the emperor's illness grew worse and there that he died.

Despite Philemon's medical diagnosis, associating excessive humors with excessive bodily heat, everyone suspected that sheer exhaustion had caused the emperor's illness. Having battled his whole life for the good of Rome, he was ready to sleep. Now that his son Constantine was present, and now that the Picts had been subdued, he was ready to pass on the baton as in the ancient Lampadedromia.

I witnessed the approach of his death several days before his passing. Visiting him with Constantine shortly after his condition had descended to the "critical," that point which physicians identify as a hinge situation, an either-or where the patient can either get well or suffer death, Constantius Chlorus was now a shadow of the man I had met back in late December.

It was clear that his soul was leaving his body and returning to the World Soul. *But what is that?* I wondered. I had read about it, but now I found I didn't really know what it meant. Does the individual man remain? If so, do the just go to the realm of the stars as Plato claimed, that province of eternal light? I wasn't sure, so I asked Constantine what he thought.

"It's a mystery," he replied. "We can only trust."

"How fragile we are," I observed.

He nodded.

"We're little more than death." I thought of Stella who had died some ten years before.

With that, Constantine disagreed. "Not we," he countered. "You and I are immortal souls."

I didn't feel it, though.

Whatever my own feelings about death and my own personal existence after dying, the emperor didn't wait for me to arrive at a conclusion. Rather, Flavius Constantius Augustus died a few days later toward the end of July. After a few last gasps for air, taken more by his body than the man himself, he rested, having earned his rest by means of an honorable life.

Constantine emerged from the chamber where his father had died and walked bravely into the antechamber where his guard, the masters of horse and foot, and other chief men were dutifully awaiting news of the emperor's demise. He told them that the emperor had peacefully expired and they all nodded gravely. Behind them, the emperor's wife, Theodora, and several of his children by her, quietly wept.

Then everything changed.

The news spread quickly. The masters of horse and foot informed their officers, and they in turn told their men so that the news of the emperor's death rapidly permeated the whole army—legions, cohorts, divisions, squads, and on down the line, man to man. It also spread swiftly throughout Eburacum so that finally, hundreds of men and women came to bid farewell to the emperor whom they had only met just weeks before.

A few hours drifted by as if in a dream.

Inside the large two-story house where the emperor had passed away, we heard a loud rumbling from without. I looked over to a window and asked Constantine what it was.

"I don't know," he admitted.

It grew louder.

I stood and walked to the window. Constantine joined me, as did Philemon who had been attending the emperor's corpse. We were surprised.

"It's the army," declared Philemon.

"It is," Constantine concurred.

It was the army marching, chanting, as if on their way to battle.

"But why?" I asked, alarmed.

It was a foolish question born of fear or born of hope against the likely truth.

"I can't say," said Constantine, though he knew. He feigned ignorance for my sake in order to steady my own apparent anxiety.

Philemon, however, wasn't as considerate. Used to diagnosing a situation for what it was, he concluded, "There are two possibilities. Following one of the bad habits of Britannia, the army has either come to eliminate you and raise one of their own as emperor, or they've come to declare you Augustus."

I swallowed hard, my fear confirmed. Eliminate Constantine? Doubtlessly I hoped for the latter of the two possibilities.

Either way, hundreds of soldiers marched our way led on by the master of foot.

Finally, Constantine did the sensible. He flung open the window to better hear and observe.

Now the chanting grew louder.

"What'll you do?" asked Philemon.

I nervously wondered the same.

"Wait," said Constantine, evenly.

What else could he do?

As for me, I thought he must act! He must act to save himself and me, and all his allies, and …

"Do you hear that?" asked Philemon.

"I do," I responded, my fear confirmed.

"Augustus!" they chanted at some distance.

It was clear now. The army had made a decision.

"They've acclaimed a new emperor," Philemon declared.

"You're right," said Constantine. "But who?"

The physician ventured a guess. "More than likely, it is the master of foot leading them below."

"No," replied Constantine, confidently. "I know him well. Bastrus would never betray my father."

Philemon countered, "Power will cause a man to betray his *own* father, let alone yours."

True, I thought.

"But he wouldn't," declared Constantine.

So we hoped.

Finally, the army stood beneath the house and window. Now the choice was clear.

Philemon turned to Constantine, and deadpan he offered, "I was wrong—forgive me."

The new emperor did.

From below, the army shouted, "Constantine Augustus, Emperor of the Romans!"

For his part, Constantine accepted their acclamation some minutes later, standing confidently before the master of foot and his soldiers—*his* men now.

And me? I nearly fainted, Theophilus. The suspense, the dénouement, and the resulting elation were far too much.

Book Three

Constantine the Emperor

July 306 to November 335 A.D.

The Cell in Tabennisi

Near Afternoon

Theophilus: ARNOBIUS STIFFENED SOME when he said the last. I could see there was something wrong.

"Would you care for some water?" I offered, thinking that perhaps his throat had gone dry.

He nodded and I poured him a cup's worth from the jar we shared. For a few moments, we sat in silence.

I took the opportunity to stand and stretch and glance out the opening of my cell. All was quiet. Most of the monks were out working beyond the walls or silently laboring in their cells, as I would have been on an ordinary day. High in a soft white sky, I saw the sun was hanging near the zenith. Imperceptibly, it traced several seconds of arc as I stood there considering Arnobius' story and wondering what more he would tell of Constantine and eventually of Papa Athanasius and the Church.

Back in the relative darkness of the cell, I glanced at Arnobius before resuming my seat. He didn't look well. His expression was one of uncertainty again, of fear and hesitation, just as it had been earlier in the morning.

"What?" I asked, sitting down on the stack of mats.

"I'm ashamed," he replied.

"Why?"

For a moment, he said nothing, before admitting, "Because I failed to be his friend."

"How?" I asked, thinking of the many times I had failed my own friends.

"I should have taken him and ..." Arnobius paused. Then sighing, he confessed, "I loved him."

I could sense the admission was something profoundly difficult for him to utter. It wasn't so much the reality of the love itself but what followed. *That* was the hard part, the failure.

"I let him down," he went on, solemnly. "From the time I had met him five years before in Alexandria to when he was acclaimed emperor, I had changed—or I *was* changing, from a loving friend to a mere ..." He stopped. Then, "It's possible everything is exaggerated in my mind. It was so long ago. Perhaps I fold back into time what came to be. If anything, I feared for Constantine. I was afraid he would change."

"Afraid for Constantine or for yourself?" I asked.

"For him," he replied. Then, after considering the matter, he admitted, "Well, yes, for me as well. I was afraid the power would alter his personality."

"And you would lose him?"

"I suppose."

"What went wrong?"

"The seed was planted at his father's funeral. There Constantine had me serve as panegyrist—a duty I warily took on."

"Why were you hesitant?"

"Because I knew that whatever I would say of his father, the whole world would apply to Constantine."

"Wasn't he worthy?"

"He was."

"Then what?"

"I should have warned him."

"What do you mean? When? After your speech extolling his father?"

He nodded. "Yes, and after the many speeches I made in praise of Constantine in the years to come. I should have been prescient. Power corrupts; it erodes the good. I know that now, having seen it far too many times. It seems no one holding power, whether imperial or ecclesial, is immune from that one simple reality."

"But you read back into the past a knowledge you have only come to possess over time. How can you be guilty of what you didn't know?"

"I *should* have known. I had read of it in the philosophers and historians."

"Yes, but that kind of knowledge is quite different than—"

Arnobius cut short my words. "I should have been like the slaves who used to ride behind the consuls in the triumphs of old Rome warning them of pride. 'Remember, *dominus*,' they'd whisper, 'you're a man, not a god.'"

"Aren't you being too hard on yourself?"

"Not at all. What happened proves the point. He came to see himself as the image of God on earth with a divine mission to unify the whole world."

"But then, you didn't know."

"True," he responded, shaking his head, "but I should've known."

When some time had passed, I asked, "What happened after the funeral?"

Arnobius sighed before shutting his eyes in order to remember what he cared not to recall.

Thirteen: Treveris

From 306 to late 311 A.D.

AFTER FULFILLING OUR DUTY to Constantine's father in appropriately sending him off to the realm of the dead, we travelled from Eburacum in Britannia to Augusta Treverorum in Gaul where Constantius Chlorus formerly had his imperial residence, and where his son, the new emperor, planned to have the same.

We reached the mouth of the Rhine, which flows down from the Alps and into the German Ocean, near the end of September. The plan was to boat up the great river in order for Constantine to become familiar with the contours of the northern border of the western Empire as well as with the commerce that bustled along its flow. We'd go as far as the Moselle. Then we'd turn toward Augusta Treverorum, which sits mostly on the eastern bank of this lesser, but not unimpressive river.

Augusta Treverorum surprised and impressed me. But then again, if I had only recalled the histories I had studied when a boy, perhaps I would not have been so surprised. So much had gone into building and sustaining the city since its Roman founding some three hundred years ago: toil in construction, blood in defense, labor in the surrounding fields, and genius in trade.

Originally, the Treveri, a tribe composed of both Celtic and Germanic lineage, built the city to be a *burg* or fort. The Treveri were then a wild bunch of men. Then again, so are all barbarian tribes before they encounter the Empire. At the time of their forced introduction to Rome under the auspices of Julius Caesar, the Treveri were hunters and fighters. Their life was in blood. Yet in fairness, Theophilus, I must add that they were principally famous for their skill with horses. The Treveri were the best horsemen north of the Alps. Nevertheless, their men on horseback could do little against the organization of the Empire and the creative determination of Caesar.

After conquest, we Romans transformed the small burg, what they had called Trebata, into a Roman city. Augustus conferred honor upon the

Treveri and upon himself by calling it Augusta Treverorum—the August City of the Treveri. Over time, local habit shortened the city's name to Treveris. It grew in significance, serving as the capital city at different times and under different capacities. As of late, Diocletian had now and again declared it his chief western city, as had Maximian and Constantius Chlorus after him. Now as we sailed upriver, Constantine planned to do the same.

Our ship was merely one of many plying the Moselle and Rhine rivers. These boats and the trade they allow make the men of Treveris very wealthy, giving rise to the geographer Pomponius Mela's remark that Treveris is an *urbs opulentissima*, a most opulent city. Ours in particular was a ship devoted to wood, one of the many niches of trade found in the land around the Rhine. Harvested from surrounding and impenetrably deep and dark forests, wood is one of the three most significant sources of wealth. The other two are wine and wool. Thus, in springtime and summer, green vineyards creep beautifully along the hills around Treveris, and sheep by the thousands bleat under the care of Gallic shepherd boys. These three, wood, wine, and wool, made and still make Treveris a wealthy city as is reflected by the population, nearing a hundred thousand, and the many buildings and architectural features that one imagines as more appropriate to the south rather than north of the Alps.

We disembarked from the large merchant vessel once the crew set anchor and ropes along the walls of Treveris. From our wood laden ship and the gently flowing waters of the Moselle, we trotted along the city walls that Marcus Aurelius had constructed over a hundred years before in order to defend against the many marauding Germanic tribes. We entered the city from the north side, through the imposing *Porta Nigra*, the Black Gate, one of five castellated gates along Treveris' walls, constructed of immense, gray, sandstone blocks rising five stories high. As we passed beneath, I looked up to see soldiers manning the Black Gate and the surrounding wall. Silently, they stood in honor of the emperor's arrival. Finally, we rode down a broad avenue to the imperial residence—the same one that Constantine would improve with palatial extensions within the next few years.

Over the following days and weeks, as I gained a broader introduction to the city, I encountered many other buildings and structures of splendor. Of greatest import are the several bridges that lead one from the eastern bank of the Moselle where Treveris mostly sits to the western side. They are hundreds of years old, going back to Caesar's original conquest. As for business, there is the large forum in the city's center. No, it's not as large as other forums scattered throughout the Empire, yet for a town in northern Gaul, it's impressive. As for entertainment, the people of Treveris have much the same as do other large cities: a circus for horseracing, an amphitheater for games large enough to seat twenty-five thousand, and baths, including those called the Barbara and the imperial baths not far from the new basilica constructed by Constantine some years later. There are also magnificent houses built in the Roman style and towering temples. I was duly impressed.

Overall, Theophilus, I observed how Treveris is a city of substance and wealth. It is indeed the urbs opulentissima of Pomponius Mela. As such, it serves as an abiding lure to the Germanic tribes that live beyond the Rhine. These same tribes feed off the empire as a parasite does a living body, though some fault, one notes, rests with the men of Rome.

For a very long time, there has been a cycle in the fortune of the northern border along the Rhine and Danube. When Romans war with one another, one citizen against another, the barbarians invade. These invasions in turn demand strongmen for pacification—a *dux* to reconquer what the tribes have taken. Following re-conquest, however, there frequently occurs further civil war, as oftentimes, goaded on by his army and his own lust for power, the victorious strongman usurps rule from the rightful emperor. Consequently, more civil war follows as do further barbarian invasions, re-conquest, usurpation, and so on, world without end.

The cycle only recently stopped with the peace of Diocletian and the hard-won victories of Maximian, first, then of Constantius Chlorus. But when the latter died, the tribes moved once again, sensing opportunity. Therefore, when I lived in Treveris, they served to keep Constantine and the legions in constant motion—drilling, fighting, and persistently defending the borders.

We settled in Treveris for the years to come and life drifted by following that pattern and cycle assigned by the gods at the beginning of creation. From the death of winter came the new life of spring, and from that came summer, hot and full of tiring responsibilities—mercantile, military, and otherwise. Everything slowed in the fall, and finally, all died once again as the snows came and the earth froze, hiding the promise of what would come.

Constantine's life during this time followed that of the legions, and theirs corresponded to the cycle circumscribed by necessity. Fall and winter were spent in supplying the army and refortifying the forts and encampments up and down the stretch of the Rhine. The men, both afoot and on horse, trained for the following year's campaign. When the Rhine thawed, if in fact it froze completely from one shore to the other, the army marched off to fight the many Germanic tribes—the Franks, the Alamanni, the Burgundians, among others.

During the half decade or so from when we departed from Eburacum to the year before Constantine was forced to march south in civil war, Constantine was quite successful against the barbarians. So much so, that after conquering them, he was able to enlist many into our ranks. Our enemies, therefore, the Franks prominent among them, came to fight for us. This, Theophilus, was no minor accomplishment. In fact, in the years ahead, when Constantine came to face Maxentius, son of Maximian, the Franks were a significant ally. But of that contest, later.

During those years, Constantine changed. Any hint of youth that had lingered from when I had first met him in Alexandria, now seemed to vanish into the work he threw himself into headlong. Although he had always been serious, he had maintained a certain sense of humor. Now, as lines of gravity permanently carved themselves into his features, those expressions of humor grew further and further apart, until finally, shortly before we departed for Italy, I feared they had disappeared forever. He became a man of responsibility—his responsibility to the Empire, to the borders of Rome, to his men. In like manner, he grew regal as the years passed by. In short, he became a different man.

But then again, Theophilus, I had changed as well, from when I was a boy of sixteen when I had first seen Constantine with my father, and from Iamblichus' lecture in Alexandria when I was nearly twenty, to now, five years after we had arrived in Treveris when I was nearly thirty. If it is as certain wise men teach and six years in a man's life are like the passing of a month in the year, I was then just entering the summer of my life. June. The spring of youth was gone and the heat of the aestival months had arrived. I sigh. Along with summer, spring's lively green had dulled into a deadish, if soft, brown. There was no longer that freshness, that sense of life I first felt when I set off for the capital city of Egypt to study philosophy. Then, I had firmly set my sights upon wisdom in pursuit of the One and the good life. Now, it seems, my mind and heart had changed. A new set of goals appeared like the snows of winter to cover my old goals, which were still there, perhaps, but like a seedling awaiting spring. I still desired philosophy, but it seems the practical concerns of life had taken precedence over the ever-patient concerns of the soul. Accordingly, I rushed along this river we call life, always desiring the stability and rest of the shore but never finding my way there among the many demands of life.

These necessary burdens were primarily the demands of imperial business, the affairs of the Empire. I worked for Constantine in different ways during those years. I practiced law. I plied my rhetorical skills in making speeches, often giving orations on behalf of the emperor and others. Otherwise, I used the bureaucratic and commercial skills I had learned from my father and in Nicomedia to further the prosperity of the Empire at large and the wealth of the men of Treveris in particular—not to mention my own family's estate in Carthage.

The trading affairs of Treveris were significant for me because my involvement with them led to something unexpected and good. While engaged in such business, I encountered the man Gaius Publius late in December of the same year we had arrived in Gaul.

Working at the Office of Permits granting men license to sail and trade along the Rhine and Moselle, I met him one cold winter's day. When Gaius Publius walked in, I instantly knew there was something extraordinary about him—a feeling confirmed over time. He was one of many wealthy men who own large estates nestled into the hills along the Moselle. His family had been in Gaul for centuries, going back to the time of the tragic loss of his name-sake, Publius Quinctilius Varus, when an alliance of Germanic tribes, led by Arminius, son of Segimer of the Cherusci, slaughtered him and a Roman army at the battle of Teutoburg Forest. What a loss that had been! Neverthe-less, over the years Gaius Publius' line had quietly labored—some along the border fighting and some in lands proffered by the Empire upon retire-ment—until eventually, the family was wealthy by any standard.

But for me, Theophilus, Gaius Publius was far more than the paterfamilias of a well-off family in the northern stretches of the Empire. Rather for me, he was the father of the young girl I was destined to marry.

Fourteen: The Games

June 307 A.D.

KATRINA. What should I say?

I first saw her in early summer, a full year after we had arrived in Eburacum after defeating the Picts and nearly a year after Constantius Chlorus had died and Constantine had taken on the imperial purple. It was a month before Constantine was to marry Fausta, the young daughter of Maximian.

I was sitting in the amphitheater with twenty-five thousand others. The sun was shining on us like an old friend, and for once, the skies were blue. It was one of those days when the whole cosmos seems to declare the well-being of everything. I say that for me, as it was not well for all.

Earlier that day, Constantine had staged a triumph in celebration of the army's spring victories against the barbarian tribes beyond the Rhine. High up and exalted in the victory car, he paraded solo. Next to him were his generals, Bastrus and Magnus, sauntering along straight and proud. Following them, the army marched and the cavalry trotted along, hailed as the defenders of peace and prosperity. Behind walked the conquered, fettered in chains. Thousands lined the road cheering.

Prominent among the conquered were two barbarian chiefs, both Franks of the Bructeri tribe. Their names were Merogaisus and Ascaric. They were brothers—Merogaisus was the older of the two.

That day those unfortunate fellows, both colossal in stature, faced a grim destiny. Constantine had sentenced them to fight against wild beasts, and so for them it was not a gorgeous afternoon.

Despite their impending demise, as I sat in the amphitheater happy and without a care in the world.

Then something happened.

Constantine had just entered the amphitheater. He was speaking with Crassus, and the two were laughing about something. Next to them on both sides stood two lines of guards, all young men, anchored some five feet from each other along the stone entryway that led to the emperor's box.

Finally, Constantine took his seat just below me.

"Next time we should play sport with their heads!" Crassus bellowed.

"No," Constantine replied, stiffly. "That would be far too barbaric."

"True," Crassus said, correcting himself.

It was then I heard the voice of a young girl. "Belanus!" it called.

I glanced around, curious to discover its origin.

"Belanus!"—again.

There she was just above the entryway, which was a sprawling arch constructed of enormous blocks cut of gray stone.

"Belanus! Look my way! It's me, your sister!"

I wasn't sure about this so-called Belanus, but I looked, and there above I saw a girl who was the image of beauty, like a goddess of the wood. The sun shone on the dark features of her face and fell on her brown hair that reached below her shoulders and touched her colorfully embroidered dress. My heart swelled with desire.

She called out again for one of the soldiers. I could tell because one responded with the snap-quick glance of his eyes. I followed her voice and saw it land on a young guard who stood fixed to the wall. He flinched. And pulled by brotherly love, he dashed his eyes upwards to where she lurked like a nymph over the arch, and then, just as rapidly, they moved back again. In that quick moment, he commanded her to be quiet. I could see it. As soon as his look fell on her, she disappeared from the wall, and I lost sight of her.

Strange as it may sound, Theophilus, but I nearly panicked, so taken was I with desire. I thought I'd spring out of my seat to find her. She wasn't far. She was above, I judged, sitting with her father or uncle or some other male chaperone. But with the thought of him—whoever he was—the hope of acting vanished. It was impossible. To behave in such a way was against every custom. She was lost to me.

Even so, she occupied my mind when Constantine stood to begin the games. "People of Treveris!" he shouted. "We've fought long and hard throughout the months of spring and early summer. Now, it's time to celebrate!"

Twenty-five thousand men, women, and children roared at his announcement. They had desired the games for months on end.

Briefly, I glanced back on the outside chance that the young girl was standing and looking out over the arch again. She wasn't.

Below me, Constantine looked to the men who organized the events on the sand down in the arena and yelled out, "Let the games begin! And may the enemies of Rome, now and forever, be vanquished to hell!"

Again, a roaring.

I didn't participate. Instead, I thought about what I would do and how I would meet her father—if her father were still alive. If not, I'd have to meet her next of kin. I wondered if they had already made an agreement with some other man. I thought about how fortunate he must be and wondered what he was like.

All the while, both men and beasts consummated several horrid, sweat and blood-filled bouts on the arena floor below. I was aware of this for reason of my own intermittent attention and because of the crowd howling at every thrust and every slash, and finally, at every kill. Afterwards, the attendants dragged them away, their bodies leaving crimson trails of blood that slowly seeped into the orange sand.

Again, I glanced back searching for her. She wasn't there. Now, I wondered what she had actually looked like. My thoughts had grown vague, my recollection dim. I looked down and saw her brother, the guard. With that, at least, I knew she was real. For a moment, I worked to imprint his face upon my mental faculties so I could later find him and so, her.

Then, loudly from below on the sand, a man called out, "These next men, barbarians both, are the enemies of Rome!"

The people crowding the amphitheater were quiet and still, listening to what the man below had to say.

"My fellow citizens of Treveris, you saw them this morning paraded in disgrace through our streets. Now," he shouted, raising his voice as if to stress the significance of his following words, "they will fade into the sand, nothing more than a stain of blood below a mound of flesh!"

He pointed to an entryway that led into the arena opposite him and opposite us. Finally, he announced, "People of Rome, I give to you the brothers Merogaisus and Ascaric. Today they will die!"

The amphitheater erupted in frenzy. It was nearly unbearable for me. All I wanted was to see her. Just once again. Nevertheless, the noise drove my eyes from the crowd around me and from that place where she sat somewhere above to the men below.

I observed their two massive bodies that would soon be nothing more than a gory mess. They were warriors, chiefs of warriors, that particular class of Frankish men whose job it is to fight their whole life. Both were strong, individually as strong as two or three men were. They were tall like giants and muscular. Their hair was long and their skin was dark, marked by the sun. Nothing hid them now except for the fresh blood that we had smeared upon their chests. There, they were dark red, for the blood had dried. Otherwise, they stood as they were born before this great crowd of men and women clamoring to see them die. I'm sure they felt ashamed. Now there was nothing to do but to resist as best as they could.

As Merogaisus and Ascaric walked just yards inside the amphitheater, three wild animals suddenly opposed them. I knew these well from my own childhood. Our nanny, the slave woman married to my pedagogue Tyrannio, used to scare the living Jupiter out of us, using the threat of this beast whenever she wanted to gain our absolute obedience. The animals that stood opposite the two Frankish men were lions—to be specific, two lionesses and one lion, the former two much smaller than the latter one.

When the attendants finally released the three beasts, they peered up into the shouting crowds, confused. Then, looking below, they spotted the two men who had backed up now against the far side of the arena. There, they were talking to each other. It appeared as though Merogaisus was directing his brother in some strategy. I glanced back at the lions. I could see they were unsure about what to do.

Then, from a few rows above me, I heard a man loudly comment, "They're fools!"

Quickly, I looked away from the lions and over to Merogaisus and Ascaric.

"No," said another in considered objection. He sat next to the first man. "It's a brilliant move."

Now I saw the two brothers were sprinting at top speed toward the lions.

One of the men above me explained. "They'll surprise them in their confusion and overtake them."

"Let'em tell that to Pluto himself!"

"They'll have the chance!"

They both laughed.

By this time, the two brothers were nearing the lions, which seemed even more baffled with the crowd above chanting loudly and the men before them running at them as if on the hunt.

Then I heard Merogaisus shout at his brother. His native tongue, one I'd learned in bits and pieces over the past year, was hardly audible over the den of the crowd, but still, I made out a few words.

"... around the side ...!"

They split. Merogaisus ran to one side of the lions and Ascaric to the other. Then abruptly, they turned and pounced.

"My god!" cried one of the men above. "He's given it his arm!"

Both had. And in a flash, Merogaisus wrapped his other arm around the neck of the beast until his hand came around to grasp the inside of its whiskered and now bloody muzzle. Then quickly, he yanked it upwards and around.

The crowd responded viscerally. When they heard the snap, the cracking and quick breaking of the vertebrae along the lioness's spine—I'm surprised we could hear it at all—the crowd groaned, "Ohhh!" at the same moment and in the same pitch, before shouting again for more blood.

There were a few in the crowd, I'm sure, who were pleased to see Merogaisus victorious. But his brother had not been so successful. Instead, it seemed fortune had come to frown on this poor soul.

"Amazing maneuver!" commented one of the men above. I glanced up their way. "Hardly believable!" he said, adjusting his tunic.

"I've never seen anything like it," revealed the other. "What luck!"

"Not his brother. Look!"

I turned to look back toward the arena where Ascaric's arm was missing. More accurately, it dangled to his side as he stumbled backwards away from the lioness he had unsuccessfully attacked just moments before.

"Run!" I heard Merogaisus yell.

But his brother could not run. He was stunned. Next to him, the lioness stood to his side, and the male lion, one and a half times her size, walked menacingly toward him. Now it looked as though the lion would attack.

Seeing this, Merogaisus dashed toward the beast, which was crouched over preparing to spring. "Ahhh!" was all I heard—the battle cry of the Bructeri and of all men.

Before he arrived, however, the lion jumped forward and caught Ascaric by the jugular, bringing him down to the sand. Just as he did, Merogaisus hurled himself upon the back of the beast, which was now busily tearing at his brother's throat.

"No!" shouted Merogaisus.

He stretched forward and grabbed the lion around the neck, around its great fiery mane, and pulled himself within a fraction of a moment so that he was straddling the lion's back and pulling up its head.

"Die!" he screamed.

But the lion wouldn't die. Instead, like a flash of lightning, its muscular body pivoted around and threw Merogaisus off its back and down to the arena floor. Then it roared. And with that, the people above responded in kind, growing even more ecstatic with their lust for blood.

Merogaisus rolled.

The lion backed off.

Merogaisus glanced at his brother. His throat was a red, soggy mess, and his arm, he saw, was beneath him, tied as if by a tether to his left shoulder.

"Ascaric!" he screamed, lamenting his brother's impending death.

I could not hear how Ascaric replied. It was lost to all. But his lips moved as he gazed at his brother for one last time.

Then Merogaisus sprang to his feet again. The muscles of his calves popped out and I could see the tendons above his ankles grow a yellowish, splotchy white.

Now there were the two lions—the lion and the lioness—against the one standing man.

One of them, the lion that had fallen upon Ascaric after the initial attack, lolled over to where Ascaric was dying or was already dead, and after one casual glance at Merogaisus, as if to tell him that he had won and the winnings were his rightful deserts, he began to eat. The man could do nothing.

Then the other lion—the lioness—began to move toward the one living brother. Seeing this, Merogaisus crouched once again.

The lioness drew closer.

"A repeat!" shouted the man above.

"By the gods you're right!"

So it was. Merogaisus had fed the beast his bloodied, left arm, and with his right, he had snapped its neck.

"How is that possible?" asked the one, in disbelief.

"He's a god!"

Again, laughter.

By now, Merogaisus was crouching on all fours panting. Perspiration glistened across his body but for where it mingled with dripping rivulets of blood.

Surrounding me, the crowd had grown relatively quiet, except for one man, up a ways from me and somewhat to my left, who cried, "Go for the kill, man!" He meant for Merogaisus to leap once again on the lion that was eating his brother.

Along with this one man, it seems that much of the crowd began to root for the Frankish chief their army had vanquished just a month before, crying, "Kill it, barbarian! Kill the lion!"

Merogaisus glanced up into the crowd. The sun was white in his eyes. Sweat dripped down from his long brown hair, now ruddy with blood. He was weak—I could see it. He was losing blood from the gash in his left forearm and was growing weaker as it dripped and seeped into the orange sand below.

Still, he stood up.

With that, the amphitheater exploded with excitement. Now everyone wanted him to be the champion.

"Kill the beast, Merogaisus!"

Now, despite the odds, it was the one injured man against the one uninjured beast, somewhat like the end of the fight in Livy between Rome's champion, Horatius, and Albas Longa's Curatius. There they were, staring at each other.

Finally, Merogaisus moved. He stumbled away from the lion, which pawed the ground casually behind, its yellowish maw covered with the blood of his now perished brother. He mumbled something, cursing the animal, I imagined. Perhaps he also prayed for his brother's shade, that it would descend bravely into Hades and there receive a warrior's welcome.

The fickle crowd began to hurl curses, booing at his inactivity.

"Turn and fight him, you coward!"

"That's no way to glory!"

"Go for the kill!"

At their insistence, he did. He turned and with all his might, he fell upon the lion, which stood up roaring. Merogaisus dove at it, striking it with all his reduced might upon its barrel like chest.

But that was it.

The man above summed it up succinctly. "It's like an encirclement," he explained. "Now the lion's got him wrapped up like a little ball."

Merogaisus fell. Exhausted, he fell to the orange sand face down. Most likely, he passed out due to a loss of blood. When he did, the lion let go, now seemingly uninterested.

The crowd, however, could not let go. "Finish him off!" they cried.

The lion didn't have the chance. Instead, a team of two sets of men jogged out into the arena in order to finish the duel. One set took care of Merogaisus and Ascaric. The other set threw a net around the last lion, dragging him off.

I glanced down a few rows to Constantine who was sitting solemnly among several leading men of Treveris. I wondered if he had enjoyed the fight as much as the rest of the crowd had. Surely not, I judged. In any event, he looked out on the arena with approval.

If it was evil, it was a necessary evil. It's what the people wanted, and as emperor, he had to give it to them. It served, however rudely, to mark him as champion, as victor. He had vanquished the enemies of Rome. Now the borders were secure, the barbarians held at bay. For a while, none would come to disturb the peace of Rome. *For a while.* Constantine, nevertheless, had to know it wouldn't last. It never did. Eventually there would be another fight.

Now, as Merogaisus and Ascaric disappeared through the entryway to the amphitheater, the fight was sometime far into the future.

Then—

Suddenly remembering the girl, I turned to glance upwards. I thought I heard her voice again and wanted to see her peeking over the arched entryway. But when I looked, she wasn't there.

I cursed.

I'd have to find her brother—the soldier. I'd have to ... I'd have to wait.

Fifteen: Katrina

July 307 to late 311 A.D.

A MONTH LATER, I thanked the gods. It was during the wedding of Constantine and Fausta, the daughter of Maximian, that I saw her again.

The wedding itself was an extraordinary affair, but admittedly for ordinary reasons. That is, they were ordinary if you happened to be the emperor of Rome. In this case, the reason for Constantine's choice of bride was straightforward. In sum, he required powerful allies. Having no other choice but an alliance or going it alone against Galerius, Severus, and Maximinus Daza, Constantine judged it best to tie himself to Maximian, the former emperor, and his son Maxentius. The latter had himself acclaimed *Princeps*, First Citizen of Rome, and afterwards he had declared the whole of Italy and Africa—Severus' territory—his. Galerius had already sent Severus to oppose him. According to several spies and various rumors, the next move would be against Constantine.

None of this filled my mind the day of the wedding when the alliance was sealed. Instead, I thought of the speech I had given in praise of Constantine. The goal of the speech was evident and necessary as he had explained to me several weeks before.

"Arnobius, you of all my friends are an honest fellow."

"And?" I shrugged, considering the implication.

"You, therefore, will give the chief oration during the wedding feast."

"I'm honored," I replied, all the while wondering what it would entail. I'd given these speeches before, and I was wary of what he'd want me to say.

"What will you declare?" he asked.

"I will tell the truth," I answered. "I'll speak of your courage and wisdom and how smart it is of you to tie yourself to such an illustrious and powerful family."

"Perfect," he approved. "But don't forget the most important element."

"What's that?" I begged.

"My tie to the Divinity. By marrying into Maximian's family, I bind myself to the hero and god Hercules, deified after his twelve labors."

"Shall I speak of those too?"

"Possibly," said Constantine. "I'll leave that to you."

He meant yes. Of course, I would. Therefore, I did.

As the wealthy of Treveris lounged about the great hall of the palace, and Constantine reclined alongside Maximian in a prominent place, and Fausta, young Fausta his bride, was god knows where, I spoke of Hercules, companion of emperors, the slayer of the Nemean lion, and the master of the Thracian horses and the Erymanthian boar. Like him, Constantine would make the world safe for mere mortals. I skillfully folded all of Hercules' magnificent labors and all of his victories into one panegyric that managed to praise Constantine, my friend, and Maximian, now retired, and his son Maxentius, who was now Constantine's brother-in-law and ally.

When I finished, everyone applauded politely, and thus relieved, I happily departed to find refreshment.

A few minutes later, I was sitting alone in another room on a long white couch. In one hand, I held a goblet of Treveri wine—quite decent—and with the other, I stroked my chin wishing I hadn't shaved off my neatly trimmed barbula as all men had begun to do following Constantine's lead. I was pleased with myself. I had done my duty in a polished and rather ingenious way, I judged. I had covered all the essential points and made all the important ties. I knew that sometime later when Constantine and I next met again he would pat me on the back and congratulate me on another fine performance. "Smart speech," he'd praise, or something to that effect. "What would I do without you, Arnobius?" "Thanks," I'd respond, demurely.

By now, I was practically talking to myself. The wine was going directly to my head, and like many an orator, I was embracing myself with pride and self-adulation.

Then a soldier fell down beside me on the couch, breathing heavily as if exhausted.

"Hello," he greeted me, panting. "I'm Belanus."

Immediately I knew his face. I knew the cheekbones, rock hard, and the forehead I'd seen furrowed, and the eyes I'd observed glancing up at ...

"You mind if I share your couch?" he politely asked.

"No, not at all," I replied. And silently, I wondered if ...

"I'll be gone shortly," he blurted out. "I've just squashed a man who was drunk—drunk as a man on a whore."

"Oh?" I asked. I didn't really care. But at the same time I did. He was …

"He was fighting with another man. Not that it was a danger to the emperor. More a nuisance. Not appropriate. Imagine getting drunk on a day like today. Whatever happened to sobriety?" Then he asked, "What's your name?"

"Arnobius," I informed him.

"Ah," he returned, recognizing me. "Now I see. You're the one who gave the speech."

I nodded.

"You're the philosopher, I hear."

"Oh? Says what man?"

"My father."

"You're father? And who is he?"

"A merchant. He knows you from the Office of Permits."

I thought about who it could be.

"His name is Gaius Publius," Belanus revealed.

Immediately, I knew him. "Of course!" I said in full recognition. "He's *your* father?"

"Well, mine and my two sisters."

Your sister, I thought.

"Is she here—I mean he … *him* … your father, Gaius Publius?"

"Yes, who else? Do you need to speak with him?"

"No," I said. Despite the wine's assistance, I couldn't find the nerve.

"But why not?" asked Belanus. "Let's go and find him. I'm sure he's bored. For him, life's nothing but wine, wool, and wood. I bet he'd like to talk a little sense."

"Sense?" I asked, not grasping his intent.

"Philosophy," he explained.

"Oh?"

"Of course."

It was then I knew. I absolutely knew I had to have her and her father and her whole family.

Five minutes later, we were speaking with Gaius Publius. I was tipsy, but I held myself well enough.

"Of course I know him!" he exclaimed when Belanus introduced us.

As for me, I had trouble focusing on what Gaius Publius had to say. Just as we joined in conversation, I glanced aside and saw her once again. The beauty. The brown eyes. Her dress was the color of a yellow spring flower. Still, I shifted back, pulling myself away from her and forced myself to listen. It wasn't easy.

Finally, it all came together. I focused and heard him.

"If only he'd written more plainly," he said, "perhaps the world would have been better off."

"Who?" I asked.

He told me and we talked about Plotinus' ideas.

A half hour later, Gaius Publius suggested that I come and stay with him sometime. "You'll have to come out to our estate," he offered. "We'll eat and drink lightly and talk about what is and what's not."

I thought of all such a visit implied and wanted nothing more.

"I'd be pleased to come," I said.

"Why not this Saturday?" offered Belanus. "I've got three days' leave."

"Then Saturday it is," declared Gaius Publius, "if, of course, you can make it, Arnobius."

I happily told him I could.

Saturday came and I rode out the ten some miles to Gaius Publius' estate, which sits in the hills outside Treveris along the Moselle. When I arrived, a slave woman greeted me with refreshment and had me wait in a spacious yet intimate and well-appointed room just off the courtyard.

"Master will be in shortly," she informed me, handing me a cup of chilled wine and a plate of food.

"Where is he?" I asked.

"Down on the dock, my lord. It's the wine boats again."

"Is Belanus around?"

No, she nodded. "He's there too."

"Thank you," I said.

She was very pleasant—the slave woman. She served as if she wished to even if she had not been compelled to do so. I saw contentment in her dark eyes.

Once she left, I sat back on a couch to wait. After a half hour or so had passed, and after I had drunk several cups of wine and had eaten the food she had given me, I fell asleep.

Then: "Sir—"

I opened my eyes, heavy with sleep and the wine and meal I had taken. For a moment, I thought I was waking up to another world. It was a dream I had often had during the past month. She was there, the beautiful nymph-like girl I had seen in the arena. She was bending down to kiss me.

"Arnobius?"

"Yes?" I replied.

It was the girl; it was Katrina.

"My father sent me to fetch you. He and Belanus are down haggling with the wine merchants or the men who actually ship the wine up and down the Moselle. I don't know—but you *must* come. I'm to take you there."

I sat up. *You?* I thought. *The girl of my dream?*

She looked at me as if there were something wrong. "Are you okay?"

"Yes," I said, smiling. "I'm just a bit groggy."

"Here, have this."

I took the water she gave me.

"Thank you."

"Let's be off!" she commanded.

I followed, and Katrina led me from the back of their house along a path down to the riverside. She was wearing a simple white dress sewn with a dark green trim around the neckline and hem. As we walked, we didn't speak again until we were finally near the river.

"Just here," she pointed.

Gaius Publius and Belanus stood alongside several bearded men who were giving orders to a whole crew of shipmen behind. "Don't topple 'em fools! Damn it! I said don't let 'em roll!" The men behind were loading a long vessel with what seemed like thousands of barrels of wine. I'd often witnessed this scene in Treveris.

Belanus turned when he saw Katrina and me trailing behind. "You've finally made it!" he said to her.

Gaius Publius saw me as well. "And so have you," he greeted me, warmly. "Did you meet Ulfila?"

"That's our dear servant," Katrina explained.

"Oh, yes," I said. "And thanks for the meal."

Another girl, perhaps twelve years old, bounded up and asked, "Is this the man, father?"

"Yes, it is," replied Gaius Publius, chuckling. Then, turning to me, he said, "See, you're already famous. Luxilla's been thrilled to have a visitor for the past two days."

"Don't forget Katrina," added Belanus. "They've both been giddy with excitement."

The two girls blushed, and Gaius Publius told them to return to the house. "Give Ulfila some help," he ordered.

Obediently, they did.

Our own return followed an hour or so later. Finishing business with the wine merchants, we turned to walk up to the house.

It was a house I came to know well over the next few years, Theophilus. Indeed, they set aside a room for me and officially called it my own. Upon my first visit the slave woman Ulfila warmly said, "You'll be staying in this room, make yourself at home." In the months ahead it was, "Go ahead and situate yourself into your room; Gaius Publius is in the library; Belanus is in the barracks until next week." Then, it became, "Welcome home master Arnobius," and nothing more. I knew where to go and what to do. It had become another home for me, and with it, Gaius Publius' family had become my own.

During those years, I happily grew older with them. I saw Luxilla grow from a young girl to a young woman, Belanus climb in rank in the cavalry under Magnus the master of horse, and Gaius Publius age like a fine wine. He grew wiser, and despite his wealth, nurtured with due care and responsibility, he cast his eyes more and more upon the Permanent, as Plotinus advised, rather than on passing things as most men did. And Katrina. The odd thing about her was … what should I say? I don't fully understand it even now. It's as though I forced my feelings underground. And when they vanished—or when I suppressed them—that sense of mystery vanished as well. It's not that she had suddenly become less than beautiful or that she had lost any of her charm. Rather, something within told me I simply had to wait. Hence, I became as a brother to her, another Belanus. We conversed and played games together after supper, and I even tutored her along with Luxilla at times. Aside from this, however, aside from the mundane and sibling-like, there was nothing more than that between us for a very long time.

+ + +

Four years passed. No, it was more—four and a half.

It was November or December and the cold had returned. I was reclining before a fire one evening near to Luxilla and Katrina who were playing the game of war on the floor below. Above them, I was reading one manuscript or another from his library, when Gaius Publius came in and sat by my side. I sat up, for I had been slouching.

"Girls," he spoke, motioning them to leave for a moment. They did.

"Good evening," I said. "Are you finally back?"

He had been away for a few days in Treveris on business.

"Yes," he nodded. "Those damn wool merchants want *everything*." He sighed. "But I suppose that's their job, right? To get what they can?"

"It's the sheep who lose," I offered, hoping to interject some levity.

He laughed.

"Arnobius, I've been thinking."

"Oh?"

"I've an important proposal to make to you."

"What more?" I asked.

My father Buteo had long before admonished me to align our affairs with those of Gaius Publius' household. I had, and things had turned out well for all parties concerned. Doubtlessly Buteo had been particularly happy. In Africa, he was rising to ever-new heights of prosperity. "Soon, we'll have conquered Carthage!" he wrote in one exchange of letters. "And next, the whole Empire!" I laughed when I had read it. I loved him. And Mother? Well, she was pleased, but when she had discovered there were two young and unmarried girls involved, she directed Buteo to advise me to make a move of inquiry at the very least, and she herself turned with even greater devotion to Tanit.

"No, no," Gaius Publius responded, chuckling. "You and your father have been superb. One couldn't ask for better partners."

"What, then?" I queried.

He said nothing for a moment. Then, he asked, "Will you be back in town in a few days?"

"I plan to be. But if you need me here, I can delay. I'll write ahead to the emperor."

"No, that's perfect. We can discuss it there."

"Fine," I agreed. "Where do you want to meet?"

"The imperial baths," was his quick reply. "We'll have a warm bath and a massage and dine afterwards."

Three days later, I sat across from Gaius Publius in one of the more pleasant taverns that stand next to the imperial baths. We sat drinking a warm, spiced wine, fully relaxed after a long bath and massage.

"I never quite saw it that way," I was saying. "It makes good sense, though."

"Of course it does. I think it fits well with what Plotinus was trying to do. In his early years, a man is the World Soul playing in the realm of materiality, in the ordinary world. But not, I say, as any old sod! No, as a man of responsibility, a man of virtue, you make your mark in the world."

"Or that of the World Soul," I suggested, for the sake of clarification.

"Better expressed," he agreed. "And after you've made your mark, you retire as it were to become the Proficient he mentions in the fourth *Ennead*."

"But what of purity during the former stage?" I asked.

"What do you mean?"

"I mean the purity he speaks of—from the world and the desires and ..." I hesitated.

"Do you mean sex?"

I nodded.

"He never condemned it, Arnobius. It's called marriage."

I conceded the point.

Then Gaius Publius shifted on the bench and had a drink out of his cup. Steam rose from a ceramic bowl of broth set in the middle of the table. Behind, a tall woman with her hair tied up casually set several gray ceramic plates trimmed with blue down for another pair of men. A black dog wagged its tail next to her feet. The other men were gossiping about the rumors of war. For a moment, I thought about Constantine. I thought about how he had changed and all the challenges he faced. Yes and no, I judged. I remembered the first time I had met him. His question—the One or the many? My mind jumped. I missed my father. It had been so long since I had seen Buteo, Mother, my two sisters, and my one living brother. Then I looked at and admired Gaius Publius and thanked the gods.

"Not bad," he remarked.

"The wine?" I asked.

"Yes. Not quite as good as what we produce, but not bad either."

I tasted the wine and thought about the many times and the many varieties of wine I had drunk over the past four years with Gaius Publius and his family. Again, he shifted across from me.

"Arnobius," he went on, "it all brings me to my point."

"What?" I asked. "The wine? I thought we'd had enough of business."

"No—we have. But the other. I mean marriage."

"What? Surely you're not getting married?"

Gaius Publius squawked with laughter. "Not me!"

His wife had died some sixteen years before in childbirth. Luxilla had been the end of her. Nevertheless, he'd always been grateful. Her death, he had revealed to me, had driven him to the consolation of philosophy.

"Who, then?" I asked.

"Well ...?"

From the looks of his expression, I thought he meant me. And equal to his own response, I balked. "What do you mean? I'm quite content with my present station."

"You are?"

I nodded. I supposed I was and supposed I knew, and yet I didn't quite.

"No, I mean Katrina," he declared.

"Is *she* getting married?"

"Yes," he replied.

No! I thought. *She can't be.* It was then that a flood of suppressed emotion welled up in my heart. I remembered when I had first heard her voice in the amphitheater, and when I had first met her in the house, and how she had led me down to the river. I recalled the many hours I had spent with her over the past years, and how I had loved those years and had come to love her. She *couldn't* be getting married. She was mine!

Yet, I thought, Katrina was nearing eighteen. She had long been a woman. Soon some man would ask for her hand or Gaius Publius would make arrangements. *My God!* I panicked, *she'll be married and go away and leave me all alone. I can't let this happen!*

Gaius Publius moved me beyond my rambling thoughts. "I hope to find someone suitable for her in the next few months."

"Like ... like who?" I stumbled. My face must have grown pale.

"That's the question," he said. "Any ideas? Among all your contacts, whom might you suggest?"

"I don't know," I answered, falling silent.

"Arnobius, are you all right? You look a bit—"

"What do you mean?" I asked.

Then Gaius Publius laughed aloud, and the men sitting near us glanced over our way.

"What?" I demanded, leaning toward him.

"You," he said. "You're more of a fool than I thought. If you want her, just say it."

"*Want* her?" I echoed.

"Oh, come now. You've always loved her. This is what I wanted to ask you. Do you want Katrina to be your wife?"

I sat up. *Of course I do*, I thought. Yet my tongue failed me.

"Well, friend?"

I must have betrayed my true sentiments.

"You will, then?"

I lurched.

"Good. But don't worry—you'll have your bachelor's freedom for some time yet."

"When?" I managed.

"I was thinking of four or five months from now. Late spring."

"I can do that," I grinned.

And with that, I was engaged to be married to Katrina. For once, Theophilus, I felt completely happy as Lady Fortune herself smiled upon me.

Regrettably, however, when it came time for the wedding in May, I was already well on my way to Italy, marching with Constantine and his army to face Maxentius in a battle that would alter the history of the whole world. It was then that Fortune frowned. But to explain, I must backtrack some.

Sixteen: Maneuverings

307 to 311 A.D.

THREE YEARS AFTER CONSTANTINE MARRIED Fausta, he put her father to death. More precisely, he had Maximian kill himself, a forced suicide. With a sharpened blade of gold, he drained his own life.

Later, after a set of trustworthy servants mopped up the blood, Constantine had Maximian's body burned and his memory damned. Then, moving on with the affairs of the Empire, he proceeded to ally himself elsewhere. I should know, because once again as with his marriage to Fausta three years earlier I made the speech praising him as a man and demonstrating his ties to other remarkable men and the gods.

"Claudius Gothicus?" I asked one day when we were going over the upcoming oration.

"Of course."

"But where's the tie?"

"He was a great man," declared Constantine, as if that were enough. "The greatest before Diocletian."

"And I'll include him as well?"

"Yes."

I understood. Truly, I did. He had to have some tie extending beyond his own father for legitimacy, a tie to one of the original two emperors of the tetrarchy. Now that Maximian was gone, this naturally fell to Diocletian. The men in his army would appreciate this. The other man, Claudius, conqueror of the Goths, had more to do with Constantine's own devotion to the divine Sun.

"And I'll include the story of the vision?" I asked.

"Oh, it's no story," he flatly averred.

As for me, I couldn't say. Yet when I made the speech a few weeks later, I spoke as if it had incontrovertibly occurred.

"Lastly," I announced, "I must mention the emperor's tie to the divine."

Those listening shifted upon their seats, and those standing gave their weight to another leg.

"You have known for a long time of your emperor's devotion to Apollo the divine Sun. This he inherited from his own father, Constantius Chlorus, and before him from Claudius Gothicus who had a special devotion to this Divinity of light. But you may not have heard of the recent visitation."

I paused to let the idea sink into the ears of those listening. Some, I could tell, slunk into their seats bored as if *this* would be another one of *those* stories; others, however, sat up with keen interest.

"Not a month ago, Constantine was praying down in the grove next to the shrine of Apollo. Pacing back and forth, he begged for divine light, that he might know what to do with his enemies. It was then he had the vision."

I extended my hand out from beneath my bleached white tunic and lifted it up to indicate the divine presence.

"Apollo appeared to him, and Constantine fell to his knees and awaited the words of the Unconquered Sun. Finally, Apollo spoke—words that came more as light than the sounds of our own speech. 'I am with you,' he shone, brilliantly. He was a body without body; he was pure light. 'Go and conquer my enemies. And when you do, you shall bring unity to the land, and peace and prosperity will follow in a way never before known.' Constantine bowed until Apollo reassumed the form of the luminous sun above."

Again, I paused. I could see a mixture of belief and doubt.

"Thus," I concluded, "is Constantine tied to his divine father—to Apollo the Unconquered Sun."

Politely, they affirmed what I said.

My work done, I descended to sit on a bench next to Belanus and Gaius Publius.

"Well done," complimented the latter.

"Is that story true?" whispered Belanus.

"Of course," I said.

In any event, the speech had its intended effect. Constantine tied himself to Claudius Gothicus who had ruled decades before, Diocletian who now passed his days gardening in Dalmatia, and Apollo the divine Sun. Overall, they were a good set of allies.

With that done, matters seemed fairly secure. But this is to ignore what had happened over the past three years and what would happen over the next year or so. What was that? I'll be brief. For like one of those games with many moving pieces, there were only a few that truly mattered.

Once Maxentius had himself declared princeps by the Senate and people of Rome and once Augustus over Italy and Africa, everything seemed to fall apart—and this despite the wedding eight months later between his sister Fausta and Constantine. If Maxentius had truly wanted to ally himself with the latter, then perhaps events would have transpired differently. Apparently, though, he had had no such long-term intention. Once he had defeated Severus—albeit with the help of his father—there was no stopping the reach of his arrogance.

Galerius had called upon Severus just a few short months after Maxentius' declaration. Following orders, Severus swooped down from Mediolanum, thinking he'd rapidly be able to take care of the matter. He neglected, however, to consider one possibility—that is, Maximian. When Maxentius heard of Severus' imminent attack, he called upon his father to take on the imperial purple once again. Poor old man. It was everything he yearned for. So he did. And with it, he regained the loyalty of his army, which was presently marching south with Severus to attack Maxentius and Rome.

Eventually, Severus camped before the walls of Rome, those built by Aurelian some forty years before, and prepared for a long siege. In the actual event, it was anything but. As soon as his army heard of Maximian's resumption of imperial powers, and as soon as the latter promised a bonus in the form of gold, they deserted in droves making their way to where Maximian was on his way down to help his son Maxentius. Consequently, his army falling apart, Severus panicked, and his advisors admonished him to flee. Thus he did, fleeing upon horseback with the remainder of his men up to Ravenna.

In just a few weeks, Maximian appeared beneath the gates of the city demanding Severus' surrender. Afraid for his life, however, Severus refused. Finally, given certain assurances, Severus agreed to leave the safety of the city walls in order to meet with the old emperor to negotiate. *Negotiate?* This wasn't exactly what Maximian had in mind. Rather, once Severus was out, he sprung a trap and the caesar became his prisoner. Still, Maximian didn't kill him as he could have; instead, he kept him locked up for later maneuverings.

It was about this time that Maximian secured the alliance of Constantine through marriage. As I've related, the latter married his daughter Fausta, and

I made the oration tying the two together as if nothing would ever stand in the way of their undying family love.

Later that same summer, Galerius arrived. No doubt, he judged Severus had behaved the part of a weak fool. Perhaps he thought he had made a mistake in his choice of caesar. At the very least, Severus required humiliation, even as Galerius had ten years before after failing against the Persians. In the end, Severus would receive no such thing. Rather, Maximian killed him, and Galerius, realizing Rome would be far harder to take than he had imagined, turned around and sped back to Nicomedia and the familiar pleasures of the court. He'd have to do something else.

Before he could work out anything, though, the pieces moved. Maxentius, to Galerius' own delight, declared himself emperor of Hispania. Or as some speculated at the time, the generals of Hispania declared for him. Either way, this drove a wedge between Constantine, who had official possession of Hispania, and his new brother-in-law. Galerius thought this would be enough to bring Constantine to war with Maxentius. But it wasn't. Instead, Maximian declared against his own son! Nevertheless, in the end, poor Maximian failed. He lost to Maxentius and so he was forced to flee to Constantine who received him tepidly. He refused when Maximian suggested they ally against Galerius and his own son. Constantine had other plans.

Then Galerius struck.

In Carnuntum, in the province of Pannonia along the Danube, Galerius called a conference including all imperial leaders. Well, most. He called Diocletian from retirement, Maximian from Constantine's side, and Maximinus Daza from his pleasure palace in the Oriens. As for the others—I mean Constantine and Maxentius—he left them out of the conference altogether. Although Galerius had previously recognized Constantine in some fashion, he now shunned him, leaving his status unclear for the moment. As for Maxentius, he ignored him like the enemy he had always been ever since his usurpation of imperial powers years before.

It was in Carnuntum that Constantine's eventual ally Licinius was elevated to the purple. Why? For all the old reasons and world without end! Galerius required someone faithful in the West, and Licinius was an old soldier friend. He'd proved himself on the field both as a loyal ally and, more importantly, as an intelligent general. Diocletian stamped his approval, as did Maximian. Consequently, there came to be Galerius and Maximinus Daza in the East and Licinius and Constantine in the West, though the latter was relegated to the status of caesar instead of the status his father's army had awarded him some four years prior.

"What do you think of that?" I asked Constantine when he received the news in the early part of the following year.

"It means nothing," he replied, shrugging. "I have a destiny, and I'm meant to fulfill it whatever Galerius has to say."

Nothing much happened for a year. Then, itching for power again, Maximian moved against Constantine.

The first time, Constantine forgave him. The second time, however, he could not. For this reason, Maximian ended his life on a cold stone floor, bleeding out to death, his old lust filled eyes staring lifelessly upon a world he had once ruled as the second most powerful man in the Empire.

"Do you think there will be peace?" I asked Constantine, sometime after my speech tying him to Claudius Gothicus, Diocletian, and the Unconquered Sun.

"No," he declared. "There'll never be peace until we are governed by men who respect the will of the god."

"Apollo?" I asked.

"Y-yes," he confirmed, hesitantly. "Yes, the divine Sun."

Still, Theophilus, there was something more in Constantine's mind, something just then forming, as if a new idea were overlapping one old. For just about that time, an old friend had arrived from Nicomedia as well as a Christian priest he'd met some years before when on campaign in southern Gaul.

The priest was now a bishop. He was Ossius of Cordoba, both a judicious and astutely political man, and he, it seems, was the root cause of much of Constantine's ambivalence at the time.

Whereas Constantine's identification of the sun in the sky with the One, with God, would have dismayed the ordinary Christian, Ossius promoted the idea with particular alacrity.

"There's no real problem at all," he avowed one day in Treveris as we reclined at supper. Ossius was visiting from Hispania.

"How not?" I asked, amazed. "He worships the sun as though it were the Divinity itself."

"Not so," retorted Ossius, smiling wisely.

"Correct," interjected Constantine. "Arnobius, you must use clearer language. And even your own points to my true sentiments."

"That you are a sun worshipper? A devotee of fire?" I said.

"Be reasonable," Ossius urged me, kindly. "You must listen to what another says rather than insisting upon your own interpretation."

"That's fair," I agreed, "proceed."

"I do not worship the sun as God but as the *image* of God," Constantine averred.

"And that," Ossius explained, "is hardly a problem. You see the sun as an icon, an intermediary, as it were, signifying or pointing to the true nature of the divine One beyond. In that sense, the sun reveals the One—right?"

"Correct."

"The only problem or danger," Ossius went on, "is tying this image to Apollo. For there you tether yourself to the whole mythological system of the Greeks."

"Exactly," I said. "My precise point. For one, you're tied to the Greeks. But for another—and here, Ossius, I respectfully believe you are wrong—you continue to promote this idea of a mediator. There's simply no need for that. To have a mediator is to sully the One, which is thereby dragged down to the level of the many—whether by the divine Sun or this Christ you speak of, the god of Israel. What necessarily follows is corruption. For the One, however, this is impossible! It defies all logic!"

"No, no, no," countered Ossius, "not impossible—that is, not if one understands the teaching correctly."

"How then? Show me it's not impossible," I challenged him.

"Well, this is where Constantine's understanding of the sun as image of the One comes into play." Ossius turned to Constantine. "Please, Lord Emperor, tell me, what is the nature of an image?"

Without hesitation, Constantine replied, "It's a reflection of the thing imaged."

"Correct. As in a polished mirror or a painting, right?"

I couldn't help but interrupt. "I know, I know," I insisted. "And there's no diminution of the thing imaged by being portrayed in a painting or reflected in a mirror."

"Right. So, what's the problem?"

I claimed it reeked of Iamblichus' theurgic system where the One is somehow enslaved to the many gods and magical rites of the Greeks and Romans, and consequently, to all manner of foolishness and immorality.

"I can understand your misgivings," allowed Ossius, "but our way is entirely different from that of Iamblichus. There's no magic involved. We're not out to manipulate the One by means of mediary gods, whether good or evil, moral or not."

"But what, then, is the Christ?"

"He reveals the One, even as the sun is said by Socrates to reveal the Good."

Constantine turned to me. "It *is* possible, Arnobius. Don't play the part of a mule. At least listen."

"Possible," I permitted, "but unlikely. The One is entirely transcendent. It *is* and has no part in our world of becoming."

"Perhaps," said Constantine.

Nevertheless, Ossius' ideas, or Christian philosophy in general, began to sway the emperor more and more despite a certain and continued note of ambiguity. Progressively, he came to see how the Christ of the Christians, the one that was said to reveal God, was quite similar to the sun, which was said to reveal the divine Apollo and so the Divinity itself.

Lactantius, the old friend from Nicomedia who had counseled tolerance along with Constantine some ten years before, agreed.

Lactantius had grown up in the traditional religion of his native Numidia before converting at some point to the Christian faith. Late in life, he had come to the imperial court in Nicomedia because Diocletian had appointed him chief professor of rhetoric. Then everything had collapsed for the old man. Just as he should have received the laurel wreath for a lifetime of accomplishment, Galerius outlawed him with all other Christians. Consequently, he lost all his money and lived the next few years a cranky old beggar, surviving by means of a few odd teaching jobs and his writing. Lately he had turned to a life of asceticism so that his flesh hung from his bones like another man's tunic might hang from his body. Finally, he moved west where once again he encountered Constantine.

As I said, Lactantius had few problems with identifying the Christ with the sun for purposes of analogy. Nevertheless, for him there was far more. He vociferously proclaimed that the light of the Christ was rising and the kingdom of darkness was collapsing all around us. He predicted this right around the time when Gaius Publius made his proposal that I should marry Katrina.

"All persecutors of Christians," he asserted, "come to a horrific end."

"Oh?" said Constantine, willing at the very least to hear him out. "And Galerius, then?"

"Like all the rest, Galerius will die an unhappy death—as will Maximinus Daza."

"By what agency?" I asked, incredulous.

"God," he stated, flatly.

I smirked.

Constantine did not. He was thinking. What Lactantius said made some sense to him. Those who had respected Christian revelation and the absolute unity of God had fared better than those who had not. He thought of his own father who had died a natural death as compared to Nero, Decius, and now Diocletian who, if rumors had it right, was going insane.

"Come now," I scoffed, "you're telling me the divine One is in the business of *smiting* people?"

Quite simply and seriously, Lactantius averred, "Yes, he is."

In my mind, if true, the One had reached a new low.

Six months later Galerius died an excruciating death. People said that the whole city of Nicomedia reeked because of his affliction, one in his gut, which caused him quite literally to dissolve.

"It's come to pass," declared Lactantius when Treveris received the news. "Another persecutor has died."

"But he rescinded the persecutions!" I countered, attempting my best to dispute what I believed to be the rather facile and foolish association of divine behavior with profane happenstance.

"True, but the One still required recompense. And besides, Galerius never came to believe."

I said nothing more. What *could* I say? Whatever, my appreciation for Lactantius fell a few notches down from where it had been—and *that* had already been low.

Constantine, on the other hand, was impressed. "You may be right," he allowed. "The power of evil is diminishing."

Lactantius seemed pleased with himself.

Later, when alone with Constantine, I asked, "Do you agree with Lactantius?"

"I don't know," he admitted. "All I know is that I have come to earth to do one thing, and *that* I must do."

I nearly yawned, for I could predict his sentiments. The reference was to his mission given by the god, by divine providence, to procure unity, and from that, peace and prosperity.

I should not have yawned.

At the time, these three—unity leading to peace, and peace leading to prosperity—were again threatened. When Galerius died, the whole game shifted once more. For then, if properly allied, Constantine could move against Maxentius and regain Hispania. Maxentius knew this, and therefore he secretly allied himself with Maximinus Daza. When Licinius learned of this pact, he immediately made overtures to Constantine, who happily agreed to an alliance. In the end, it became Constantine and Licinius, now both declared full emperors, pitted against Maximinus Daza in the East who coveted Licinius' lands, and Maxentius in the West who had come to rule as a tyrant. The agreement was that Licinius should hold Maximinus Daza in check while Constantine would worry about Maxentius.

Worry, he had to do. We knew that Maxentius was preparing his armies in the south for an attack on Constantine. The latter, however, believed he couldn't allow this to happen; he must strike first, marching into Italy against his brother-in-law.

"We'll strike at the tyrant," he said confidently to his generals. "We'll win with the sponsorship of the god, of the divine Sun, Apollo!"

Still, behind closed doors, Constantine agonized. The ambiguity of his allies—both in the profane and divine realm—ate away at him. Was Licinius trustworthy? Would he hold against Maximinus Daza?

Then there was the question regarding the Divinity. Above all, he agonized over what god would lead him against Maxentius. Who would be his *comes*, his divine partner? Would it be Apollo the divine Sun as I had declared in the speech after Maximian's forced death, or some other god? Whoever, whatever, he desperately required clarity.

One evening, in a moment of weakness, Constantine shared his uncertainty with me. I told him he shouldn't be so worried, that if he had justice on his side, then he'd prevail. Surely, I asserted, he did. Maxentius had wrongly taken Hispania—clearly, he was a usurper.

"Still," Constantine countered, "I must know who marches by my side. I must know who protects me so that I may give proper devotion and gratitude. Whoever it is, the god leads me along this path, along this mission I have been given to accomplish."

We both said nothing for a moment. Then, I broke the silence by changing the topic somewhat. "If you want to know what I think," I said, "I think Ossius has poisoned your mind."

"Poisoned?" he asked. "How?"

"No—that's too strong a word," I clarified. "He's confused you."

"He has," Constantine confessed. "But he may not be wrong."

"On the other hand, he may not be right."

"Then what should I do?"

"What you've always done," I suggested. "Live by the light of reason. If nothing else, it's reason that mirrors the divine Mind."

"Agreed," he said, "at the very least, you are right in that."

I could tell, nevertheless, that Constantine had not answered the question in any final way. The following months proved this suspicion true, for he continued as ever in agitation.

As for me, I couldn't help but judging that the divine One was indifferent to our affairs. Aloof. My sun was different from Constantine's. Mine shed its light in silence, I thought, shining indifferently upon the great river of time in all its turns and falls and slow moments of stillness. I doubted whether the One had any real disposition one way or another regarding human activity. For me, human life appeared to unravel in dark silence.

There were times when I even wondered if perhaps the Epicureans are right after all. There's no providence, they claim. All is the product of blind chance. And as proof, they offer the flaws of our world. Lucretius suggests these flaws demonstrate a lack of design; therefore, he concludes, there's no designer.

It's possible, I thought. In the end, there's nothing more than atoms and the void.

During those times, it seemed to me that God is the void; God is silence itself. But I didn't know what to think.

The Cell in Tabennisi

Midday

Theophilus: ARNOBIUS STOOD, TROUBLED. Or was he? I watched him as he passed from the relative darkness of my cell to the noonday light outside. Eventually, I got up as well and joined him there.

Above us, the sun shone brilliantly, making the sky seem white. He moved away from me and paced back and forth a short distance from the cell. I was afraid I had lost him, that he would turn to me and call it quits. I felt for him. He had come to the monastery to forget it all. But now, like a pitiless doctor, I was pulling at his innards. You, however, had asked me to do it, Abba, and so I did it.

Standing there, I felt the intensity of the sun upon me, its heat bearing light. Considering what Arnobius had earlier recounted, I wondered what the sun revealed of the divine nature—*if* anything.

"Arnobius," I called after a while.

He turned.

"I can't fathom it either."

"What?"

"The nature of the One."

"Oh?" he replied, though more out of courtesy.

"I too am tempted. This temptation is what's behind my own inability to commit. Over and over I ask, is our faith real?"

Arnobius didn't reply. Preoccupied with his own thoughts, he stared out beyond the walls of the monastery to the desert beyond and to the horizon far away where the earth shimmered and seemed to nervously merge with the air above.

As for me, Abba, I continued to speak. I had to. Here was a man who was similar to me, with similar questions and doubts. We both knew the impossible challenge of committing to the invisible, to the silent—to God. In this way, Constantine was remarkably different from both of us.

"I've never been able to give all," I admitted. "Even now, I'm here more at the insistence of my mother. *She's* the saint, not me. Instead of putting to use the Catechetical School's sacred formation, I turned to rhetoric and theater. I've been far more concerned with what others think of me than …"

Arnobius turned to me. "Than what, Theophilus?"

"God," I replied, "or, like you say, the silent One, the One who seems more an absence than a presence."

"It's the great temptation," Arnobius declared. "You go on living as though there are two realities—one distant and one nearby, God's and ours."

"And there's no real meeting place between the two," I said.

"That's what I thought."

I wondered how it was that our own silence participates in the great Silence. Then I shared something I recalled from my years at the Catechetical School.

"I remember one of my instructors once suggesting the One is like the author of a vastly long scroll—one nearly infinite."

Arnobius nodded, having heard this as well. "A finite-infinitude," he remarked.

I went on. "The author lives and thinks outside the reality of the scroll. Then one day he writes, and in doing so, the story springs to life, coming to be from nothing."

"But his thoughts," Arnobius added.

I agreed. "His thoughts become written words, a script, extending into the void and enduring through time."

"It's the story we endure," said Arnobius.

"What do you mean?"

"I mean that our living, our becoming—the story itself—is suffering."

"But not *all* is suffering," I countered. "There's much good."

"Really?" Arnobius' eyebrows turned up. "Look at it this way. On the one hand, you're right. The author's words are truth, goodness, and beauty; they're life; they're the blue sky and green trees, and health and wealth for living, and beautiful people, wives and children, and peace, and all manner of ordered things engaged in all manner of ordered activity, along with the knowledge that seems to correspond. But everything comes to an end. So on the other hand, there's evil. There's change, flux, and death, and the confusion and ignorance that corresponds to these. The sky storms; trees and men die and putrefy; wealth is spent or stolen; beauty morphs into old age. Life is constant warfare, Theophilus. Recall what Heraclitus said. *War is the father of all.* This is our story, the chaos; and this, we men suffer."

I stared ahead, feeling low.

Then after briefly reflecting upon what he had said, Arnobius continued by remarking, "Sometimes I can't help seeing more of randomness in this long scroll than I do of rational composition. The rhetorician in me shivers. Where's the order? Where's the symmetry, the proportion? Are the apparent truth, goodness, and beauty of the cosmos only a surface reality? Where is God, the author? Why all the evil? Why all the suffering? Why all the silence? Such is the fruit of my poor understanding."

My head and heart fell. He's right, I judged. And so had I speculated in the past. I had even made a similar argument to the instructor who gave to me this image. "If there's a divine author," I challenged, "then why all the disorder?"

"What'd he say?" asked Arnobius.

"He went on about the significance of free will. This, he said, is what brings evil and disorder to life."

"But that's just it," countered Arnobius, "don't we feel powerless in doing the good?"

I shook my head. "We do."

"Is God to blame, then?"

I couldn't answer him.

Still, I thought there must be something to this image. Therefore, I said, "For the sake of a theory, then, if this author were there outside the scroll of our world, how would we know it?"

Arnobius shrugged. "Despite all the usual arguments, I can't say. How can a character within a story know the author outside?"

"I don't know," I responded. "But I wonder if the silence you speak of has anything to do with it? Is it somehow characteristic of the divine author?"

"In some sense it must be," he declared. "The oracles admonish us somewhere *to be still*, or to *be silent, and know that I am God.* We must live that silence to know God—in both the good and the bad. We mustn't understand it; we must live it. But what exactly do you mean, Theophilus?"

"Perhaps you're right," I said. "But here's what I was thinking. I wonder if we simply fail to see or hear in the way that's required."

"How do you mean?"

"Think of it this way. We can tell a play written by Sophocles as compared with one composed by Aeschylus because of differences in style."

"Of course," said Arnobius.

"But why not with the divine author? How are disorder and suffering and the accompanying silence part of *his* style?"

"I can't say," Arnobius said at first.

Neither, of course, could I.

Then Arnobius added, "Look, Theophilus. I believe you're analogy fails in a few important ways."

"How?" I asked.

"For one, these problems as we experience them—disorder and suffering and the like—may simply be part of the conditions of creating *anything* rather than the actual style of the creator. Think about it. Even Sophocles was limited in his own play writing."

"By what?"

"By things like language or proper themes or the duration of his plays, not to mention the materials he wrote with and on. Also, think about how Aristotle suggested that any good play would have a beginning, middle, and end. A play can't be *all-end* or *all-middle* or *all-beginning*."

"No," I said, "then the all-end or middle or beginning would be meaningless. These parts require the other parts as contrast. But are you suggesting that the omnipotent God is limited in some way?"

"Not in himself."

"How, then?"

"In his creation—or better, the actual conditions of creation. In creating, that which is not springs to life. What is it originally? Nothingness. Finitude. That which is radically limited—the dark chasm Moses mentions. This is what God has to work with, and thus he is limited in some sense. Creation is the expression of the infinite God in finite terms, just as a play by Sophocles is an expression of Sophocles, the man himself, in limited, theatrical terms. Do you think *Oedipus the King* completely captures the mind and thoughts of Sophocles?"

"Of course not."

"Neither, then, does creation completely represent the mind and thoughts of the infinite Creator."

"But is that the right way to look at it?"

"I don't know," Arnobius admitted. "But it *is* one way to solve the problem of all the disorder and suffering we know. They are part of the limitation of creation itself, of the act of creating. In writing, the divine Author becomes limited. As such, the Creator suffers limitation even as we do."

"Possibly," I said, considering this novel idea.

Then Arnobius suggested, "The other problem with your analogy is that there's no other author to compare ours to. As far as we know, there's no other scroll like ours."

"Is there not?" I asked.

"Well, I for one can't say—despite Lucretius' claim that there are an infinite number of worlds."

"Fine," I allowed. "But what of a probable truth? What would the scroll look like if there were no author? What if the background of all was silence, absolute silence? I mean, isn't that the great temptation—whether one thinks there is no author at all or that there is just too much distance between the One and the many?"

"If there were no author, then I suppose there wouldn't be a scroll."

"If that's so, then we know there must be an author and this author must, at the very least, be of a certain character."

"Of course," Arnobius affirmed. "I know that somewhat circular argument: since there's creation, there must be a creator—an effect must have a corresponding cause."

"Well, then?"

"I guess that's not really the point," he said.

"What is?"

"I guess it's really what you mentioned before, Theophilus—that is, what distinctive marks of the author do we find in the unraveling of the tale? And do they all fit?"

"I can't say," I admitted, "except to mention those marks which have been given for ages. The creator is known in the powers of the sky, the nourishment of the earth, the apparent order of things, in the love that pulls all things together, and most appropriately," I finished, glancing up to the sky while shading my eyes, "in *that*, which gives light to all."

"The sun?"

"Ambiguous, I agree, but so are all signs," I remarked.

"It requires faith, no? A choice."

I nodded. "That and reason—interpretation. But yes, Arnobius, faith."

"Do you have it?" he asked.

I didn't answer. Instead, I redirected the question to him. "Do you?"

"Now? Well, I suppose now is quite a different story," he responded, tentatively. "Then, thirty years ago when Constantine was casting about wondering *what* was God or *who* was God, I didn't have a clue."

We reentered the cell. It was positively dark compared to the light outdoors. For a moment, I found it difficult to see, but then, when my eyes had adjusted, I took my seat on the stack of woven mats. I glanced up and saw that Arnobius was already sitting, drinking a cup of water.

"Did *he* have faith?" I asked.

"Who?"

"Constantine."

"Oh, yes, he did," affirmed Arnobius, smiling. Then, after considering the question, he added, "But not so much in some precise understanding of the nature of the One, the author of the scroll, as he believed in the storyline the author had composed for him."

"His role in bringing unity, peace, and prosperity to Rome?" I suggested.

"Exactly," he answered. "In that, he had a faith that was burning and full of trust. It was a divine madness."

With that remark, Arnobius continued the story.

Seventeen: Revelation

Winter and spring of 312 A.D.

AS I HAVE SAID, Theophilus, it was becoming more and more evident that Maxentius was planning to move against Constantine. The latter had it from trustworthy informants. The only question was what he should do.

His first step was most sensible. Constantine went to his advisors in the army and asked them if they thought he should march against Maxentius.

Magnus, Constantine's master of horse, spoke first. "Lord Emperor," he admonished, "it would be a fool's errand."

"Agreed," said Bastrus, the master of foot. "Maxentius has far more men. And look at what happened to Severus and how Galerius was made to look like a moron in running away after a siege of what ...?"

"Hardly a week," finished Crassus, still chief of guard.

"But we have speed on our side," Constantine countered.

"What? Like Caesar against Pompey?"

"Yes," he affirmed.

Nevertheless, they were all overwhelmingly against the idea. They advised Constantine to dig in and face Maxentius defensively. Make him come to Gaul and fight in his own land among his own people. Why tempt fate?

"Why not?" Constantine said to me later.

"I can't say. It seems to me, however, that they speak with wisdom derived from experience."

"Oh, experience can rot in hell! What I've got is greater!"

"What's that?" I inquired.

"A divine voice that speaks to me. I hear it and it drives me on!"

"You actually *hear* a voice?" I asked, incredulous. I waited briefly for his reply, before saying, "I worry for you, my friend."

He defended himself. "No, not exactly a voice, Arnobius. And don't be such an ass. You know what I mean. I've spoken of it for years."

"I know—and it's a wonder you're not yet crazy."

"Perhaps I am," he admitted.

I stopped—though I could have said something nasty. It was the one time in all the many years that I heard Constantine express a doubt regarding his mission in life.

Then: "But I'm *not* crazy! I know it! I've felt and heard it for so long! The voice leads me in a mission to unify Rome. No one will tell me otherwise, Arnobius, I won't allow it!"

I said nothing in reply. He'd transformed from open and intimate a moment before to closed and imperial.

"I'm simply not satisfied," he went on, "I *must* have another answer."

"How will you get it?" I asked, cautiously. "The men you should trust have already given theirs in the negative."

"True. But are they the *right* men?"

"Who else?"

"I see two possibilities. One traditional and one not."

"What do you mean?"

"I mean I could ask my chief haruspex to read the future."

"I thought you'd given up on that."

"I have. Still, isn't it the Roman way?"

"Of course," I admitted, "but what would Ossius say about it? Or Lactantius? Or any of your other Christian friends?"

"They won't be happy. But unlike me, they're not the emperor." Then, as if decisive, he declared, "And I'm no Christian."

Not yet, I thought.

Then, considering the more traditional way of determining the future, I said, "But really, Constantine. The haruspex? You can't be serious."

"Why not?" he asked. "It's our way."

Absurd, I judged, knowing what he intended to do.

The following morning, I met him near the temple of Apollo. There was Constantine, and there by his side were several priests of Apollo and three *haruspices*, including the chief haruspex a fellow called Gallo. I didn't care for him. Not that I truly knew him, Theophilus, but whenever I had spent time in his presence I couldn't help but smell blood and the unpleasant inner parts of this or that beast.

When I approached, the men were standing in a semicircle around a great white ox. Gallo was chanting, calling down the power of the god, asking that Constantine might know the will of heaven in the signs exposed in the beast.

Oh gods, I thought. He's lost either way. If the answer is, "Yes, by all means go and conquer," then he'll be elated, but he'll also be tied to this superstition. I thought of Iamblichus and his magical mediators and concluded that one might as well roll the dice. If on the other hand the signs reads, "No, don't go," then he'll be crushed. I assumed he'd march anyway. After all, he was set on going.

Gallo finished his incantation while one of the priests plunged a razor sharp blade into the beast, first cutting the animal's throat. It grunted a few times and finally squealed when the priest made the other cut from just above its testicles up to the rib cage. Blood spurted red everywhere, and there was the horrible combined stench of cold iron and feces.

Gallo reached inside the animal to extract its steaming liver.

Constantine stood transfixed.

For my part, I stood back watching, knowing how it would turn out. The emperor asks for knowledge and the sign always comes back in favor of the emperor's intended course.

This time, however, it was different.

"It's hard to see," reported Gallo once he had cut open the liver and made the proper inspection.

"Hard to see?" asked Constantine.

"Well—" stalled the other.

"Well, what?"

"It's negative."

"No?"

I raised my eyebrows and suppressed a smile.

"Correct. It positively says you *shouldn't* march."

"But I must!" observed Constantine.

Gallo said nothing. I thought I saw a slight trimmer in his now bloody hands, a trimmer that grew into a shiver when Constantine demanded that he check the other parts.

Gallo did.

"And?"

"Nothing, Lord Emperor, I'm sorry."

"Neither a yes nor a no?"

"No," he clarified, "it indicates you must not attack."

"Damn it all! It *must* say yes."

"I can keep looking, Lord."

"No," said Constantine, "don't bother. I'll look elsewhere."

"Where?" I asked, as we returned to the imperial residence.

"I've been a fool," admitted Constantine, contritely. "Ossius warned me."

"Oh?" I said, wishing not to betray the *I told you so* I felt.

"Yes. He told me not to ask Apollo. He said that I'd probably get an answer that is diametrically opposed to what I should do."

"But how would you know?" I asked.

"That, I don't know."

That night, Constantine had a dream—or so he told me later on. It was a vague dream, he explained, but somehow, in some way, it answered his question in the affirmative.

With that, the feeling to march returned. Consequently, he marshaled together his men—it was then late winter—and began to train in earnest for what he knew would be a near impossible campaign.

Still, Constantine wished for divine clarity. He prayed privately and fervently as Ossius had shown him for some revelation that would confirm his intuition and show him the way he must go.

Eventually, his desire was fulfilled. Or so he claimed. I wasn't there, and to this day, I must admit that I'm uncertain of the reality of it all. Still, *he* was sure. And relative to what happened afterwards, that's all that mattered.

One day in late March or early April, a few weeks after he had had the dream, Constantine was out with his generals and the rest of his army drilling in the field. It was near to that point in the day when the sun reaches its zenith high in the sky. While the other generals trained their own men, the emperor commanded a division of horse in various exercises. Presently, they were charging at each other with wooden lances made with breakaway and blunted tips and wicker shields strong enough to withstand the blow.

There he was, Constantine upon his horse, shouting orders. "Okay, men, form up next to one another!"

They did. There was a long row of horses on one side and another long row on the other.

"Now when you ride, do so at just under full speed."

"Aye!" they cried out.

"You know the drill! Pass between each other. But give it a good shot!"

Again, they shouted their understanding.

"Now, when I say go, ride!"

"Aye!"

"Fix your lances!"

"Fixed!"

"Go!"

The horses facing one another began at a trot. Then they sped up to a canter and finally a gallop as they approached.

Constantine shouted, "Drop your lances!"

Some seventy-five lances dropped on either side. Simultaneously, the men raised their shields to absorb the attack. Exercise or not, it was a dangerous affair. Constantine must have heard the thundering patter of six hundred hooves pound the earth and the invincible exclamations of the men now that they were nearing each other.

"Go!"

Now they were just twenty-five yards apart. They braced. Equine eyes gaped widely. Then, crash! Lances thudded against shields, snapping, sending their splintered cries to the sky above.

There, just there in the sky—

Constantine glanced above. *How odd.* The sky had grown brighter. Now his eyes drew upward toward the sun. For a moment, he tried to shade them, raising his hand above his eyes. He couldn't see. He couldn't look to determine if the sun had in fact grown more luminous. It was so bright.

"My God, Arnobius!" he revealed to me later. "I thought I was going to die! The sun was like a million fires!"

Then, however bright it was originally, the sun grew dimmer. Now he was able to drop his hand from above his eyes and look directly at it.

An eclipse, I thought, or some other natural phenomenon. I told him. But Constantine assured me it was not.

And more. Just above the brilliant crown of the sun, he saw a cross, like the ones upon which we crucify criminals, and words written in the sky. He claimed they commanded his army to march.

"What did they say?" I skeptically queried.

He replied, "*In hoc signo vinces*—by this sign you will conquer."

I nodded. It was the sign he'd desired.

By this point, the men were done with the exercise. Perhaps a quarter were on the ground, having been knocked down by the force of the other lances; the rest were riding around whooping and hollering in the excitement of it all.

They looked at Constantine who was by now on his knees looking up.

"What is it, sir?" asked one.

"Look!" the emperor cried. "Look, men!"

A hush fell on the field and hundreds of men peered up into the sky.

The same one asked, "What, Lord?"

"A sign," said Constantine.

"What sign?"

Another shouted, "There in the sky! It's Apollo the divine Sun!"

Constantine quietly read the words he saw. It seems, though, that no one heard him—or that's how I later understood it.

"Is that what you see, Lord? The divine Apollo?"

Seemingly unaware of those around him, Constantine slowly mouthed, "*By ... this ... sign ... conquer.*"

Then it vanished.

That afternoon, Constantine admitted to uncertainty just as soon as the sign had disappeared. It wasn't so much that he doubted the vision itself, as he was unsure of its precise meaning. There had been the sun, the cross, and the words. But was it the divine Sun of Apollo, he wondered. Or was it the cross of the Christ? Or was it both somehow?

Later, when Constantine consulted Ossius, the bishop explained that it was the Christian cross. I was there.

"It's what I've been suggesting all along," asserted Ossius. "Now, God has confirmed it. The two signs are not contradictory. Rather, the cross is the fulfilling sign of the sun. While the sun is an image of the One, the cross and the one crucified is a fuller image, more exact."

I said nothing at this absurdity. I couldn't imagine how the cross could possibly be the image of the One. The cross, by contrast, is the image of suffering and ignominy. How can it possibly point to the One that cannot suffer? How can passability and corruption signify impassability and incorruption?

Constantine was also unsure but for different reasons. If Ossius was right, then he had to adhere to the god of the Christians. Apollo, it seemed, would no longer do.

Still, uncertainty did not entirely rule his heart. About one point, he was relatively confident. Whether Apollo or the Christ, he had received the sign he had longed for. Heaven had commanded him to go and conquer.

As for me, I ranged from uncertainty about what Constantine should do, to certainty that the cross and this man Jesus could not represent the One.

That night, Constantine's uncertainty evaporated. He told me so in the morning. Then I could tell something had altered considerably. Aside from his story, I could tell by his eyes that something had changed overnight in some significant way.

"I had a dream last night, Arnobius."

"What of?" I asked, bracing myself for more.

"I'm confident now. We should go. We *will* go and vanquish Maxentius."

"How so?"

"He appeared to me."

"Who?" I asked. "Apollo?"

"Jesus," he declared, flatly.

I confess that I nearly rolled my eyes.

"The Jew—right?"

"The Christ," he said.

I nodded, politely.

He clarified. "Jesus appeared and confirmed it was in fact him in the vision. He sent the sign of the cross, the sign to go and conquer. He explained that he had long prepared the world for my coming."

"Do you mean *his* coming?" I asked.

"No, *mine*," he said, perfectly serious.

As I later discovered, Theophilus, Constantine more precisely meant the Roman Empire represented in himself as emperor.

He went on. "The Christ commanded me to fix his sign as our insignia when we march out against the enemy."

I didn't ask what this sign was. I was afraid to ask because I thought my friend had ventured into the rather fuzzy realm of lunacy. Moreover, what would he have said or done if I had dared to ask?

From that moment on, Ossius became Constantine's right hand man, as well as many other Christian priests he had gathered around him. And from that moment on, I'm sad to say, I seemed to fall in Constantine's estimation. As a result, Theophilus, our friendship slowly began to die.

Constantine's was a certainty I couldn't embrace. It's not that I disbelieved him—not entirely. My real problem was more basic than whether or not he told the truth. For me it was the old thorn of philosophy. What did the many have to do with the One? How could the finite possibly grasp the infinite? Said another way, how could the infinite be expressed in finite terms? Whether through the gods, or the divine Sun, or this Christ as Constantine had encountered him, I believed it was impossible. And with my belief, came my reality, one I'd numbly grown used to. The One was silent; the One was indifferent; the One had nothing to do with the many; the Infinite was infinitely beyond.

In contrast to me, however, the men of the army believed in the vision. Many, in fact, affirmed they'd seen it, including hundreds of men who'd been on an adjacent field.

Why not, I thought. *Their emperor had.*

Ossius, of course, confirmed it as well. He explained that God had oftentimes made use of such signs. He cited Moses and the burning bush—a story I had not yet heard—and the apostle's encounter with a similar bright and shining light, which had led to his profound conversion and his manic mission to convert the whole world.

Still, I wondered, was it real? The men of the army claimed to see it, doubtlessly, in order to support their emperor. That, of course, was fitting. Since the majority was uneducated, they could be forgiven and even lauded for their loyalty. As for Ossius and his gang of priests, there was no surprise with them, too. The vision fell in line with what they already believed and with the theory of fulfillment Ossius had repeatedly explained to Constantine. In the end, the emperor was my biggest problem because he spoke of the vision as if it had actually occurred and claimed the Christ had visited him in the spirit realm of his dream.

Yet what was *I* to make of the vision and dream? Were they merely the expression of his desire, or was the whole thing somehow the confluence of reality and metaphor? We—Constantine and I—had heard many a lecture on this in Alexandria. Metaphor has a real bearing upon reality. Perhaps, I thought, this is how Constantine saw these signs. Or maybe he just took the metaphor too far.

Still, something argued against this relatively flimsy interpretation. It was Constantine himself.

Of this, I am certain. From that time forward, from the day after he had the vision and the morning after he had the dream, Constantine was a different man. Whatever the vision and dream's reality, he came to believe it. From that day forward, he adhered to the One who had answered his call for revelation; he followed the Christ of the cross who appeared above the sun of Apollo and spoke the words commanding Constantine to conquer. Consequently, he met with his generals once again.

Now the mission was clear and so the command. They were going to war. More than that, Theophilus. I was going too.

Eighteen: Civil War

Summer and fall of 312 A.D.

I SPENT SEVERAL DAYS WITH Gaius Publius, Luxilla, and Katrina before leaving for Italy. Given what was imminent, that I would be marching off to war, they were surprisingly happy days full of peace and contentment. Belanus was already away with the army where he trained the cavalry as one of the staff officers for Magnus, the master of horse.

"Will you fight alongside Belanus?" Luxilla asked me the evening of my last night with them. She was now sixteen.

"I doubt it," I said, not exactly lying.

"Arnobius plays the role of an advisor," Gaius Publius offered.

"But you'll fight, right?"

"I'll be with the army—what else?"

I saw Gaius Publius smile.

Katrina sat nearby sewing. She had recently turned eighteen. "I imagine you'll be back by winter," she said.

"It's what Constantine hopes for," I replied, "though we may have to stay on longer."

"Will he want you to remain with him?"

"Possibly. At any rate, I'll be back by spring."

"Then you'll come and marry Katrina," declared Luxilla, elated with the proposition, imagining the flowers in her hair, the wedding banners sailing in the wind, and her sister as pretty as a full moon.

Blushing, I saw Katrina glance over to Luxilla. Then she looked at me.

"That's up to your father," I remarked. "But certainly, it's my wish too."

Gaius Publius agreed, adding, "Don't be too anxious, Luxilla. Betrothals don't expire. It'll happen when the god wills."

Katrina glanced down again. I could tell she was pleased with her father's reassurance.

Later that evening, I sat out with Gaius Publius in the courtyard. By then it was dark and the stars sparkled brightly above despite the competing moonlight. Although we had been drinking wine together, I was quite sober.

"What will happen if I don't return?" I asked.

"What do you mean?"

"With Katrina—what will you do?"

"Let's not speak of it," he suggested.

I let go of the question, though I could not help but wonder.

We sat there lost in our own considerations. I would miss him, I thought. I had spent so much time with Gaius Publius and his family over the past years. They were now my family. I was happy, at least, that Belanus would be traveling with me. Still, I would long for the rest.

Gaius Publius interrupted my meandering thoughts. "Would you like to see her before you leave?"

Although I'd be leaving in the morning, I didn't grasp his meaning.

"You *are* betrothed," he went on. "I'll call for her."

He stepped into the house, and a few minutes later Katrina came out and stood next to me in a white dress embroidered with dark blue, red, and orange flowers.

I felt awkward. We had never been alone—or at least not like this. "Please," I invited her, "please sit."

She sat next to me.

For a while, we were silent. I tilted my head back and peered up into the sky wondering if the early philosophers were right. I wondered if each of the stars reveals the light of the heavenly sphere beyond the edge of our own dark cosmos, like light coming into a dark room through many keyholes.

Finally, Katrina whispered my name and asked me to disclose my thoughts.

I did.

"I was thinking about something similar," she revealed.

"About the stars?"

She nodded. "I wonder if we'll be together someday in the brightness of the heavenly realm."

"It's what some say," I ventured, not betraying my true feelings. "But first we must …" I hesitated.

"What?" she begged.

"Nothing," I replied.

I wanted to declare that we had a long life ahead of us, but I didn't. I didn't want anything as simple as presumption to spoil our future.

"Arnobius?"

I turned to her.

"Will you hold me?"

I held her and she began to weep.

"I'll be fine," I assured her, stroking her dark brown hair.

"You will?"

"I'm confident."

She smiled and looked up to me. Her mouth was now inches from mine, and more than anything, I desired her.

She giggled and declared, "When you return, you'll be Arnobius the Conqueror."

"Something like that," I demurred, knowing better.

She laid her head against me again. She must have felt my heart beating with desire, for not long after she raised herself and said, "Kiss me."

I did. I kissed her, I held her, and I wished to the gods that I didn't have to go away.

Nevertheless, I had to go. It was my duty to the Empire and my personal obligation to Constantine, my friend, however much we had recently disagreed.

The following morning, I bade farewell to my friend Gaius Publius, to Luxilla my dear sister, and to my betrothed love, Katrina. Then I rode to Treveris.

A week later I marched south with Constantine to conquer and kill Maxentius. The army seemed exhilarated at the adventure, envisaging glory and honor at the end of the road. Yet I wondered. Perhaps we were the foolish marching to destruction. After all, Constantine's generals had advised against the action. More, the odds were against us. Maxentius could field a larger army, at least twice that of our numbers. That wasn't all. Even if we successfully passed through the Po River valley, we'd still have to face a long siege at Rome. That alone had caused two recent emperors to fail. Constantine, however, was obstinately certain.

I experienced this firsthand one evening when on our way through the Alps. We sat together in his field tent. Casually, I suggested some kind of compromise, a power sharing arrangement between all the emperors. Constantine would have nothing of it.

"It's moved beyond that option," he asserted.

"But couldn't you achieve peace with a few victories in the north?" I offered.

"No," he declared without giving reason.

"Why not? Once Maxentius sees you mean business, he'll sue for peace."

"Absolutely not!"

"Why are you so adamant?" I asked.

Constantine grew indignant and slammed the palm of his hand upon the table that separated us. "Damn it, Arnobius! Don't you see? There *must* be unity!" he announced as if a command. "And *I* have been chosen to render it!"

Indeed, he had. Or so he believed. It was that sense he had first had in Nicomedia while still hostage to Galerius, the one that had sustained him these many years, and the one now confirmed by the vision he had seen in the sky and the dream of the Christ. Now, marching into Italy, his soldiers had the Chi Rho monogram painted in red upon their shields and marched beneath Constantine's standard, the *labarum*, which was similar to the old Roman standard but with the addition of a wreath above surrounding the Christ's monogram as specified by the vision.

Constantine calmed some before saying, "We march to free the Romans from slavery to Maxentius."

I nodded. At the very least, I agreed with *that*. Over the years, Maxentius had become a tyrant.

We marched beyond the Alps through a pass near Mount Cenis and finally into the Po River valley where we faced the enemy for the first time. Constantine successfully took the garrison town of Segusio by burning down its wooden walls. Afterwards, we passed on to Augusta Taurinorum, and following a brief fight, we trailed Maxentius' army eastward to Mediolanum, expecting a full-fledged battle there. But there was no battle. In fact, the city's people joyfully welcomed us as liberators.

Meanwhile, Maxentius' army sped on toward Verona in order to prepare a final northern stand. The fight there was ferocious and thousands perished on both sides. Nevertheless, by the end of the day, Constantine was victorious, and Ruricius Pompeianus, one of Maxentius' most skillful commanders, lay dead on the field. Then after some relatively light work to ensure the defense of our backside, we turned south toward Rome.

I wrote several letters shortly after the battle of Verona. One was to Katrina. In it, I hinted at my affection for her and told her not to worry. Another was to Luxilla, whom I advised to be good to her father. As for Gaius Publius, I told him about Belanus and how he had fought bravely alongside Constantine. His son, I reported, was like a torrent blasting his way through the enemy. I'm sure he smiled when he read about it.

A month later, we pitched camp at Saxa Rubra along the Tiber River some nine or ten miles from the heart of Rome. Overtly, the plan was to lay siege to Rome and force Maxentius to surrender; covertly, Constantine and his agents worked to loosen his despotic grip on the city. In the end, thanks to Maxentius' and his priest's own hurried reading of the Sibylline Prophecies, Maxentius marched out from behind the protection of Rome's walls in order to meet our army in the open field. It was a foolish move.

Nearly two months after camping at Saxa Rubra, Constantine's covert maneuvering was beginning to work by eroding Maxentius' support in Rome—as if such erosion required much help. By then the wealthy few hated him for behaving tyrannically. Consequently, rumors burned through Rome like a fire through rows of wooden apartment buildings. Some questioned Maxentius' abilities, his manhood. Some argued more pragmatically, suggesting the city would be better off once the whole question was resolved. And why, they inquired, wouldn't Maxentius march out and decide it? He had the greater army, they said; surely, he would win. A last group openly called for a change of alliance. They argued the city would fare better with Constantine.

Afraid he was losing the support he required to hold out during a long siege, Maxentius fled to the temple and priests of Apollo where they keep the Sibylline Prophecies and begged their direction.

The reply? After quickly scrolling through the prophecies, Apollo's priests solemnly announced, "Tomorrow, the enemy of Rome shall perish."

Maxentius sighed with relief. "The sacred books have spoken!" he declared. "Constantine shall die tomorrow! His army shall perish with him!"

That night, the prefect Rufius Volusianus worked long and hard by candlelight to devise the offensive strategy for the following day. One matter must have been certain as he worked with other officers late into the night— they weren't going to get much sleep. This was so because the attack would take place in the early hours of morning. But that didn't matter, he thought.

He'd have more than enough time to sleep the following night after Maxentius had successfully defeated Constantine.

Well, yes, Theophilus, but in his own bed?

The following day, the fifth before the Calends of November, Maxentius took our entire army by surprise. Most of us were still sleeping when the trumpets blasted the call to arms.

As for me, I stumbled out of my tent in the near dark, hardly aware of the early morning sliver of grayish-yellow just above the mountains and a shadowy army of thousands of men and horses positioned below, with thousands more to their rear, streaming across a makeshift pontoon bridge. Maxentius had torn down the other bridge, the Milvian as Romans called it, sometime before our arrival in order to prevent our crossing.

"Armor up, men!" I heard centurions roar.

There was frenzy in our camp, but an ordered frenzy—Roman.

"Get your weapons! We fight today! We fight now!"

After quickly preparing myself, I walked over to Constantine's tent at the center of camp, and after greeting the guard, I stepped in. The emperor sat with Magnus, Bastrus, and the other officers giving orders. Belanus stood some distance behind. I nodded hello and he winked at me.

"We'll spread out," commanded Constantine. "Magnus, we'll take center. It'll be our job to cut down the *kataphraktoi*."

These are men armed from head to toe, Theophilus.

"Yes, Lord," said Magnus.

"Bastrus, I want you on our right. You'll swivel just as soon as you can and push them against the river."

"They'll drown!" he responded.

"Exactly," said Constantine, coolly. "Ptolemy, you'll take the left. Just hold them until the rest of us can turn them toward their deaths."

"Will do, sir."

"Crassus, you'll ride with me. And Belanus, I want you on my weak side."

"Yes, Lord!"

I could tell Belanus was excited.

Constantine stood. "To victory, we go!"

"To victory!" they cried.

They all passed through the door of the tent. When Constantine did, I followed him, wishing him luck, believing it might be the last time I saw him alive.

Moments later, riding swiftly toward the field of battle, Constantine pointed to my right and a row of low-lying hills not too far away and shouted, "There, Arnobius, you can perch yourself there."

"I will," I agreed, relieved. Shortly thereafter, I turned my horse toward the hills.

Seeing our men approach, Maxentius ordered his archers to rain down a host of arrows. Many of our own fell. I saw them squirm and heard their loud cries born of pain from my position not too far away. Nevertheless, the devastation didn't last for long. Soon, Constantine ordered a charge.

On our right, Bastrus led his men against the age-old Praetorian Guard. They swung out, swiveled, and finally hit them head on. I heard the clash of arms and felt the ground tremble beneath my horse. Men on both sides yelled and maneuvered, cutting away at each other, sword clashing against sword, shield, and body. Many died.

Our right shoved against their left. The other side gave way. I heard Bastrus shout, "Our advantage, men! Press on now!"

They pushed and pushed. The enemy's left began to merge with their center.

My eyes naturally followed. There, Constantine, Belanus, and Crassus fought valiantly against the kataphraktoi and the others with them.

I shouted for them from my perch on the hill. "Go!" I shouted. "Cut those sorry bastards down!"

It was as though I was back at the racetrack in Treveris rooting for my team.

"Kill them, Constantine!" He did. I saw him, arrayed in brilliant red, slashing through his opponents.

"Careful, Belanus!" I cautioned, although he couldn't hear me. He rode on Constantine's left, defending the emperor.

"Crassus, your back!" I cried. He turned, but another of our own defended him, dropping a man with a cutting jab to his unarmed neck.

Our right pushed in, as did the center. Slowly, Maxentius' whole army was forced eastward where the brown Tiber loops out and southward, and in again to where the old Milvian Bridge had stood.

Just behind Crassus, I could see Constantine's standard raised high against the enemy. *By this sign, you shall conquer.* They *were*, I judged. Our shields, decorated with that magical sign of the Christ, blocked all manner of weapons: swords, lances, maces, arrows, stones, and fists when everything else failed. Imagine a tall, red X vertically intersected by a P, the Greek letters *Chi* and *Rho,* the first two letters of the Christ's Greek title, *Christos.* That's what the sign looked like. And leading the men into battle, I admit that the Chi Rho now seemed to have so much power.

Pondering it, I glanced back at the sun rising over the range of mountains behind. It was now riding high in the sky. I confess it, Theophilus, in the exhilaration of the moment I hoped to see something there, some confirmation. Consequently, I foolishly stared, my sight transfixed just above the sun.

But of course I didn't see a thing.

Not only that, I was soon blind. Because I had stared for far too long without anything to shield them, my eyes burned with the sun's bright luminosity, as they were flooded with its light. Then I panicked. Suddenly, I couldn't see!

In momentary darkness, I quickly turned back toward the battle. In that time—no longer than it would take for a man to make suitable libation to any one of the gods—I relied on my ears to gain news of what was happening below, hoping to the gods I'd soon be able to see again. I felt alarmed. What if the battle moved my way?

Below me, there was a great den. Shouting. Clashing. The rapid clip-clopping of horse's hooves. Raspy, urgent voices giving orders. Shifting lines. Marching. Hitting. Sounds of shields clanking. Swords whipping and thrusting through the air. Arrows flying. Lances piercing. Sounds of suffering, of dying. Groaning. Moaning. Screeching with pain. It all grew louder. Was it drawing closer to me? I grew heavy with fear.

Then, though hard to believe, as I stood at some distance, I heard Constantine's voice. It came clearly as if through a section of a plumber's lead pipe.

"Belanus!" he cried.

With anxious anticipation, I wondered what it was. My eyes were just now recovering. Slowly, form and color returned. Still I could not see well enough.

Then from a distance, I heard again, "Belanus, my back!"

I feared for Constantine. Sweat poured down my forehead and neck. I wiped it from my brows and eyes. It was abnormally warm for fall, and I was nervous.

Finally, I saw more or less distinctly. A soldier was jabbing at Constantine's backside. The emperor's left arm held his shield with the Chi Rho swathed across it while his right defended against another man in front.

"Belanus!" he shouted again.

Belanus cut down the man in front of him. Then as quick as a strike of lightning, he swiveled and turned on the man who was threatening the emperor from behind. The move, however, was too quick—he didn't have time to consider it. He was still young like that. Rash. Spinning, he met the armored man who had swiveled just as quickly and caught Belanus in the groin. I saw him lifted up. He reared in his horse and attempted to pull rein away. But it was no use. Another man rode in from behind and hacked his neck just below the helmet. I couldn't believe my eyes. I was helpless. There was nothing I could do.

Finally, Crassus thundered in and fell on them. He cut the horse from beneath the first man and decapitated the other. I saw the man's head spring up into the air and fall again as a young boy's ball might fall, bouncing on the hard ground below. Then Crassus sidled up to Belanus who had slumped down in his saddle. He pulled him to his own horse and bolted from the thick of it.

Seeing him leave the battle, I wrenched my feet into the side of my horse and galloped down to Crassus who was now kneeling aside his horse next to Belanus. The latter was flat on the rocky ground. As it happened, he lay dying.

"Belanus!" I cried out.

I jumped from my horse and cradled him. His blood leaked onto me from the back of his neck. He said nothing, but I could see he was still alive.

"Belanus," I said at a whisper, "you fought bravely."

His eyes spoke to me. They spoke of his pride, about the glory and honor he had won. He was happy to die for Rome. I grabbed his hand and squeezed it hard.

His lungs heaved. He gasped for air. Blood gurgled from the cut in his neck just above his shoulders.

"Father ..." he exhaled. "Tell him ... and Kat ... and Lux ..."

"I will," I promised. "I'll tell them everything."

The corners of his mouth curved slightly upwards. Then he died.

There was no last breath and nothing to indicate that he'd really gone. Like a mist, he simply vanished, and I realized he was no more.

Glancing up, I saw that our army had advanced well away from us. What had it been—a quarter or half an hour? Whatever, they were pushing against Maxentius' men relentlessly. Constantine was there in the middle commanding his men to give no ground, no mercy.

I felt hot. I felt sick. Again, I wiped the sweat that poured down my face. I couldn't believe Belanus was gone. Then suddenly, beneath the intensity of the sun and amid the war god's horrors, I faded.

When I woke up, I lay in a dark and stuffy field tent. For a moment, I thought I was dead and in Hades. But I was wrong. I saw the faint light of a lamp, and shortly thereafter, a man loudly called to me from above.

"Arnobius!"

Giant Crassus stood there over me.

"What's happened?" I asked.

"You fell asleep next to your horse, old man! *That's* what's happened!"

"But …?"

"We've won!" he declared, elated with the fact. "Constantine has won!"

"Where is he?" I queried.

"His tent."

"And Belanus?"

"Dead, I'm afraid."

Dead, I pondered. I knew that. Poor fellow. So young. It all came back to me. His death in my arms—a good death. I thought of Gaius Publius and his sisters. They'd take it hard, but they'd also be proud.

"I got the two men who did it," Crassus bragged.

I wanted to tell him that I'd seen him do it, but I didn't feel the strength. Instead, I was quiet.

Crassus was in no such mood. "You should see Maxentius!" he exclaimed.

"Oh?" I allowed.

"Waterlogged. We found him a few miles downstream, still in his armor, the bastard."

"What happened?" I asked.

"A rout! Panicked, they tried to flee across the Tiber."

"By the pontoon bridge?"

"Well, yes, for a while. But the bridge began to sink under the weight of all the wretched men. When Maxentius rode for it, the bridge was hardly there. He fell into the river fully armored—cuirass, helmet, greaves, and all. Imagine that!"

"I can't," I said, weakly. I felt numb at it all.

"Imagine trying to swim the length of a hundred flowing yards fully armored!"

"Impossible," I agreed.

"He learned it firsthand! The fool sunk like a rock!"

"Where's he now?"

"Don't know. But word has it he'll be paraded tomorrow."

"Tomorrow?"

"When we enter Rome."

I stared above me at the roof of the leather tent.

The following day, Maxentius' body was set up on a pike like a piece of butchered meat on a spit. Then it was paraded through Rome to prove the tyrant was dead six years and a day after he had usurped power.

Constantine was in his tent most of the day issuing a variety of commands. The most important was that none of his soldiers should harm anyone. "There'll be no pillaging, no burning, and no rape!" he commanded.

The people of Rome were not the enemy, he declared. No, he had come to set them free. The emperor had come under the sign of the Christ to give Rome unity, peace, and prosperity.

It appeared, Theophilus, he had done just that.

As for me—or for Constantine and me—our friendship seemed to deteriorate after the conquest when he focused more on Ossius, the other priests, and the Christian faith.

In contrast to them was my own inability to believe, the skepticism I had nurtured like a fire made up of dying embers. I could not countenance the emperor's broad assertion that it was the Christ and his sign that had wrought victory that day near the Milvian Bridge. However much it seemed that way, the claim didn't fit into my neat philosophical categories.

Consequently, in just a few short months our friendship grew intolerable. With his newfound faith and certainty, Constantine became imperious. Gone was open conversation where I participated as an equal rather than as a cautious adviser.

In the end, I had no desire to be around a fanatic—and most certainly not one with power. If the western Empire now had its unity and peace, Constantine and I sadly did not.

Nineteen: Separation

313 to 324 A.D.

I WAS DEPRESSED AND IN CARTHAGE by the end of January the following year. Just three months after our victory, after *Constantine's* victory, I ran from him as if he were a tyrant. Why? you ask. Simple. At the time, my reasons for staying on with him in Rome seemed to vaporize like a fog in late morning. *His* morning, I daresay, his sun, his light, his vision. But more. I unexpectedly lost my reason for returning north to Treveris as I had hoped and longed to do. Like a sudden bend in a river, my future altered course. There would be no wedding, no wife, no life of domestic love and children. Katrina had died. And just like that, she vanished from the horizon of my life. So too had her father, my dear friend, Gaius Publius. They both had died of the plague.

I received word of it from Luxilla shortly after the Calends of January. She reported that their lungs had filled with bile and their bodies had grown hard and lumpy here and there. Finally, beset with coughing and burning with fever, they perished. There would be no reprieve. Death stubbornly called from the world below.

When at first I read of it, my heart turned to stone. It wasn't real. I'd go north and they'd be well. I'd marry Katrina and spend many an evening with Gaius Publius discussing philosophy. Soon, that same heart turned to water, and I wept and wept, devastated. I desperately wondered how they could be gone. The family I had come to love was no more. I felt like I had when Stella the slave had suddenly died nearly two decades before. Life was radically unstable and insecure; life was impermanence.

I returned Luxilla's letter a week later. By then, I had already made the decision to venture on to Carthage. I knew she would be devastated, but what could I do? Aside from Luxilla, my second family had perished, and now I wished only to see my first family. Later, Luxilla told me she understood my need. Nevertheless, she was lonely and sad and depression filled her with gloom for months. If not for Ulfila the slave, she might have surrendered to the darkness of grief. With her admonishment, though, she bore up, entrusted herself to the divine One, and vowed to live on bravely.

Luxilla and I exchanged letters for some time thereafter, but after a while, perhaps a year or two, the correspondence fell to a trickle, and then it stopped. Finally, Luxilla and her whole family exited permanently out of my life. Or so I then dejectedly believed.

But that's to journey years ahead of my story. Presently, Theophilus, that is, before I traveled to Carthage, I was in Rome living in the Imperial Palace and executing this or that bit of business for Constantine, who was vibrant with what had happened and what was happening. Licinius had come to join him. Soon, he would marry Constantine's sister, Constantia. Together, Constantine and Licinius had issued an edict of toleration in response to Galerius' legislation of intolerance a decade before.

For Constantine, the law was a move against those ideological contentions that pitted one faction of Romans against another. No longer would the imperial government set itself against any particular religious disposition; no longer would it persecute. As long as a religious practice was peaceful and as long as it gave proper gratitude and service to the Divinity, the Empire would tolerate it.

As such, the edict was reasonably ambiguous. In my judgment, this was good. While mentioning Christians in particular, it did not mention the Christ, their god. Instead, it stuck to the broader outlines of belief. For example, the law simply named "the Divinity" rather than any particular god. For this reason, I favored it. Still, and for this reason precisely, I could not do what Constantine begged of me—not in good conscience.

What he asked for was not unusual in itself. He simply wanted me to give another speech even as I had done many times over the past years. But on this occasion, I refused.

"I can't do it," I said to him upon the asking, shaking my head back and forth to punctuate the point. "Not in the manner you wish."

"And why not?" he demanded, irritated with me. "How does it differ from what you've done before?"

"It's too much."

"What is, to use the name of the Christ?"

"Precisely."

"But you've named the deity before! Don't forget, my friend. You've called upon Hercules and Apollo. Do you remember *those* divine names?"

"I do. But it's a far cry from what you ask now. Those are traditional names. We Romans have used them for hundreds of years and people knew I didn't really intend to imply their actual existence." I paused. "Or at least those with any education," I finished, snidely.

"And what then? Are you suggesting I lack that education, the ability to see into your complexities?" He was growing angry.

"Of course not. But—"

"But it's not real, right! You don't believe I saw the sign! You don't believe I saw him in the dream!"

"Well?"

"You're blind, Arnobius! You can't see for all the knowledge you've collected over the years!"

"Perhaps," I allowed, attempting calm. "Nevertheless I must remain faithful to what I do see."

"Or don't!"

"Granted. However, if you wish for me to speak, I cannot introduce the name of the Christ into my oration. The men of Rome will think you've gone off."

"But Maxentius was a Christian and—"

"And *he* was a tyrant to boot!"

"Still, they must know!"

"What? That you've gone off?"

Abruptly, Constantine stood and hovered over me. For the first time since meeting him in Alexandria—or perhaps the second or third—I felt physically threatened by him. "You blaspheme, Arnobius!" he shouted. I saw the veins pop from his thick neck and to the side of his wide brows.

"I do no such thing," I responded, continuing my attempt to maintain an even temper.

"You do! I say it, and thus it's so! You impugn me and the One who appeared to me. You are an offense against the Christ—you and your skeptical distance between the One and the many!"

I said nothing. What could I say? It's not as though I had created the distance!

He went on. "The vision commanded *by this sign, conquer.* I was obedient! I did it! The Christ was the victor at the bridge! I was merely his instrument!

And now you wish me to be silent, to rob the Divinity of proper and just recognition!"

"No," I countered. "*I* just can't do it!"

He shouted over me, "But you must!"

For a moment I froze. Finally, I stood up and stepped back from the emperor. "Pardon me," I excused myself. "I'm afraid we can't speak now."

Then I turned my back on him, on the emperor, on Constantine my friend, and walked out of his chambers and toward my own apartment a few buildings away.

"Stop!" he commanded.

But I didn't stop. Rather, I walked away one heavy step after another. As I did, I quietly wept. I wept not so much for me as for death. I mourned Constantine, his passing. He was no longer the man he'd been. It seemed my friend was gone. And still heart wrenched over the news I had so recently received from Luxilla, I wept for that too. My gods, what would be next?

In the end, Ossius persuaded Constantine that I was right. He said that as emperor of Rome, the ruler of a vast empire of people with many beliefs, he must be more subtle in his proclamation of victory. While he should give orations proclaiming thanks to the Divinity, he should do no more. To name the Christ would exclude others. And that, reasoned Ossius, would somehow be contrary to the Christian faith. I respected the bishop for this.

Unfortunately, or fortunately, depending on the vantage point, I had already declined the job of giving the speech. When the emperor asked me again a few days after our dispute, I informed him that I was going to return to Carthage to see my father Buteo and Mother and to check up on family affairs. I wanted to imply that it was nothing personal, but it was. I'd be back, I assured him, after some months or maybe a year in order to work for him and the Empire. But in truth, I didn't believe it, as I had no such intention.

Magnanimously, as if we had never quarreled, he conceded. Then I said goodbye to him.

"I'm sorry," he offered, knowing my feelings.

"I am too," I returned. "But there's little that can be done."

"Yes. But don't be so pessimistic. I just wish you could see."

I frowned.

"Even so, you're my friend, Arnobius."

I wasn't so sure.

There was an awkward silence between us. Then he asked, "Do you remember the first supper we shared together?"

I said I did.

"You claimed you didn't care much for wine, that it softened the mind. I agreed, but argued that it also softened the heart. And that, I suggested, was good."

"I remember distinctly," I said, a faint smile curving my mouth.

The emperor called the server who walked over with a golden pitcher of Falernian. "Would you like some more?" asked Constantine.

I thought about it but not for long, having already had a cup or two. "Of course," I said.

Each of us drank from our cups before Constantine asked, "Do you think Galerius' change of heart was real?"

"I'm sure it wasn't," I declared with little consideration. "The man was political through and through. Knowing the people weren't happy with his persecutions, he *had* to alter course."

Constantine reflected before saying, "I'm not so sure. I think it's possible. A man can change, you know."

"I suppose."

Constantine sighed. "Will you truly return, Arnobius?"

"I will," I lied, unsure whether I would or not.

"I hope so," he said, "I really do."

I wondered why, for he had very little use for me anymore. There were Ossius and the other priests, and lawyers, accountants, and speechmakers were a denarius for a whole lot. Even so, I replied, "I'm sure Carthage will be far too boring."

"I'm sure," he agreed, before explaining, "it's not so much that I need you, Arnobius. You know that. It's just that ..." He trailed off.

What? I wondered. But I didn't beg it of him. Instead, our last time together came to a sudden end when a man came in demanding Constantine's attention.

"It's fine," I countered when he asked me to wait. "I have to go."

"No, stay around. It'll be just a moment."

But I didn't stay. I couldn't any longer. Carthage beckoned me.

The following day, I traveled to Ostia, and later on that evening, I set sail for Carthage, where we made port in just a few days.

+ + +

I lived in Carthage for ten years working with my aging father who was as profit oriented as ever, and submitting to Mother who schemed as she had never done to find a wife for me who would replace Katrina and bring honor and wealth to our family. None of her plans interested me, however. No one could take the place Katrina had occupied and still held in my heart. All the while, I grew older, passing through my fourth decade and advancing into my fifth.

During that time, I missed my old friend Constantine. Yet happily, I was not far from his thoughts. He wrote every few months letting me know the details of what transpired in his life, and I wrote to him, too. Over those years, he became the sole ruler of the Empire. He also had several children by Fausta, progeny that would guarantee his family line, even as Crispus, his son by Minervina, grew older, stronger, and wiser. In fact, Crispus played an important role in his father's drive toward absolute power. But I get ahead of the story. Or do I? The details of what passed are not as important as compared to the end.

The letters composed by Constantine over the years became more and more Christian in both overt expression and implied tone. Sometimes, I admit they were hardly tolerable, at least for one who did not share his convictions. He would harp on about unity, that old theme, the drive for one empire, for peace and prosperity all under the one Divinity—now the Christ. Constantine, of course, was his image on earth, his vicar. I could hardly read of it. In my view, he wasn't led on by the Divine or the gods or whatever. Instead, the events themselves drove him along.

What were those events? I'll be brief. First, there was Licinius' victory over Maximinus Daza at Adrianople ending in the latter's death. Then there was the betrayal. His own brother-in-law Licinius—recall, Theophilus, that Licinius had married Constantia, Constantine's sister—conspired with Bassianus, another brother-in-law whom Constantine had appointed caesar over Italy. It was a year after Maxentius had fallen at the Milvian Bridge. Constantine pursued Licinius and Bassianus to Pannonia where he soundly defeated them. Yet it wasn't over. Foolishly, they persisted, and so they fought again in Thrace, the battle ending in a draw. Despite the ambiguity of the conclusion, Licinius was in no position to make demands. Consequently, he surrendered Bassianus' head along with all of Thrace.

Nearly a decade of tenuous peace followed. In that time, Diocletian finally died. Officially, then, there were only Constantine and Licinius who had or hoped to have any real power, as everyone else—Constantius Chlorus, Maximian, Maxentius, Galerius, Maximinus Daza, and Severus—had already perished.

As for me, I continued living in Carthage. Occasionally I'd go to Alexandria, Pelusium, or one of the other cities along the coast on business. Otherwise, I never ventured to Italy or Gaul to engage any of our western interests. Buteo understood with kindness.

"She must have been quite a woman," he would remark.

Mother's reply, if she were in the same room, would always be, "Yes, but we must find another."

One day my father encouraged me to leave Carthage.

"Will you ever rejoin Constantine?" Buteo queried. He said nothing about profit, but I knew it was likely at the fore of his mind.

"I'm not sure," I replied.

"Well, it wouldn't hurt," he suggested, popping his mouth.

"No, it wouldn't."

"But nor does your care of the eastern provinces hurt."

I smiled.

Eventually, Constantine came to reign as the sole emperor of Rome. My father broke the news to me one afternoon. He'd just come from the city's port, when he burst into my office where I was working counting numbers as it happened, and proclaimed, "He's done it!"

"Who?" I asked, imagining he referred to my one living brother who'd been in Sicca working on a legal matter that had stubbornly refused to go away.

"Constantine—your old friend!"

"What's he done?"

"He's defeated Licinius!"

"Again? Where?" I asked.

My father shrugged. "I can't say."

Over the next few weeks, we learned the details. Constantine confirmed them in a letter I received a few months after the great battle. Licinius had challenged him after Constantine had strayed into his territory in order to take care of one barbarian tribe or another. The two battled with over two hundred fifty thousand men between them. They first fought at Adrianople not far from Byzantium. Licinius was defeated and retreated eastward. Constantine informed me that his son Crispus was the real hero of the war. When Licinius fled to his ships in the port of Byzantium, he found them destroyed. Crispus had annihilated Licinius' navy some time before in a great naval clash in the Hellespont. Nevertheless, Licinius and the remains of his men crossed the Bosporus and fell back to Chrysopolis where he lost once again. When Constantia later begged for her husband's life on soft, bended knee, Constantine refused. Therefore, like Maximian before him, Licinius committed a forced suicide. Afterwards, Constantine marched back to Byzantium and from there he wrote to me.

Glancing up from the letter, I informed Buteo that the emperor had asked me to join him in the New Rome. It had been nearly eleven years since I had last seen him.

"The *New* Rome?" my father asked, bewildered. "What in the name of Jove is he referring to?"

"Apparently he's constructing a whole new city to celebrate the victory he's won. It'll rise over what is now Byzantium."

"Byzantium?" he said with raised brow, calculating. Then there was a broad grin. "Not so bad," he concluded. "No, in fact it's quite a strategic site for a capital city. And not a bad place for trade, too."

I agreed, before asking, "Do you think I should go?"

"Do you?" he replied. It was a ploy, of course, knowing I'd eventually surrender.

"I'm not sure," I said. "I don't know if I want to entangle myself in the affairs of the Empire again. Or his life."

"I understand," rejoined Buteo. "But think of the good you accomplished the first time around. Our business had never fared so well in Gaul. You could go and solidify affairs along the Bosporus—if only for a little while."

I thought about it.

"Look at it as an obligation to your old man," he added, hoping I'd bite.

"Old man?" I retorted, laughing. "You work more than I do!"

"Yes—but it's my nature." He popped his mouth again as if he couldn't help it.

"It is," I concurred, grinning. I loved my father. But what about my own nature? I wondered. My old self that had hungered for wisdom and a steady life had vanished. I'd become much more like my father. A realist. A business man. A profit seeker. Not enough, of course, to merit his nickname, but enough.

Still, where had my old self gone? Nowhere, I judged. Like all the rest—Stella, my younger brother, Belanus, Katrina, Gaius Publius, and the old Constantine—that Arnobius was dead and gone.

Raising a cup in quiet desperation, I thanked the gods for work as distraction and wine to end the day.

In the end, Theophilus, I told Buteo I'd go. At least my father hadn't died, I thought, happy of that. With a smile and a heart full of resignation, I explained I'd go and check up on family affairs—to solidify things as he had said.

My real motive, however, was quite impractical. I went in search of the past. My heart yearned to see Constantine once again, if only for a while. And perhaps I'd find something there of me as well.

Twenty: The New Rome

Late 324 A.D.

WHEN I ARRIVED IN BYZANTIUM around the Ides of November, I was surprised at how difficult it was to see Constantine.

The problem was no one recognized me at the Imperial Palace. "I'm Arnobius," I said, introducing myself. "I used to work with the emperor. How in the god's name am I supposed to speak with him?" The reaction was shrugged bureaucratic shoulders. I told them I came from Carthage, that the emperor had invited me. In response, the officials, several young men swaddled in pristine tunics, stared at me with cocked brow as if every day many a man claimed just that. "You're probably a long lost friend," they drolly remarked. "Well?" I replied—it wasn't too far from the truth. Then, thank Mercury, an older, roundish, balding man came springing up, and immediately I knew I'd be recognized, for this man knew everything and everyone. He was Pila—old Pila from Nicomedia.

Straight away, as if we'd never been apart, he said, "Arnobius! Whatever are you doing?"

It'd been nearly twenty years.

"Pila!" I exclaimed. "My God, you've hardly changed."

"Don't be so flattering," he said.

We embraced.

"What brings you to—?"

"Constantine," I announced without allowing him to finish. "He wrote a letter demanding my presence as it were. So I obliged. But I'd have more luck killing Death himself than I've had in seeing the man."

"You're right," explained Pila, "it's nearly impossible. Do you recall Galerius' rules?"

I did.

"Constantine has become even more—what shall I say—*off.*"

"Why?"

"He fears assassination."

"So how does one get to him?"

"Arnobius, my dear fellow, Pila stands before you and yet you ask how you'll have access to the emperor or to anyone else for that matter? Fear not. As always, *I'm* your man. But first, let us have a meal together to celebrate your coming."

We went and dined together. It was just as it had been so many years before. I told him what had happened in my life, though sparing many of the details, and he told me about his own. When finally I asked him how he ended up serving in Constantine's court, he smiled and averred, "Pila has his ways."

I shouldn't have asked. He always had.

"It's too bad," he told me, "you missed the inauguration of the city. It was quite magnificent, dear man. If nothing else, I give it to Constantine. His vision is splendid."

"So it seems," I replied, parroting my father's own remark. "Byzantium is brilliantly situated for defense and trade."

"Did you say Byzantium?" he asked. Without allowing me to respond, however, he went on, "You did. But *don't*. That'll really anger him. No, quite firmly it is *Nova Roma*, the New Rome. And the brilliance goes far beyond defense and trade. For Constantine, it's a city meant to recognize the new reality, the new age."

"What do you mean, Pila?"

"I mean it's meant to be a *Christian* city—the antitype of the old Roman past."

"How so? I've noticed nothing particularly Christian about it."

"Not yet. Presently it only has the usual forum, palaces, hippodrome, baths, and so on. But construction has only just begun. When it's finished, he'll have built one of the greatest churches. He'll call it the Hagia Sophia, the church of Holy Wisdom. And there's talk about building one to the twelve apostles."

I shrugged my shoulders. "The followers of the Christ?"

"Those—but only the first dozen. Now there are millions."

"Are you one, Pila?"

He grinned. "I am what everyone else is—and *quite* devotedly."

"Then you are not?"

"Possibly."

We finished our meal and Pila assured me that I would see the emperor no later than the following week.

"Next week!" I exclaimed, perplexed. "But he's personally invited me."

"Still, Arnobius, he's *very* busy. Moreover, he's not the man you used to know. He's the sole emperor of Rome now. Even so, show up tomorrow morning and I'll see what I can do."

I told him I would, and after thanking him and telling him how good and pleasant it was to see him again, I walked off to rent rooms.

The following morning I walked to the palace hoping I would find Pila and hoping he would tell me I could see Constantine straight away. When I arrived, however, several of the young men from the day before told me that both Pila and the emperor were away. Constantine was hunting, they informed me. As for Pila, he was pursuing one bit of business or another. When I asked when the two would return, they couldn't tell me. I told them I'd come again the following day and left word for Pila as to my whereabouts.

Later that evening, Pila came knocking at my door.

"Hello," I said, surprised but welcoming him nonetheless. "Thanks for coming."

"He's ready," he responded mysteriously, without a greeting. "Come with me."

We walked to the palace through several empty and dark streets. Trailing Pila, I asked if the emperor seemed pleased I was coming.

"Pleased?" he asked, his voice full of irony. "He doesn't yet know."

"He doesn't know?"

"It doesn't matter; he'll see you—trust me."

Upon arriving, we passed straight through the palace complex to the imperial quarters. Finally, Pila turned to me and said, "When we see him, kneel before him."

"Kneel?" I objected. "But he's an old friend!"

"Still—it's protocol. He's now the sole emperor, my dear man, and he's rather taken to eastern ways."

I couldn't believe it. Even so, when two colossal golden doors were heaved open and I saw the fifty-two year old Constantine standing there in full regalia towering over me even from a distance of ten paces, I quite naturally fell to my knees and bowed just as Pila did.

"Arnobius!" he bellowed. His voice had changed. It was older, distinct, and distinctly confident.

I looked up.

"Well, rise!" he commanded. "My old friend, rise to your feet and let me see you!"

He looked at me.

"Ah, yes," he judged, "still the philosopher."

I wanted to tell him it wasn't exactly true anymore, but I suppose he intended something quite different at any rate.

"Come here and sit with me."

I did. We embraced, and I sat, and after some time, once we had moved to a private chamber somewhere in the depths of the palace, we passed the evening together drinking wine, eating a meal, and conversing as we had on so many occasions about just as many things.

From that moment on, we fell into our old pattern of friendship. Not in every way, of course, but I could sense that I meant what I had always meant to him. We spoke of old times and laughed far too much, and for a long while, we steered away from those issues that were like barbs to us.

At last, however, as if he could not restrain himself any longer, he quietly said, "I've done it, Arnobius."

"You have," I acknowledged, wishing to be agreeable.

"I've achieved the unity that I was meant to achieve."

I nodded.

"My new city is meant as a sign of that unity."

"I'm happy for you."

"And for Rome, I trust."

"Most of all."

"But ..." he hesitated.

"What?" I asked.

"It hasn't come off as planned."

"Why not?" I shrugged. Now I was genuinely interested.

"Well, politically, defensively, we are one. The borders are secure despite the barbarians who, as you know, are an ever-present threat along the Rhine and Danube. But more than that, there's a division of soul."

"What do you mean?" I queried.

"I mean that in the practice of religion there's great rancor. We're not at peace. We're not one."

"Is that a problem? Whatever happened to tolerance? I thought that was the official policy. Don't tell me you're calling for persecutions."

"No, of course not—whom would I persecute?"

"I don't know—those of the old religion?"

"No, no, no. I *wish* that were the problem. You're right—we could simply be more tolerant and hope they'd learn to live with it. No, the real problem is in the Christian communion. I've had to wrestle with them ever since you left Rome."

"How so?"

"How not!" he retorted, frowning.

How not? I wondered.

Then I recalled the dispute in Carthage between one Donatus, a prig of a man who'd begun a new kind of Christian religion, and Caecilian, one of the traditional sorts. I'd never quite understood the details of the differences, but just as Constantine was presently telling me, the fight was severe. In fact, it led to rioting in Carthage on several occasions. One time it was so bad we had to evacuate our townhouse in order to take up residence in our villa in the country. I laugh now. It was then my father Buteo remarked, "See what I mean about theoretical speculation? Instead of building up, these lunatics are tearing down." I saw it; I did. Their rioting destroyed much property. But after it had blown over, I hadn't given it much more thought.

Finely I asked, "Do you speak of the sect in Africa?"

"Partly," he confirmed. "You know of the Donatists?"

I smiled. "I do. They're loud and intolerant themselves, and from what I've heard and seen, they've given quite a bad name to their religion."

Constantine sighed. "They claim to be the only *real* church, and therefore the only licit dispensers of divine grace. Everyone else—the *traditores* they call them, the traitors, the ones who had surrendered the holy books and sacred vessels during Galerius' persecution—requires rebaptism. They declare that traitor priests are no longer able to mediate the divine life. Their sacraments are not valid—baptism, the Eucharist, and so on."

I stopped him, asking him to explain the latter, as I hadn't yet studied the Christian philosophy in any detail.

"Oh, nothing," he responded. "What I mean is that's not the problem. With the Donatists, it's more a matter of property. They want the churches."

"The physical buildings?"

"Yes."

"What've you done?"

Constantine thought for a moment, recollecting the past. "I held several meetings. The first was in Rome with the bishop there, Miltiades, presiding. Rather than judging fairly, though, he stacked the court with his own men, those allied with Caecilian, the so-called traitor bishop of Carthage."

"What'd the council find?" I asked.

"What else? It negated the Donatists' claims as unfounded."

"And?"

"I gave in."

"To Miltiades?"

"No," he clarified, "to the Donatists."

"Why?"

"Because they appealed again. So I held another council in Arelate just a year later."

"What'd you find there?"

"I found the Donatists are no better than weasels."

I laughed. "The same with most men, no?"

He agreed. Constantine, however, did not share in my laughter as the whole matter weighed heavily upon him. "In the end," he went on, "I judged in favor of the Roman Christians who allow a greater scope for mercy."

"So they got the buildings?"

"It was the only just solution."

I nodded. Then, seeing he had little more to say on the matter, I casually concluded, "So, that's that. What's the problem?"

Without hesitation, he explained there was another dispute that was even worse.

"Why worse?"

"Because it's about more than property—or I can't reduce it to such. This one is a doctrinal dispute involving all sorts of heady, philosophical speculation."

I thought of my father, before asking, "Can't their holy books decide the matter?"

"No," he sighed once more. "It appears they can't. It's far too complicated, or so they've made it. And now it's the one thing that disrupts the unity I've longed for."

"This *religious* dispute?" I said, incredulous.

Fortunately, Constantine didn't notice the tone of my remark. Rather, he assured me, "Oh yes, Arnobius. You know how they are in Alexandria. They'll come to blows over ideas and over the constituent words forming their every complex conception."

"So, this other dispute is centered in Alexandria?"

"That's where it broke. The opposition, however, is centered in Antioch in Syria and Nicomedia in Bithynia."

"What do you plan to do?"

"I plan to put a stop to it," he answered with simple determination.

"How?" I asked.

He smiled. "By means of your old friend Ossius, the bishop of Cordoba."

The Cell in Tabennisi

Theophilus: IT WAS EVIDENT, ABBA, THAT ARNOBIUS was speaking about the controversy that erupted some twenty years ago. Sadly, it continues to affect the Church today. Early on, Arius was the chief protagonist, but as it developed, Eusebius the bishop of Nicomedia, quickly took hold of the reins.

"I've never quite seen it in that light," I remarked.

"In what light?" Arnobius asked.

"That the Church's dispute turned into a nightmare of disunity for the emperor and the Empire."

"But that's just it. Constantine wasn't concerned with some theoretical orthodoxy as the partisans on both sides would have it. Instead, as always, he was driven on by the goal of an actual, concrete unity, one founded on the Divinity and Rome rather than on mere abstractions. For him, the disputes were an attack on the new city and empire he was building in obedience to the mission he had been given. The New Rome wasn't just a matter of defensive boundaries or politics or even material prosperity. There was something supernatural to it. And since the Empire was moving in the direction of the new religion, the Church had to be at peace. In that sense, the dispute was a clear violation of the new city he was building and the walls he put up to defend it."

"So he despised Athanasius as a trouble maker?"

"No. Don't get me wrong. Constantine didn't despise him at all. Sure, there were times and certain characteristics of the man he wished were different. But overall he had great respect for the bishop. That's why, once he recognized him, he agreed to hear him out."

"Recognized him?" I asked, unsure of the reference.

"I'm sorry," said Arnobius. "I jump ahead."

"To when?"

"That's the question. How many years separated my arrival in the New Rome and that time?"

I shrugged while Arnobius did the calculation.

Finally, he said, "It was just about ten years."

"To what?"

"Ah, yes. Be clearer man. Ten years to when Athanasius bravely met Constantine before the walls of the new city."

"What happened?"

"With Athanasius?"

I nodded, "With you as well."

"Me? That's simple. Standing next to Athanasius, I felt nervous."

As for what happened with Papa Athanasius, Arnobius shut his eyes even as he had in the early hours of morning. Then he explained.

As the emperor and his entourage approached us on the road leading into Constantine's new city, and as everyone else moved aside, including the gruff looking man with his old, brown mule and the boys with their goatskin ball, Athanasius knew the emperor alone could grant justice. Still, perhaps he understood this differently than did Constantine. Indeed, he did. Nevertheless, it had always been common for Christians to see earthly rulers as the representatives of God on earth. The Christ had admitted as much as well as the apostle. However that was, Athanasius audaciously stood in the middle of the road as Constantine's guard bore down upon us, swords drawn.

Finally, Athanasius boldly called out to the emperor asking for justice by means of an imperial hearing.

"Who is that man?" Constantine demanded.

"Whoever," replied one of the guards brandishing his sword, "I'll give him justice!"

"No!" the emperor countered. "Put that away and don't be a fool!"

The soldier did.

Then to Athanasius, Constantine shouted, "Who are you?"

The emperor could not have recognized him because Athanasius, like all of us, was dirty and ragged in appearance.

"I am Athanasius!" he bellowed in response, "the rightful bishop of Alexandria!"

Constantine stopped along with the rest of his party just shy of the bishop and not far from me. He studied us. It was then that he saw me and stared at me in frigid recognition before his gaze turned toward the bishop.

Athanasius once again called out, "I appeal to the judgment and justice of the emperor of Rome!"

The emperor walked his horse forward. "Justice?" he repeated, as if that word had particular significance.

"Justice!" Athanasius echoed.

Constantine's features assumed a grave expression. Gesturing with his muscular right hand, he declared, "The bishop of Alexandria shall have it!"

Then, turning to several of his attendants, he ordered, "Bring horses for these poor men to ride!" And after briefly resting his eyes on me again, he further directed, "Add enough refreshment for all—bread and wine. They look like they've had a rough time of it."

We had.

I wanted to smile or give some sign of recognition, but I did not. It had been far too long, and anyway, his eyes suddenly turned from me when, grasping the reins of his horse and bidding us farewell for the moment, he trotted off with the others leaving a few attendants behind.

Eventually, sometime after the emperor and most of his men had trotted off and after the horses had been delivered, we rode to the Imperial Palace expecting to find some kind of resolution for our troubles. But expectations, Theophilus, hardly ever find proper fulfillment.

Arnobius paused. I took the opportunity to suggest to him an idea that had been taking shape in my own mind. Admittedly, Abba, it was less than well formulated, but I thought I would share it with him anyways. I suggested the meeting of the bishop and the emperor before New Rome's city walls was like the incarnation, where the divine met the profane.

Arnobius immediately disagreed. "It's a tempting metaphor," he allowed, "but not workable." He chuckled. "I laugh because it is similar to what Constantine believed of himself."

"Truly?" I asked.

"Yes. Just as God had come into the world as man in order to bring man back to the divine realm, Constantine saw himself as the philosopher king descending into the darkness of the cave in order to lead the many out into the light of unity and peace." Arnobius reflected before continuing. "In a way, this idea was harmless with respect to Constantine. Though driven on, and though he had plenty of defects, he nevertheless had a certain humility lacking in other men."

"Humility?" I asked.

He nodded. "The emperor had a genuine respect for other positions."

"Of what kind?"

"Religious. Philosophical."

"Always?"

"Not always," he admitted. "Although his genuine stance was one of tolerance as it had been for a very long time, his vision began to sour toward the end."

"Why?"

Arnobius considered this before saying, "His trust in others and the reciprocated good faith he expected were violated time and again."

"Did he grow intolerant? Was he ever as bad as his son has been?"

Ignoring the first question, he replied to the second. "His son Constantius, of course, is quite different."

"Quite," I concurred.

"He doesn't have his father's humility; nor does he possess his sense of toleration—thus, the terror we've seen in Alexandria and the ensuing program of coercion."

I shuddered. Then after thinking about the Empire and the Church for a moment, I queried, "So what is the right relationship between the power of an emperor and the authority of a bishop?"

Arnobius thought about this while I pondered how I should next steer our conversation. Then, he spoke about Bishop Athanasius. There was a time, he said, when Constantine demanded something of him and he refused.

"What'd the bishop do?" I asked.

"He declared that the emperor could not make the particular demand."

"Why not?"

Arnobius explained in a general way. "There are two spheres of power; the Empire has its proper affairs and the Church has hers. The operation of each, however, is different. The Empire, it seems, is built upon raw power and force."

"The sword," I suggested.

"Exactly. It's the enforcement of borders and laws and dignities and so forth."

"It was the Empire that crucified the Christ," I added.

"Yes. And the Church must not crucify others."

"No," I agreed.

He clarified. "The Church is not about power. On the contrary its power is different—that of persuasion. It does not force; instead, it proclaims and lives its vision of the truth in love in order to draw souls to God."

"What about the role of the emperor?" I inquired. "Hasn't he called councils? And what about the many exiles? And now, Constantius is using this power for his own ends against the Church."

"You're right," he admitted. "There is a role—but it's a small role and one that can be abused. But take this example. It's the problem I've already mentioned—the Donatists in Africa."

"Okay," I consented.

"They were a thorn in Constantine's side for years. Nevertheless, he governed well in giving the churches and other property to the right side."

I nodded. "Isn't this also true with the Arian controversy? Can't the emperor simply allocate property and be done with it?"

"Yes and no," Arnobius replied, circumspectly. "Certainly there are property issues."

"It seems so," I remarked, "if Constantius' bullying is indicative of anything. As you know, he's robbed the church in Alexandria in favor of the Arians. And now Gregory of Cappadocia reigns as a pseudo bishop, while Athanasius is on the run."

Arnobius sighed. He knew all this because he had been there that night before Easter. Then he explained, "Still, it is more, Theophilus. It's more now as it was more then, when Athanasius begged for justice."

"I imagine so," I granted.

"And beyond legal issues, those of property and ownership and the like, the Empire, I would venture, has a very little role."

If so, I wondered why Athanasius had gone to the emperor.

"If this is true," I said, "why did Athanasius approach Constantine for judgment?" The question was the same one I had asked earlier in the morning.

"*That's* the question," Arnobius recognized. "Most of what happened, properly speaking, was a matter for the Church to decide. Athanasius didn't budge on doctrine and he refused to admit Arius back into the Alexandrian fold. Discipline and doctrine, he affirmed, are a bishop's solemn charge. But the reasons for Athanasius' trouble and his request for justice were far more sinister. They were criminal. In this sense, they affected the whole Empire."

"How?" I asked.

Arnobius sat erect on the stool and adjusted his lebiton. Then he crouched forward and heaved a sigh again before looking at me. I could see he was exhausted from talking so much. It was warm in my cell. The afternoon heat had set in with the passing of the sun along its lengthy diurnal course. I felt for him.

"Perhaps," I suggested, "we should take a break."

He smiled, relieved. "I'd like that," he revealed.

"Why don't we reconvene after a few hours?"

"Good," he said.

And so we went to rest. He went to his cell and I remained in mine.

It was only later on that Arnobius told me what Athanasius had done and how the Eusebians had sought to trap him.

Book Four

Athanasius the Deacon

297 to 326 A.D.

The Cell in Tabennisi

Late Afternoon

Theophilus: THE BLAZING SUN causing limbs to wither and water to dry had nearly run its midday course before Arnobius and I sat before each other once again in my cell. We both had rested our weary eyes in silence, and together with the other brothers of the monastery we had gathered for mid-afternoon prayers to God, the eternal Sun. Inside we experienced a coolness that was foreign to the heat outside.

Arnobius glanced at me refreshed. He was ready to speak. "So," he began, "where did we stop? It seems we may have lost focus before the break."

I looked at the notes I had taken and told him.

"Of course, now I remember," he said, and he smiled.

"Why the smile?" I asked, furrowing my eyebrows. "I can't imagine why the Arians would provoke such mirth."

He shook his head. "I smile not because of the Arians, but because I remember Athanasius. However imperfect he was, he always strove for excellence, as he still does today, I presume. I miss the man."

"When did you last see him?"

Arnobius considered it. "Just before his departure for Sicily. He was on his way to Rome when I bade him farewell."

"On account of the emperor Constantius?"

"Yes. It wasn't long after he drove Athanasius from Alexandria."

I knew this. Although I had not been there in the church of Theonas, I knew it. The whole city knew it. The Christians were fighting again. At least, Abba, that's what my unbelieving friends had declared.

"How long did you know him?"

"I first met him at the great council of Nicaea."

"Fifteen years ago?"

"Perhaps a bit more. I can still see him." Arnobius closed his eyes and portrayed Athanasius as he was. "There's that that strange growth of dark auburn hair crowning his finely shaped head. Below are his eyes, equally dark, intense and brilliant, yet soft and kind. When I first saw him, Athanasius of medium height was sitting next to silver haired Alexander who was then bishop of Alexandria. Alexander was quietly listening to him speak, though he was many years Athanasius' senior. He was animatedly discussing a theological matter with Eusebius the bishop of Nicomedia and, I should add, a follower of Arius. Athanasius argued like a sheepdog guarding its sheep. In that way, he's a typical Copt. You know what I mean, Theophilus—the way they bargain in the market, not giving up before reaching the desired price."

"Of course I do," I warmly affirmed.

Arnobius continued. "I don't exactly recall what it was they were discussing, but no doubt it had to do with the Christ. Eusebius, a heavy man, stood smirking as if his mere expression would be sufficient to put down this worthless deacon. Athanasius maintained his poise. Even then he had a wisdom that far surpassed his twenty-seven years."

I thought of that, Abba. I thought of the fact that he was then just a few years older than I am now, and I wondered how it was that he came to be so learned and influential at such an early age.

Finally, I put the question to Arnobius. "How," I asked, "did Athanasius come to be a significant player in the struggle against Eusebius and the Arians?"

"How?" he echoed, as if gathering his own thoughts. Then Arnobius relaxed some upon the stool and began to tell me what he knew of Athanasius' past.

Twenty-one: Athanasius, Arius, and Alexander

297 to 318 A.D.

AS I REMEMBER IT, Athanasius was born sometime around Lucius Domitius Domitianus' failed uprising. When Diocletian and Constantine thundered through Alexandria on their way to defeat the usurper, Athanasius was no more than a babe at his mother's breasts. Later, when I went to study philosophy in Alexandria, he was little more than a clumsy lad, and so he was perhaps half a decade old when Constantine first pulled me into his circle.

Athanasius was born into a pagan family that was wealthy, or wealthy relative to the many that eke out their existence in Alexandria. He was born a Copt in every way. I say this in contrast to what he was not—meaning he was not exactly Greek. This was evident given his stubborn and intense commitment to the Christian religion as a concrete, actual way of life and cosmic renewal as compared with the many more abstract, theoretical Greek ways competing in Alexandria at the time of his birth. This stubborn commitment flourished despite his own mother's traditionally pagan and I daresay rather obstinate intentions, which were driven along by a certain perceived necessity, as Athanasius' father had died sometime early on in his life.

When Athanasius was merely fourteen, and after he had been educated in the typical manner, crowned with the wisdom and mysteries of the old Heliopolitan masters, his mother suggested he help with the family business, which was then operated by an incompetent uncle who squandered the family's wealth on his own dissolute ends instead of dutifully making increase. Contrary to his mother's desires, however, Athanasius demonstrated little interest in family affairs. Not that he was unconcerned. Instead, as the years passed by something else tugged at his mind and heart. He had become interested in a set of ideas and a way of life he had encountered in the famed Catechetical School of Alexandria.

Eventually, Athanasius came to study the philosophy of the Christ and wished for nothing else than to continue his studies in order to receive initiation into the mysteries and finally go off to the nothingness of the desert in order to live a solitary life seeking God.

His mother's response? I can only relay what Athanasius told me later on. She was not pleased with his heady aspirations. She wanted him to take charge of family affairs and leave his newfound religious ambitions aside. To ensure it, she hired young dancing girls for his good pleasure in order to steer him clear of his eventual aim to seek God in the desert—a goal that required moral purity. As though a young schoolboy, Athanasius was ordered to sit still and watch these beautiful girls dance, made up as they were, scantily dressed, with golden anklets, bracelets, earrings, nose rings, and more, he reported, seductively hanging and jingling from every conceivable body part. His mother's hope was that their beauty would serve as fuel to ignite in him lustful desires that would turn his gaze from the One to the many—though perhaps she would not have put it that way. It didn't work. When Athanasius told me about it later on, I recall him laughing. "The poor woman," he said. Then he thanked God for the grace of purity.

But his mother wasn't yet finished. A month later, in a desperate last attempt to sidetrack him, she aimed her arrows once again. She hired a prostitute who, like the earlier dancing girls, was thoroughly divine in appearance. She had dark hair and milky white skin. She ordered the young woman to join her son in bed late at night after sleep had already encumbered his soul, leaving him weaker than he would have been during the light of day.

She did it. Sometime after midnight, the young woman slipped into his bed followed by a cloud of sweet perfume. She was naked. When she finally joined him beneath the covers, she lifted his undergarment and touched him. Then she kissed him on his mouth.

Startled, Athanasius woke up as if from a bad dream.

His response? Once fully awake, he batted her away. God, he claimed, protected him. And so his mother's plans failed.

Frustrated and desperate now, she didn't know what to do. Finally, she decided she would go and speak with a Sabaean wise man, a magician in the Rhacotis Quarter's market.

"What should I do with my son?" she begged. "My husband has died and he refuses to marry and look after me and the rest of the family." She went on to explain how he was learning foreign ideas and participating in foreign rites.

The Sabaean wise man considered it before saying, "Let me eat bread with him."

He did. They dined together, eating and drinking, and passing the better part of an afternoon and evening.

The following day, the Sabaean wise man met with Athanasius' mother. "Woman," he advised, "do not be anxious over what you cannot change." She protested, weeping, while he continued. "You will not have power over your son; you will not persuade him. By the gods he is a Galilean and a Galilean he will remain."

"A Galilean?" she repeated, unsure.

"A follower of the Christ," he explained. "An adherent to the doctrines of Jesus the Jew."

She wept.

"But do not fear," he went on, "your son will be a great man."

She tentatively raised her head. Through tears, she managed to plead, "A great man?"

"Yes. And you'll be taken care of," he promised.

"But he'll leave me!" she protested, returning to her fears. "He's said it. He'll go to the desert and leave me here alone!"

"It won't happen," he stated flatly.

Therefore, after a moment's reflection, and trusting his words of prophecy, she declared, "Then I must join him."

She did. She too began studying in order to be initiated into the Christian mysteries, and that's how Athanasius' whole family came to know the Christ.

I can't say exactly how old Athanasius was at the time of his baptism, but it seems he wasn't yet connected to Bishop Alexander. That came some time later when Athanasius attracted his interest in a rather divine manner. One afternoon, on the feast day celebrating the martyrdom of Peter—the former bishop of Alexandria who had died under Maximinus Daza in the persecution of Galerius—Athanasius and some of his believing friends were walking along the beach discussing the rite of baptism nearby the bishop's residence. Although they were all initiates, there was some dispute among them as to how the rite was accomplished. Accordingly, in the manner of a bishop, Athanasius was demonstrating precisely how it was done amid the waves of Our Sea. Alexander observed this from the porch of his residence and beheld something unique in the young man. He couldn't exactly say what it was. Nevertheless, the Spirit prompted him to approach Athanasius and his friends. He did, and with the ongoing recognition of something unique, he invited Athanasius to live with him at the bishop's house so he could give his own special attention to his education.

From that day forward and with the permission of his mother, Athanasius lived with Alexander. Over the next three years, the bishop educated and formed him. Foremost among all other areas of knowledge he studied were the divine oracles—the law, the prophets, the books of wisdom, the memoirs of the apostles, the epistles of Paul, and all the other sacred writings. Further, he served the bishop and the Church in different ways, becoming known and loved among the people of Alexandria.

Then, when he was just eighteen, Athanasius went to live in the desert with Anthony the monk. There he hoped to compete as an athlete of the Christ under the direction of that holy man. He sought holiness in the measured path of dying to oneself. It was a simple life of spiritual exercise, replete with study, much prayer, and ordinary labor, and if Athanasius had been his own master, it would have lasted to the end of his days. But it was not meant to be. Instead, he was called back to serve in Alexandria.

The bishop—but more now, his father in the faith—required his assistance. For by then, by the time Athanasius had rounded out two full decades of life, he had already surpassed Alexander in many ways. More specifically, he was his superior in philosophical and theological wisdom. Consequently, Alexander called Athanasius from the sweetness of the desolate desert in order to help refute a priest who was seemingly irrefutable. The priest was at the center of a dispute, a raging sand storm that had broken over Alexandria, one that was causing serious divisions in the Church.

Arius, the priest, claimed that the Son of God was not God. Not truly. Christ Jesus, he said, was not truly God.

It seems Arius had learned these ideas from a priest, a martyr no less, called Lucian. I mentioned him earlier this morning, Theophilus. He was immensely popular at the time, and Arius studied with him in Antioch along with others who would eventually ally with him in the years to come. Among these were Eusebius of Nicomedia, Eusebius of Caesarea, and the Libyan bishops Secundus of Ptolemais in Pentapolis and Theonas of Marmarica, just to name a few. They all referred to themselves as fellow Lucianists—a tight circle from all appearances. Labeled by some the party of Eusebius, this group of men grew to have much philosophical influence in the provinces of

Syria and Asia. But in Egypt and in Alexandria, their influence was more like a trickling stream until Arius came along like a rushing torrent, intellectually powerful as he was, flooding men and women with his Lucianist teachings.

Many assume that Peter, the earlier martyred bishop of Alexandria, had given Arius leave to go study with Lucian shortly after ordaining him deacon at the beginning of his episcopate. When Lucian died under the persecution of Maximinus Daza, Arius returned to Alexandria to serve the church there and—as it became clear—to spread his Lucianist understanding of the Christ. Were his intentions good? Judge not—right Theophilus? In any event, Achillas, the bishop of Alexandria after Peter, soon ordained Arius to the sacred priesthood. Thereafter, he maintained a large following due to his brilliant and charismatic personality.

Arius was a tall man and well spoken. He had a long, thin face, which ended in a chin that didn't quite signify manly strength but it seemed a kind of ascetic pride. On the opposite end was a crown of gray hair, as he was then over half a century old, which lent him the airs of august wisdom. By all accounts, this made for an attractive man. Accordingly, the women adored him. I say that not to impugn his character, but there *were* rumors. Yet let us banish them as we have all sinned.

Eventually, Achillas entrusted Arius with the church of the Baucalis, a wealthy neighborhood, as you know, Theophilus, near to the Bruceum and the royal palace. There, due to his smart appearance and his extraordinary manner, he was instantly successful in attracting many to the Christ—at least to *his* Christ.

As I said, the issue centered on the nature of Christ the savior. Specifically, it had to do with the Christ's relation to God the Father. If the Christ were God in some way, how, exactly, was it so?

As for who was to blame for the controversy that ensued and which continues to disturb the peace of the Church worldwide, the accounts vary, though I suppose I have already strongly implicated Arius. To be fair, however, there were other explanations.

I'm thinking, for example, of Constantine's account. When he caught wind of the disagreement, the emperor's first response was to laugh. What foolishness! Then he cried. He wept in anger at realizing how this one small philosophical matter had reached to such great proportions and how it threatened the unity of his empire and therefore his mission under the one

God to bring unity to the world. Then, after stifling his feelings, he penned a letter to Alexander and Arius blaming them both. Against the bishop, he advised that he should have never raised such a question in public—a question of such subtlety and of such inconsequential significance. Why, he asked, did you force Arius' hand? Why did you make him commit to his views in the arena of popular judgment where he had no choice but to stick by them doggedly or risk ridicule? As for Arius, he cautioned that he should have never raised his sentiments above the din of his own private thoughts in the first place. You ought to keep those kinds of heady reflections to yourself, he chided. But little did Constantine know. Even then, he was a babe in thought relative to the maturity of the overall train of Christian philosophy. Yes, perhaps they were both to blame. Yet both were the product of Alexandria, which esteems the intellect above all and argues minute points of philosophy until the truth, however hidden, prevails.

Still, in his defense I must say that Alexander acted out of a sense of humility and fairness. He knew that if Arius had in fact strayed into heresy, then he should be gently guided back into the fold according to the advice of the divine oracles where Paul advises the servant of the Lord not to quarrel but to be kind and to teach without resentment. If someone does stray, says the apostle, the shepherd must gently instruct, hoping God will lead him to the truth. If anything, Alexander's mistake was the forum he chose for his instruction and, I should add, the form.

In this sense, Constantine was right. Whereas Alexander should have privately educated Arius as his bishop—his shepherd—due to his sense of objective justice, and so, the need to hear all sides, he chose instead to settle the matter by means of several public dialogues, imagining he—or the truth of the Christ—would win Arius over. This, perhaps, was his greatest mistake. In the end, it would have grave consequences.

Alexander held the first dialogue in the church of Dionysius. Though he had not advertised the proceedings, the news spread so that a significant crowd of some five hundred men watched as though they had transposed themselves from the usual marketplace of ideas in Alexandria to the church in order to follow this debate between two eminent Christian philosophers. In fact, the whole matter had become a point of derision for much of the non-Christian populace. You could even see it lampooned in several of the local theatres, where men pranced about on stage, one taking the side of the homoousians and the other that of Arius. Of those who came to the first public dialogue, half, I gather, were not even remotely Christian. The other half? Hard to say. Many, of course, were bishops, priests, and deacons, and those hoping to be such.

When Alexander ordered the church to a relative silence, he stood to introduce Arius and begin the proceedings. Some cheered; others booed. The bishop waited patiently. Then as if conducting a class at the Catechetical School, he began, "Arius, would you please state your major thesis."

Arius stood. The skin of his jutting chin pulled tightly as he grinned and assured Alexander that he would be pleased to do so. "My basic contention," he explained, "is that Jesus the Christ is not God."

"Not God?" asked Alexander, patiently, while some hissed and one cried "Blasphemy!" from the back of the church. But not the bishop. Unperturbed, he asked for clarification, and Arius obliged.

"He's not God in any natural sense. By the will of God, yes, the Christ is God—that is, by God's choice, by the One's election. Moreover, he is morally divine given his perfect will and life. But he's not God by nature. In that sense, the Christ was only a man who had the same human nature we have—the same ordinary human being."

"And what, may I ask, drives you to such a conclusion?"

Arius, I was told, glanced out among the crowd, his eyes shining with candlelight, before declaring, "First, the divine scriptures. Second, logic."

Alexander nodded. And probing more for the source of Arius' ideas, he queried, "Is this your own thinking or another's?"

"Mine," huffed Arius. Then smirking, he added, "As well as another's. Logic is something available to all men. Heraclitus of Ephesus claimed as much centuries ago when he wrote that the divine Logos is common to all."

Half the crowd erupted with laughter. Others whispered indignantly.

The bishop replied by saying, "Yes, yes, of course, but—"

But Arius went on, "Alexander, dear man, leaving aside the scriptures for a moment, you *must* recognize that the nature of the One logically demands this conclusion. For how could the One suffer as we all affirm the Christ has done? And if the One cannot suffer, then the Christ who did suffer cannot possibly be identified by nature, by being, with the self-same One."

There was a great murmur throughout the crowd. Some agreed; many, however, did not. Instead, they demanded a reply from the sacred oracles, which Alexander delivered by saying, "We cannot simply set aside the memoirs of the apostles or the letters of Paul as you suggest, Arius. For it is among these and in the earlier testament that we find our doctrine of the Christ. *There* it is clear! The Word was God. And there the Son identifies himself with the Father."

"Yes, yes—of course!" cried Arius. "But we have to properly understand that identification! We must see the whole! It is my contention that the primary, most significant data in the divine scriptures is that the Christ suffered for our sins. Again, how in the name of reason can we reconcile a passable Christ with the impassable One? It's impossible!"

"So, what of the points of identity found therein?" Alexander asked.

"I've already answered! The identity of the Word with God and the Son with the Father is not one of nature, of being. It merely reflects the divine elective will and a moral unity."

"Is it no different, then, from that unity with God we Christians hope to achieve?"

"In terms of its beginning, no. God chose the Christ to be one with him just as through the suffering of the same Christ, God chose us to be one with him. But in terms of the Christ's own will, it is different."

"How so?"

"He was sinless, whereas we sin. Although from nothing, his will was always aligned with the Father's will."

"I see," acknowledged the bishop. Then after a moment, Alexander followed up on a side point Arius had just made. "From *nothing*—you declare the Christ is from nothing?"

"Yes. Again, logic points us in this direction. If the Christ is not God, not the One, then surely he is a creature. For everything that is not the One was at some point no-one or no-thing. It follows that the Christ too was created from that which is not."

"The Christ, then, is a creature?"

"Is that so bad?" asked Arius, grinning. "Surely it is good. For Moses says that when God created, he declared his creation good."

"But how, then, does the Christ save?"

"By suffering. By example. He becomes our divine guide to the One. He is the divine exodus from God that points the way back to the beatific return. Unified with the One in will and by God's election, we too, like the Christ, will eventually return to our heavenly abode. Then, like the Christ, we too will be God—or, to say it differently, we'll be one with the One."

For the moment, Alexander granted his answer. Then pursuing another tangent, the bishop asked, "You said the Christ was *in fact* sinless. Are you suggesting he could have sinned?"

Arius quickly responded. "Theoretically, yes. As a creature existing in time as any other man, the Christ could have sinned. But only theoretically. In reality, his will was protected from all eternity by the will of the One who had chosen him from all eternity to save."

"From *all* eternity?"

"Indeed. The Christ's relationship to time is different from ours. As the scriptures say, he was created before time and thus from all eternity. But as produced, as having an origin, the Christ is not eternally existent, that is, he does not exist from all eternity as the One does except for as the will or the choice of the One."

"Ah," said Alexander, thinking he may have found a gap in Arius' logic. "Isn't the Christ, then, at the very least identified with the eternal will of the One?"

Arius nodded. "In a sense."

"So, are you proposing we introduce division into the nature of the divine One? Are you willing to separate the divine will from the divine being?"

"Not at all. But remember, when we speak of either, we use images. They are projections of our own limited will and being. The divine will and nature are truly beyond all comprehension. To fully comprehend would be to limit, and to limit the Divinity is out of the question, just as to introduce suffering or passability into the divine nature is unthinkable. This, my dear bishop, is why we must not allow the suffering Christ to be one in nature with the unsuffering, impassable God. As philosophers of the Christ and of the Divinity, we must take care to guard the One as though guarding the most sacred treasure. If we allow Christians to say that the Christ is identical to God in nature, in being, in *ousia*, then we might as well say that God is passable, that God suffers! And if we permit this, what will come next?"

"What?" someone shouted from the back of the church.

"Idols!" replied Arius passionately. "All sorts of perversion! Next the One will appear as every conceivable created object down to the most profane, just as pagans manifest their many gods. Gold, silver, and pieces of wood shaped in the form of man and animals and parts of man shameful to mention. You've seen it! You know it! *I beg you*—the Divinity must be protected!"

"But so too, must the integrity of the divine oracles!" countered a frustrated Alexander. "There, we find that God is Father. Now, if Father, then eternally Father. If that is so, then he eternally had a Son who was likewise eternally existent, even if begotten."

"No, no," said Arius, shaking his head. "There's where you are wrong. We must not allow the Peripatetic theory of relations to obscure our way. For when one is a master, then yes, there must be a slave. But in this case, the Father was not always Father. First and always, he is God, the One. He's 'I AM,' as he revealed himself to the prophet Moses, not I AM *to*."

"Then the One is not three?"

"Now, yes, but not always."

"Then your position leads you to deny the sacred Triad?"

"Again, you oversimplify my position. I make no such denial. However, we must understand the Triad properly. First is the One, the Monad from eternity. Then there was the Dyad, the Son who was begotten of the Father. Lastly, came the divine Spirit sent to lead us into all truth."

"I see," replied Alexander, perplexed.

But the crowd of men swelled. Many of them weren't as understanding or patient. Some were calling for Arius' head. Blasphemy! How could he utter such nonsense! Others took the alternative side, suggesting he made sense. In good Alexandrian form, there was nearly a brawl.

Alexander, ever sensitive to his flock—whether Christian or not—took notice. "Arius," he said, having returned to a tone of fatherly moderation, "I believe we'll have to take this up again in another month. For now, you have given me and all of us present something to consider, something to ponder in light of the divine oracles, and, as you say, in the light of reason."

Arius smiled as though he'd won.

Then, turning to the crowd, Alexander begged of them mutual charity and ended the proceedings with a blessing, after which he departed to his chambers to write a letter to Athanasius.

As I have said, Theophilus, by this time, Athanasius was in the desert with Anthony living a simple life unto the glory of God, a life that would shortly be embroiled in complexity, even as it still is despite his desire for peace.

The content of the missive was simple. Alexander knew Arius was wrong. But where—exactly—and how, he could not precisely identify. Arius' logic seemed irrefutable and so too his interpretation of the divine oracles. For this reason, the bishop explained, he now required the help of his young protégé.

Athanasius, for his part, was doubtlessly sad to leave Anthony and the pursuit of holiness that the desert alone could afford. Still, he was pleased to return the good his own spiritual father had first given to him by taking him in and forming his heart and mind according to the revealed light of God. Immediately, he set out for Alexandria where he hoped to preserve the Church and save Arius from his erroneous thinking. He suspected, though, that the battle wouldn't be easy.

Twenty-two: Condemnation and Calling

318 to spring of 325 A.D.

ACCORDING TO ATHANASIUS, who was now back in Alexandria, Arius' problem was simple and straightforward. It was his emphasis. Arius' concern—one might even suggest his noble concern—was the integrity of the doctrine regarding the One.

As we discussed earlier, Theophilus, this concern is quite ancient, originating some thousand years ago around the time when the freedom loving Greeks fought the despotic Persians. Following Xenophanes of Colophon, Parmenides of Elea first suggested a unified Absolute, outside the march of time, complete in itself, without parts, and so, unchanging. Melissus of Samos went on to spell out what this means. Unchanging, the One cannot suffer, because suffering implies change from wholeness, integrity, and health to dissolution, decrepitude, and unhealth. Therefore, the One is wholly and simply *what is*. Being itself is radically simple. It's not *this* thing in *this* way or *that* thing in another or during this time or that; Being itself simply is, beyond all things altogether. For Parmenides and his followers, the One is reality, and the many that we see, hear, and can touch is nothing more than an illusion.

Others took up this definition of the One, of Being itself, and modified it in one direction or another. Some, attempting to save the plurality of reality, as it were, tried to understand the One as many while retaining the characteristics of the One for the many. Everlasting reality is small bits of matter, entirely simple, they claimed. They called these bits of reality atoms, because in themselves, they're indivisible or un-cuttable, *atomos*. The major proponents of this theory were the atomists Leucippus and Democritus, and later on, Epicurus and his Roman admirer Lucretius, who wrote an epic poem on the nature of all things. They posited atoms drifting in the void, from which all things arise.

Others continued to see the One in much the way that Parmenides seems to have viewed it. Socrates, of course, is the most famous, Theophilus. Recall his notion of the Beautiful in Plato's *Symposium*—it has all the characteristics of Parmenides' One and is thus radically beyond human knowing and language. A vast gulf separates the One and the many, which participates somehow—as shadow, as image, as echo—in the one, everlasting, unchanging light and life of the Good and the Beautiful. The only way to experience the One is by a mystical leap into its distant reality—a reality transcending the limited grasp of both the senses and reason. Plato followed along with Socrates—or as some say, he shaped Socrates in his own image.

However that may be, as things developed past Plato, the gap between the One and the many grew to vast proportions. Why? Simple. As Arius declared, logic demands it. The characteristics of the One insist upon the distance. Therefore, as Arius put it, if the One is absolutely transcendent and absolutely impassible, that is, incapable of change or suffering, then the Christ cannot possibly be God in the way that the One has been understood by philosophy from Parmenides down to our own day. This is true because the Christ came to suffer and *did* suffer, dying a horrible, humiliating death.

So what, then, you may wonder is the answer? Well, as I've reported, Athanasius' reply was that Arius' gaze was on the wrong problem. In a sense, Theophilus, Athanasius' response was like your classmate who answered your master professor and the paradox of Zeno when you were a boy. Remember? The paradox states that one cannot possibly walk from the back of a lecture hall to the front, for it would require reaching the halfway point first, and the halfway point of that halfway point before that, and that repeatedly all the way to infinity. Your classmate countered the paradox by standing up and walking forward. He left logic alone and simply did it. In the same way, Athanasius affirmed with the divine oracles that God the One did in fact become man and did indeed suffer. But that's not all.

For Athanasius, the point was the purpose behind God's becoming man—what some call the incarnation and what he likes to call the inhomination. Why did God do it? Why did the infinite Word become finite, suffering flesh? According to Athanasius, he did it in order to restore creation. Man had fallen from his initial state of being and faced either corruption and destruction if God did nothing, or he could be raised up to new life as the restored image of God. Athanasius' contention was that the inhomination was really about creation—or, better said, re-creation. When the Son became man, this act allowed man once again to know God and so reflect God perfectly in mind, heart, and soul as his image.

This wasn't Athanasius' only criticism of Arius. He further insisted that the Son is not merely a kind of protection for God the One. The Word is not some mediary being that fills the gap between the distant, ever-transcendent One and the messy, complex world of the many. He's no demiurge, as Arius seemed to suggest when he spoke of two Words and two Wisdoms, one set internal to God and one set external, doing God's dirty work as it were. In this sense, Athanasius judged that Arius' Christ was more like the prevalent conception among the educated of Jupiter and the gods as the workmen of creation, as if the One wills and these other gods, however immortal, do all the filthy work, besmirching their hands with the mortality of human affairs and this world. No, countered Athanasius. God created by his own internal Word and Wisdom who became external as well. And when this creation went astray in the will of man, the crown of creation, God, the everlasting and unchanging One, created anew with this same internal Word and Wisdom, who humbled himself, becoming man in order to lead creation to God the Creator.

Unfortunately, Arius refused to see Athanasius' wisdom—wisdom that held on dearly to reason on the one hand, and yet on the other, transcended it. Consequently Arius, it seemed, was stuck. Was he to blame for this? I can't say. This is the way of Alexandria, where one holds stubbornly to whatever light one possesses. In like manner, Arius clung to his own ways of thinking, his own logic, his own view of the sacred writings.

As bishop, Alexander came to see that he had no other choice than to anathematize Arius for his false views. Therefore, he did.

At another proceeding again in the church of Dionysius, Alexander listened to Athanasius both question and refute Arius. When Arius refused to capitulate, he dismissed him and all the other spectators in order to have a vote among the bishops. They voted to condemn him. Arius was condemned for teaching that the Son was not God and that the Christ was a mere creature from that which is not. Accordingly, he was cut off from communion with the Alexandrian church.

When Arius learned of his condemnation and excommunication, he thanked Alexander with begrudged courtesy and huffed out of the church, out to a crowd of mostly women, though some men were present as well. Then he disappeared.

The following morning, Alexander discovered that Arius had fled the city of Alexandria altogether.

"He's gone!" reported the priest Macarius who had been asked to keep an eye on his whereabouts and activity.

"Gone?" inquired the bishop. Athanasius sat by his side.

"Yes! Friends say he's gone to Palestine. He departed sometime around midnight under cover of darkness, right out the Canopic Gate toward Pelusium. He'll be in Caesaraea Palestrina in a week if he travels rapidly."

"Of course," said Alexander. "He's gone to Eusebius."

Eusebius, you'll recall, was the bishop of Caesaraea. He died just a few years ago. I must say that he wasn't a bad man. Still, his record was somewhat mixed despite the best of intentions. Nevertheless, it was to Eusebius that Arius fled at first, though this wasn't his final destination. No, although allied with him after a fashion, Eusebius of Caesaraea was far too mild a man for Arius' present needs. He was a quiet, retiring, bookish man, who lived among and breathed the refined air of the many scrolls he and others had gathered in Caesaraea. What Arius required was nothing less than a full-on partisan who was equally convinced, even as he was, of the truth of his own teaching, and equally motivated to act on it. He required another fellow Lucianist, one who had been associated with him in Antioch when he first heard of and believed in these ideas about the impassable One and the irreconcilable nature of the passable Christ. He needed Eusebius of Nicomedia.

After some time in Caesarea Palestrina, Arius traveled on to Nicomedia in Bithynia, the then-eastern capital city of the Empire—for this was before Constantine converted Byzantium into the New Rome. There he went to Eusebius, its then dubious bishop.

As I've seen him over the years stretching from the great council of Nicaea to when I last saw him in the New Rome, when Constantine agreed to grant justice to Athanasius, the most evident feature of Eusebius of Nicomedia is his appearance. He's a large man—fat, to be plain, Theophilus. Yet while this may betray a certain disorder among the desires of his soul, his external appearance is always and without fail nothing short of perfect. He's immaculately dressed, fastidiously even.

You may wonder why. In reply, I say this. I once heard him assert that his dignity demanded it, that is, the dignity of the Christ in him as bishop. I wonder. However that may be, he *was* bishop, and I suppose a certain way of appearing was therefore appropriate. Even so, I always wondered whether it was a matter of substantial, interior reality for him, or merely one of external appearance. I wondered this because Eusebius of Nicomedia was a man of incredible political ability. I say this because the political man, the man whose business it is to shepherd men, is necessarily a man of appearance in order to gain the attention and loyalty of his followers. This was—this *is*—Eusebius. He's a man interested in power.

Evidence, you ask. Simple. Contrary to all ecclesial norms, Eusebius was a *see* changer, shifting from one diocese to another as if they were fashionable cloaks to be discarded at will season after season. He first began his episcopal tenure in Berytus in Syria. Then, detecting opportunity where another man would have shuddered, he transposed himself with the help of others to the prestigious See of Nicomedia. He did this so he could have more influence. As it is today, Nicomedia was then one of the most dominant cities in the Empire. Finally, once Constantine moved the capital to Byzantium, Eusebius maneuvered to be installed there after Alexander, its aged and courageous bishop, passed away just a few years ago.

At the time, when Arius fled to him over two decades ago, Eusebius was still bishop of Nicomedia, and therefore, one of the most influential men in the Church. His rule happened to coincide with Licinius' sole tenure in the East, after Licinius had defeated Maximinus Daza near Adrianople and before Constantine had destroyed him at Chrysopolis. As events unfolded, this was a stroke of luck for Arius. By the time he arrived, Eusebius had already grown thick with Licinius' wife and Constantine's sister, Constantia. In her, Eusebius possessed a willing ear, and consequently, he had the attention of Licinius who was beholden to her both as his wife and as the sister of the man who had forestalled invasion of his half of the Empire on her behalf. Accordingly, when Arius spoke to Eusebius about the violation of his rights and power as a priest in possession of his own church, the latter in turn whispered the whole story to Constantia who, in turn, demanded action from her husband. Licinius' response was immediate and rather severe. By simple command, he forbade all church synods, thereby protecting Arius and others from further condemnation.

In a way, it was a wise move. Whatever his intentions and whatever his motivation, the edict had the effect of bringing peace to the East. Perhaps if Constantine had joined him, what happened over the following years up to now would not have occurred. But presently it's a moot point. He didn't. And only God, I suppose, knows how matters will unravel over the great stretch of time.

Still, at that moment, one matter was clear. Arius was a free man. Thanks to Licinius, he was safe with Eusebius of Nicomedia, and Bishop Alexander of Alexandria could do nothing aside from writing letters, which he, Eusebius, and many others continued to do rather prolifically. That all changed, of course, when Constantine soundly defeated Licinius. When the latter died, so too did his edicts.

It all seems so strange now looking back on what happened. When I arrived to visit Constantine in the New Rome shortly after his victory over Licinius, Eusebius was already on good terms with the man who had forced his former friend and ally to drain his own life's blood. This one abhorrent fact apparently didn't move Eusebius one way or the other. Life is flux, and as it shifted violently, so too did the bishop. So too did Constantia, the emperor's sister.

Constantine, by contrast, wasn't pleased. While he moved with the flux and even flourished as perhaps no other man could do, he desired above all a state of rest, both for himself and for Rome. His sole aspiration was for unity, peace, and prosperity. Hence, it was a severe blow when he had to face the disunity of the Church so soon after bringing unity to the Empire.

One day, after years and years of bitter strife with the diocese of Alexandria, Eusebius of Nicomedia approached Constantine with the idea of using his power to further his and his allies' goals. He asked Constantine to have Arius reinstated in Alexandria. "To his rightful place," he suggested, "the one unjustly stolen by Alexander, who overstepped long accustomed precedence in order to silence the traditional"—or so he asserted—"teaching of the priest, Arius."

Constantine refused despite the fact that the whole matter bothered him tremendously. Instead, he composed a lengthy letter commanding all parties involved to stop fighting. "You embarrass yourselves and the holy Church," he wrote, "which should be one in mind and heart. You are no better than children or old women arguing over useless matters." Then he urged them to take their direction from the pagan philosophers who, despite their disagreements on small matters, adhere to one another overall. At letter's end, his admonition was a simple command. "Stop!" he insisted. "Stop the impiety of this absurd philosophical wrangling!"

But little did he understand. And even less did their arguments come to an end. Rather, each side became more entrenched in the rectitude and pride of its own position. As a result, Constantine finally asked Ossius to go and settle the controversy.

"What shall I say?" asked Ossius who, as I've explained, had climbed the ranks of Constantine's advisors ever since the vision of the Christ in Gaul and the subsequent battle of Milvian Bridge in Italy.

"What shall you say?" gasped Constantine. "That's the question I put to *you*. It's not my area of expertise, you know, but yours."

As for me, I wasn't asked to accompany Ossius. This, of course, was no surprise in itself. I hadn't come to the New Rome to be a philosophical emissary for Constantine. No, I had simply come to be with him, pursue my own affairs, and help him, perhaps, as an afterthought. Still, it bothered me. There was a time when I would have been the one to go, a time when Constantine trusted me above all. But that was a time long before. Then, after the vision and dream, and after I had refused to give the oration signaling the Christ's victory, Ossius and the other priests edged their way inward toward the center of Constantine's innermost circle. After Milvian Bridge, their position was secure and mine was not. Even though I shouldn't have, I felt betrayed, jealous.

I say all this, I suppose, to explain why I don't know many of the details about what happened in Alexandria that late fall and onward into winter. What I do know with any certainty is that Alexander, along with Athanasius, was able to convince Ossius that the dispute between the bishop and the priest was far more than *mere philosophical wrangling* as Constantine had claimed. In fact, as Athanasius made amply clear, the matter was paramount to Christian understanding and therefore to the salvation of the whole world.

In the end, a synod composed of Alexander and many other Egyptian bishops, with Ossius at the helm, condemned Arius and several of his colleagues *in absentia*, including Arius' dear friend Euzoius. They were condemned for heresy. Rather than accepting the proposition that Arius' thesis was simply another way of looking at the one mystery of the Christ, they resolutely affirmed the Son's essential Divinity.

Perched in Nicomedia, Arius refused to surrender. Understandably, he was upset. But when Eusebius received the news, he told him not to worry.

"Easy for *you* to say," Arius countered. "They haven't taken *your* church and *your* people away."

"No, they haven't," returned the bishop. "But what's mine is yours, dear man. And what I have is far superior to Alexandria, despite its history and magnificence."

"True," Arius agreed. Nevertheless, it was *his*, he insisted.

Eusebius reasoned on. "Whatever they say, you mustn't submit. They no longer have jurisdiction over you. In fact, they haven't for quite some time now."

When Constantine heard Eusebius' line of reasoning, he strongly disagreed. There are not *many* jurisdictions, he told me, in the one Church. There is only one. Perhaps each ruling bishop differently and independently expresses it, but it is one nonetheless.

"So what do you propose to do?" I asked him one evening when we were dining together.

"I'm not sure," he responded. "But I have an idea." He looked worn with worry.

I invited him to share it.

"What's required is a gathering on a large scale, a council that will truly reflect the totality of the one Church."

"With *all* the bishops?" I asked, doubtful of the idea.

"If possible," he said.

Constantine, never afraid to consider his affairs on the grandest of scales, determined to summon a council that would finally end all the bickering.

By chance, I was there when he gave the order some weeks later. We sat together with Ossius in the great hall of the palace. Eusebius was there, as well as several other priests. He had just been complaining as he often did about the rude behavior of the Alexandrians and the consequent ill-treatment of Arius' allies—*his* allies. Constantia sat nearby dripping with agreement along with Basiliana, Constantine's sister-in-law. Then quite to their surprise, Constantine stood from his golden chair, and towering over them, he boomed, "If everything is so horrible, then there shall be a meeting to end all meetings!" Loudly he went on to declare, as if by command, that the Church would be one.

I glanced over at Eusebius who suddenly wilted. It wasn't what he had hoped for.

A moment later, he was gone. As he breezed out of the great hall with Constantia, Basiliana, and the others in tow, I heard him lament that there would surely be another condemnation as he knew there wasn't enough episcopal support to grant Arius freedom, let alone his church in the Baucalis.

Behind him, where I still sat by Constantine, Ossius immediately confirmed his own support for the proposed council.

"Good," nodded Constantine, quite soberly. "You'll preside over its course."

In the next few days, Constantine suggested that Ancyra, the chief city of Galatia, should host the council. Accordingly, we sent out invitations to all bishops throughout the Empire, both in the East and West, in order to call them together.

But with the warming of winter and the coming of spring, Constantine changed his mind. He decided it would be far easier for the bishops to travel to a port city. Consequently, we sent out a new invitation, this time calling them to Nicaea, which is a hard day's ride from Nicomedia.

Then he rested, feeling reassured that all would work out well. The One, he believed, had operated through him to unify the Empire. Now, the same Divinity would move to unify the Church.

Twenty-three: The Council

Spring and summer 325 A.D.

BISHOPS, PRIESTS, AND DEACONS, as well as many others following along in train, began arriving in Nicaea of Bithynia in May. They came from every corner of the Empire and world, from all the churches in Europe, Africa, and Asia, from Syria and Cilicia, and from Phoenicia and the distant land of the Arabs. Still more distant was the one Persian bishop who came and the one Scythian. From the opposite side of the world they arrived from Hispania and Gaul. The prelate of the old imperial city, that is the bishop of Rome Sylvester, was not able to attend because of his age. Even so, he sent the two priests Victor and Victorinus in his stead. Closer still to Nicaea were those from Pontus and Galatia, Pamphylia, Cappadocia, and Phrygia. From the immediate west came the Thracians and Macedonians, Achaians and Epirots. From the south large parties arrived from Libya and Egypt, and from my own city, Carthage.

There were many who compared the gathering of men to that occasion in the deeds of the apostles when Peter, inspired by the Spirit of God, addressed an assembly of men gathered from throughout the entire created world. Gone was the hubris of Babel. God was drawing men together again in newfound harmony. Certainly, the hopes were as high—that the one God would once again breathe a kind of divine unity upon those gathered, the three hundred-some bishops, and all the others who attended for a variety of reasons and in different capacities.

All of these arrived by conveyance of the public system. Constantine generously provided for its usage—for horses and wagons, mules for baggage, and in many instances, travel by boat across Our Sea.

We—Constantine, Ossius, the rest of the emperor's entourage, and I—arrived in Nicaea toward the end of May. We traveled leisurely from Nicomedia early one morning and passed through the North Gate of the city upon our arrival the following day. In a way, Nicaea is much like Nicomedia, though on a much smaller scale. It too was built upon the shores of the Sea of Marmara. Likewise, it is surrounded by towering walls that have given the city a sense of security ever since its founding some six hundred years ago, shortly after Alexander of Macedon died. As I came to discover in one evening's conversation or another, the city was named after the wife of a prominent general. She had been called Nica in honor of the goddess, the patroness of victory in both war and peace. In Nicaea, this woman is reputed to have been as beautiful as Helen of Troy. I cannot say, of course. I can confirm that Constantine looked upon her, or the story of the woman Nica itself, as a kind of portent of what would come: victory's peace after war.

As we passed into the city through the low arch of the North Gate, Constantine was in high spirits and full of hope. Not only was he eager for what was ahead—peace in the Church—but he was also pleased with what had already transpired. Work was flourishing in his new capital. Like the busy hive of bees in Virgil, builders were rapidly constructing a New Rome that would last forever. As he reminded me on several occasions, the strong arm of the Almighty had unified the Empire. Now the same Divinity would work through him and the bishops to bring unity to the Church. When this was accomplished, the one truth of the one God would act to enlighten all men instead of serving as a point of derision for those who refused to believe.

The actual situation in Nicaea challenged this confidence and hope on the very first day of our arrival.

We were sitting in the Old Palace of Nicaea when Constantine received word that a number of bishops, priests, and deacons, along with many non-ordained men, self-described philosophers and dialecticians, were engaged in what several termed "metaphysical contests"—in other words, the very same intellectual wrangling they had been gathered together to eradicate. I was well aware of these contests. I'd spent many a day in Alexandria and Nicomedia engaged in similar matches of intellect. In the end, I had come to loathe them, these battles of words, without quite knowing why. Now, I think I understand. But of that, later.

At that time, Constantine demanded surveillance of the nature and severity of these disputes. Consequently, he called Ossius and, to my surprise, me, and asked us to go and see what was happening in the newly constructed church of Holy Wisdom where they met.

It was then that I saw Athanasius for the first time. There he was, a deacon now, with that odd dark auburn hair—for a Copt—and those brilliant eyes, heatedly engaging Eusebius of Nicomedia. As I earlier said, Theophilus, I didn't hear the details of their conversation. Although I knew Eusebius— indeed to the point of disgust—I didn't then know Athanasius personally, and so, I didn't know to listen to him. Nevertheless, Ossius and I meandered around the church attempting to appraise the situation for Constantine.

After some time, we returned and reported what we had seen. Ossius was the first to speak. "My dear emperor ..." he began, attempting to lessen the blow of what we'd witnessed. "Where there's a negative, a positive's soon to follow."

"And the negative?" Constantine demanded.

"As the rumor goes. It seems everyone is involved in a variety of disputes dealing with highly obscure metaphysical puzzles."

"Everyone?"

"I'm afraid so," answered Ossius, apologetically.

I added, "Your dear friend Eusebius is at the center of the fray."

"And there's more, my Lord," Ossius said.

"What more could there possibly be?" asked Constantine, deflated.

"It's taken a very personal turn."

"That's new? Ha!" he disclaimed. "It's been personal from the begin- ning—and to their shame!"

"True," agreed Ossius. "Nonetheless, now that they've gathered together, it seems even worse."

"How so?"

"They openly insult each other. And some have made threats, violent threats, to have their opponents physically harmed."

"Has there been open fighting?"

"Not yet."

"I shouldn't hope it'll last for long, though," I declared. "You recall how it was in Alexandria, right? We always escaped—and you, to your credit, Constantine, for you could have crushed anyone. But I remember how many times sharply thrown words led to sharply thrown objects—elbows to guts, fists to cheekbones, boots to shins. And do you recall the one time when Detrimos of Chios claimed he could prove the whole of the cosmos actually existed upon the exterior of his eyeballs? It led to brawls so severe that the governor had to forbid discussions of that sort in the market for two weeks. And that, the gods forbid, was like taking away the city's supply of wine!"

"I do recall it," said Constantine, revealing a slight smile, as if those days when we were both younger and when the cares of the world had not yet engulfed our souls were superior to these.

For a moment, there was quiet between the three of us. Then I commented, "It's too bad. It seems the more urgently we seek the truth, the more and more distant it becomes."

This, of course, was more a commentary on my own internal condition than on what was occurring in Nicaea. Beneath it all, in the depths of my soul, I still yearned for the light of the Real just as I had when a young man. But in the fog of midlife I suffered from that disease of soul we call cynicism, the near relative of skepticism, which like Janus looks both ways toward the light and toward darkness.

Constantine ignored my general pessimism, as he had grown used to doing. He had found the truth and intended to serve it fully. Feverishly anxious for the good of the Church and Empire, he barked, "However that may be for you, Arnobius, this childish fighting must come to an end!" He called for his guard.

Ossius, however, knowing the emperor's mind, intervened. "Lord," he admonished, "you mustn't!"

"Why not?" bellowed Constantine. "If it's a fight they want, then it's a fight they'll receive!"

"But it wouldn't be right!"

Constantine heaved a sigh, sitting down once again upon his throne. "No, I suppose not." Then glancing down, he inquired, "What's your advice, then, Ossius?"

"Patience, my lord, forbearance." It was how Ossius had always treated Constantine.

In the end, the emperor resolved upon humility and patience. He would not fight fire with fire. Instead, he said he would utilize water to quench the fire. For of all the four elements, he explained, water is the one that always seeks the lowest place, overcoming rock and fire with meekness and long-suffering.

With his resolution, Constantine's confidence revived. All would work out well in accordance with the divine will.

In the end, this confidence proved to be prophetic. Some days into the so-called metaphysical wrangling, an old man, a martyr-confessor who had lost the use of both hands during the former persecution, entered the church. He walked through the crowd of disputants even as the Christ had done when threatened by the mob in his hometown. Having made it to the other side of the crowd, he stopped just short of one philosopher who had been making sport of several of the more learned bishops and priests.

"May I speak with you?" he asked, humbly.

Gazing at him, the philosopher agreed with a wicked grin and eyes that betrayed his hope to cut down the old man like an enemy of war.

Later, many admitted to fearing for the old man. He was, after all, a simple man of little education. But little did they know, Theophilus. I was there and was astonished at what followed.

The old man began with a simple command. "In the name of Jesus the Christ, listen to the truth!"

The philosopher made no verbal reply. Yet suddenly, as if strongly influenced by the other man's mere presence, his manner shifted slightly. He was like a plant turning east toward the rising of the sun.

The old man continued. "There's one God who made heaven and earth." As he said this, he raised his now-lame hands toward the sky as if to trace its breadth, and then he carved out the circle of the globe.

He went on. "This one God gave breath to man—your breath, mine! For I ask you, wise man, what are we in ourselves? We're a mixture of earth and water, that's what! We're mud and yet we live! How do we live? We live, O Philosopher, by God's breath! Consider it! He has made this mud to live by his very own breath!"

To everyone's surprise, the philosopher listened intently and considered his words as the man fearlessly kept on.

"Once that breath seemed to lessen, covered over with layers of our own mud, God sent his Word and Wisdom, his one and only Son, who was born of a virgin, and gave us life for a second time. Do you believe it?"

The philosopher didn't say.

"You should believe it, my friend; you are beloved of God! The Son has set us free from the muddy suffocation of sin and death. And now, if only you'll receive it, you may live by the Holy Spirit of God once again—by God's own breath!"

The great hall was silent as the martyr-confessor kept on. His words were nothing logical. His was not an argument constructed dialectically. Rather, what he said, what he intended to convey, was simple truth. It was alive, this truth, and by it, the old man was living.

Then, in the midst of a silence that had momentarily vanquished all the wrangling, the old man issued his challenge a second time. "Do you believe?"

Everyone in the great hall absorbed the full force of that one simple question. *Do you believe?*

When I answered it for myself in the quiet of my own mind, I found I *didn't* believe, Theophilus. I couldn't, I judged. There were far too many questions.

But with the philosopher, it was different, for demurely he gave his affirmative answer. When he did, there was no longer any of the former pride. Hubris, it seemed, and the desire to outdo everyone, had vanished. Humbly, he added, "It *must* be so."

The old man responded, "If you believe that it's so, then rise and follow me to receive the seal of this holy faith."

He did. The philosopher followed him to be baptized.

Before he did so, he turned to his own fellows and confessed, "For so long, men, I have argued and argued. I've set clever words against other words in dialectical fashion, and I've defeated arguments with my own rhetorical skill. But now that this old and venerable man has set the power of the one truth against mere words, I feel powerless and defeated. He has a way of life, whole and entire, whereas I only have arguments—empty speech it seems. As for me, I now leave sophistry behind. Rhetoric is dead. And I trust I'll be wealthier for doing so."

With that, the philosopher turned away along with several of his friends and followed the old man who led them to the waters of purification and illumination. Later, someone reported that he rejoiced and gave glory to God at having been finally vanquished.

In the end, this story inspired Constantine to take a certain path of action. He too would set aside all the disagreements, disputes, and personal accusations, and simply assume unity in the power of God. He himself would believe for everyone.

I suggested this might not be the most effective plan of attack. For one man it had worked, I admitted, but for the many gathered there in Nicaea to settle substantial philosophical differences, it would never work.

He went ahead with his plan anyway. And I have to say, that despite my skepticism, I admired him for this.

Early in June, Constantine made his first official appearance at the council.

As for me, I had already been in and out, observing a variety of meetings, usually at the side of Ossius, the emperor's chief representative and president of the council. By then, Theophilus, I had warmed up to him more, even if I didn't accept his beliefs. I had come to know that he was truly a generous and open man. On the day of Constantine's entrance, I was in the great hall sitting just behind Ossius and several other of the chief men, including Alexander of Alexandria and the two Eusebii, among others. Athanasius sat next to me behind Alexander. Up to that point, we'd hardly spoken at any length aside from the demands of courtesy.

That day, the bishops had been discussing several matters. One, an ongoing debate, was about the correct day to celebrate the resurrection of the Christ. The other was a heated discussion about virginity.

Regarding the latter, one man stood, and citing the authority of the martyr Methodius of Olympus and his *Symposium on Virginity*, he asserted that those ordained in the service of the Christ should remain virgins in order to be fully dedicated to the Lord. If married, they should live chastely. The response? There was murmuring all around. Some assented; some, however, vehemently disagreed. Then Paphnutius of Thebes stood. He was a witness who had lost his right eye and had been condemned to the mines in the last persecution. Constantine had a special affection for him. He used to call Paphnutius to his side in order to gain wisdom from him and kiss the sunken socket where his eye had once been before Rome had plucked it out. "Men," Paphnutius admonished, "it is not ours to burden our fellow servants. Virginity was no command of the Lord. And certainly when Paul advised it as a superior way of life, he neither meant it for all men nor did he issue his advice as a command. Consequently, in the name of the Lord, I trust we'll not overstep the bounds of practical wisdom and demand virginity of all clergy. If a man is unmarried before confirmed in orders, then let him remain so. If not, he shouldn't be separated from the woman with whom he has been made one in flesh." In the end, however, the council voted against Paphnutius' position as one can read in the council's canons.

But that vote, Theophilus, was weeks away. On that day, or thereabouts, when the emperor made his first appearance, the bishops had yet to cast their votes. In fact, despite having been urged toward simplicity and away from the complexity of words and dialectical disputation, there was yet more arguing, and insults flew like missiles on a battlefield. As a result, bad feelings and ill will grew. Into this atmosphere, Constantine entered boldly as a demigod set on making peace. He was arrayed in dazzling garments that glowed from within and shone from without. His robe was a deep purple, embroidered with the brilliant splendor of gold and studded with the sparkling glory of precious stones. Rather than his usual retinue, an armed guard, he casually strolled into the hall surrounded by allies in the faith he had come to embrace. Bidding them farewell, he silently walked across the great hall toward a low chair made of gold, his eyes downcast.

Once the emperor had reclined at the invitation of Eusebius of Caesarea and the other bishops, the same Eusebius briefly addressed the council, invoking the blessing of almighty God and admonishing those present to proceed toward unity with an attitude of peace and charity above all.

Then Constantine stood again to speak, and I with him, as he had asked me to interpret for him. You see, Theophilus, although his Greek had grown more functional over the years, he thought it would be best on this occasion to speak through an interpreter. As for why he chose me, the reason was simple. Everyone knew I was neutral, that I didn't have a position on the Christ, and so I favored neither Arius nor Alexander. This bolstered the emperor's own professed neutrality.

"My dear friends," he began, gesturing to all the bishops and other men present. "It has been my greatest desire to see you gathered together as one. Presently this desire is satisfied thanks to the mercy of the One who loves and unites us all. But more. I feel bound to express the highest gratitude to the almighty Ruler, because presently we are united not only as one body but also in common sentiment. This, brothers, is no small achievement."

Constantine paused to allow this alleged reality time to sink into the hearts and minds of those present—what was truly more of a hope, and so as coming from the emperor, a declaration of how things ought to be. Then, with eyes closed and as though praying to the Divinity, he continued.

"I pray, therefore, that no treacherous adversary may from this point forward interfere with this newly achieved happy state of the one Church. Now that the tyrants have been vanquished, now that those persecutors of the saints who follow this holy religion have been scattered by the strong right arm of the Lord, may that spirit which delights in evil never again draw up an army against the one Church of God."

He opened his eyes and glanced around the great hall. My eyes followed and everyone's gaze was a mirror to our own.

"Sacred men!" he called out. "We can't allow ourselves to give fodder to those who would malign the faith. No longer shall we invite blasphemous calumny by fighting among ourselves. To do so is a great evil! Indeed, in my judgment intestine strife within the Church of God is far more evil and dangerous than any other kind of war or conflict. That's why I have called this gathering. As the instrument of God for peace and unity, I have deemed it necessary to put disagreements behind us and move forward together in unity. Your work is to follow me. Delay not, my dear friends! Delay not in discarding the causes of disunion! Embrace the principle of peace! This will please the supreme God while at the same time bringing great joy to my heart, which yearns for peace, as I have been fighting one battle or another for the greater portion of my life."

When Constantine was finished with the body of his oration, he motioned that I could resume my seat. I did. Then, in mostly fluid Greek and with a tone that was full of both hope and concern, he made a gentle request to the bishops that, as I have said, I doubted from the first moment of its inception.

"My dear fellows," he said, "I've heard that you have grievances with one another. This, of course, is only natural. We are men after all; our natures are disordered."

Athanasius, sitting next to me, leaned over and remarked, "That's a fine piece of understatement."

I nodded, thinking of the ignoble horse in Plato's *Phaedrus*.

The emperor continued. "Because of this, I wish to make a simple request, one which will eventually prove, I trust, to be of immense utility to both you and me, and hence, to the whole of our fellowship."

The bishops waited, wondering, I presumed, what he'd ask. Then, the command. "If you have any grievance with your brother, please bring it forward to me in the form of a written petition."

With that, Constantine was abruptly finished.

As if on cue, a page stood to announce that the meeting would reconvene in two hours' time. At that time, he explained, the emperor expected to receive the petitions of each bishop, the complaints of each, whether personal or doctrinal in nature.

Meanwhile Athanasius turned to me and asked, "Do you know the emperor's mind?"

I could sense he was puzzled as I imagine most were. Still, I didn't reveal Constantine's plan. "No," I said, despite knowing.

"Doubtlessly he has something beneficial in mind," he suggested.

"Doubtlessly," I agreed.

Then, bidding me farewell for the moment, Athanasius stepped forward to speak with Alexander.

Two hours later, the same page gathered all the petitions and placed them before Constantine. I could see that the bishops waited anxiously to learn how the emperor would proceed. I'm sure everyone hoped Constantine would read his own petition first so that its grievance would take precedence in that afternoon's discussion. But none of that happened.

Constantine shuffled the petitions until he had an ordered stack sitting before him upon a long gilded table that had been set up during the intervening two hours. Then he said, "You see this pile of petitions sitting before me?" The bishops and the others nodded, quickly glancing at each other and back to the emperor. "It is this which is the enemy of the Church. This stack of petitions is the wall that divides one man and faction from another." Constantine tossed up his hands before exclaiming, "May it no longer be! From this moment forward, I banish your dissension! May your grievances with one another be gone!"

With that, he literally set them aside. From the center of the table, he shoved the stack of petitions to his left side. "There," he motioned. "Now we have set aside our differences."

A gasp erupted throughout the great hall. As might be expected, the many present were astonished at the emperor's behavior. They couldn't believe he'd simply set aside their substantial differences. Beyond this, however, and more importantly, he had humiliated them. For some this led to an authentic humility, and so the result was positive as they came to see things anew. But for many others, most perhaps, his act served to ignite the passion of dissension.

Nevertheless, the emperor was used to making difficult decisions. In his mind, he knew what he must do in order to accomplish the all-important goal of unity. Consequently, ignoring the factious hubbub, whether for good or ill, Constantine shifted to his left and called a soldier to come take the petitions away. "Burn them," he commanded so that all could hear.

He did. The soldier took them outside to a courtyard and set them afire.

Back in the great hall, Constantine declared, "Now, we can act as one."

The crowd of churchmen, however, belied the veracity of his assertion—as did Athanasius sitting next to me.

"Indeed," he whispered, his voice full of irony. "We'll be one in body but not in mind. And where there's no true agreement, there's only the semblance of unity. What's required, what the Lord asks for, is a substantial unity of heart and mind."

"Makes sense," I offered, but only to be agreeable.

Before us, the emperor stood and dismissed all the men after ordering them to rejoin the following day in order to begin work on a statement of belief that all men could accept.

After everyone began to disperse, Athanasius faced me once again and began to speak with me at length.

Twenty-four: The Homoousion

Summer 325 A.D.

ATHANASIUS' EYES FLASHED with fire. They were always like that—a fire that consumed all before its path, with an intensity I could never quite fathom and a compassion that revealed true sympathy. He cared for me. I couldn't deny it.

"Arnobius, may I get your view on something?" he politely asked.

I gave him permission, if hesitantly.

"How do you think true knowledge leads to fullness of life?"

O gods, I thought. My initial urge was to say I didn't really have time for such a conversation, that I had to go attend some important matter or another. But I didn't. Instead, I told him that I didn't know. I told him that at one point in my life I thought I did, that knowledge of the Good as we find it in Plato would lead to union with the One. Soon, however, I foundered. I had changed. "It's knowing this truth and living it that seems so impossible," I finished.

He told me that he agreed with much of what I had said, both in terms of its substance and in the difficulty of practice. Then he explained his own position.

"We are revived as images of the one God," he said, "the one Good. But how? In short, it is faith itself, a kind of knowledge that mirrors truth, that comes to serve as a true reflection of the One. This is where the Greek tradition falters," he explained. "For in order to be revived, one must have a correct understanding of the Logos, the Word."

"How do you mean?" I asked. By then I was curious, despite myself.

"I mean this—the Word is the perfect image of the One."

"But that's long been part of the philosophical tradition," I countered, thinking of the divine Mind and Reason, which are emanations of the One.

"True," he allowed. "Yet there's a significant difference. We must not see the Word as some abstraction, some *thing* or speech or underlying rational structure of reality."

"Why not?" I challenged.

"Because it's not so. The Word is not an impersonal abstraction. Like your voice and mine, the divine voice is full of life. It's like when you yourself think or speak. Your thoughts and voice carry you wherever they go; they *are* you, fully alive, fully personal. As such, the Word *is* the One who restores our own faded image. When by faith the Word dwells in our midst in mind and heart, then the living image of the One purifies us in such a way that we ourselves come to reflect the Divinity. This is how true knowledge leads to fullness of life. Thanks to the Word, we grow to be what we were intended to be by the Creator. It's a re-creation of sorts. Man comes again to be the image of God."

But that's just the problem, I thought. However appealing was his idea, the flux of life seemed to disprove its reality. I said so, shrugging. Then as always, the problem for me was the seemingly unbridgeable gap between the One and the many.

Noticing my frustration, Athanasius didn't press. He smiled and said, "Enough for now. I suppose one can have too much of philosophy in a day."

I agreed.

Then he asked, "How long have you interpreted for the emperor?"

"Oh, I usually don't," I demurred.

"No?"

"Today was more of a …"

"So you don't normally work with him?"

"Not as much anymore."

"But you used to?"

"A long time ago," I revealed. "Once, we were very good friends."

"Are you originally from Nicomedia?"

"No," I laughed. "I'm not. And the gods only know why I ended up there." I thought of my father, Buteo, and explained how I had met Constantine in Alexandria decades before.

"But you're not Alexandrian," he observed.

"No," I disclosed, "you're right. I'm from Carthage."

"Of course you are," he said. "It's the Latin accent of your Greek."

"Is it bad?"

"Not at all. It's just not exactly Greek."

"I suppose so," I grinned.

"Do you miss Carthage as much as I do Alexandria?" he asked.

"I do," I admitted.

"It's not that I'm attached," he clarified. "I'll go wherever God wants me to go."

I thought about my own travels. Originally, I suppose they were for God—to know God. Now, I wondered what they were for?

"Still," he went on, "it's my home, it's where I belong. I love the people of Alexandria."

"I understand," I said, wishing I had the same clarity of mind and motivation instead of my own muddled thoughts and life.

He smiled, his eyes flashing compassion.

Soon after, we said goodbye and went our separate ways. I presume Athanasius went off to confer with Alexander. As for me, I went on a long walk and thought about Athanasius and considered what he had said.

In the following days, as June passed into July, the council worked toward an agreeable conclusion on several issues including, most importantly, the nature of the Son relative to that of the Father. For my part, Theophilus, I soon grew weary of listening to their discussion. It's not that it wasn't interesting in itself—it *was*. The problem for me was the scarcity of progress. They debated the same minute points again and again. First one of the Alexandrians would make their case—Alexander or Athanasius of Alexandria, Hermogenes of Cappadocia, Ossius of Cordoba, or even Victor of Rome, among others. Then one of Eusebius' party would defend: Arius, Euzoius, Ptolemais, Theonas, Theognis of Nicaea, or Eusebius of Nicomedia himself.

For a time this proved interesting. However distasteful, Eusebius' party was rather ingenious. To give just one example, one day sometime after the council had been moved from the smaller church of Holy Wisdom to the larger *Senatus Domus*, the Old Meeting House, Eusebius challenged Alexander to find a simple layman untrained in philosophy to explain the Alexandrian position. Alexander consented, but only if Eusebius would do the same. Eusebius agreed. Later on, they met, each with his lay representative.

"Shall he go first?" Eusebius asked. He motioned to a diminutive man who sat on a plain wooden bench behind him.

"If you wish," Alexander offered.

Eusebius beckoned him and the man walked to the center of the hall. "Don't be nervous my good fellow," he coached. "Just give your understanding of Jesus, the Son of God."

For a moment, the man looked as though he might faint with the fear of speaking before so many important men. But he didn't. Instead, with what seemed like the sudden possession of a god, he began to sing:

> *God, the Monad, ungenerate, unborn—*
> > *he without parts; Logos and Wisdom, internal.*
> *The created Logos, in contrast, external—*
> > *the Son from nothing, generated by God's will.*
> *Begotten, he was, but not like God—*
> > *not in being; the one a man, the other divine.*
> *The Creator, uncreated, producing—*
> > *not so the Son, a creature, produced by choice.*
> *The Dyad, existing from before time—*
> > *by whom the Father creates all things in time.*
> *Glory to the Father, to the One—*
> > *Father, because Son; and glory also to the Son.*

There the man stopped in his starkly simple yet verbosely complex recitation, and I for one was astonished.

I had long heard of this song. People said that Arius had put his philosophy to verse—to Sotadean verse after a man called Sotades who had long ago written verses of a bawdy nature, sarcastic and obscene, the kind you might hear in a tavern washed down with several cups of undiluted wine. Although it wasn't impressive in terms of poetic specimen, the song seemed to have accomplished Arius' desired end, for this poor and uneducated man was able to recite his complex teaching in just a few simple verses.

Once the man was finished, Eusebius haughtily turned to Alexander and invited him to have his own man step forward. "Don't feel too bad," he taunted, "if your man can't convey your position with similar precision."

Alexander balked; his face grew flush. It was the first time I saw him come near to losing his temper. "But your man doesn't understand!" he protested. "He's memorized your creed like a child memorizes any song!"

"Enough of your excuses!" snapped Eusebius. "Let's see your man."

Alexander refused. He said his man hadn't memorized anything, and he'd be made to look like a fool.

"Well," huffed Eusebius, "it appears our view at least has *this* to its advantage—even the unschooled can learn it. And why?" He turned to the other men present at this particular session. "Simple," he advanced. "Because it's no violation of common sense. The Christ as God by nature? Pah! It's laughable! Contemptible! It's contrary to logic and any levelheaded reading of the divine oracles!"

"Perhaps simpler," retorted Alexander, flustered, "but untrue! And besides, if we're seeking the simple, we'd worship a rock rather than the divine Spirit! For God, all is possible—not merely the logical, but that which surpasses reason as well!"

Eusebius laughed. "Beyond reason? How is *that* possible?"

Alexander attempted to explain.

But on that note, I slipped out of the gathering into the streets of Nicaea. I'd heard it all before. Now they'd retrace their arguments. They'd go back and forth, each side adamantly asserting the truth of its own position. However intriguing it was, I was sick of it. And so, leaving the meeting hall, I hoped to escape it. Yet oddly, no matter where I went, I couldn't get away from what I'd left behind. It was as though the whole argument were haunting me like a wicked spirit. Everywhere I could hear one person or another—now a man, now a woman, now a small child—singing that song Arius had devised to spread his doctrine. *God, the One, ungenerate ... in contrast, the created Logos ... from nothing, generated by God's will.* Others answered in jealous reproach, protective of the divine union of Father and Son. And I? As always, I was unsure. Consequently, the certainty of both sides haunted me.

At first I walked along the walls of Nicaea. I wasn't quite sure where I was going except for I wanted to drive the whole controversy out of mind for at least a few hours of mental peace. Eventually I found the theatre, and realizing that something was going on inside, I paid for a pass and went in to see the spectacle. As it happened, the show was a display of various hunting skills. You've seen the kind, Theophilus. A man stands at one end while an animal, say an antelope, boar, or another powerful beast, escapes through a small gate at the other end. The man throws a net, shoots an arrow, or hurls a javelin through the air, the javelin whizzing until it reaches its desired end. Cleanly, it enters the animal's flesh with a punch, and in moments, it dies. It's horrible. But the many enjoy it—the sport, the action, the competition, if one can term it such.

After taking all I could stomach—which turned out to be less than half an hour—I left the theatre and turned south. Once I came to the southern gate called the Great Gate, I walked on toward the countryside. By this time, the council's competition had mostly passed out of mind. In its place, I thought about my old home in Carthage and my family's estate south of the city and decided I'd much rather be there than in Nicaea listening to these discussions which never seemed to ...

But there they were again! The debates were haunting me! I could hear them, the disputants, arguing and arguing. I thought about the absurdity of it all. Why did the one mediator need to be both God and man as the Alexandrians insisted? Why couldn't the Christ be created? To me it seemed that Arius and his side made the better half of the argument. Didn't their view protect the One?

But what did I know? Besides, what concern did the One really have for us? For me? The One was distant, silent. That's what I believed.

Still, Theophilus, I wanted to know. Despite my own skepticism, I cared. Perhaps it was possible after all. Perhaps Alexander and his men were right.

Sometime in the middle of July, I put the question to Athanasius, for by that time we had come to be rather decent friends sitting next to each other day after day.

"Why," I asked, "is it so necessary that the Son, the one mediator as you call him, be both true God and true man?"

His reply was to the point: "So that we men can become divine."

I grinned. "Even *if* that's possible," I countered, "Arius' way seems satisfactory."

"What? That the Son serves as a moral example, exemplifying the way to God?"

"Sure, why not?"

Athanasius shook his head. For him, it was a matter of fact. "We've had many moral examples," he explained. "Recall Socrates, or Diogenes the Cynic, or Epictetus the Stoic, or more recently, Plotinus, who was famous in Rome. They're not enough, Arnobius. What we men need is the God-man— not one who has merely approached the divine in whatever mystical manner."

"But why?" I begged, not convinced.

He thought for a moment before declaring, "In order to truly restore us, to replace our own corruption and mortality with incorruption and immortality. There can be no mere approximations for these. Presently, we men suffer corruption as disease in our bodies and vice in our souls; mortal, we all die. This is not what God intended. No, he created us for the opposite. God made us for fullness of life, for himself—the infinite God. I ask you, Arnobius, is there any other being which can restore what we have lost?"

"I can't say," I admitted.

"You're right—on our own it's hard to know. But we believe the incorrupt and immortal Word of God became a mortal man so that we might become divine. We know this because it was revealed."

I thought about this for a moment before shrugging and confessing I didn't know. But more, I gave Athanasius all my old arguments. The idea of the God-man as mediator smacked of all the old myths, I claimed. And how could the One suffer, or even the image of the One?

Nevertheless, Athanasius argued as though there were a certain logical necessity to his position. To that extent, it made sense to me. Yet so too did Arius and the Eusebians. This was my problem—I could hardly make up my mind. Both sides were reasonable, both coherent. Moreover, both sides marshaled passages from the sacred oracles. Not that I accepted the latter, but they were then becoming fashionable in higher social circles, and so they were coming to carry a certain authoritative weight, even as Homer and the other poets had always done among the educated elite. But which side was right? For me, Theognis the bishop of Nicaea was correct when he declared that to speak accurately about God is to walk on the clouds. There we were, Theophilus, foolishly attempting that very walk. Or so I thought.

Finally, not many days after my conversation with Athanasius, Ossius suggested—at the urging of Constantine and Alexander—that the term *homoousios* be used to bar any ambivalent explanation of the nature or substance or being of the Son. The problem was that many of the council fathers objected to this word—not least of whom there were Arius and Eusebius of Nicomedia, among others.

"The term is unsound!" cried Eusebius, rather theatrically. "Suggesting the Son is of the same substance as the Father is to suggest that God's simple being is liable to division! May we never teach this! It's no better than what the Gnostics have done!"

"Exactly!" Arius agreed, dramatically tossing his hands aside. "The Gnostic Valentinus long ago argued that the Dyad was thrown forward by the Monad. Imagine that! It's absurd! As if a gushing torrent! And Sallius was condemned for saying the same Monad had parts, as if the One were a son-father or a father-son of the same divided substance."

The historian of the Church, Eusebius of Caesaraea, joined the fray by suggesting it was actually Mani who had spoiled the idea of consubstantiality when he had argued that God was some kind of rarefied, light filled matter capable of separation and distribution.

The other Eusebius added, "Paul of Samosota was condemned some seventy-five years ago for the use of the very same term. God is of one substance, he claimed, revealing the one God-being under different aspects: God-Father, God-Son, and God-Holy Spirit."

George of Laodicea interjected, "If God the Father is the creator of all, then the Son too is created. If this is so, and yet they're somehow the same substance, that is, generated being, then reasoning backwards, the Father too must be created. But what lunacy! Let them be separated! Let there be no confusion!"

"I agree!" affirmed Paulinus of Tyre. "The Christ is a second God. He's not the first—and thus not the same in being. He has become God even as we shall. George is right!" he declared. "Let there be no confusion, no mixing of the first and second Gods!"

At this point, however, there was much confusion among the Eusebians, who sat along wooden benches on one side, and the Alexandrians, who sat on the other side. Many chanted, "Same in being, homoousios!" Others vociferously asserted the opposite. "Not one! Not like!" They stirred, stamped feet, and shook fists. For a time, Theophilus, I feared these church-men might give themselves over to violence and join in a brawl.

Before this could happen, however, an old man, another bishop and one I didn't recognize, stepped forward and soberly granted the truth of the Eusebian point. "There must be no confusion," he said.

Everyone grew quiet because of his age, if nothing else.

"Yet," he went on, "your conception of the Son as created drags the Word into the world of corruption, of sin, of suffering. The Son is a creature, you say. The Son is fallen like the rest of us."

He sighed as he glanced around the room eying each of us. Then simply, he begged, "How can a creature *possibly* save?"

It was then that Alexander stood forward. "You're right," he admitted to Eusebius and the others. "You are right in suggesting that this word homoousios has been abused in the past. Or better said it has been used differently than we would like to now employ it."

"But won't that introduce confusion?" demanded George of Laodicea, reiterating his major point.

"No, it will force clarification."

"How?" asked another.

Alexander answered. "By saying the Son is homoousios, that is, consubstantial or of one being with the Father, we declare it is God who creates and God who saves. When man went astray, it was God alone out of his great love for us who deemed it right to restore. Consequently, the Word became flesh so that flesh might share in the one life of the Word, in the one life of the Son, true God."

Standing, Arius balked. "But your own philosophy runs contrary to Alexandrian custom! Hear what your predecessor Dionysius taught."

We all listened while Arius read from a scroll with his usual charm. Then, summarizing its major points, he declared, "Dionysius said that the Son does not belong by nature to the Father, but by his own nature is alien from the Father, just as the vine itself is other than the planter of the vine, and the ship itself is other than the shipbuilder."

"I admit it," allowed Alexander, sighing with a heavy heart. "Dionysius did say that. And in humility I admit that I too have made erroneous statements regarding the nature of the Son. Yet this is the very point upon which this controversy turns. We—all of us—must recognize our need to repent. If we've said what is incorrect, what is blasphemous in the sight of God, we must exchange our words of mere opinion for those of divine revelation. For the scriptures declare the Word is true God. And as the beloved disciple taught, this same Word became flesh—not some external, secondary Logos as you teach."

"But the scriptures also say otherwise of the Word," Arius countered.

To which Alexander made reply.

Then Eusebius.

And Hermogenes.

George followed.

In my mind, they imitated a dog madly chasing its own tail. One side argued logically. The other responded in like fashion. Then one made an argument from the divine oracles, and the other rebutted it from the same. Round they spun. A creature; not a creature. Different in being; of the same being. Not God; true God. I wondered where in the name of all the gods this mess would find its end.

Finally, at the bidding of Constantine, who desired unity and peace above all, Ossius, with the help of Alexander, Athanasius, and Hermogenes of Cappadocia, drew up a creed. It employed the unequivocal word—or so they claimed—homoousios. Consequently, the Alexandrians won—if indeed that is how one should speak of such an outcome.

The creed averred the Son of God is *gennetos*, the only begotten of the Father, that is, born of the Father's nature or substance or being. Hence, as the creed proclaims, the Son is, "God from God, light from light, and true God from true God." The latter, by the way, is no redundancy as many have claimed. In the mind of the council fathers, it was a further clarification of the former "God from God" by declaring that the Son is *truly* God, that is, according to nature rather than by God's elective will. Begotten of the Father, the Son is the same in being with the Father, homoousios, rather than being or becoming God in some other manner as Eusebius and Arius and their faction would have it. In response to Arius' claim that the Christ is merely a creature, or that there was a time when he was not, the creed affirmed the opposite. In point of fact, the fathers cursed anyone who would dare assert the contrary, appending statements of anathema that were directed like well-aimed arrows at the heart of Arius' ideas. The Christ is God, eternally existent, without beginning, *agenetos*, even as God the Father is agenetos. The council fathers declared that they would cut off from communion with the Church those men who claim that, "there was a time when the Son was not," or that "he was made of nothing," or that "the Son is of another substance or essence than the Father." They added that no man should speak of the Son as being created or susceptible to change.

When the council fathers were done, and after Ossius had read the creed aloud, Constantine stood to make a brief speech.

"Brothers! Today, the God and Father of our Lord Jesus Christ has revealed himself, making clear the true nature of the Son. Now, let us imitate the divine Being by placing all division behind us, advancing forward together as if we've vanquished a great enemy in the field. Indeed, we have, brothers! God has inspired! The One has spoken! Let us therefore be united!"

The emperor looked around the hall before sternly adding, "If any bishop or priest dares to go against the will of the Divine as expressed by the creed drawn up by the whole Church, then let him know that he will no longer be allowed to reside in his own diocese. If any bishop refuses to affix his signature to this creed, then he shall not only be cut off from our holy fellowship by the power of the bishops acting together, but he shall also suffer exile by my own authority! In the name of God, so be it!"

In response, well over half of the bishops gravely intoned, "So be it!" Others, of course, were not as pleased. Even so, most went along with the emperor, if tepidly, and signed. The most prominent example was Eusebius of Caesarea, who felt compelled to explain to his own diocese the council's precise usage of the term homoousios—that it was intended to connote shared spiritual substance unique to the divine nature instead of physical matter.

At the end of the council, the fathers anathematized and the emperor exiled several bishops and other men. Most significant, of course, was Arius, who persisted in his obstinacy. Constantine was especially angry with him. He went to great lengths to rid the world of Arius' ideas by forbidding ownership of his works and consigning those found in Nicaea to a great bonfire. This act reminded me of Galerius' fires of persecution some twenty years before. Others exiled included the two bishops of Libya—Theonas of Marmarica and Secundus of Ptolemais—and the deacon Euzoius, Arius' longtime friend. Eventually, there were others, including a man I admired, Theognis, the bishop of Nicaea. Eusebius of Nicomedia's exile to Illyricum in the West followed some months later after the emperor's great feast, when Constantine finally recognized the insincerity of his commitment to the new creed.

The whole affair disturbed me. In my mind, the council's conclusion evinced a severe change in Constantine—though perhaps not as severe in reality as I imagined in my own mind. Contrary to his earlier policy of toleration, I felt he had exhibited a side of his character that could tend toward intolerance. More and more he was shifting away from the man I'd known so many years before. This became far more apparent over the next year. Violently so.

Still, Constantine had achieved the unity he had longed for. The Empire was one and at peace, and so he could finally rest. It was the kind of peace, though, that a volcanic mountain like Vesuvius has before it erupts. But I ask you, Theophilus, what other sort of peace do we experience in this life? By your own silence, I know the answer.

Twenty-five: The Royal Banquet

July 325 A.D.

THE END OF JULY CAME. It was the last day of the month and I was sitting next to Athanasius of Alexandria as I had so many times over the past few months. We pleasantly reclined, light of heart, in a relative state of joy amid hundreds of bishops as well as countless other men. Presently, Athanasius was making one rather mundane point or another—or mundane as I remember it.

"I'm not so sure," he said, "that Constantine is shown in the best light."

"How do you mean?" I asked.

He clarified. "It seems as though Fausta has received a better treatment, and thus, woman is shown to be superior to man."

"Yes," I agreed. But revising his generality, I remarked, "Not just *any* woman over *any* man. Here you have a depiction of married woman as superior to married man." I thought of Mother and my own father and had no doubt about who had the better half of their partnership.

"Ah, right," he conceded. "Perhaps it is so. But what do you make of his expression?"

I glanced up and studied the large mosaic covering the wall opposite where we sat in the banquet hall. It depicted Constantine arriving in the East upon a great white horse, with Fausta to his side carted along in a gilded litter sparkling with jewels. Inside the litter, her expression was one of ease, a lightly worn smile. His expression, by contrast, was strained.

"Not so happy," I commented.

"Exactly."

"But what's to be expected?" I said. "I mean, it's a display of the truth. Constantine's conquest of the East was no easy matter."

In fact, this accomplishment is precisely why he had called us all together. Thinking he had finally achieved success, the emperor held a great feast to celebrate. The feast served two purposes. One, it celebrated Constantine's vicennalia, his first twenty years as emperor, which included the achievement of unifying the Empire under his sole rule. Otherwise, it honored the bishops who had struggled to restore peace to the Church at what many were now calling the great council of Nicaea. The feast, then, recognized the unity of the Empire and the unity of the Church founded upon the unity of the divine Monad. As such, it was an appropriate sacrifice offered up to the One. At least, that's how Constantine saw it.

There we reclined, all of us, on couches more fitting for nobility and men of royal descent than the servants of the one Church. Guards stood dutifully nearby, swords hanging aside. It seemed Constantine realized how matters truly stood—both within the Church and without. The peace was tenuous and its ongoing existence required force. If so, however, he made this known to no one, not even me. Instead, he was all smiles. As representative of the One, Constantine had seemingly ushered his people toward peace and everlasting realities.

At the conclusion of the long meal, the emperor stood to give a speech. Dignified, perfectly sober, and arrayed in purple and gold, he boomed, "I breathe easily today, my friends in Christ the eternal God! I breathe easily, because like David of old our enemies have been vanquished on all sides. Like Moses and the people of God, we have escaped that slavery of mind, which ties us to our own petty thoughts. We have been released into the glory of the splendor of truth, which gives light to everyone everywhere as does the divine Sun. At peace, our hearts have joined in one steady beating like the heels of a well-trained army—though marching not *to* war, but *from* war, from the din of battle to everlasting calm! Now our arms hang upon the rack, retired and forever at rest, and we enjoy the succor and plenty of the one God. Ours is harmony! Love has vanquished strife! Today we know the peace of God! What you see around you is a foreshadowing of the great kingdom of Christ to come! This is a foretaste of the eternal feast when we shall taste of the divine reality forever and ever!"

At his last words, the whole hall erupted in applause. The bishops and all the others congratulated one another and praised the Divinity.

Then, as it grew quiet, Athanasius leaned over to me from his couch and whispered, "I pray so."

I turned to face him. "Are you that set on unbelief?" I wryly asked, thinly smiling.

Peering into my own skeptical eyes, his expression one of perfect gravity, Athanasius responded, "Faith in God is one matter, Arnobius. For with God, all is possible. Yet optimism," he said, "is quite another matter. It can be a kind of blindness."

The smile disappearing, I agreed.

He continued. "To put it simply, the emperor is overlooking human nature and human pride. Once set upon the course of wrong, we fall as though tumbling down a never-ending hill. What's required is repentance, which springs from authentic conviction from faith given by the Spirit of God. A command *cannot* work. It's like those myths you always speak of, where the gods abrogate human nature. To work, God the Word must become flesh. If not, man remains man. He is corrupt and falling headlong into greater corruption, the abyss of unlikeness, until ..."

"Until what?" I asked.

"Pray God we never know."

"Right," I said. Yet I knew where he was heading.

We were both quiet, thinking our own thoughts.

Soon, however, once Constantine sat down and once the hall grew loud again with the noise of hundreds of men communicating with one another in newfound unity, we talked about the future.

I told Athanasius that we would be returning to Nicomedia and on to Byzantium within the week, and that the emperor was already planning a trip to Rome to stage an even greater celebration of his vicennalia.

"Will you go?" he asked.

"I suppose so," I replied.

"After that, what will you do?"

"I can't say. What about you?"

"I'm returning to Alexandria with Bishop Alexander and the rest of our entourage in the next week or two."

"Back to the ordinary life of the Church?"

"Yes," he said.

Then he invited me to visit him in Alexandria the next time I was there on business. I told him I would.

"At the very least," he said, "we should correspond."

"At the very least," I concurred.

"I'll hold you up in my prayers, Arnobius. I've no doubt you'll come to understand as God wishes."

"I trust so," I allowed.

At the time, however, I doubted it. More, I had little faith in Athanasius' intercession with the Divinity on my behalf. How could his flying words possibly move the immovable God?

Still, in some measure I hoped they would. And although tainted with disbelief, I imagine this small amount of hope served as a kind of prayer all its own demonstrating my own wary earnestness.

Some five days later, I said goodbye to Athanasius.

"You *will* visit—won't you?" he asked.

"Of course I will," I promised, though I had no idea when I would.

I felt sad to be leaving him. Later that day, we were on our way to Nicomedia and then on to Rome to celebrate, as I have said, Constantine's twentieth anniversary of rule.

"I'll hold you to it," he said, grinning.

"You won't have to," I promised.

I meant it.

As it happened, we corresponded over the next few years before I went to visit him just after he had been ordained bishop.

But by then, Theophilus, everything had abruptly and violently changed between Constantine and me. It all happened in Rome.

Twenty-six: Murder and Separation

326 A.D.

ROME. I REMEMBER PILA DESCRIBING the eternal city to me nearly twenty-five years before when Diocletian had gone to Rome to celebrate his own vicennalia. Over cups of wine, he said Rome was pure grandeur, magnificence. What was once a town of brick and mortar, a town of soil-loving, hard-working, rough-handed farmers, had become the great city of polished marble, the capital of senators, generals, and emperors with hands as soft as those of any patrician woman. I laugh. The reality, I'm afraid to say, is quite different. Oh sure, Theophilus, there are hundreds of magnificent marble buildings, the many built over the centuries we Romans have been lords of the earth. And they do glimmer and shine. Nevertheless, I couldn't help but notice a stifling poverty. It seems everyone is poor—or poor relative to those in the East. No wonder Constantine removed the capital from its old seat to the New Rome along the Bosporus. The old Rome, it seemed, was no longer what it once was.

This, I believe, is what explains the difference between my experience of Rome after the great council of Nicaea and Pila's telling some twenty-five years before. The city was in decline. It had been.

But more. While in Rome with Constantine and his whole retinue, everything collapsed. My whole life; Constantine's. Afterwards, I truly wanted nothing more of the Empire and nothing more of the emperor.

The reason for this was simple. It was because Constantine put his wife and son to death.

Looking back, I don't know that I can blame him—although what he did was atrocious in itself. Still, people had betrayed Constantine so many times over the course of his life that he had become paranoid. He was no longer one who trusted others implicitly. Rather, Galerius and a whole line of other men had introduced him to the realities of human nature, that most men are out for gain, for power, and the pleasure these afford. Often—thanks to God and his own skill, he would say—these same men had come to a dreadful end. Among others, there were: Lucius Domitius Domitianus, a suicide; Aurelius Achilleus, beheaded; Galerius, disemboweled by disease; Maximian, bleeding out on a cold marble floor; Maxentius, drowned and impaled; Licinius, another forced suicide; and Bassianus, also beheaded.

But would Constantine always be so fortunate against his enemies? This one question haunted him.

Prudently, therefore, the emperor concluded he must keep a vigilant watch. He must be on guard. He mustn't trust. Or not overly much.

Over time, this prudence morphed into an excessive suspicion. Now that he had attained the one goal he had sacrificed and suffered for over the stretch of twenty long years, he grew anxious for all he had achieved. Not only did he fear for his own life, that someone would betray and assassinate him, but he feared for the unity he had won as the hand of God.

The result was that Constantine grew harsh. He dealt with anyone who seemed to betray him or act contrary to the good of the Empire in rather summary fashion. No one person was worth more than the Empire.

The tragedy occurred after we had been in Rome for some time, when the months of the year had already passed the end of spring into early summer. Now that it was warm and unpleasant, we would oftentimes retreat to the imperial estate just outside the city where a breeze blew off the Tiber and brought respite to our tepid existence.

The vicennalia festivities were over. The emperor had celebrated in a manner worthy of his accomplishments. Now, exhilarated by it all, Constantine was manically making plans for the future—a brighter one to be sure. But then, everything went dark.

One evening, I was dining with the emperor and a few other men on a porch overlooking the slow brown flow of the Tiber. There we were, eating, drinking, and happily conversing, when the empress Fausta burst onto the porch having easily pushed by the few guards stationed at the entryway.

It was then she betrayed the emperor.

"Constantine! I must speak with you!" she demanded.

Immediately, he stood to his feet. "Fausta, dear wife, what is it?"

"He's betrayed you!" she screamed, warm tears rolling down her reddened cheeks.

Constantine moved toward her, concerned. "Who has?"

"Your son!" she wailed.

"My son?" he echoed.

"Yes!"

Growing even more bewildered, he asked, "What do you mean? *Which* son?" For then, as today, Constantine had many sons. Most, however, were then hardly old enough to betray him.

"Which son?" she mocked, wickedly laughing and wailing at the same time. "Who else, but the one son old enough!"

I saw that Constantine was confused. I saw it in his poor dark eyes. There was only one. And *he* couldn't have. Surely, he wouldn't have.

Constantine grew impatient. "Be plain, woman! To whom do you refer?"

"Crispus!" she roared. "Your son by that whore, Minervina!"

There was silence. There was a painful silence beneath the portico that covered the porch. Not far from us the Tiber flowed on toward Rome and then on toward Our Sea. Whatever breeze there had been vanished.

Then, hardened to the outcome, Constantine commanded, "Specify yourself, woman! What did he do?"

She did. She accused Crispus of seducing her. "Just now," she revealed, "I was bathing. I was fully disrobed when your son came in and made a forced attempt to join me. I declined, of course, but he insisted!"

Constantine's eyes narrowed.

Fausta went on. Raising her voice, she shrilled, "He wished to rape me! He disrobed himself, and I saw him, his … and he climbed down the steps into—"

"Stop!" demanded Constantine.

She did—for the moment.

He furiously thought. The emperor considered his son and all that Crispus had done for him. It was Crispus who had brilliantly, heroically, and most importantly, successfully, defeated Licinius' navy outside Byzantium in the Hellespont. That was just two years before. If not for this one son by Minervina, the love of his youth, he wouldn't have been able to defeat his enemy. Or unify the Empire. Or build the New Rome. Or unite the Church. If not for him …

After a moment, Fausta burst into his thoughts. "I'll stop my speech," she angrily sobbed, "but first you should know what he did! You should know how the one you so adore, the one who helped you reduce Licinius to nothing, the son you hope will one day succeed you as emperor—you should know how Crispus has betrayed you, how he has seduced your wife. And although I don't mean as much to you as that whore with whom you conceived him, it is nevertheless shameful and contrary to my honor and dignity. And because I am your legal wife, it's a blight upon yours too, dear husband!"

Again, there was quiet beneath the portico. Then Constantine asked, "Did he succeed?"

"Gods, no!" cried Fausta, wiping warm tears from her face.

But Constantine did not believe her. There were rumors. There *had* been. Raising his voice, he pressed, "Tell the truth! Did my son succeed?"

"He did not!" she insisted. Then taking a slightly different tack calculated to bring condemnation, she suggested, "Nonetheless, as you are well aware, I'm sure, he's been far more fortunate with many other women."

"No!" exclaimed Constantine, deceiving himself. "I *cannot* believe it! He's become ..."

"Christian?" asked Fausta, smirking.

"Yes," he said.

"Has that stopped other men?"

Constantine didn't answer. Instead, before she could say another word, he abruptly sent Fausta off from the porch under guard and called for Crispus and Fausta's bath attendant.

An hour later, Constantine sat in judgment in another hall, now elevated upon a chair plated with gold and encrusted with precious stones. He had already questioned Fausta's bath attendant who had confirmed Crispus' presence in the empress's bathing chamber earlier that evening. Even so, she hadn't seen anything inappropriate. Now he interrogated his son.

"Have you betrayed me, Crispus?"

The son looked confused. "What do you mean, Father?"

"Tonight, with my wife?"

"Father?"

"Were you in Fausta's bathing chamber tonight?"

"I was," he admitted.

"And why were you there?"

"She called me to speak with her."

"When no other man should see her?"

He shrugged. "I didn't know."

"Didn't know what?"

"That she was bathing. If I had, I would have waited."

Constantine paused for a moment before saying, "Fausta says you disrobed and attempted to seduce her."

Crispus, too startled at the outlandish accusation, said nothing. He simply repeated the charge in the staggered form of an astonished question. *"Seduced her?"*

"Yes."

"No!"

But you admit you were there?"

"I was."

"And she was bathing."

"She was, but—"

Constantine cut him short. "Do you believe she is beautiful?"

Crispus blanched, too embarrassed for words. He must have thought that he was trapped, that he could say nothing. If he admitted yes, that naked she was a beautiful woman, then his words amounted to guilt. Yet if he said no, then it was another kind of admission but similar. He had considered it. He had asked himself this very question as he looked upon her bathing in her natural form. Either way, he could not simply draw back in disgust as if she were his own mother, as if to think in such a way—that she was beautiful— were incestuous, as if he were Oedipus and she Jocasta. No. She was not his own flesh and blood. Furthermore, she *was* beautiful. And more, she wasn't much older than he.

For Constantine, this long stretch of silence was enough, and so he turned to the other charge. "Have you seduced other women, son?"

Crispus shifted, dropping his head. "I'm not yet married, father."

"Indeed," said Constantine. And a warm tear fell down his now pale cheek. "You are not. You are nearly thirty years old and not yet married. What a grave error I have made."

Later that night, despite belated cries of innocence, Crispus was surreptitiously put to death for adultery. For betrayal. For seducing the empress and bringing shame upon the emperor and upon the Empire. The son he admired and adored, his firstborn son, the one born of Minervina his first and only love, Constantine put to death on grounds of a suspicion.

From that moment on, Theophilus, the emperor was in a state of inner discord. Not external, I say. No, in fact he was even more fastidious about his appearance and the outward show of calm. But it wasn't real, and he knew it. Something had gone terribly wrong.

Early the next morning, Constantine's mother Helena ruined him further, though with good intention.

Having heard the accusation against Crispus from one servant or another, but having not heard of his death because it had been accomplished in secret, she informed her son that his wife had lied to him.

Constantine asked for evidence.

"It was *she* who called him to the bath," she explained.

"I know."

"And *she* who attempted to seduce *him*."

"Impossible!" he cried, standing and shaking his thick right fist.

"Have you asked her bath attendant?"

"I have!"

Undaunted, she queried, "And what did she say?"

"That he was there in her bathing chamber when she was naked!"

Helena stepped toward her son. "But w*hy* was he there?"

Constantine looked away. He trembled slightly as he used to when scolded by his mother a half century before. Mutely he said, "I *know* the reason he was there. My son implied it himself."

"Then you know the truth?"

He was quiet and looked down. Then firmly staring at his mother, he asserted, "I know what he did. When I asked him if he seduced her, he was silent! That was evidence enough! That along with all the other women ..."

"But it was her," Helena countered. "It was Fausta! *She* did it! I tell you Crispus is innocent!"

"He wasn't!"

"He *is*—you must admit it and tell him so."

Constantine would admit no such thing.

"You *will* tell him, won't you?"

He wouldn't.

"Then *I* will!"

"You can't!"

"I must!"

"He's dead!" he finally shouted, revealing the horrible truth.

"He's *what?*"

Constantine stared through her.

"Did you—?"

He didn't answer. And quietly, Helena wept.

After his mother left the hall, Constantine sent a guard for Fausta. Soon after, she stood before him. He looked at her. He studied her eyes, her manner. Had she told the truth or a lie?

Finally, he inquired, "Did you do it?"

"What?" she asked.

"Was it *you* who seduced him?"

She gasped.

"Well?"

"But why would I?" she begged.

"For the same reason that—"

"What, Constantine?"

"All the other men you've been with. And ..."

But as he told me about it later, he couldn't bring himself to say it. He couldn't accuse her of murdering Crispus so that her own sons could eventually rule the Empire.

Fausta shifted uncomfortably. Then, as though telling the god's own truth, she claimed, "No. *He* did it. He came in unannounced, and dropping his tunic, he forced himself on me!"

"You're lying!"

"I swear it before the virgin goddess Diana!"

"She's no goddess!" he shouted.

"Perhaps not," she admitted. "Nevertheless, your own son rubbed his body against mine as I stood begging for something to cover myself."

"I see," said Constantine.

"I was weeping!" she cried.

"Oh?"

"Figuring out how I could throw him off!"

"Impossible!" he interjected, shifting his tone.

"Why?" asked Fausta.

"Because your attendant swore that you yourself had called him to your bathing chamber. It was *you!*"

Fausta froze. "Yes, yes, *that's* true!" she confessed. "But then, quite against my own will, he dropped his white tunic and I could see ..."

"But you swore he came unannounced!"

"His … he was pulsating with desire …"

"Unannounced, woman!"

"… his …"

"Silence, Fausta!"

She was.

And shaking, the emperor cried out in judgment, "You've betrayed me! You've killed my son!"

"He's *dead?*"

Up to then, Theophilus, she didn't know.

"Dead," he confirmed.

He wept—just a bit. Tears of sorrow, of anger.

Then, rapidly stepping toward her, he hit her across the cheek with the back of his right hand.

"You bitch!"

She dropped to the floor, stunned and sobbing.

He stepped back again and there was silence. Finally, a guard led Fausta away just as Crispus had been led away the evening before.

A week later, after having been absent from court for some seven days, Fausta was found dead.

"What happened?" I queried the servant woman who discovered her body.

"She was burned to death," she explained.

"Burned?" I asked, astonished. "In what fire?"

"Not burned," she corrected herself. "Boiled. I found her in her bath, in the hot bath, the *caldarium*. They say it was a suicide."

A suicide? I wondered, feeling sick. I knew better. I knew her death was no different than Maximian's or Licinius' had been. Constantine had put Fausta to death. He had ordered her into the bath where she had attempted to seduce Crispus, and slowly, she was boiled to death.

Now they were both gone. Crispus was dead and now Fausta. With them, Constantine seemed to die as well. And when I learned the grisly truth, I too died my own death in my own apartment.

I was sick for several weeks with an ill-defined ailment. The doctors told me they had never witnessed anything with my precise symptoms. Nor could they find any help in their manuals. But I knew what it was. Indeed, it was quite simple, perhaps too simple for a physician. I was tired. I was exhausted. I had come to the realization, both mentally and physically, that I had had enough. Consequently, I fell into my bed and didn't get up for twelve days. Day after day, I slept and slept hardly eating, drinking, or accomplishing those tasks that are necessary for life.

Then, suddenly on the thirteenth day, I awoke. I mean I got out of my bed and emerged from my sleeping chamber a new man.

It all came with a sudden realization. I realized one morning nearly two weeks after I had taken ill that I had to leave Constantine and the imperial court and return home to Carthage.

Yet when I went to leave, I found it was difficult to depart.

When I approached Constantine to broach the subject of leaving, I discovered that in the several weeks that had intervened between Crispus' and Fausta's deaths and then, the man was entirely transformed. It was as though he himself were the living dead. His face was pale and his body had suffered the loss of a considerable amount of weight—of muscle—and he looked the ghost of a man, mere skin on bones, compared to the man I had known and loved before.

"Arnobius," he whispered upon my entry. "Raise yourself."

I did.

"What is it?" he asked.

I didn't have the courage to say what I wanted to say. How could I tell him that I wished to leave him all alone? Therefore, I didn't tell him—not then.

But I had to. The thought of departing, of escaping him and his Empire, had become my one obsessive thought. I hoped a more opportune moment would arise—one in which he wouldn't be crushed, and one where, I had even come to fear this, he wouldn't feel betrayed. Nevertheless, as I bided my time, Constantine continued to change for the worse.

Finally, however, my time came to go. An excuse arrived that would allow me to depart without rancor and, I hoped, without offense to my longtime friend. I received word from Carthage that my dear father Buteo was nearing death. As it happened, he had been ailing for some time. He had steadily begun to lose his mind and control over himself—over the normal function-ing of his body.

"Constantine," I said, when I finally worked up the nerve to tell him I must leave, "Buteo is seriously ill. He's dying."

The emperor hardly acknowledged my words. It was as though he had forgotten who I was and about the olive oil man Buteo, the very man who had introduced us so many years before.

"I see," he said.

I moved to the point. "I'm here to bid you farewell."

"Just like that?" he asked.

"What do you mean?"

"I mean, you simply wish to inform me?"

I didn't grasp his meaning.

"Most," he clarified, "come before me asking for this or for that. If it is in my power, I grant it; if not, I don't. But *you* …"

Me? What did he want? I could see he had come to mistrust me as well. Constantine, my heart bled, what had happened to us? What had happened to him? To me? Was it worth it?

Finally, he said, "If you must go, then be gone."

Gone? I wondered. "No," I protested. "You misunderstand my meaning."

"How?" he asked. "I understand perfectly well. Like all the others, you wish to leave me."

I could say nothing. Even though I wished to, I now *had* to go. My father was dying.

Then abruptly, as if it didn't matter anymore, he announced, "I have other matters to attend, Arnobius."

He turned away.

And with that, I was ushered out of the great hall of the Imperial Palace without so much as the opportunity of a backwards glance at him.

Sad, I walked toward my own apartment believing it would be the last time I saw him.

Days later, I made my way by horse to Ostia and boarded one of the many ships that sail back and forth between Carthage and Rome.

Goodbye Constantine, I whispered. I looked back to see the shore of Italy shrinking in the distance, and I cried—if only a bit.

Book Five

Athanasius the Bishop

326 to 335 A.D.

Twenty-seven: Corresponding in Carthage

326 to 328 A.D.

WHEN I ARRIVED IN CARTHAGE, Buteo was already gone. My father who had worked so hard for my own well-being was no more. My family had burned his mortal remains in one of the crematoriums along the coast and had dedicated his soul to the immortal gods. Now, presumably, his shade walked among the great crowd of the dead in Hades. With a grin, I imagined him pursuing profit even there, making contacts among the deceased and perhaps even becoming friends with Pluto himself, the god of the dead, whom some also call the god of wealth.

For her part, Mother was heartbroken at my father's departure and afraid of what it would mean for her and the rest of us. Contrary to my own expectations, my arrival did little to bring her good cheer, though I knew she was pleased to have me home.

"We'll all be ruined," she would say, "now that Buteo is gone."

I would try to reason with her. "He's been gone for some time," I pointed out. "You said so yourself. Hasn't he?"

She, however, wouldn't listen to reason. Instead, she simply begged me to stay on, never to leave, and to act as the head of our family.

"That's what I intend to do," I assured her. And over time, this finally gave her some measure of comfort, even though we all keenly missed my father—she more than anyone of us.

Months passed by and I dutifully worked at family affairs. I made deals with other men, accounted for them in the books, and organized the men who worked for us as they pursued our work. Eventually, with the passing of time, I came to be satisfied after a fashion. At the very least, I began to feel the great burden of life with Constantine lift. And yet, Theophilus, I must admit that sometimes I was bothered by thoughts about him. Although I had written to him and had attempted to keep up with him—with his return to the East after his vicennalia, with his legislation, and with how he continued to deal with the Church—Constantine never once responded. Finally, I realized we had grown irreparably apart. This is what bothered me; this is what hurt.

All along, Mother kept at me to marry. Above all, she wanted me to have children, to sire offspring that would keep the family going. It was her belief that she would only remain happy—that is, in the afterlife—if all was well with the family. Poor woman, I thought. But I did my best. Indeed, for a time I had the notion that I would marry. Yet fear held me back. Deep down, I didn't want to experience the loss of love again. It was a feeling that traced its origins all the way back to Stella. More than that, of course, it was Katrina and the sentiments I still felt for her and the family I had lost, although more than a decade had passed since they had died. Sometimes I thought of Luxilla and wondered if she had married. Surely, I thought. In any case, I concluded that if I didn't love, if I didn't lend my heart to vulnerability, then I'd be better off. But how?

Sometimes, Theophilus, as the sun passed beneath the earth and darkness came on, that old feeling I used to get when I was a child crept upon me like a ghost. Then, when I was a young boy, I used to fear the dark. The unknown. But now it was greater. It came over me, haunting me, suggesting my life was meaningless, that I would work, marry, and have children perhaps, but when it was all done I'd descend unto the dead like any other man, unfulfilled and unhappy.

On those nights, I'd consider how my life had unfolded up to that point and wonder what I could have done differently. I would wonder if I had made the right decision. Had it been best to give up on Alexandria in order to go to Nicomedia with Constantine? What if I'd stayed on and found the way of truth? Some nights, however, when the fear wasn't as thick, I would wonder if things had actually happened as they were meant to happen. I was meant to go to Nicomedia, and from there to Britannia and Treveris, and from there to Rome and home again and to the New Rome ten years later, and finally—*finally*, I would think—to Nicaea, where I met Athanasius. Perhaps he was the solution, I conjectured. Of all the people I'd ever known, Athanasius had a philosophy that proposed both an understanding of the truth and a way to live it.

One night while following this train of thought, I wrote Athanasius a lengthy letter studded with all manner of questions. I hoped and trusted he would reveal just what I needed to know. I was disappointed, however, with his response because he answered none of my questions. Instead, he simply pointed out that the Christian way of life works, whereas pagan philosophy has always failed. I asked him how that could be in another letter. Athanasius explained. In short, he said, the way of the Christ succeeds by making men better, whereas pagan philosophy, although successful with the few, fails with the many. It succeeds, he claimed, by actually improving those who adhere to the Christ and to the sacraments of his Church. It succeeds by leading one into a higher way of life, into the way of virtue, and most importantly, he finished, into the way of the highest virtue, the way of the heart, that of love.

Love, I shrugged, when I read his letter. Dropping it on my knees, I laughed aloud thinking of those Christians in my own city, half tied to Donatus and half tied to Caecilian, who were far from loving. They seemed far more concerned with who had the most property. Where was love? I laughed as well remembering the many bishops in Nicaea who were more interested in being right than in loving their opponents. Where was love?

Still, I judged, it was possible I misunderstood. Perhaps Athanasius was getting at something else. There was, after all, something I had noticed that was different with men who truly follow the Christ as opposed to those with power. A different quality. But what was it?

Sometime later, I received an extraordinary letter. It was an encyclical intended not only for me but also for many others, mostly churchmen—bishops, priests, and deacons. Although Athanasius' signature and a brief greeting were appended at the bottom, the letter was not from Athanasius himself but from his new secretary, the priest called Macarius. In it, Macarius announced that Athanasius had been elected the bishop of Alexandria.

Immediately, feeling a kind of inexplicable elation, I composed a brief letter of congratulations. Then I sat back and thought about it. *Bishop*, I marveled—and at such an early age. He was just thirty years old as I later learned.

A month or so later, Athanasius himself wrote thanking me for my kind wishes and inviting me to visit him in Alexandria. It was time, he wrote, that I turn the life of my soul toward the light of the One in the Christ. Soon, he suggested.

I returned that I couldn't. Not any time soon. I told him about Mother, and how she would die of worry if I left her.

He responded that my sense of obligation was admirable, but he would pray that Mother would have a change of heart. If you came, he said, we would better be able to carry on with our philosophical discourse.

I returned: intriguing. Trust me. And I was intrigued. I wanted nothing more than to talk to him about the matters I have mentioned. Of truth, of God, of salvation—if such were possible. Therefore, I gave him my permission, as it were, to pray for Mother.

A month later, I was on my way to Alexandria.

What had happened? Definitively, I cannot say, Theophilus. But of this I am certain. Three weeks after I sent off my post giving Athanasius permission to intercede on my behalf, Mother approached me in an odd mood.

"Arnobius," she said, "I've been thinking."

"What is it, Mother?"

"You've been faithful," she went on. "You've earned a great fortune for the family and have tended well the estate your dear father left behind."

I nodded, acknowledging that it was true.

"Still," she said, "I believe you could do more."

"*More?*" I asked in disbelief.

"Always more," she confirmed, with a serious nod of her head.

"How so?" I queried. There I was, faithful Arnobius, always asking what more could be done.

She eyed me. "How long has it been since you've been gone from Carthage?"

"Some time," I replied, vaguely.

"And do you believe all of our affairs are well attended elsewhere?"

"I do," I asserted. "We have men in every major city."

"I know that," she said, as if she knew *everything* about our business. "Still, it might do for you to attend our affairs personally."

"Oh?" I asked. "How do you mean, Mother?"

At the very least, I knew I must hear her out. Even if it ended with me doing nothing at all, I must appease her anxiety.

"Take Alexandria, for example," she went on.

I did. I took it and agreed with her, and the next day I purchased fare to go to Alexandria. Ha! I exulted. What a stroke of luck!

Or—?

Without delay, I happily wrote to Athanasius letting him know I was coming. On business, I said, knowing he'd know my real meaning.

So it was, Theophilus, that with the blessing of Mother, I was on my way to Alexandria the very next week. As I left, she smiled. I knew what she was thinking. Mother thought that I was just like her husband, like my father, Buteo the Buzzard. It was just as he would have done. I was pursing opportunity wherever and whenever it could be found.

I also smiled. Yes, I conceded. In some ways, I had become like Buteo. But now, unknown to her, I was returning to Alexandria to search for Arnobius the nineteen year old who had once harbored great aspirations.

Twenty-eight: Up the Nile

328 A.D.

I ARRIVED IN ALEXANDRIA just in time to leave.

"Business can wait!" Athanasius declared, imploring me to sail up the Nile with him.

It was late at night. I'd arrived from Carthage a few days late due to poor weather and the death of two crewmen lost overboard. Wearing a simple, white tunic, Athanasius grasped me by the shoulders. His eyes shone with that compelling light that draws one toward him and in the direction he wishes you to go. Two deacons flanked him.

Up the Nile? I considered. The last thing I wanted to do was to board another boat—not after what I'd just experienced and given how exhausted I felt. But knowing he would be gone for several months and that I'd be left alone in Alexandria with nothing to consider but the distribution of olive oil, I agreed.

"Of course I'll go," I consented despite my own immediate feelings.

Athanasius grinned and patted my back. "We leave tomorrow, friend."

With that, he turned toward evening prayers, and one of the deacons showed me to my room where I crawled off to bed.

The following day we departed. We boarded a large boat, typical for the river, manned with tens of sweaty oarsmen rowing in two shifts. Leaving the city, we sailed up the relatively placid Alexandrian Canal toward the Canopic Branch of the Nile. With us were many churchmen and others who had a variety of tasks to accomplish for the bishop and the rest of us onboard. Noteworthy among them were the priest Macarius, who was Athanasius' secretary, and the deacon Timotheos, who had a full head of curly, black hair. Early on that morning, I rode in the fore of the boat just beyond the great rectangular sail and the cabins, which housed the pilot, Athanasius, me, and others of the pilot's crew. From there I observed the sights of the narrow

Alexandrian Canal that would take us out to the westernmost branch of the Nile. Behind me, the copilot called direction from the castle post to the helmsman who steered us away from incoming boats, both large and small.

Leaving the dock, we sailed along the city walls of Alexandria. When they disappeared in the distance behind us, great vistas of cultivated land opened up before us. There, the people of Egypt—mostly lean peasants organized by muscular foremen—toiled in the fields growing wheat and barley. Most were scarcely dressed aside from dirty white loincloths. They were dark, these men toiling beneath the sun.

"Beautiful, no?" remarked Athanasius, sitting down next to me. "I look forward to this every year."

"Is this an annual trip, then?" I asked.

"If God so wills."

I thought of Hapi, god of the Nile, of his universal provision providing every need to the people of Egypt.

Athanasius interrupted my thoughts. "I've been making it for many years with Bishop Alexander. Now that he's asleep, the duty falls to me."

"What's the purpose?"

Athanasius smiled looking to the shore. "Do you see those goats over there?"

I told him I did.

"The people need a goatherd, or they'll be devoured."

"Devoured?" I repeated. "By whom?"

"By all sorts of wild animals. Lions, packs of dogs, crocodiles. What I mean, of course, is they'll revert to all the false gods they used to follow, the ones who demand perversion for worship."

I nodded, for I knew what he meant, Theophilus. The processions holding high the sacred phallus. Men having intercourse with consecrated prostitutes. They call it worship. Herodotus describes women engaging in sexual orgies atop great wooden barges plying the Nile. Drunk, they bare all—round shoulders, supple breasts, bellies divoted with mystery. Men rage with passion below the barges, amassing themselves along the shore. They shout at them. *Let us come aboard!* They do. And inspired by base desire, every shameful act is committed on behalf of the god of lust—called Aphrodite by the Greeks and Venus by Romans.

In reference to those toiling along the shore, Athanasius explained, "I'm their goatherd. Their pastor. It's my duty to ensure their safety into the divine fold. We visit the whole of Egypt stretching along the Nile, attempting to share the love of God and the way of restoration."

He finished by explaining the Church's provision for the poor.

And *that*, I thought, was unique. Aside from the temples of Asclepius, there was nothing like it in the Roman world in which I grew up.

We sailed on. In just a few hours, we reached the Canopic Branch of the Nile and turned southward from our previous eastward direction. Our first major stop would be Heliopolis. But that was a full five days row and sail upriver. In the meantime, we anchored each night and sometimes even more frequently, in mid-morning or afternoon, alongside a small village that typically possessed just one mud brick and thatch church and perhaps a deacon and priest of the Christ. People, as if ants emerging from some underground maze of tunnels, surfaced from the village and surrounding fields to see the new bishop. The news of his election had already spread upriver, and along with it a reverence for him and his life. "The bishop lived with the hermit Anthony for a time," I heard people whisper. "He's a holy man. Touch him and you'll be cured." Athanasius blessed them with his presence and his counsel. "Follow the way of the Lord," he admonished. "Reject the ways of evil and devotion to evil spirits."

Along the banks of the Nile, however, I saw where many had not rejected these evil spirits as Athanasius conceived of them. There, one could see small altars and votive offerings to the great beasts of the river—to the ferocious hippopotamus, the so-called river horse, and to the crocodile, the devourer of children. There were also gifts to the river god himself, Hapi the god of fertility, who graciously provides the magic of food grown from the dark soil, and offspring for mothers and fathers wanting care in old age and immortality through their children after they've died. These manifestations of the old religion greatly sorrowed the bishop. It's not that Athanasius didn't understand their desires, their need for security and hope for plenty. Rather, he believed the old religion actually carried them in the opposite direction of what they wanted.

"Why?" I asked. "If they believe they receive these goods, then isn't their devotion at least in some measure useful to them?"

"In some sense," he allowed, "but not ultimately."

"How so?" I asked.

"Because it's shortsighted. Their good is a mirage; what they truly long for is the fully good."

Perhaps, I thought. But how can these poor peasants, let alone anyone else, attain that?

We continued our voyage upriver. By the third day, and just two days away from Heliopolis, I felt like I had come to be one with the gentle movement of our craft beneath the sun, which shone brilliantly above without an excess of heat. We passed by and visited village after village, and each time the many of Egypt came out to welcome their bishop. "Athanasius!" they'd cry. "Papa!" The bishop loved them as a father loves his own children, eating with them and speaking about matters both mundane and divine.

Finally, we came to the ancient city of Heliopolis, city of the divine Sun, of Re, who rises from behind the earth in the morning and falls again in the evening as Re-Osiris—as death. Here, the mighty flowing Nile splits apart into many fingers that flow on and eventually sink into Our Sea. That night, Athanasius gave a somewhat lengthy lecture. I was there, Theophilus, and as he began to speak, sitting before us clad in a simple white tunic behind a plain wooden table, I listened with keen interest.

"It is possible you have already heard, my dear brothers in the Lord, that I have recently finished two works which should be of great assistance in preaching the truth of God in Christ Jesus."

Many of the men—priests and deacons, and perhaps one other bishop, and monks drawn from the desert near to Heliopolis—nodded their heads. They *had* heard. I, for one, had not.

One of the works, he clarified, was written for the sake of those men who are still caught up in the nets of traditional religion, worshiping the Divinity in wood, rock, and stone, and in man-made paintings and statues. Among others, he meant the Greeks and Romans, Indians and Ethiopians, and not least, of course, the Egyptians whose pantheon of deities mirrors the heavens above, the earth below, and the underworld further down. The other work was written for all men—Jews and gentiles alike. He explained that it was about the incarnation of the Word. Later, before I had actually read it, I told Athanasius that most men are perfectly at home with the idea of the gods becoming man or animal. In this work, however, he meant something entirely different.

Athanasius made a promise to the men sitting before him. "My hope is to have scribes make copies. Then I'll distribute them far and wide so the whole of Egypt will know of the goodness and love of God and the work of his salvation, the restoration accomplished in the Christ when we men had sinned."

That's it, I surmised, the simple claim of those who follow the Christ. Man sinned, and somehow this Christ—this demigod, as I still imagined him—died on a Roman cross making things right again in some mysterious way. *How did it work?* I wondered.

My mind drifted back to that embarrassing incident so many years before, when I sat in the lecture hall in Alexandria with Constantine listening to the ever-elevated Iamblichus speak of theurgy and all those divine works that could somehow lead a man to unity with the One. Those magical mediations. Those gods upon gods, spirits upon spirits, and daemons upon daemons. The One there, way up there in the heavens, and we men here, way down here on earth.

It puzzled me.

I wished I could fit it all together. I wished I could see the difference between Iamblichus and Athanasius for the obvious reason that the latter was not like an ordinary man. I could tell he genuinely cared for me, for my soul, whereas Iamblichus and others seemed only to care for their own reputation and wealth. Something nevertheless held me back. Confusion? Skepticism? Cynicism? Whatever, I couldn't see the difference between their ideas. Life, it seemed, had inured me to truth. Even so, I turned to the bishop who was gesturing with his hands as he spoke. Presently, Athanasius was speaking of evil. The others listened rapt with attention.

"Evil doesn't exist in of itself," he explained. "Instead, it is a reality by choice—and that, a kind of unreal-reality. How so, you may wonder. You claim you positively see and hear evil every day. And so it is. But it's because we have made it so. We men have turned from what is, from God, to what is not. Rather than basking in the light of the One, which gives form and structure to all, we've settled for the darkness of the many, turning away from order, concord, and harmony, to their opposites, to disorder, discord and disharmony."

Athanasius paused to allow his abstract words to find concrete meaning in the mind of each of his auditors. What kind of disorder? What manner of discord and disharmony? I thought of what I had read about in Herodotus and several others, about how the Egyptians had always yearned for order, that remedy for chaos. Accordingly, they had devised stories to explain how it, what they called *ma'at*—order, truth, justice—had come about. The divine

Sun Re shone giving light and life to the many. When illumined, all was well; when dark, all was chaos, formlessness, disorder, and untruth. The pharaoh served as an image of this light and order. Indeed, he brought political unity and order to Egypt for thousands of years until the Greeks invaded under Alexander of Macedon and we Romans finally drew Egypt into our own system of order. The priests taught that the pharaoh, like the divine Sun, shined. In their own language, they call it *khay*. This shining was political order. It was life itself. And if all was well, the illumination of Re and the shining of the pharaoh was reflected in the soul or *ka* of each individual Egyptian. Consequently, there was *ma'at* throughout the cosmos, the kingdom, and each soul. When disrupted, however, it was tragic. There was chaos, evil. This, I supposed, was something of what Athanasius was referring to.

He went on. "It is like a man who stands in the light of the sun, the light which reveals all, the blue sky above, the green surrounding the flowing brown of the Nile, the dark and fertile soil, and the orange, barren desert beyond. Evil is like the vision of this man when he closes his eyes. Then, all is darkness. Though he still possesses the power of sight, the light vanishes, as does the glory of what he has beheld. Now he must live inside the darkness of his mind. And as time goes by, this darkness becomes even darker as all traces of light slowly disappear.

"'God—where are you?' he asks.

"The reply, of course, is weak. Through his eyelids, he can still make out a faint trace of the light, but no more.

"'Well, then, I'll work out matters for myself,' he defiantly says to himself.

"And so he does. He turns from the light of the sun, from the beautiful truth of the Good, of God, to the darkness of his own imagination. Rather than reflecting this great light and seeing reality as it is—the ordinary and intended work of this remarkable mirror we call the imagination or the soul—he instead begins to imagine a different reality altogether. This new reality is not entirely devoid of the one that we call the True, the Good, and the Beautiful, but any light or life that was once truly there, becomes darkness and death in that it's covered over by things of sense.

"Now, the man turns to a reality fashioned by his own hands. He moves from knowing the one and only God, the light and source of all, to knowing a world of phantasmal appearances—one of his own devising. What is this reality in plain language? It is the gods we have made, the idols that are an unreal-reality. They are the embodiment of our base desires, of our darkened, evil inclinations. Therefore, to use the Greek names, we find Ares enthroned as war, Aphrodite as lust, Dionysus as drunken mindlessness, Zeus as power, Hera as vanity and envy, and Hades as death itself, craving the dead souls of men. It's as the apostle wrote three hundred years ago:

> *For although they knew God, they neither glorified him as God nor gave thanks to him, but their thinking became futile and their foolish hearts were darkened. Although they claimed to be wise, they became fools and exchanged the glory of the immortal God for images made to look like mortal men and birds and animals and reptiles.*

"But more! Along with this turn to idols, we began to be oriented more and more toward bodily things, to realities sensed with eye and ear instead of the clear light and comprehension of the soul. When this happened, the once pristine mirror that had been good, beautiful, and true as the image of God, became darkened.

"Yet I ask you? What happens when the light disappears? In time, we grow used to the darkness. In a way, we begin to see, possessing a kind of dark vision, one shadowy, tenebrous, and funereal. With this, we are habituated to the dark and so our desires change. Rather than desiring things of light, things of God, we begin to lust for finite realities, for bodies, for things of sense. Again, it's as the apostle wrote:

> *Therefore, God gave them over in the sinful desires of their hearts to sexual impurity for the degrading of their bodies with one another. They exchanged the truth of God for a lie and worshipped and served created things rather than the Creator ... Because of this, God gave them over to shameful lusts. Even their women exchanged natural relations for unnatural ones. In the same way the men also abandoned natural relations with women and were inflamed with lust for one another ... Since they did not think it worthwhile to retain the knowledge of God, he gave them over to a depraved mind, to do what ought not be done. They have become filled with every kind of wickedness, evil, greed, and depravity. They are full of envy, murder, strife, deceit, and malice. They are gossips, slanderers, God-haters, insolent, arrogant, and boastful; they invent ways of doing evil; they disobey their parents; they are senseless,*

faithless, heartless, ruthless. Although they know God's righteous decree
that those who do such things deserve death, they not only continue to do
these very things but also approve of those who practice them.

"Dear brothers, when we become habituated to these realities of the body, to its many desires, to those of the belly and groin, and the lusts of our hearts—our fallen hearts which above all wish for honor and power to dominate other men—it's the body alone which satisfies. So we think. Therefore, we fear the death of the body. In fact, death becomes the greatest cause for anxiety.

"Nevertheless, along the way, the body is worn out with the disease of immoderate satisfaction; it becomes hardened like the skin of a dead animal left out to dry in the wind, and our hearts become like stones instead of the warm flesh they were meant to be.

"To reiterate, brothers, *we* are the cause of this evil; we are the cause of this darkness, of this great malady that can only end in greater darkness, in death, in the movement toward the abyss of nothingness, of non-being. Still, we cannot despair. There's a remedy!

"God, let it be known, is good. He is light, life, and love. From the beginning, the Creator has always shed his great love upon the world. He intends his creative light to lead creation, and most significantly we men, to him. From the beginning up to now, to this very day, we are his beloved, his spouse who has gone astray. To use another image, he's like the father of the prodigal son who was lost upon receiving and wasting his inheritance. God is that ever-loving father who patiently and lovingly awaits our return."

Finishing, Athanasius bade, "Let us return brothers. Let us turn to our Creator, our Father! Let us open the eyes of our soul to the light of God, the light shining upon his own creation! It's simple! He's waiting for us, right here, right now!"

But for me, as always, Theophilus, it wasn't so simple. In short, I remained unconvinced. As an idea, it made sense having a certain coherence and logical plausibility. But that's just it. It was no more than a logical *possibility*. For me, however attractive, it was no more convincing than other philosophies of return to the One. Athanasius' words didn't reach down and take hold of my heart.

I admit it—I find this is odd, Theophilus. I can't fathom why some men end up convinced and why some do not, why some believe and some falter. I leave it to God.

However that may be, for that night Athanasius was finished. Consequently, the church in Heliopolis became a storm of deacons, priests, and monks pouring forward in order to speak personally with their bishop.

As for me, I sat aside the swirl of men pondering what I had heard and what I should do—if anything.

Three days later, Athanasius and I stood beneath the great pyramids of Egypt, the three that are perched on the western bank of the Nile not too far from Heliopolis and Memphis. Have you ever seen them, Theophilus? They ascend one enormous limestone block upon another reaching high into the sky. We stood there as ants beneath a towering boulder, and I for one marveled at how the pyramids had possibly come to be. How had they been constructed? How had the blocks been hoisted one atop the other? By what ingenuity? According to Herodotus, the pharaoh Khufu was responsible. Yet standing there, I was puzzled. It seemed impossible for one man—nay thousands—to erect such an edifice. In fact, if someone had told me that some god had granted the pyramids as a gift of heaven, I might have believed it. I mentioned my aberrant thought to Athanasius, and he laughed.

"Yes," he said, "some god indeed!" Then he remarked, "It does go to demonstrate that something so big and so magnificently structured requires an ordering mind and constructing power. For surely it cannot happen by accident."

"No, it can't," I agreed.

"It's like the point I made the other night in Heliopolis. The visible order and harmony of creation necessarily reveals an ordering and harmonizing power, if only we'd open our eyes."

"God the Creator," I suggested.

"Right," he confirmed. "But more specifically God's Word by which he created and by which he continues to create. The Word is the Father's structuring wisdom and working power that mixes contraries to form a harmonic whole. The Word is like a conductor over a choir drawing all the voices together as one, or like the ruler over a city who rules for the common good. It is by means of this same Word who is the true image of the father that we men are declared the image of God. In him, we have our being; apart from him, we die."

"And so when we close our eyes," I said, repeating what he had earlier taught, "there's nothing but darkness; the light of the Word disappears."

"You listen well," he smiled.

"Thank you," I responded, bowing in jest.

Then I asked a question I'd been considering over the past few days. "If the light of the Word is God, and that light is the means by which we are the image of the Word and so declared the image of God, then how is it that we are restored?" Before he could reply, however, I went on to explain something of what I meant. "I too understand this world is an image or shadow of the divine realm. If anything, Athanasius, I adhere to Plato and the philosophers who have followed him—Plotinus and the rest. I believe in his allegory of the cave, where we prisoners sit in the bottom of a dark cavern staring at a shadow world caused by a fire and puppets above. There we are, bound to this dark world of dancing apparitions. We see shadows and hear echoes, yet chained, we are unable to turn to see the light above, and so our life is a seeing-darkly, even as you have explained."

"But that's where we diverge," suggested Athanasius. "Notice Plato and the others teach that our souls are caught up in this shadow world against our own wills. Our ignorance binds us involuntarily. Plato said that no man knowingly does evil. It's not so with our own faith. Rather, we see man's condition—his sinfulness and the moral evil he knows, that is, the loss of the light of the Word—as his own choice. It is we men who have chosen this dark world."

I thought about that—this nuance, this difference. The Christian doctrine suggests a willed ignorance and evil as opposed to the Platonic tradition in which man never quite wills evil but knows it by ignorance. "You're right," I conceded. "I grant the difference. But how is it that Christ the Word becomes the means of our restoration to the world of light, to God himself?"

Athanasius considered my question before asking, "Do you remember how the philosopher in Plato's tale, the one who arduously makes the climb out of the cave, ends up returning to its darkness to save his friends whom he'd left below in the shadow world?"

"Of course," I said.

"And do you remember his fate?"

"I do. The poor man died because of it. His so-called friends, the ones bound in the darkness below, thought he'd gone off when he spoke of a world of real light and real forms illumined by the sun. But more, they were grossly offended by his accusation that their world was none other than a dark shadow world."

"Exactly," Athanasius corroborated. "And so the poor man was put to death for speaking the truth, for telling them of the light above."

I nodded. "Doubtlessly Plato had Socrates in mind when he described this man's fate. It was Socrates who thirsted for wisdom, for those things above; it was he who spent his whole life telling others of a knowledge which is not mere opinion, but unmediated wisdom about the truly real."

"Which is invisible," Athanasius added. "Invisible to those, at least, with eyes shut—to those with a mind shut up in darkness."

"Plausible," I concurred. "The real isn't known by the senses; it's neither seen nor heard nor touched; it's known by means of a kind of inward, super-rational vision."

Athanasius shook his head. "The men of Athens weren't pleased with him."

"Not at all," I agreed. "To them, he was like a bothersome fly. In fact, that's how he described himself—as a biting gadfly. His mission was to prod others along toward a higher life, the life of virtue according to reason rather than a life focused on base pleasure, wealth, and honor. And what was his reward for all his effort?" I laughed. "He asked for free meals!"

"He did," said Athanasius, laughing too.

Then I grew sober and sighed. "His reward was death. Like the wise man that went down to warn his friends in the cave, Socrates was put to death."

"Voluntarily?"

"Sort of, yes. He chose to stay rather than flee Athens like his friend Crito begged him to do and like he could have done."

"Did it help?"

"What do you mean?"

"I mean, did his death help his fellow Athenians?"

"I suppose it helped a few, if by help, you mean it made his fellows wiser."

"But what about the majority?"

"Do you mean to ask whether or not his death helped the majority of men?"

"That, yes—and his teaching. Did his death and teaching help those beyond his small circle of friends?"

I thought about this before declaring they did. "His death has inspired many a man during the throes of his own passing. But most importantly his teachings have influenced the whole world. Plato and Xenophon, among others, went on to record them in their dialogues. Plato in turn affected the scholarch Speusippus, his successor at the Academy, and Aristotle who taught Alexander of Macedon. And they, in their different ways, whether through instruction or conquest, swayed the thought and behavior of all men down to our own times, including Plotinus and his followers."

Athanasius pressed. "Of *all* men, Arnobius?"

"No," I shifted upon reflection, "just some."

He nodded. "They've only influenced the few. For the rest, for the common man and the slave, not to mention women, there has been little effect."

"I suppose so."

"Until recently, the majority, whether free or slave, has continued in the darkness of the traditional religion—local cults tied to local deities of sense, full of darkness."

"What, then?" I asked.

"It's clear, isn't it? I don't mean to disparage Socrates. He was a good man and wise, and his death was admirable. But it wasn't enough."

I looked at him as if I didn't quite understand what he was getting at.

"What I mean is that for the rest of us, it wasn't quite enough. If it had been, then the whole world might have changed by now. But that was eight hundred years ago, Arnobius! Think of it!"

I did.

Athanasius went on, "Why are the majority of us still the way we are?"

I didn't know. But he had a point. "It's true," I allowed. "Hardly a thing has changed, except for the wealthy few who have the leisure to read and contemplate. And even then ..."

"Even then!" he repeated. "Who marches us off to needless wars? Who hordes all the wealth?"

"The rich do," I said.

"Yes, their interests have remained the same. But now, since the coming of the Word made flesh, hundreds of thousands are converting—the wealthy few and the many poor. It's no exaggeration to declare that the world is changing. Now the many pursue the light of God and the life of virtue. Imperfectly, perhaps, but it is true. And even the wealthy are now tempered in the pursuit of their interests."

"What's the difference?" I asked.

Athanasius began to answer. Just then, however, the priest Macarius called to us from some distance as he rounded the corner of the pyramid. "Athanasius!" he shouted. "We must go!"

"What is it?" he asked, once Macarius was closer.

"A woman is ill and has asked for your blessing."

"Can she wait?"

"Possibly not," Macarius pronounced, "she's near death's door."

Straightaway, we went off to where the woman lived, leaving our abstract questions and thoughts behind to give assistance to this real soul in immediate need.

Twenty-nine: A Portrait Restored

328 A.D.

WE DEPARTED FROM THE VILLAGE nearby the great pyramids a few days later just after the woman died and Athanasius committed her body to the care of the earth. When a day had gone by, we came to Arsinoe, oftentimes called Faiyum, *the Lake*, because of its proximity to the grayish-blue lake called Moeris where the Egyptians used to keep the sacred crocodile, the god Sobek. It was there, Theophilus, I fell dreadfully ill. Athanasius and the others believed I was going to die.

"He's been struck by the god!" claimed a local man. "For irreverence!" he shrieked. He was an old toothless man who possessed the knowledge of illnesses peculiar to the lake and to Arsinoe.

"Nonsense," countered Athanasius.

Nevertheless, he anointed me with sweet smelling oil and blessed me to fend off any evil spirits.

"What should I do?" I begged, weakly.

"Rest," said Athanasius, "and pray."

The old man, however, told me I must swallow a cup of water from the sacred Nile in order to counteract whatever it was I'd done that was irreverent. I did. He forced it on me one spoonful at a time.

Even so, my fever worsened and I grew unconscious, fading in and out of knowing and not knowing. What was reality? What was a dream? Both were full of sweat, both disturbing. Finally, burning up and feeling an unquenchable thirst, I felt I was drawing near to death.

They gathered around me. Athanasius prayed alongside Macarius, the deacon Timotheos, and the others. I was awake and there was light; I was asleep and there was darkness. An older woman bathed me with cool water. She washed my head and my limbs with water and kindheartedness.

Time passed by. Moments. Hours. A few more days.

Sensing my end, Athanasius prepared me for the next world by consecrating me according to the sacred rite. I had given him permission with the nod of my fevered head. I was now ready to sleep forever.

Yet I didn't die.

Another day went by.

My burning and heavy eyelids drew open to a man sitting by my side. He was young and had a full, black beard composed of dark curls upon dark curls like the waves that roll in one after another from the sea.

"What's that?" I asked, my voice lathered with heavy aspiration.

"A portrait," he replied.

I smelled freshly ground pigments and hot bees wax warmed over coals. I imagined he was painting Athanasius who sat nearby. Unknown to me, however, he was painting my own portrait. The locals, fearing I was close to death, had kindly commissioned a death portrait according to their custom.

"Why?" I later asked Athanasius.

"I just let them," he said. "I was too busy interceding for you to bother asking them not to. Besides, what could it hurt?"

Finally, health returned. Its rapid restoration was almost as abrupt as the onslaught of sickness itself.

After another few days passed, I was myself again, healthy. I felt right again. Athanasius gave thanks. As for me, I pondered how it was that a body exchanges health for disease then disease for health.

Eventually, once I was well enough, we continued sailing up the Nile. Leaving Arsinoe, we sailed past Oxyrhynchus and toward Hermopolis Magna, the city of Hermes the messenger. From there we headed for Coptos where the Manichaeans planned their revolt so many years before during the reign of Diocletian. Then, eight days after we had departed Faiyum by Lake Moeris where I nearly died, we came to a great bend in the Nile.

"We'll be at Tabennisi in a day," Athanasius declared to me. "The monastery will be our final destination."

We sat next to each other on a long bench grafted into the side of the boat. Along the green banks of the river, sunbaked men worked beneath a wide blue sky.

"What would you say drives most men to enter a monastery?" I asked.

Athanasius thought for a moment, before answering, "I don't know if I can speak for most. I suppose there are many reasons. But if a man has the right goal in mind, he enters to renew himself in the Lord."

"How does it happen?" I queried. "I mean I understand the first half, that is, your theory about how our souls have grown dark. We've closed our eyes, shutting out the light of the sun. Consequently, we're no longer the image we're meant to be, I mean the image of the Word of God. Now what I wish to know is how the image is restored. And what does that have to do with entering a monastery?"

Athanasius gazed at the shore that passed by slowly, considering my question.

I pressed. "What's the process?"

He smiled. "Process? It's not easy, but thanks to God, Arnobius, it's possible. One has to become pure again," he explained. "That's the purpose of the monastery. Simply put, your soul has to once again reflect the light of God, the pure light of Being itself, of Love."

"But how?" I shrugged. This, above all, was a point I couldn't understand. "How is it possible if our souls have become darkened? What can a man do? What can *I* do? As I see it, it seems the only option is to free ourselves from our own shackles and make the arduous climb out of the world of darkness and shadows into the light of the sun."

"Impossible," countered Athanasius, shaking his head.

"But how, then?"

"Well, impossible in any final sense."

"Why?" I asked.

"Because we're not our own creators."

"But you said we've created our own darkness."

"True, but that's different. It's secondary. It's not within our power to create the light. What we require is a kind of re-creation or renewal by the Creator."

I nodded, listening, bidding him to continue.

"It's like this, Arnobius. God created. Why you ask? Why did God create? God, after all, was perfectly fine without creation; God was whole, complete. But like a wise man without a student or a father without a son, or perhaps even a beautiful woman without an admirer, he created out of love. God loves; God shares. That's the nature of God's being—the nature of Being itself, the Good. God is not jealous! God wants everything to be good, to attain fullness—the fullness of being! Plato declares as much in his own account of creation—do you remember? Jesus said much the same. 'I have come that men may have life, and have it to the full.' Therefore, we who were not came to be in God's loving light; when we first existed, our souls originally shone with his love. 'It is good,' he said. This was our reality until we turned away toward what we had formerly been, toward that which is not."

"Toward nothingness?" I asked.

"Yes, our natural state. It's what we are in and of ourselves."

"And so our present darkness," I suggested.

"Right."

"But how, then, the restoration of light?"

"It is love."

"Love?"

"Patient love. It's like the father who waited for his own son to return from a life of debauchery. The son who had been secure in the wealth of his father went off to experience the pleasures of the world as if they were somehow greater than the security, pleasure, and love he had known at home. Soon, however, he became tremendously poor and nearly died. Finally, wasting away and living the life of a beast, the son chose to return to his father. Whereas the father could have begrudged the son of his prior choice, he was manifestly delighted. When he saw him from far away through clouds of dust, he ran to meet him, joyfully welcoming him into his life again. Because of his father's love, the son was restored to his former life and existence. But now it was really more, Arnobius. Now the son was wealthier than before. For then, not only did he possess all he required for a good life, but now he truly knew the measure of its worth against the poverty and want he had experienced."

"But why? Surely the father didn't have to?"

"You're right. Neither did God. Rather, in a sense, God had several choices."

"Which?"

"Well, for one, God could have overlooked what had happened."

"Unlikely," I said. "The very idea seems to go against our conception of justice, that true harmony has to be restored instead of the mere appearance of harmony, the overlooking of discord."

Athanasius agreed. "That would be to allow everlasting corruption, injustice. The image of the Word would remain forever hidden. In point of fact, man's nature, as well as the rest of creation that yearns for man's restoration, would be more like chaos than order."

"What else, then?"

"Another option would have been to simply allow man to sink back into the nothingness from which he was drawn."

"Possible," I allowed, for it seemed to match the reality of life and our world. But truly? Something in my heart felt that this too would be a tremendous injustice. I told him so. "I think not," I proposed. "The return to nothingness would amount to a kind of failure on God's part. It would be like the builder of a city who begins with grandiose plans only to have his greatest, most important building collapse. And, as you said, the Word would remain obscure beneath the ruins."

Athanasius agreed. "How could God allow that? How could the immutable One determine to share his love and light with us only to allow us to fall back into dark nothingness?"

"Impossible," I declared, hoping it was otherwise.

With that, we came back to where we had begun. God gave light; we shut our eyes; now all was dark. And yet, Theophilus, I felt we were somehow closer to discovering how it was that a return or restoration was possible.

Athanasius led the way. "Listen to what we've said."

"What?"

"Man chose this fate, this evil."

"Right," I conceded. I had already—at least theoretically. But really, it was too much for me. And so, I asked, "Why did God allow the choice in the first place?"

"Of necessity," he replied.

"How do you figure?" I asked.

"Think of it this way," he suggested. "The first time around, when God created the heavens and the earth and man along with the whole of creation, he didn't do it in conjunction with our own choice and cooperation, right? I mean tell me Arnobius, did you ask to be created?"

"Of course not," I responded.

"No. How could that which *is not* ask to be from that which *is?*"

"Ah!" I said, catching on to what he was getting at. "But this time around it must be different. The first time was without our choosing; the second must be with, just as the son didn't choose to be born, but chose to return home to the father."

"Precisely."

"But how?"

"Again, we are faced with several possibilities."

"Let me guess. For one, God could simply make the choice for us. He could force open our eyes."

"That's one option. He could, but he doesn't."

"No," I agreed. "That would be a violation of our will, of who we are as men."

"Still," averred Athanasius, "God *must* do something. In that, we are agreed. He can't simply turn a blind eye or allow us to sink back to our natural condition."

"Then what?"

"Consider it this way," he offered. "The first time around, in the first creation, man was made in God's own image. As if a fine painter, God painted by means of his own Word, his own reflection, and man was the resulting portrait."

"An image of the Image of the One?" I asked.

"Yes," he grinned, realizing how abstract it sounded.

I grinned too.

Then Athanasius said, "It was as though the Word sat for a portrait. Or rather God the artist looked into a perfectly reflective mirror in order to paint a self-portrait."

"I see."

"Now, what would happen if the painting suddenly turned away after the portrait was finished?"

"How strange," I commented. "What do you mean?"

"See it like this. Does the one sitting for a portrait stay around once it's finished?"

"Of course not."

"So, what if while he was gone, the painting suddenly fell from the easel to the dirty ground below? What if it purposefully caught a gust, like a sail greedy for wind, and was carried away?"

"Well," I said, "I imagine it would be covered with dirt." Then I laughed.

"What?" he asked.

"I can't imagine it."

"I know," he allowed, chuckling, "but recall, Arnobius, no analogy is perfect. All I ask of you is to imagine."

I closed my eyes and saw the portrait dirty on the ground by its own choice.

"There it is, unclean. Perhaps some of it is torn. Then what happens?" he asked.

"There it'd stay," I concluded, opening my eyes.

"But we agreed it wouldn't—at least not forever."

"So we did."

"Well then, that wouldn't be the end of it. Yet powerless to lift itself again to the easel, consider what would happen. The portrait would stay there in the dirt where the many passersby would step on it. Finally, trampled by so many feet and ground into the dust, it would be worthless. But what would happen when the artist returns longing for his own self-portrait again?"

"I suppose he'd curse it before picking it up."

Athanasius laughed. "Indeed he did curse! But would he leave it there—I mean, assuming he truly thought it had been a good portrait?"

"You mean after threatening to assign it to a place deep in a pile of trash?"

"I mean just that."

"No—I doubt he'd leave it there."

"I agree. Rather, he'd see what he could do to repair it."

"That makes perfect sense, unless the portrait was beyond restoration."

"Sure. But haven't we agreed that the artist wouldn't let it go that far?"

"Did we?"

"I mean when we said that God wouldn't let us fall back to nothingness."

"I suppose," I consented.

"So here's where we get to the restoration. The painter picks up the portrait, and after dusting it off—no simple process—he sets it back upon the easel."

"And then?" I raised my eyes.

"Well, first he must call upon the man who originally sat for the portrait. In this case, it's the Word himself or his own reflection, his own image in the perfectly reflective mirror."

"And after that?"

"Then he paints again. But it's really more, Arnobius. It's here where—if it hasn't already done so—the analogy breaks down entirely. What I mean is

320 Tim J. Young

this. In order for it to work, the man portrayed would actually have to become the portrait itself. Do you follow?"

"I believe I do, but it makes little sense to me."

"So now we must speak plainly."

I waited for him.

"The truth is God the Word became man so that man might become God."

I thought about this, puzzled. I'd heard this slogan many times before, but it made little sense to me—little sense beyond what Greeks had always said about the gods entering our world.

Athanasius tried to explain. "God the Word became man, descending into the nothingness of death, into the wood itself and the pigment and wax of the portrait, in order to restore the whole."

"The whole?"

"Yes—the image of the man portrayed. *His* image."

"I see," I allowed. But still, I wasn't sure.

"And now, Arnobius, now that God has become man, man need not ever fear death again. Now his destiny is life; it is light once again."

I thought about it before asking, "How does it happen? In your analogy, the painter finds the painting and decides quite on his own to restore the portrait. Does God restore by fiat?"

Athanasius shook his head. "Not at all."

"But it seems he does," I countered.

"Remember. God became man. Here's the point—*as man* he chose to open his eyes to the light of God."

"But how can he make that choice for all men? I mean, it seems to me that he did it for himself alone."

"True. If he were only a man, this would be the case, even as it was with Socrates who opened his eyes to the light above and who doubtlessly wished to choose well for all men."

"So how?"

"Let's approach it from another angle."

"Which?"

"Adam. Do you recall what our holy writings say about the first man?"

"Remind me," I bade him.

"They say he acted contrary to God's command."

"If so," I responded, "then he did so for himself alone."

"Not quite."

"Why not?"

"Because he was the first man in the old creation, and in him was the whole human race, just as an oak tree with its many branches is in an acorn."

"I see," I conceded, willing to go along with this for a moment. I recalled the Stoic doctrine of the one nature we share as human beings, the one community we are. "So when Adam made the choice, we all made it in him?"

"Yes."

"And now, what has changed?"

"Now, with the Christ, it is much the same as it was with Adam. But now all things are new. We are restored in him who is the image of the invisible God, the firstborn of the new creation. In him, God creates all anew."

I nodded my assent, but it all seemed too neat, Theophilus, too logically parallel. The old restored in the new; Adam remade in the Christ. That's not to say I didn't find it attractive. I did. But in the end, it just didn't seem workable, and so I enlisted that one simple question I had asked so many times before: "How?"

"How, you ask. Let me venture an answer," he said, "but I warn you, it may not be to your liking."

"I'm sorry," I apologized, "I don't mean to be difficult."

"Not at all," he assured me. "It's just we speak of things that are beyond our natural capacities. They're mysteries—not contrary to reason, but beyond."

I accepted the conundrum.

Athanasius hesitantly began. "It has to do with the fact that human nature is one. But mind you," he said, as if to explain his hesitation, "I'm now going beyond the firm bounds of tradition and straying into the unsettled lands of speculation."

In my mind it didn't matter; we had been there all along.

"To understand you cannot think sequentially, that is, from the beginning of time in Adam to the end. Instead, you must consider our nature as coming from its true beginning point or source."

"And what's that?" I asked.

"It is Christ the Word."

"But isn't that what we've been saying all along?"

"Partly, yes, and partly, no."

"Why partly not?"

"Follow what we've said. In our analogy, we began with the first portrait, the one that existed before it fell to the ground. Let's call it Adam."

"Fine."

"Fine, yes, but recall the reality of our true nature. We are the image of God the Word. But more. We are the image of the Word made flesh made God once again, the firstborn of all creation."

I looked at Athanasius, confused. "What do you mean?"

"I mean this. In a sense, the true or final or fullest beginning of all, of history, of us, is this Christ the Word of God who is one with God in being, and yet one with man, possessing both the fullness of divine and human natures."

I granted him the point, Theophilus, if only to allow him to advance his explanation.

"Well, when he did so, the Christ lived an ordinary life as a man in our world before preaching the kingdom of God and finally dying a bloody death on the cross. Why was this? It was to satisfy justice by making the decision as a man, for men, to be one with God."

"But how can his death possibly accomplish this?"

"That," Athanasius expounded, "has to do with the mystery of death."

"Meaning?"

"Meaning that left to ourselves, dying is our natural state. We are radically limited. We are mortal. Isn't that what the poets have always said in contrasting our own human being with the diving being of the gods? Thus, as mortal, we are more non-being than being; we're practically nothing. Think of it! And worse, we are trapped in this nothingness."

"The dark cave," I suggested.

"A fair analogy. And so in dying, in entering the dark cave, as it were, the Christ descended into that nothingness we had chosen by closing our eyes; he became *our* nothingness, our suffering, Arnobius, so that you and I and all other men might be released and come out into the light of God."

"I see," I said. "And so his dying descent is the act of creation *ex nihilo*, from nothing, as Christian philosophers say?"

"In a sense, yes. In a sense his death was *the* act of creation—of the new creation from the nothingness we had chosen. And in this sense, then, Adam was only a step to this real or full beginning, as if Adam were the moment when a carpenter pulls the hammer away in order to hit a wooden peg."

"So the Creator had this in mind all along?"

"It's conceivable," allowed Athanasius. "But remember, I'm only speculating. Perhaps it's like the Peripatetic idea of the unmoved Mover. Are you familiar with it?"

"Remind me."

"According to the Peripatetics, the unmoved Mover moves us from ahead as the object of desire rather than from behind. We desire and so we come to be. Adam's true and fullest cause was not yet born according to the usual sequential thinking of history, and yet the Christ existed from before all time, from eternity."

I scrunched my brows and said I understood—*mostly*.

And yet ...

As we continued to row up the Nile toward Tabennisi, I couldn't let go of the sentiment that Athanasius' explanation was so theoretical, so abstruse, and so heady. I daresay it seemed unreal to me, however sensible. It was like one of those abstract ideas of Plato or Plotinus. Indeed, I felt I could have found it somewhere in their body of ideas if only I had searched long and hard enough, if only I had teased out all the right conclusions. But in the end, Theophilus, it wasn't enough. I didn't need a new idea. What I required was something far more down to earth. As I always had, I wanted a way of life.

Finally, as night approached some hours after our lengthy discussion and we anchored alongside a small village, I shared this sentiment with Athanasius.

"You're right," he consented.

"You agree that easily?" I asked.

"Absolutely. It *is* heady. But that's where our religion is different. It's far more than a mere theory. And how do I know this?"

"How?" I asked.

"I know," he said, "because the love of God has actually changed lives."

I nodded, supposing that I couldn't disagree with that. *Still*. I still wanted to beg of him how that love could change *me*. How could *I* be restored?

"Look around you, Arnobius. What do you see?"

It was three or four days after our last conversation and we stood in Tabennisi amid dozens of mud brick monastic cells—the monks call them *larvae*. The sun shone brightly overhead.

"I see the monastery," I said, declaring that which was most obvious.

My simple answer, however, wasn't quite what Athanasius had meant in asking what I saw.

"What, then, do you mean?" I asked.

He smiled before saying, "Look beyond the outer form—the buildings and the labor, the men and Abba Pachomius; look at their lives. It is their lives that are the strongest argument."

Immediately, as if someone had lit a candle in a dark room, I knew what he meant. He spoke of the monastic life. Yes, I knew, for having been at the monastery for several days, I had witnessed it. He meant to say that it was their simple life. It was their struggle to convert, to move from darkness to light. Yet it was more. It was more because they actually lived in the light. I saw it. Above all, I observed their brotherly love. It was Love itself, palpable, knowable, and real. And there, standing next to Athanasius, I finally knew the remedy, how the image could find restoration. My hunch had been right. It wasn't an idea, I required, Theophilus; I didn't need another abstraction—not even *the* Abstraction. Rather, it was a way of life I required. Standing there, I knew these men had changed because God was living in each one of them. Expressed in each one of their lives was Love itself.

Over the next few days and weeks I knew a measure of tranquility again for the first time in my long, adult life. Not that I fully possessed it, mind you—not at all—but I tasted of it in a way I'd never known before, not even before Stella the slave had died. Somehow, peace was there among the monks in the monastery.

During this time, I followed their daily routine, praying and laboring. Much of my time was spent in silence—God's silence, Theophilus—reading the sacred oracles and considering their meaning. Oftentimes, I sat out beneath the great blue sky alongside the flow of the Nile and contemplated the One. I thought about the divine Artist, the Logos, the Word made flesh, and I considered his work of restoration. I struggled, and for once, I trusted. And *that*, Theophilus, set me free—for the moment, at least.

In time, however, we had to leave. And so as if departing from the calm of a peaceful harbor, we pulled anchor in order to return downriver to Alexandria. On the way, I told Athanasius I was ready.

"Ready for what?" he asked.

"To be initiated," I revealed.

For a moment, he said nothing in reply. Then, grinning widely, he extended his hands and prayed, thanking God and blessing me.

Upon our return to the city, I planned to receive instruction in order to obtain final initiation into the Christian mysteries. I thought I had finally come to that place of peace I had yearned for since I was a young boy in Carthage. I'd found my home. I believed once again. The river of life was mostly still.

But then, Theophilus, the river abruptly plunged over a falls, and I failed—or others, rather, failed me. Either way, I was falling headlong into the chaotic white of the crashing, rushing river below. I felt I was drowning.

The Cell in Tabennisi

Early Evening

Theophilus: LIKE SO MANY MOMENTS IN TIME along the lengthy stretch of that day, Abba, Arnobius grew quiet once again and his expression grew dim. I could see he was upset, sad, and yet he seemed resigned to this sadness. The skin sagged moistly beneath his eyes.

For a time I looked outside the cell and wondered about what had happened to him. I saw the sun was setting. I could tell because the blue shadows had grown longer.

Finally, after turning to Arnobius, I asked, "How did the others fail you?"

At first, he didn't answer. Instead, he asked for a cup of water and so I poured him one.

When he was finished drinking, he dried his mouth and said, "I was scandalized."

"By what?" I queried.

He looked up at me. "Think of it, Theophilus. What argument had Athanasius made for the Christian religion?"

Foolishly, as if forgetting everything he had just said, I tried to sum it up by expounding the restoration made possible by means of the Word made flesh. I got lost in abstractions. Being and non-being, I explained in the manner of a philosopher—Being itself becoming non-being so that non-being might become Being itself.

He laughed.

"What?" I asked, knowing his laughter somehow came at my own expense.

"Nothing at all," he said, before asking, "what else?"

I thought about it. Finally, I concluded, "Ah, of course—the argument concerning the lives of men."

"Precisely."

"Precisely," I echoed, "but what about it?"

He stared past me. Then obscurely, he remarked, "It takes truth, Theophilus, innocent as it is, bright with light like the face of a child, and tears it apart."

"What does?" I asked, seeking clarity. He spoke as though a Pythian priestess.

"Scandal," he replied.

"Scandal?" I repeated.

Arnobius went on cryptically. "You think you have it, you think you know it, when scandal comes along slashing through the middle of truth like cold iron through warm flesh. You cry! You scream! The pain, the terror! The one thing you wish for turns out to be other than it seems. And there, behind the truth, you discover deception. It reveals darkness behind the light. Because of that, things go from good to evil as all of reality not only fails to make any sense, but reality itself is finally turned inside out in such a way that it's impossible to make it right again. Reality has become a monster. It's a dark chasm like Tartarus. And there you're left falling as if in a nightmare, falling forever and ever into the darkness, down into the abyss."

"What happened?" I asked.

He didn't answer and I could sense he didn't want to speak of it. Still, after some time, I again whispered, "What happened, Arnobius?"

He turned to me. "Men," he declared. "The lives of men."

I nodded. "But who?"

"All men," he stated.

"All?"

"Not all," he admitted.

"Then which men?"

Finally, he declared, "Athanasius himself."

"The bishop?" I said, surprised.

"My friend."

"What happened?" I asked.

He answered vaguely. "There were waves of accusations, tall, dark, crashing waves. And for a time I suspected that Athanasius acted more the part of a thug than—"

"A thug?" I interrupted, hardly believing it possible. *Papa Athanasius?*

Arnobius' expression was flat. "So I suspected."

"Why?" I begged.

"I'll tell you."

I waited.

Then, drumming up the necessary courage and resignation, Arnobius began. "The immediate occasion occurred as we neared Alexandria. On the way downriver, we received word that a man called Ischyras was acting the part of a priest."

"I've heard of him," I revealed.

"I'm sure you have. He and the wretched Meletians have been the cause of great strife in Egypt."

"Didn't he have a large church built in his honor?"

"He did," Arnobius confirmed, "but that's to get well ahead of the story."

I nodded. "So, what happened?"

Arnobius explained that a few men had gone to investigate Ischyras who lived along the lake.

"Lake Mareotis?" I asked.

"That's the one," he said. "While we waited onboard the boat, the priest Macarius and a few others made the short journey to the small village where Ischyras dwelled. There, they discovered the truth, that he was in fact playing the part of a priest."

"What do you mean? Wasn't he ordained?"

"No," said Arnobius. "At least not canonically. A man called Colluthus had merely granted him a pseudo-ordination."

"And so the scandal?"

"Not exactly," he explained. "Colluthus was more like an old bone in search of flesh. Rather, it was what Macarius and his fellows did."

I leaned closer. "What was that?"

"First I should clarify." Arnobius leaned toward me as well. "It's what Ischyras *claimed* they did."

"What did he claim?"

"He said they burst into his church, the one in his house, and cruelly shoving him aside—abusing him, he later vouched—they violently over-turned the altar upon which he celebrated the holy rite. Then they broke his sacred chalice by hurling it in anger against the floor and stomping on it."

"My God!" I exclaimed. "How horrible!"

"It was. And afterwards, Ischyras came running up to Athanasius. He jogged up to our boat from his house in the village not far away, and scream-ing incoherently, furiously—pulling at his dark hair, his dark eyes wide—he demanded the bishop do something about the outrage."

"Sounds fair," I judged. "What did Athanasius do?"

"Nothing."

My mouth fell open in surprise. "Nothing at all?"

"I'm afraid not," he shrugged. "He refused to see or speak with him."

"And so?"

"And so, with Macarius and the others back onboard, we sailed on."

"What happened next?"

"I confronted Athanasius."

"What'd he say?"

"He claimed that Macarius had done nothing wrong."

Arnobius paused.

Then: "But *I* saw him. I saw Ischyras screaming like a mad man. And I knew it. *Something* had happened."

"What do you think?"

Arnobius' eyes flashed with thought. Then he admitted, "It's possible that Macarius didn't commit a crime; it's possible, as Athanasius asserted, that he didn't do anything wrong. But had he done what was right? That's what I wanted to know. Had he failed to do the right?"

Arnobius shrugged his shoulders, leaning back once more.

"And so you went home?" I inquired.

"Yes. Instead of remaining in Alexandria for instruction, I returned to Carthage and to Mother and my sisters and my one brother, and I figured I would simply take some time to reflect upon what had occurred."

"What'd you come to think?" I asked.

"I didn't know what to think," he admitted.

"So, what happened?"

He sighed. "What happened?"

I shook my head.

Arnobius sat across from me in my cell as the sun began to dip beneath the earth and the shadows grew longer. He sat there until after a long while he began the story again, as though he must, as though a duty, as if to trudge through it all would bring him finally to his end. Whatever had happened, it pained him.

Thirty: Conspiracy

328 to 335 A.D.

ISCHYRAS WAS ONLY THE BEGINNING, Theophilus. Although he came to have grave significance for Athanasius' future, Ischyras the pseudo-priest was only a single brick in the construction of accusations built up against Athanasius over the next decade. The Eusebians had gathered. Those allied in mind with Arius and following the clever leadership of Eusebius of Nicomedia had collected themselves together in a well-organized body, readying themselves to move against the bishop of Alexandria.

According to them, they did so for the sake of justice. Athanasius had been falsely ordained, they said—or so went their immediate claim. Actually, their alliance against him was for an earlier offense. Athanasius had lobbied against them at the great council of Nicaea. He had opposed Arius, Eusebius, and their allies, and had favored the creed expounding the homoousion Christ. But there was more—and for them, it was of greater significance. Athanasius had been directly involved in the excommunication of those who were anathematized. He had also supported their humiliating exiles ordered by Constantine, during which many had lost the ear of the emperor—besides the honor and prestige of ruling the Church.

But all was not lost to them. Rather, just a few years after the council, and shortly after Athanasius was ordained, Constantine permitted Eusebius to return from exile. Consequently, he was back in the Imperial Palace demanding Arius' restoration to his church in Alexandria.

As for me, Theophilus, I was back in Carthage during that time working for my family and mulling over what had happened. Whatever I learned, therefore, I learned through correspondence with Athanasius or an occasional visit to Alexandria. For though I suspected him of injustice, I retained a strong sense of respect for him, and despite my misgivings, a strong sense of friendship with him as well.

I learned Eusebius had written several threatening letters to Athanasius. His tone was such as to reveal the attitude of a certain aggrandized power, as if the bishop of Nicomedia had somehow come to possess more ecclesial authority than that of Alexandria, the ancient See of Mark. "Restore Arius," he demanded, "or face the consequences!"

"The consequences?" Athanasius retorted in written response. He explained to me that Eusebius had no jurisdiction in Alexandria. But not only that. More importantly, it would be wrong—both morally and pastorally—to allow Arius' return. "I can't do it," Athanasius wrote in reply to Eusebius. "I *won't* do it. The council excommunicated him, and therefore it is not within my power to restore Arius to our holy communion."

Eusebius went to Constantia, Constantine's sister. Complaining, he begged her to speak with her brother. "Remind him of his past errors," he suggested, "of Crispus and Fausta, and how he put Licinius, your husband and his own former friend and ally, to death. Suggest that perhaps a little good would atone for his own sins."

"I will," she agreed. Off she went to the emperor, her delicate white feet carried her to accuse the bishop of Alexandria by whatever means. "Constantine, dear ..." she reportedly said. She went on to beg for Arius' restoration, proclaiming that Athanasius was an irresponsible prig and that Eusebius had every right to see his friend restored to his church in the wealthy neighborhood of the Baucalis.

On some level, the emperor must have agreed. At the very least, he saw the need to act. As a result, he dictated a letter to Athanasius demanding Arius' return.

When I learned of this from Athanasius, I wondered if it had really been Constantine's desire to write the letter. I suspected someone else had composed it after gaining access to the emperor's signature and seal. One of Eusebius' men, perhaps. But it was not the case. I know, because it sounded far too much like Constantine to have been otherwise. As Athanasius described it to me, the emperor demanded that Arius be restored. Why? Can you not conjecture, Theophilus? He demanded reconciliation for the sake of unity of the Church and so the Empire. I'll say no more. At end, Constantine reduced his demand to its simplest form: either you, Athanasius, bishop of Alexandria, restore the priest Arius to his rightful place, or I will depose you.

I understood and felt his motivation; there had been far too much of philosophical wrangling in the Church. Yet the nature of the Christ was not merely a matter of opinion. As Athanasius had explained, everything seemed to hang upon it. But deposition? Wasn't that going too far? Had Constantine the power to depose a bishop of the Church? Of course not. Athanasius reminded him of this.

Constantinus Augustus, he wrote, must I remind you that you are the emperor of Rome and not a bishop of the Church? It follows, then, that you have no jurisdictional power in the Church. Bishops shepherd, not emperors. Therefore, my conscience before God, I cannot allow Arius, that wolf, that offspring of the antichrist, to come among my flock once again.

Nor would he.

Constantine, for his part, was appropriately chagrined upon receiving Athanasius' admonishment. This, to his credit. Although he quite sincerely viewed himself as the bishop of external affairs—as he termed his own position—he knew he was no ordinary bishop. Thus corrected, he was appropriately tempered.

Still, his sister was not. Instead, reports had Constantia complaining to her brother like the steady dripping from the corner of a tiled roof. There the *drip drip drip* splashes upon the paving stone of the ground. Eventually a groove appears and finally a hole. "He must have his place!" she insisted, repeatedly. "It's unjust! Quite horrible, brother! Arius is a good man—if only you'd get to know him! You must let him return! Remember your own sins. Are *you* one to judge?" On and on, *drip drip drip*.

Doubtlessly, Eusebius was behind this steady campaign of protest and grumbling. Rather than realizing the error of his position—if in nothing else than in overstepping proper episcopal bounds—Athanasius' bold refusal to readmit Arius served as a trumpet call to gather Eusebius' party together in order to pounce on all those who were allied with Athanasius and his homoousion Christ. "Orthodox!" he mocked. "The fools! Their teaching is no better than the doctrine of an irrational child!" With a flood of letters, therefore, Eusebius rallied his party to act.

They did act, and their purpose was straightforward. It was to depose Athanasius and his allies. Their reasons? Complex, to be sure. But in short, they moved to retain their own episcopal positions toward the end of preserving their own theological opinions—as the Church and Empire, it seemed, were only big enough for one side or the other.

In time, the contours of the Eusebian plot became more and more evident. Consequently, my suspicion about Athanasius and his own behavior

lessened and I came to trust him more once again. What else could he do—
really—than stand up for his own episcopal rights and the doctrines of the
Church?

Over the next few years, the Eusebians brought charge after charge
against several bishops who were all allied with Athanasius. In Antioch, for
example, where Iamblichus had died a few years before and where Eusebius
and Arius had long-ago studied with the martyr Lucian, Eusebius marshaled
together the whole of his party. They assembled to make their first hit as if a
mob of criminals abusing an innocent shop owner. Their target was Eustathius the bishop of Antioch.

Now Eustathius was a holy man, Theophilus. Or so his friends claimed.
His enemies, on the other hand, painted quite a different image—and for
good reason, I suppose. What I mean is that he declared himself their mortal
foe at the great council of Nicaea. During that time, Eustathius stationed
himself against them in mortal combat as a furious champion of the homoousion Christ against Arius' own doctrine of the created Christ. Ever since
the council, Eustathius had continued fighting against the Arians. In fact, he
was perhaps a bit overzealous, as, for instance, when he harangued the other
Eusebius, the bishop of Caesaraea, for his alleged cooperation with them. In
consequence, for this and his other work hounding Arians anywhere and
everywhere, he paid a significant price. In a synod called by the authority of
Eusebius of Nicomedia and hosted by Eusebius of Caesaraea, Eustathius
stood trial before the Church. They demanded his deposition.

"For what?" he countered stridently.

Eustathius asserted he was positive that his was the one and true theological position of the one Church.

But that wasn't the issue, they claimed. Rather, they accused him of
adultery. Although chastely vowed to the Christ, he had slept with a beautiful
young woman the age of his own daughter had he had one.

"Have you ever seen this woman?" the prosecutor, a man handpicked by
Eusebius of Nicomedia, asked Eustathius.

The woman in question was a whore. She stood before them all, draped in
a modest tunic the natural color of wool so as not to inflame the lusts of
anyone present. She was of some beauty, yes, or so people said, but nevertheless a woman who offered her body to men for coin.

Firmly, Eustathius declared, "I have not."

"Never, huh?" said the prosecutor, smugly.

"Never!" he snapped.

Then, turning to her, he asked, "Have you ever seen this man?"

Meekly, she nodded.

"Where?"

The woman nervously grinned. "He's our bishop."

"*Your* bishop?"

"Mine."

"Are you, then, a believer?"

"I am—though I haven't yet been baptized."

"But you *are* a Christian?"

She dropped her head as if in shame, covering it with a mantle she pulled at from behind.

"What is it?"

"I have fallen."

"How?"

She was silent.

"In adultery?" he suggested.

She nodded.

"With whom?"

The woman looked up; she pointed to Eustathius who gasped.

The prosecutor turned to the bishop. "What have you to say?" he demanded.

Eustathius breathlessly denied the accusation. "She's ... she's lying!"

It was then that Eusebius of Nicomedia stood from behind. The prosecutor stepped aside in order to allow him to speak.

"You know a bishop must be above reproach," he admonished.

"Of course I do," Eustathius announced. "And I am!" he insisted. "Neither have I seen this woman, nor have I ... slept with her!"

Still, Eusebius feigned not to believe it, which allowed his majority party to insist upon Eustathius' guilt. The result was predictable. Eustathius, the patriarch of Antioch, was deposed.

In his place, the Eusebians installed another bishop, Paulinus, who was allied with them and their plan of moving the Church forward according to their own vision of the Christ.

I wish I could say this was the end of their maneuvering, but it was not. Rather, as I went about the affairs of my own family, sometimes in Carthage and sometimes in Alexandria or another city, and as I continued to correspond with Athanasius when I was not there with him in person, I heard that the Eusebians were persisting in their strategies against the other bishops allied with him. In all, they were successful on several counts. Indeed, in time, it seemed to me that Athanasius himself was poised to fall. I told him so on one occasion when I was in Alexandria on business. He, for his part, disagreed.

"I don't think so," he countered. "I've done nothing wrong. And as for deposition, they don't have the right."

Nevertheless, I reminded him, they discovered a way with Eustathius and several other bishops.

Still, he wasn't worried. Instead, Athanasius turned the conversation away from his problems toward me. "If anything," he said, "I'm worried for you."

"Why?" I asked. But I knew. He always kept at me as a goatherd does a stubborn goat.

"You've put it off for so long, Arnobius."

"What can I do?"

"You can make up your mind and begin instruction."

When? I thought. That I didn't know. I had lost the clarity I had experienced during the voyage up the Nile a half decade before.

"I'll pray for you," he said.

I thanked him and I meant it. Yet how could I join an assembly that was not one, it seemed, but many? How could I be party to a love that was so full of discord? I couldn't. Not then. And perhaps, I thought, not ever. The One, it seemed to me, had very little to do with the Church—or churches, rather, which better reflected the desires and power struggles of the many.

Meanwhile, as Athanasius prayed for my soul and I remained uncertain, both sides kept at it, fighting. A few years after the Eusebians achieved their victory against Eustathius, they allied themselves with another breakaway group in Egypt. Odd, that. The two really had very little in common except for their antipathy for Athanasius. Which group, you ask. They were the Meletians.

The Meletians had long been divorced from the one Church in Egypt. In short, Meletus, for whom they are called, had been passionately dissatisfied with the way Peter, the former bishop and himself a martyr, had dealt with apostates during the persecution of Diocletian and Galerius. Peter, he complained, had treated them with far too much compassion, allowing their return to the embrace of the Church when, he argued, they should be set aside for the fires of hell. Because of this, Meletus broke away from Peter, who rightfully occupied the chair of Mark, and he established himself as the bishop of his own breakaway church. Ever since then, his faction has grown, supported by rigorists everywhere who believe less in the creative mercy of God than in his righteous judgment.

It was the all too familiar story, Theophilus. There was rancor; there was hatred. Lies flew like swarms of arrows occluding the light of the sun. Maneuvering followed as well as battling for victory. Then at the great council of Nicaea, the Meletians were restored to proper communion with the Church. This, of course, didn't work. It did for some, but not for the majority. Instead, when Athanasius was ordained bishop—improperly, the many Meletians vehemently asserted—they used his ordination as an excuse to sever themselves once again from the one body of the Christ.

So why the alliance with the Eusebians you wonder? One point is certain. It was not a matter of belief—for their original dispute with Peter, and later with Alexander, was a matter of discipline rather than doctrine. As I have indicated, their cohesion rested upon an intense disliking of the bishop of Alexandria. On the one hand, the Eusebians wished to dislodge Athanasius as their chief enemy and as the one who refused Arius his proper place; on the other hand, the Meletians envied him, for they believed Athanasius had robbed them of the episcopal election, and that his power as bishop therefore was somehow theirs by right.

However it was, that is, however their alliance formed, the Meletians and the Eusebians finally joined to bring charges against Athanasius and others—including the priest Macarius—over a period of several years. Let me give you some idea of these.

First, there was the pseudo-priest Ischyras. Of this, I have already said a few words, but allow me to say a few more. Now allied with the Meletians and the Eusebians, the man officially accused Athanasius of ordering his secretary Macarius to desecrate his household church. He claimed that Macarius had abused him, that he had entered his house uninvited as Ischyras lay ill in bed, and that he had overturned the holy altar of the Eucharist, smashing his one chalice, and spilling the sacred blood on the ground. Macarius balked. As did Athanasius. Still, there was no real conclusion. Next, Athanasius was accused of extortion. Several Alexandrians gave witness that the bishop had instituted a kind of tax on linen in order to bring more gold into his own coffers. What did he allegedly do with this gold? The answer to this question formed part of the next charge. His enemies claimed that Athanasius had allied himself against the emperor—the Coptic bishop against Roman rule. Purportedly, he had given gold to a thug called Philumenus in order to support a revolt. Philumenus was just like Lucius Domitius Domitianus, they claimed, some thirty years before. Again, Athanasius balked.

In the end, he was exonerated. Having received word of this serious accusation, Constantine sent his own men to investigate. They found nothing, and subsequently, the emperor wrote a letter declaring Athanasius innocent of all charges.

Still. I have to admit that at the time, even I wondered. Despite Constantine's grant of exoneration, which he could have approved for any reason, there was just enough plausibility to leave room for suspicion.

Exoneration or not, the Eusebians and Meletians maneuvered again. It was then I became sick with suspicion. They brought a charge so concretely demonstrable that I myself nearly abandoned Athanasius to these vultures. I didn't, though, and I feared for my friend. But more, Theophilus, I feared for me. If the accusation were true, if Athanasius or his men had in fact committed such an atrocious deed, then I knew this one fact would be the end of my own searching. The light would go out, and I'd be left in the dark. If Athanasius was guilty, then in my mind, his God was guilty as well. Rotten fruit would prove a rotten tree.

What was the charge? The Eusebians and the Meletians accused Athanasius of murder. You laugh. But to substantiate their charge, they offered solid evidence. Moreover, aside from murder, they accused him of sorcery, of practicing black magic, of using the poor murdered man's dead withered hand as a kind of charm against them.

When I first heard word of the accusation, I wondered if it were true. How could one man be accused of so much if he were truly innocent of all? I thought of Constantine. I remembered when he put his own son and wife to death. And for what? For a suspicion. And wasn't *he* a good man?

When I later queried Athanasius about the truth of the matter, he assured me the accusations were false. At the time, I was passing through Alexandria.

"But how can I know?" I asked. I'd seen too much of the ways of men, both in the Church and without, to know with any certainty.

"You can't," he admitted, "you can't be certain."

No, I thought. Like everything else, we can't know.

Once again, I planned on returning to Carthage and forgetting it all. I comforted myself with the thought of duty, and I hoped to work hard for my family until I died. When my time was up, when Clotho called for the end of my role in the play, I'd go sleep with my father Buteo and my younger brother among the rest of the dead. And if I was lucky, I'd meet up with Stella and Katrina again.

Athanasius, however, intervened in my meandering, despondent plans. "If you truly want to know, then you should come with me."

"Come with you?" I asked. "Where?"

"To Tyre," he announced.

"Why would I do that?"

"To join me in support," he explained. "I've been commanded by the emperor to go."

"But why? You've mentioned nothing of this."

"No—but you've only been here for half a day."

I had. I'd just arrived from Carthage and was on my way to Pelusium on business.

"He's ordered you to Tyre?"

"Upon pains of exile," threatened the commanding letter. "Or worse!"

"Worse?"

"That's what the missive said."

"My God!—what's at issue?"

Athanasius smiled. "The Eusebians and Meletians have succeeded in having a council called in my honor. They hope to depose me just as they deposed Eustathius and the others."

"My God!" I exclaimed again. "So it's finally come down to this."

"It has," he confirmed.

"And you're certain they'll not succeed?"

"Not certain," he admitted, "but confident."

Confident, I thought. I wished I could have such confidence. In Athanasius. In other men. And yet there was something that told me he was telling the truth.

"When do you leave?" I asked.

"Me?" he replied.

"Yes," I returned, not getting his meaning.

"So you won't come then?"

I laughed. "Really, Athanasius, why would I?"

He hesitated. Then he said, "The emperor should be there. He's on his way to consecrate a new basilica in Jerusalem.

"Constantine?" I asked, surprised.

As it happened, he wasn't at the council in Tyre, Theophilus. But at the time, neither of us knew this would be the case.

"Yes," Athanasius confirmed. "And I thought that perhaps you could vouch for me."

But did I want to see him again? Did I wish to see Constantine? "I haven't spoken with the emperor in years," I revealed, "nearly a decade."

"Nevertheless, don't you think you might be of some use to me?"

"Perhaps," I allowed.

"And," he went on, "don't you have other interests in Syria?"

"Sure," I disclosed after a moment's deliberation, "I do, but—"

"Perfect then—it's settled," he concluded as if it were the case.

Yet it wasn't. I told him I would think about it.

I did. The more I considered the possibility of going, Theophilus, the more it made sense. First, as he suggested, I could check up on family affairs. Although we had a man in Tyre, it wouldn't hurt for me to see how our business fared personally. Mother would doubtlessly appreciate this. But more. As I thought about it over the next few days, this is what I realized. I wanted to go with Athanasius to witness the council first hand in order to know if he was guilty. I wanted to know so that I could believe—or not.

It was three days later.

"When do we leave?" I inquired, straight-faced.

"You're coming?" Athanasius asked, smiling.

"For a bit," I responded. "Just to check up on business." I knew, however, that I'd be there for the council's duration.

"I'm glad," he admitted. Then, returning to my initial question, he said, "Soon. They've already taken Macarius to Tyre in chains."

"In chains!" I exclaimed. "Will you travel in like manner?"

"Not me. I assured them I was no risk of flight, and they agreed to let me travel as I wish."

"Well, then, I'm at your disposal."

"Thank you," he said.

We departed a few days later. The whole way I wondered what would happen.

Thirty-one: Tyre

Summer 335 A.D.

IT HAD BEEN YEARS SINCE I had last passed through Tyre. The last time had been with Constantine some thirty-five years before when we had travelled with Diocletian toward Nicomedia. I reflected on this as we passed through the great triumphal arch that leads into the city. As I studied the orange sandstone blocks that one by one make up the arch, I thought of all those years that had gone by bringing me to that singular point.

We entered the city passing through a great colonnade, its columns topped with Corinthian capitals. Below us were large, marble paving stones. Eventually the road led into the old city, which has stood for thousands of years. If Herodotus is right, then we can trace its existence back to the faintest memory, to the time when the great pharaohs were first creating order in Egypt some three thousand years ago. Sometime later, Tyre sent out men to colonize Our Sea. They sailed far and wide, settling along the stretch of every coastline, establishing cities including my own, Carthage. We made our way through the old city, meandering along its narrow corridors between old houses and new and past marketplaces and rows of apartment buildings that rise several stories into the air. Finally, we came out into an open space again, passing by a rectangular theater before eventually coming to the church where Athanasius would be tried.

We entered the church's colonnaded courtyard where we first caught glimpse of its magnificent facade, including its three great doors. There, we stopped.

"Shall I accompany you?" I asked Athanasius.

"No," he said. "It's better they see me alone."

I nodded my understanding, and suggested I would remain waiting for him next to the marble fountains in the middle of the courtyard. Athanasius turned and walked into the basilica. When he opened the center door and light flooded into the church, my eyes passed down the basilica's column flanked nave to the elevated sanctuary and the altar positioned there. Before it, a few men hunched around a table. As the door slowly began to close behind him, Athanasius walked toward these men. I imagined what would happen next. He would tell them of his arrival, and sternly, they would inform him of where he would reside during the council and how things would proceed. Finally, because I could neither see him nor inside the basilica any longer, I strolled around the courtyard and waited for his return by the streaming fountains.

It was an hour or more. Now, he wasn't alone. Rather, when Athanasius emerged from the church, he did so with a guard of two rough looking men.

"What's this?" I asked, eyeing the other men as he walked up to me.

"Safety," he assured me laconically before motioning he'd explain later.

When later came, when we had come to our lodgings not far from the church—an apartment—and when we were at last alone, he explained, "They don't trust me."

"No?" I said.

"No—and so the guards."

"Guards?" I motioned, chuckling. "Those two men look ..."

Athanasius finished for me. "Like drunkards—I know. Still," his voice dropped to a whisper, "we must keep them on our good side."

"We must," I agreed. "And what of Macarius?"

He sighed. "I inquired of a man in the basilica. He reported that they have him locked up in a room not far from here."

"Another threat?" I suggested, my brow elevated.

"That's the supposition."

"And the rest of our party?"

"The rest!" Athanasius laughed. "Do you mean Timotheos and Philip?"

Timotheos is a deacon with a head full of black, Coptic curls who has worked for Athanasius for many years. I mentioned him earlier on, Theophilus. He is a tall man with a gentle soul. In contrast to Timotheos, Philip is short and intense. Feisty. He reminds me of the dogs I used to see the Gallic shepherd boys use to corral their sheep. Keen eyes. Sharp attention. Impatient. Refusing anything out of line.

"Are there no more?" I queried, for I knew others had gone before us.

"None," he responded. "I guess I failed to tell you. They've barred all our allies."

"The other bishops?"

"Everyone," he said. "Aside from you and me—if indeed I can presume you are with me," he smiled, "we have Macarius, Timotheos, and Philip."

I remained astonished. "They've allowed *none* of your bishops?"

"None."

"But now the council is stacked against you!"

"Possibly."

"What of the others?"

"As for Macarius, you know how he fares."

I did.

"And as for Timotheos and Philip, they're two floors up."

Just then, there was a knocking. Athanasius swiveled and opened the door.

"Yes?" he said.

One of the guards was there. Athanasius told me he smelled strongly of old spoiled wine.

"I've been asked to tend to your needs," he declared, roughly.

Athanasius turned to me. "Do you need anything?"

"Perhaps some wine," I requested, winking, "and a loaf of bread."

Athanasius relayed the request and the guard turned to leave. As he did so, Timotheos and Philip appeared.

"Ah!" exclaimed Athanasius. "The two deacons! When did you arrive?"

Timotheos replied, "A few days ago, Papa. I'm sorry we couldn't make better provisions. They wouldn't allow it."

"What, this? This is perfectly fine. And more," he went on, grinning, "we like the guards. If nothing else, they make us feel safe."

Timotheos and Philip entered the apartment.

"I was just telling Arnobius how few of us they've allowed."

"A scandal," said Philip. "But it is what it is."

"Have you learned Macarius' fate?"

"Locked up—no?"

"He is. And when he's out and about, they have him in chains."

"But isn't that how *I'm* supposed to behave?" joked Athanasius. "I thought I was the one that locked people up!"

The rest of us laughed. But it was forced. And over the next few days, any true sense of humor faded as the council got underway.

+ + +

The beginning of the council of Tyre was innocent enough. As it happened, there was initially little in the proceedings that had to do with Athanasius. Instead, the sixty or so bishops discussed a variety of ecclesial issues having more to do with the Orient. Above all, they discussed the inauguration of the new basilica in Jerusalem. They decided that Eusebius of Caesaraea would give the inaugural oration and that Asclepas, the Arian bishop of Gaza, would read the inaugural prayers. Once they put this and other rather trivial matters to rest a few days in, the council turned its attention to church discipline.

It was the end of the day when the *comes* Dionysius, a man of consular rank, stood to give a brief speech. He was neither a priest nor a bishop, but a man in Constantine's service whom the emperor had appointed *conductor* of the council. When he stood, his guard stood with him. They seemed to take their duties quite seriously, for they stoically stared through all of us as if we were nothing but bloody meat if we decided to cause any trouble. There were more guards stationed at the doors of the church and around its perimeter.

"Why all the trouble?" I motioned to Athanasius at one point.

"If only I knew," he retorted.

As it happened, however, the men in arms *were* useful on several occasions, Theophilus. But of that, later. For now, Dionysius stood clad in senatorial white, his toga fastened by a golden brooch, and looking out among all those present, he disdainfully declared, "Today begins our investigation."

Investigation? Indeed. It was the beginning of a trial.

As he said this, I heard one bishop behind me murmur to another that he expected the proceedings to lead to Athanasius' deposition. I wondered if Athanasius had heard.

The *comes* Dionysius continued. "I shall not lead the proceedings noblemen; rather, that will be done by Lord Bishop Eusebius of Nicomedia and his prosecutor. My sole purpose is to keep order. And order, mind you, *will be* kept."

I looked to the guard. I glanced around at all the churchmen, then back to the *comes*.

Finally, after he was done explaining how matters would proceed, he said, "The day is nearly done."

"It is," I heard someone whisper from behind.

Ahead, standing before us, Dionysius licked his rather dry lips, evidently yearning for the moisture of wine. "Consequently," he ordered, "we'll stop for today. Tomorrow, we reconvene at the third hour."

He dismissed us, and there was a collective sigh.

Athanasius glanced over to Timotheos. "Then, tomorrow it is."

Thirty-two: The Trial

Summer 335 A.D.

THE FOLLOWING DAY BEGAN EARLY. We awoke with the sun and went to a church to pray. I say *a* church, because it was not the same as the one where the council was being held. According to local lore, the small church can trace its lineage back to the apostle Paul, to when he met with a small group of early Christians at Tyre. It was there also, or nearby, that Peter confronted the deceiver Simon Magus, the magician, whose consort hailed from Tyre. In any case, we prayed the usual morning prayers. I followed along, Theophilus, not out of a habit of prayer, but from a habit of sociability. After prayers, we broke the fast and finally made our way to the basilica of the council.

When we arrived, many of the bishops were already present along with many priests, deacons, and others, and there was a certain buzz of excitement among them as if they were finally going to achieve a long held and much cherished goal. Athanasius would finally fall in disgrace.

After making our way down one of the side aisles, we took our seats alongside Timotheos and Philip. Macarius was not present. In fact, we didn't see him until the third day of the trial, for they kept him in his room under lock and key until then.

The third hour came and went. The *comes* Dionysius, it seemed, was detained on other business, and so we waited for the proceedings to begin, some of us more impatient than others. Finally, however, we began. Dionysius arrived and opened the day by reading a brief letter from the absent emperor, which commanded all present to work in the light of truth toward the end of unity and peace. I smiled. The same old man, I thought, my old friend Constantine. I wondered if he would come to Tyre, not then knowing that he would not.

At the end of his reading, Dionysius sat down and Eusebius of Nicomedia, as large as always and as magnificently attired as ever, stood to begin his party's long list of accusations. In a way, I was surprised that he was involving himself so intimately with the trial. If anything, I imagined he would want to distance himself from the dirty business of bringing down another bishop.

"Athanasius of Alexandria!" he bellowed. "Stand and present yourself to the council."

I noticed he didn't refer to him as bishop.

Athanasius obediently stood, and with a show of magnanimity, Eusebius continued, "Athanasius, it is with gratitude that I welcome you to these proceedings."

Eusebius grinned widely and extended his hands as if in brotherly reception toward Athanasius who stood there as a lamb led on to slaughter. Then quite suddenly, the expression of his face altered slightly toward malice, and Eusebius raised his right hand so that his palm now faced Athanasius as if to punctuate his former welcome with caution.

"For as you well know—and certainly it is known throughout the Church and the Empire—you have not always been so malleable. Indeed, it was not very long ago that you refused to attend the council held at Caesaraea. Despite the insistence of the emperor, you stubbornly refused."

Eusebius paused. As he said the last, stressing the *refused*, he held his gaze upon Athanasius who remained standing there humbly. Then he glanced about the church.

"You refused, it would seem, due to a general failure of character. You are an obstinate man, contumacious. And why?" Eusebius shrugged for effect. "It seems obvious. Instead of being a shepherd who cares for the good of his flock, you go about seeking your own good, your own increase and power."

I nearly laughed aloud. *And you, Eusebius?*

As for the bishop of Nicomedia standing there and gesturing before us, he made every effort to appear as though he didn't think about his own desire for power at all. Rather, he stepped closer to Athanasius who remained unmoved.

"You, Athanasius, are possessed by a rather unfortunate lust for domination. We have witnesses who tell us that when you were last called upon to attend the council—the one organized by none other than the emperor himself—you cast about violently, insisting upon your own freedom, your own authority, and your own right to go where you pleased and when you pleased. But that's not all!"

Eusebius shook his head. And I admit it, Theophilus, I hated the man—or I felt a strong antipathy toward him.

"These trustworthy men reported to Hyginus, governor of Egypt, that you behaved in a way that is nothing short of treasonous to the emperor."

Impossible, I thought. And yet I wondered what the specific content of the charge would be. I remembered the former accusation of treason, that is, the one asserting that Athanasius had given gold to the traitor Philumenus. But this matter had been put to rest when Athanasius had been exonerated. Was there something else?

"Yes!" Eusebius went on, as if in response to my own silent thoughts. "*Treason.* They say that in raging response to the emperor's demands, you threw stones at the statue bearing his image. Consider that! You picked up rocks from the dust of the ground and hurled them at the image of our august emperor—the same one who has done so much good for all of us, for both the Empire and the Church!"

Athanasius said nothing in reply. As he later told me, he knew these charges made by the Meletians to the governor were empty, and so, as with the Christ before the procurator of Judea, Pontius Pilate, he knew it would be best to remain silent. "Still!" I protested, later on. "One must stand up for oneself." "True," he allowed, "but on the right points and at the right time. I could tell Eusebius was just blowing smoke. The real fire would come soon enough. And that," he confirmed, "would require the waters of spoken truth." So it was.

For the moment, Eusebius allowed these accusations to seep into the ears of his auditors before saying, "That's not all—although this treason alone is enough to rob you of that which you most desire, episcopal power. Beyond a desire for authority, for lording it over other men as our Lord emphatically commanded the Church's shepherds *not* to do, and beyond the desire for honor and those trappings of honor attending power, it seems you cannot control your other passions. Which ones? I ask. In reply, I say those of the groin, the lowest of them all, those most diametrically opposed to the mind and the virtues. It seems you have not been chaste."

There was a murmuring among the crowd of men present. I suspect many were thinking that if only the others possessed omniscience, then they would find them guilty of the very same offense. Eusebius, however, presented himself as pure of all sin. He knew we didn't know. Or so I supposed.

Then, turning to a man who was sitting behind him, he asked him to stand. He did. "I present to you our chief prosecutor, the priest Demetrius."

Demetrius stood. He was draped in a perfectly clean tunic the color of an elephant's tusks, and his dark brown leather sandals were tied up fashionably to the knee. He bowed to the gathering. Meanwhile, Eusebius sat down on a golden chair behind. Without another word, Demetrius carried on with Eusebius' initial prosecution as a second runner might in taking the baton from the first.

"Athanasius," he announced, "the council charges you with rape."

"No!" shouted several of the councilmen rather dramatically from behind, and it occurred to me that they had planned their protest long before.

Rape, I wondered. Why? I mean, adultery is one matter, Theophilus. But *rape?* Given the number of women and even boys for hire in Alexandria, why would a man—let alone Athanasius—resort to force? The charge was absurd. But there it was.

Then an odd twist. Before Demetrius could say another word, the deacon Philip stood to object. "Demetrius!" he called out.

The latter turned, and looking upon Philip with disgust while recognizing he was one of Athanasius' two counsels, Demetrius demanded, "What is it?"

"The *bishop*," Philip said, to underscore this one fact, "must not be made to stand throughout the duration of this trial."

Demetrius objected.

Philip, however, continued over Demetrius' own flabby protest. "If you and your side insist on heaving empty claim upon empty claim at the bishop, then Athanasius must, at the very least, be allowed to sit. This is custom."

Demetrius squawked. "You must not call him the *bishop* of Alexandria!"

"But he is!"

"It's the very question at issue—among others!" Demetrius countered.

"Still, he must be allowed to sit!" Philip insisted.

Demetrius hesitated.

Then, from behind, a flat command: "He may sit."

We all looked beyond Demetrius.

Again, "He may sit." The tone was that of an order. It was the *comes* Dionysius speaking from behind Demetrius. "Noblemen," he explained, "we must not allow ourselves to get bogged down by such ludicrous squabbling."

Demetrius nodded. *Of course not.*

Therefore, Athanasius sat down next to Timotheos and just in front of me. Philip, however, remained standing as Demetrius began again.

"Let it be according to the conductor's will," he conceded, bowing to the *comes* Dionysius. Then, turning to Philip, he said, "And yet, I beg to differ with your characterization of these charges. They are far from being empty. In fact, as we shall now demonstrate, Athanasius is guilty of rape. This we shall prove with the most concrete evidence."

Just as he finished saying this, Demetrius pointed to a side doorway leading into the church. All eyes followed. Amid all the churchmen, there appeared a lone woman who was led by a short fat deacon into the hall. Poor woman, I thought. Who was she? Whoever she was, she was plainly dressed from head to toe. From what I could see of her face, which possessed relatively attractive features—dark eyes and wisps of dark hair that fell to either side—it was not painted like the usual woman for hire. Rather, purposefully, I assumed, her face was shorn of all décor. The fat deacon led the woman to stand next to Demetrius. As she entered, I saw Athanasius turn to Timotheos and whisper into his ear. What is it? I wondered. I couldn't hear.

Demetrius asked Athanasius to stand. When he did, Timotheos stood next to him. Then, to Demetrius' panicked surprise, the woman, unbidden, began to speak.

"It's *that* man!" she shouted, pointing.

Demetrius intervened. Or rather, he tried unsuccessfully as she went on.

"He's the one who burst into my room just a month ago! I was sleeping in bed when he knocked down the door and came after me!"

The other deacon, the heavy one who led her in, moved to quiet her. But the woman easily dodged him to the left and shouted, "I sat up in bed. My gods! I screamed. And he lunged at me, tearing apart my pure white robe before ..."

"Silence!" cried Demetrius.

"I was naked! And he looked at me and felt me, and then he ..."

Demetrius moved to silence her along with the other deacon.

But Athanasius intervened. "No, let her go on!"

"It's you!" she accused, pointing and sobbing now. "You're the dog who violated me! You stole my virginity and now I'm ruined!"

"Him?" asked Athanasius. He said it evenly, as though he were the counsel and not the one on trial.

"Yes!" she cried, pointing at Timotheos. "He's the dog!" And gesturing downwards, she finished, "And hardly a man, too!"

"Quiet!" commanded Demetrius.

The fat deacon grabbed her from behind. But for the rather theatrical sobbing of the poor woman, there was quiet.

Then Athanasius countered, "But *I* am he."

The fat deacon tightened his grip.

"Who are you?" she asked.

Demetrius intervened. "She's confused," he suggested. "It's dark ... it's hard to see ..."

"Who!" she insisted.

"Perhaps her mind has grown dark," offered Athanasius, "along with yours."

"Not at all!" Demetrius' protested.

"It's clear she has no idea what she means or whom!"

Athanasius turned to the woman.

"Who are you?" she asked quietly, clearly confused, afraid of some error.

"I am Athanasius, bishop of Alexandria."

Her face flushed.

"Now, tell me the truth!" he insisted.

The woman realized her foolish mistake. "The truth?" she peeped. As she had done before as an act, she continued to weep, her tears now fearfully genuine.

Finding his feet once again, Demetrius intervened. "You can't pressure the witness! Although it's your usual tactic, you can't here! This is not *your* jurisdiction!"

"Still," ordered the *comes* Dionysius from behind, "if she has made a false claim, then we must know."

"I ..." she began.

"Then I shall ask the questions," Demetrius insisted.

Athanasius ignored him. "Who put you up to this, woman?"

Demetrius objected. "The poor woman is not on trial!"

But Athanasius went on. Or rather, he tried to. For just then, ten or so rough men allied with the Eusebian party began to make trouble from the back of the church. At first, they attempted to quiet Athanasius with heckling. "Leave the woman alone!" they cried. But when that didn't work, when Athanasius persisted in his line of questioning, they began to grow physically disruptive. "She's just a weak woman!" they shouted. And crash! One threw something! It was a chair. Then another overturned a table. "We won't stand for it!" they cried. "Athanasius won't get his way!"

Now others joined in. "He's got no jurisdiction!"

Soon, stamping forward they turned toward our party, toward Athanasius, Timotheos, and Philip, with the evident intention of beating them into submission. They were large men. Clearly, Theophilus, they were not churchmen, for they were neither appropriately attired nor did they possess the manner of a priest or deacon.

In front of us Dionysius stood. He understood their intent and loudly called them to order. But it didn't work. His words went unheeded, and the men advanced forward crashing now through empty chairs and over several wood tables and anything else in the path that separated them from us.

It was then I heard Dionysius' command to the guard. Calmly, he ordered, "Bring these men to silence!"

They did. The armed guard rapidly fell to action and within a few minutes, and after a brief battle in the middle of the basilica, they knocked out all the rabble-rousers on the floor. A few lay dying—they'd never get their coveted silver. Their number was nothing against the swarm of guards.

At the end of the violence, I sighed, relieved. Then the *comes* Dionysius stood to command the obvious. "We'll recess for a few hours," he directed. "Then, gentlemen, there will be no more of this nonsense!"

But nonsense there was. When at last the council reconvened after the heat of the day had passed, the priest Demetrius stood as he had in the morning and rather gravely read from a new series of charges. "Athanasius," he stated, "you are charged with the following: one, of an irregular ordination. Instead of following the laws promulgated by the council of Nicaea, laws that require a majority of bishops to ordain one into the office of chief shepherd, you instead gathered just a few bishops, those allied with you and the former primary, to ordain you covertly in the church of Dionysius." After glancing up, he read on, "Two, you are charged with extortion. For years, you have garnished wealth in the form of gold by means of an irregular tax on linen—irregular in that it is beyond your ordinary jurisdiction. Three, of treachery for purposes of gain. You gave a portion of your inordinate wealth to Philumenus so that he would be able to instigate rebellion against the lawful rule of the emperor and Empire. He, of course, has already met his fate. Now you shall meet yours."

The deacon Philip stood to his feet. I could see he was incensed, and yet he struggled to contain himself. "I can't let this stand!" he cried. "As I shall prove to you in just a moment, these groundless accusations have already been put to rest by the authority of that very same emperor, Constantine Augustus!"

Demetrius gestured insolently, "Well then, make your demonstration."

Philip stepped back to the wooden table next to us and retrieved a small scroll. Then, moving forward, he confidently announced, "I read to you from the emperor's own hand."

To the church at Alexandria under the care of Bishop Athanasius
From Emperor Constantine, servant of the one Church and Empire

I have searched into the matters that have been brought to my attention and I am pleased to say that they were worth very little of my time. Believe me, my brothers, the wicked men who brought these charges against your bishop were unable to effectuate any suspicion in my own mind. Rather now, in contrast to these empty allegations, I confirm his character. Neither is he guilty of plotting illegal taxation nor of planning treachery against the emperor. Consequently, I enjoin you to put all such matters behind as unworthy of your own time and consideration. Look unto the one God and love one another in peace and unity of mind. As for me, I joyfully welcome Athanasius as your bishop and as a man of God.

Given the month of April in the twenty-fifth year of my reign

Philip finished reading and began to speak. Before he could utter another word, however, Demetrius stood, and as though one covering his tracks, he said, "Just so. I have only mentioned these former charges to indicate Athanasius' character, or a general pattern of suspicion regarding his character. Indeed, there are far more serious charges—and we will get to them."

Apparently, Theophilus, he had suddenly decided to drop the other charges—I mean those of an improper ordination, irregular taxation, and treachery.

Pretending nothing had gone awry, then, Demetrius went on as if all were well. "Since you presented a letter, I will also read from a recent letter, one just four months old, from a man who was brutalized by Athanasius and his goons."

"Is this a new charge?" queried Philip. "What is its relevance? Who is it from?"

Demetrius didn't answer. Instead, brusquely turning away, his voice sonorously filling the basilica, he began to recite from a papyrus scroll he had secured during Philip's own reading moments before.

> *From the monk Callistus*
> *To Apa Paieou and Apa Patabeit*
>
> *It is under sad circumstances that I write, dear brothers, and yet you must know what has happened here as of late.*
>
> *It was not long ago, on the evening of 24 Pachon, that Athanasius' vicious dogs pursued Isaac, bishop of Letopolis. On the previous day, the attack had begun just as he was leaving Heraclius the recorder's house. That day, thanks to God, he escaped. But he was not safe. They continued their pursuit the following morning, making their way to Nicopolis, a suburb of Alexandria, and finally to the military camp just outside the city. There, Isaac was innocently dining with his host when the adherents of Athanasius attempted to kidnap him. The truth is that these men—perhaps four or five—were intoxicated as the attack began. Nevertheless, they succeeded in breaking into the camp in order to search for Isaac. The latter, thanks to God, escaped due to the sympathies of a few soldiers. But for these men, drunk with wine and with blood lust, it wasn't enough. Having lost their main prey, they transferred their drunken ire to four other brothers. They maliciously beat these before going to a hostel nearby the west gate of Alexandria where they abused the hostel-keeper for hosting Meletian monks.*
>
> *I write this as a warning, brothers. Beware of Athanasius and his men. Pass this along to other like-minded fellows. And may the peace of the one God be forever with you.*
>
> *Given the second day of the month of Paoni*

Demetrius glanced up from the letter. Then, frowning, he asserted, "This is clearly evidence of Athanasius' own brutality."

"Athanasius' own brutality!" objected Philip, repeating Demetrius' own words. "What's the charge?"

"It's obvious," asserted Demetrius.

"That may be, but according to custom you must give precise form to your accusation."

"I have."

"Then will you please do so again?"

Philip, I could see, was making every effort to compose himself with patience.

"I will," he huffed. "I shall do what I have already done." Then, after clearing his throat, he announced, "We charge Athanasius with brutality and offer this recent letter as evidence."

Philip turned from him. Looking at the rest of the men in the basilica, he judged, "How preposterous!"

"Preposterous?" remarked Demetrius from behind. "This is a real letter from real men who truly live and have truly suffered at the hands of the man you call the bishop of Alexandria!"

"At the hands of Athanasius, you say?"

"No other."

"But Demetrius, the letter says nothing of Athanasius; it simply makes a claim."

"A claim?"

"One of association. In fact, what it refers to are a few violent, drunken men. Then it goes on to claim a tie between these men and our bishop." Philip turned to Demetrius who stood facing him with his arms crossed. Then he asked, "What do we actually know about these men? Very little. Nothing more than one fact: they don't care too much for Meletian schismatics. Do we know from this letter that they are definitively allied with the bishop? Can we ascertain that Athanasius himself sent them to do such an admittedly horrible act of violence? Do we know that *he* ordered it?"

Demetrius shifted uncomfortably. Once again, Philip turned toward us in the hall of the basilica. "No, we don't. Instead, this is simply your feeble supposition. Therefore, here's what we should do. We should ask Athanasius, who happens to be here with us, whether or not he had anything to do with these drunken men."

"No, no, no!" answered Demetrius.

"But why? He's right here!" Philip pointed back to Athanasius.

Demetrius countered, "It's unnecessary. And perhaps you're right. Still," he went on, "the behavior of these men fits a certain pattern."

"A pattern?" asked Philip turning away from Athanasius and toward Demetrius. "What pattern?"

"It is a pattern of violence, of coercion, of rule by any and every means."

"But what you've offered as proof is insubstantial!"

"Possibly," allowed Demetrius. "And yet, the whole is punctuated by a crime so horrible, and I daresay so demonstrable, that once known these other incidents will prove more conclusive."

"What is that?" demanded Philip, indignant. "Is it another new and likewise baseless charge?"

"That," Demetrius claimed, "will have to wait."

"Yes it will," yawned the *comes* Dionysius.

Both Philip and Demetrius turned toward him and our gaze followed.

"For today," he declared, "this confusion has gone on quite long enough. We shall recess until tomorrow."

Philip was incensed. "But he can't make such empty allegations!"

Demetrius, on the other hand, was pleased. Cutting Philip short, he thanked Dionysius, groveling before him.

Dionysius, however, was stiff in his response, essentially ignoring him. Standing up and turning to a servant just behind, he ordered a cool jug of wine prepared for after his bath. The servant ran off to satisfy his desires.

As for Athanasius and the rest, they were soon speaking to one another in whispers.

Philip spoke first. "Do you think it will be——?"

"It's obvious," whispered Athanasius.

"The Meletian bishop," confirmed Timotheos.

Philip nodded.

With that, we returned to the apartment to plan for the following day. There to greet us, sitting in the courtyard, were the two guards who were already well on their way to a pleasant, if vicious, state of drunken oblivion.

Thirty-three: Arsenius the Bishop

Summer 335 A.D.

THE FOLLOWING MORNING, Eusebius of Nicomedia stood as he had the day before and gave the opening address for the prosecution. That morning he was especially well groomed and seemed quite pleased with himself as if something good would happen that day, that Athanasius would unequivocally come to terms with guilt, and, therefore, that they—the Eusebians and the Meletians—would depose him and install their own man in his place.

"Yesterday," he began, "the priest Demetrius was able to establish a general pattern of abuse relative to Athanasius' characteristic manner of behavior. Although it saddens me to recognize this, for any bishop's fall is in some sense a fall for the whole body of Christ our Lord, it must nevertheless be investigated and, once discovered, purged like a cancerous bulb. Today, my dear fellows, Demetrius will conclusively show how Athanasius has not, indeed, behaved as a noble bishop must, but instead as any commoner behaves, he has conducted himself in the lowest and vilest of manners."

Eusebius sat down upon his perch of gold near to the *comes* Dionysius, and Demetrius stood to begin the day.

"Athanasius rise," he commanded.

He did. As he did so, I saw him quickly look off toward a dark corner of the church where there was a small chamber veiled in shadows. Inconspicuously, he motioned to someone there with his right hand. Then he faced the prosecutor.

Just as he had done the day before, Demetrius officially—or officiously—read from a small, flattened scroll. "Athanasius, this court of the Church, in conjunction with the imperial power of Rome under the careful eye of the *comes* Dionysius, representative of the emperor Constantine, charges you with murder and sorcery."

A murmur. A whispering. Then aloud as if staged, "Murder! How can it be?"

"He's a bishop!"

"No, he *was* one!"

"He's evil!"

Once the crowd of men quieted down somewhat, Demetrius continued, first nodding to Philip as if giving a dog a bone, then to Athanasius, he said, "You may sit. For I would not have you stand during the shocking description of this crime."

Athanasius sat. Then:

"It is well known by now that you are responsible for the murder of Arsenius, bishop of Hypsele. It is the same as with Bishop Isaac, whom you harassed by means of your drunken thugs—"

Philip bolted from the bench. "That was never demonstrated!" he countered. "And neither is the other well-known as you say."

Demetrius waved his hand. "No matter," he said, calmly.

"Then you cannot mention it!"

"Perfectly fine," replied Demetrius. "I only mention it to better delineate the form of behavior deliberately obscured."

"A form you have yet to prove!"

"Perhaps. But if you would take your seat and exhibit a small measure of patience, I shall now show you and the others just why he is guilty of something far graver than what the monk Callistus reported to Apa Paieou and Apa Patabeit."

Reluctantly, Philip took his seat once again, and the prosecutor Demetrius turned toward Athanasius. "As I was saying, you had Arsenius kidnapped and killed. Why? Sadly, for one reason alone. It was because he was Meletian. Having disagreed with you and Alexander, he had allied himself with the bishop Meletus. Then, when Meletus died, he gave his allegiance to John Arkaph."

Philip stood. "Do you have proof of these allegations?"

"In time," retorted Demetrius.

Philip sat again and the latter continued speaking to Athanasius. "You took Arsenius and you detained him in a house, one far from his own diocese. Then, when his friends learned of his whereabouts, you murdered him in order to dispose of him permanently."

Again, and as would happen later, many shouted their disapproval as if cued by someone sitting among them in the nave of the basilica.

"How could he? He's a shepherd of the Church!"

"He'll pay in hell!"

"Athanasius doesn't deserve to rule!"

But Demetrius, as if above all such protest, motioned for quiet, and once the basilica had come to relative silence, he went on, "That's not all! Once the poor man, the servant of God Arsenius was dead, murdered by your own thugs, you personally came and sawed off his arm at the elbow."

There was a concerted moan, and Demetrius swiveled to those sitting in the church.

"Imagine that! A bishop behaving in such a violent manner!"

"Unimaginable!" they cried.

"Yes—and may it never again be so!" Turning back to Athanasius, he accused, "You hacked at his arm until drained of blood it fell from his corpse. Then, retrieving it for magical use, you and your thugs vacated the house and you ordered it set afire."

Again, the many trying Athanasius cried out with horror.

Demetrius persisted. "Running now, the flames behind you, those of hell which you so richly deserve ..."

I saw Philip stir ahead of me. He wanted to rise and shout objection, but Athanasius stayed him with a gentle touch to his hand.

"Running back to Alexandria, you had your chief magicians embalm Arsenius' precious arm so you could use it for wicked ends, for black magic, for sorcery."

My God, I thought. How can he say this?

"Therefore," he concluded, "we charge you with murder and sorcery."

Demetrius stood back.

In front of me, Athanasius quickly leaned over to Philip and whispered into his ear. As he did so, Demetrius stepped forward again and taunted, "Well?"

Philip, for his part, stood and walked over to the side of the church, disappearing into the shadows. Then Athanasius stood to defend himself.

"Dear brothers," he began. "I know it looks grim for me. And if true, then by all means I am among the most evil of men and deserve nothing less than death in some horrible manner."

"Agreed," judged Demetrius, shaking his head along with many others.

"But let's look at the facts. What evidence do you have to substantiate your charge?"

Demetrius smiled. Walking over to a table near to Eusebius, he retrieved a small wooden box, which looked like a miniature casket, and stepped over to Athanasius. Then slowly he opened it manifesting its contents to the whole church.

As he did, the entire council gasped and moaned in disbelief. My God, Theophilus, it *was* horrible. For there, lying in the box was the severed arm of Arsenius all dried up and withered like a grape under the sun.

"Indeed!" cried Demetrius in full agreement. "I too shiver with revulsion and disgust. And yet, I must show this horror to you because it's *his* arm!"

"Murderer!" shouted one from the back. The stone walls of the basilica echoed with the accusation. Another called, "Athanasius himself should die!"

Athanasius, however—the murderer, the sorcerer, the sadist—turned to Demetrius and to the arm resting stiffly in the box, and inquired, "So, Demetrius, you say before God that this is the very arm of Arsenius?"

"It is," he confirmed, gravely.

"And it is I who hacked off that arm?"

"None other than you," he confirmed.

"I wonder," said Athanasius. Then he looked away from Demetrius to where Philip had disappeared. "Philip!" he called out loudly.

Out of the shadows, Philip appeared.

Athanasius turned to the men of the council and asked, "How many of you know the bishop of Hypsele, Arsenius?"

Many raised their hands.

Athanasius further clarified, "What I mean to say is how many of you know him personally, that is, you would recognize him in the street if you saw him?"

Now fewer men raised their hands.

Turning around, Athanasius queried, "And you, Demetrius, do you know him?"

Nonchalantly and shrugging his shoulders, he averred, "Yes, of course I do. But I'm not quite sure I know what you're getting at."

"Would you recognize him if you saw him right now?"

"I suppose. But it's impossible—the man's dead."

Athanasius ignored this, asking, "Would you recognize just his face or his arms and feet too?"

Demetrius huffed. "Just his face, I imagine."

"Well, then, let's see. May I hold that?"

He pointed to the box holding the withered arm, and Demetrius gave it to him after first hesitating.

Opening the box once again, Athanasius asked, "Does this look like Arsenius' arm?"

"Well, no," replied Demetrius, grinning, "plainly not. No man runs around with shriveled arms!"

A few laughed at this.

But Athanasius was anything but joking. "Clearly," he conceded. "But let me ask you this."

"What?" Demetrius said.

Pointing toward Philip, Athanasius asked, "Do you know *that* man?"

"Of course I do," declared Demetrius with a smile full of disdain. "He's your chief counsel."

Athanasius shook his head. "No—I refer to the man behind Philip."

"Which man?" asked Demetrius. Neither he nor any of us could see him.

Athanasius commanded, "Come fully into the light, Philip. And bring him with you."

The two walked forward and stood next to Demetrius and Athanasius in the light. It was then that Demetrius flushed white and his lips turned a pale blue.

Athanasius pivoted, and pointing to a priest who had claimed personal knowledge of Arsenius a moment before, he queried, "My dear man, you said you were familiar with the appearance of the bishop. Is this he?" Athanasius pointed to the man standing alongside Philip.

For a moment, the priest said nothing. He just sat there, I imagine, not quite knowing what to say. Then, slowly, "Yes," he admitted. "It *is* Arsenius. I know him and this man is Arsenius, the bishop of Hypsele."

Now several men stood forward and emphatically confirmed the identification. "It's him!" they said, genuinely surprised, for not many had known the truth. "Glory to God, it's Arsenius! As if by some miracle, it's him!"

Athanasius turned to Demetrius who was still white with shock. "Look!" he commanded. He lifted the box and shriveled arm up to his nose. "Is *this* Arsenius' arm?"

Demetrius, wordless, began to sweat rather profusely.

Eusebius of Nicomedia, however, stood from behind as if nothing were amiss. He stepped forward, asking, "And what if by some force of magic, some sorcerer's trick, you've raised Arsenius from the dead? Whatever the case, *that's* still his arm in the box."

"Ridiculous!" cried Athanasius.

Philip agreed. "You lack proof!"

"Proof!" huffed Eusebius. "It's in the box!"

"Well then," advised Athanasius, "there's nothing left to do but to check for his arms."

"You can't!" cried Eusebius. "It's a trick! Egyptians have long been able to manifest things from nothing. Think of the magicians who battled Moses and Aaron! They were able to call forth serpents …"

Athanasius ignored him. Turning to Arsenius, he asked him to reveal his left arm to the council, for this arm was still tethered to his body—or so went the story.

He did. Arsenius stretched it high for everyone to see, wiggling his fingers.

"There it is," judged several of the councilmen, relieved.

"And the other?" Athanasius inquired.

Arsenius hesitated. He glanced at Demetrius then to Eusebius, both his erstwhile allies.

"See!" cried Eusebius, stepping forward to him.

"I see nothing!" cried another.

"I'm waiting," Athanasius kept on.

Then something began to emerge from beneath his cotton tunic. As a lodestone works on certain metals by means of some unknown property, Theophilus, so too did our collective gaze serve to pull this object from beneath the tunic's folds so that it was revealed for the whole world to see.

"It's magic!"

"It's sorcery!"

"It's a fake!"

"No," declared Philip, laconically, "it's an arm."

Athanasius nodded, as did many others.

Eusebius stood back as if repelled.

There it was, Arsenius' right arm, quite naturally attached to his right shoulder and to the rest of his body.

Then Athanasius turned toward Demetrius who looked sick. "If *this* is Arsenius' arm," he demanded, shoving the box and severed arm toward him again, its withered fingers pointing upwards at Demetrius as if in condemnation, "then whose arm is that?" He pointed to Arsenius.

Eusebius vociferously objected, waving his arms, his wide arms sagging with fat, the finest linen draped from them. He pronounced it was impossible. "You've deceived us somehow by the black arts!"

From behind him, we all heard a terse command. "Sit down you fool!" But he did not. Eusebius didn't even turn toward the *comes* Dionysius. Rather, for a moment, we all stared at each other, both sides, wondering what would come next.

You no doubt wonder what happened, Theophilus. I would have too, had Athanasius and the others not revealed it to me beforehand. Still, I was nonetheless shocked to hear the groundless accusation. How could other churchmen make such claims? And I wondered where the other side had secured a shriveled arm for the exhibit.

"What in God's name!" I exclaimed the day before when Athanasius informed me of the charge they would likely bring on the following day.

"What do you plan to do?" I asked.

"The only thing I can do," he drolly answered. "I'll produce the body."

"Dead?"

"No!" assured Athanasius, laughing, "quite alive!"

"But how?" I inquired. "Is he not deceased?"

"No," he explained. "He's very much alive."

"Where?" I begged.

Athanasius glanced over to Philip. "Nearby," he revealed.

"But what happened?"

"Let Timotheos tell you. He was there."

Timotheos chuckled. Athanasius, for his part, stood and walked to the other side of the room where he began to pace back and forth.

"What happened?" I asked.

Timotheos shrugged. "What shall I say, Arnobius? When they first leveled the charges against Athanasius some time ago, Constantine wrote to his half-brother Dalmatius and ordered him to investigate. After making his way to Alexandria, Dalmatius first met with the bishop in order to interview him. Athanasius, of course, denied having anything to do with it. In fact, since he had never even learned of any harm coming to Arsenius, the charge set his mind to wondering. What had happened? Who was responsible?

"So it was that Athanasius called Philip and me and asked us to do our own sleuthing. He didn't exactly trust Dalmatius and the others, and the story sounded far too suspicious. He wanted us to discover the whereabouts of Arsenius, whether dead or alive, and to ascertain if he still possessed both arms.

"Immediately, we set off up the Nile toward Antaeopolis in Upper Egypt, a day's journey before Lycopolis, an area which is dominated by Meletian monasteries. At the first monastery, we struck gold. Encountering Pinnes, the abbot of the monastery, he ushered us into a room in order to await a longer inquiry. Presently, he claimed there was a matter of business that could not wait.

"Indeed, it could not! For as we later learned, he went off to warn Arsenius to flee. Further, he jotted off a quick note to John Arkaph, the Meletian leader. 'They know!' he wrote. 'It's all exposed!'

"So it was that Arsenius fled. When the abbot returned to us, we shared a simple meal together, spoke of monastic life, of living solely for God, and suddenly—quite suddenly, I must say—the abbot had a change of heart.

" 'He was here!' he contritely wept, referring to Arsenius, the same one supposedly murdered and hacked apart by Athanasius.

" 'Here?' I asked. 'When?'

" 'I'm sorry,' he said, 'for though I cannot approve of Athanasius' treatment of our party, setting us aside as outcasts, neither can I approve of this heinous accusation against him.'

"I nodded before demanding his whereabouts. Pinnes told us. Arsenius fled to another monastery—or so he believed, down river.

"The following day, we departed early and arrived at the other monastery just before noon.

" 'He's no longer here,' declared one of the monks.

" 'He's not here?' we asked, surprised. 'But Apa Pinnes revealed that this is where he told him to go.' We didn't know if the man was telling the truth.

" 'He's not. You must believe me. Rather than staying, he went down river.'

" 'Where?' I queried.

"But the monk wasn't sure. 'Perhaps he's gone to Apa John,' he offered, in reference to John Arkaph. But it was only a guess.

"Well, at long last we ended our journey. At the very least, we knew Arsenius was alive and that Athanasius would be happy to know that."

"Was he?" I glanced over to Athanasius who was pacing and praying.

"Of course he was," said Timotheos. "The only difficulty was in further securing knowledge of Arsenius' whereabouts."

I laugh, Theophilus. They discovered Arsenius in Tyre just before Athanasius went before the council. Timotheos and Philip found him in hiding.

You can imagine what happened after they revealed his body and arms to the council all alive and all attached. Everything erupted into chaos. After Eusebius of Nicomedia rose to accuse Athanasius of deception by means of the black arts, and after he refused to take his seat again at the command of the *comes* Dionysius, and after we all stared at one another wondering what would come next, a gang of men descended on us from the back of the church. It was a repeat of the day before, as though a recurring nightmare, and I wondered why Dionysius hadn't better secured the proceedings. I could scarcely believe it.

Athanasius cried out, "*Comes* Dionysius!"

He need not have. The latter was already standing, confidently commanding. Soon, after a brief brawl during which the goons came after us, one landing a solid blow against Timotheos and striking his head with his large right fist, they were once again scattered, half of them having fled out the door, and half sprawled out around the altar of the church.

As for me, thankful I hadn't been hit, I rushed to Timotheos who was lying on the floor. Philip was already there kneeling next to him.

"I'm fine," Timotheos assured us, though he was in evident pain.

"Thank God," declared Athanasius.

"But what'll happen?" asked Timotheos, his eyes shut.

I wondered the same.

At last, Philip said, "If nothing else, I hope this fraud will soon come to an end."

Later it didn't quite happen that way.

Having been absent from the church for the better part of the afternoon, we gathered again ready to end the proceedings against Athanasius. Once the hall of the basilica came to a relative condition of tranquility—as there was still much confusion over what had earlier occurred—Philip stood to demand a full dismissal of the council.

"It's been a sham!" he cried. "Doubtlessly this is all we can expect, *Comes* Dionysius! What's the goal? It's obvious. Eusebius, Demetrius, and the others wish to depose Athanasius. 'Guilty!' That's the only verdict they wish to hear. Instead of seeking justice, as any real trial must, they actually prefer injustice."

Comes Dionysius nodded his head, tired of it all and weary from the earlier melee. "What is your wish, then?"

"My wish," demanded Philip, "is this. I call for a full dismissal of each one of the charges brought against Athanasius, bishop of Alexandria."

Comes Dionysius raised his eyebrows at this demand.

Eusebius and Demetrius both stood to object. The latter spoke first. "It's impossible!" Eusebius added. "The trial cannot be dismissed!" Then, waiting until all was calm again, Eusebius assured all present that there were other urgent matters which required investigation.

"Of substance?" asked the *comes*, doubtful.

"What else?" countered Eusebius, shrugging.

Dionysius laughed. "By the gods, what else, indeed!"

I could see he was bored. Standing up he ordered, "Then we shall adjourn until tomorrow."

Once again, as with the day before, he motioned to his servant to prepare a jug of chilled wine. It was now time to drown in a far more pleasant oblivion.

That evening, we all sat rather soberly in the apartment discussing what ought to be done. The nature of the council had become patently absurd, and we all knew it would continue as such. The fear was that the Eusebians would be able to find a way to catch Athanasius off guard, even as they had done with Eustathius the former bishop of Antioch. Already they had come dangerously close but for the fortunate discovery of Arsenius' whereabouts.

"I can't imagine how," observed Athanasius, "but I wouldn't put it past them."

"Not at all," agreed Philip.

Timotheos nodded his head—half of which was bruised.

Nevertheless, there was nothing they could do. Dionysius had ordered the council to continue, and so it would. Still, our party didn't rest at that. Philip, Timotheos, and Athanasius began to devise another preemptive plan. If justice were the goal, then justice they would have.

Thirty-four: Ischyras *Ex Parte*

Summer 335 A.D.

I AWOKE THAT NIGHT with a start.

It was Katrina and Belanus. I had just dreamed about them, as they had been twenty years before. Katrina was young and alive and Belanus brave. They were sitting next to me, speaking with me, laughing. I held Katrina for a moment and I remember she kissed me; I felt her wet lips on mine. But suddenly, they both vanished. Where they went, I cannot say. In their place was a rushing army clashing with another mass of men; they slaughtered each other down to a man. Then, as quickly as they died, and as soon as the blood flowed from their veins and seeped into the brown earth, their bodies disappeared. It was into the ground, I believe, but I'm not sure. What is certain is that Luxilla now stood before me draped in a divinely white tunic, freshly bathed as if a Vestal virgin. She was purity itself. "They're dead," she announced. I was quiet. I remember wondering how—*how was it that they had died?* She didn't answer. "You too must die," she revealed. *Me?* I thought. But she vanished, and all was dark.

That's when I woke up. That's when I sat straight up, my heart pounding, wondering what I had seen. What did it portend?

For a few minutes, I tried to return to sleep, but I couldn't. And the more I could not, the more I wondered what hour it was. How much time had to pass before morning would come and the trial would begin anew?

Finally, in order to know, as we didn't have a water clock, I decided to step outside into the courtyard to see the stars and the moon—if in fact they were visible and not behind a cover of cloud. When I did, the first thing I saw was our two guards sprawled out along the paving stones, snoring. Cloaks loosely wrapped them, and I imagined each was sleeping off his drink, as every evening they drank enough wine for eight men or more rather than two. I stepped around them out into the courtyard, and I finally peered up into the darkness of night. But ah! Theophilus, it was hardly dark. Rather, there were thousands, nay millions, of stars, and there was the moon, a quarter full. I smiled. I did so because I recalled that night deep in the past when Katrina had asked me what I was thinking. I had told her about the stars and how Plato believed that each star is the soul of a just man. She had asked me if we would end up there together shining from the heavens. I said she shouldn't think of it just yet, that first, we had a long life together. Then I wondered if that wasn't the meaning of my dream. I wondered if Luxilla had somehow come to me to let me know that my death was soon to come and I'd finally rejoin Katrina in the realm of the stars. If so, I was happy. Reflecting the light of the moon and the stars above, my heart shone with joy.

Suddenly, however, I was jolted out of my pleasant ruminations.

"What are you doing here?" growled one of the guards. I turned and he was standing behind me with a short dagger drawn.

"I live here," I explained.

"You?" he asked. "Come closer."

I did.

"Oh, right. And so you do."

I could smell the vinegary wine on his breath among other less pleasant odors. He stumbled before commanding, "Then why don't you go back to the apartment!"

I obeyed thanks to his knife—although strictly speaking, I wasn't under his command. I went back to bed and finally fell asleep, though not without difficulty.

"Wake up!"

It was Athanasius hovering over me.

"What is it?" I asked, groggily.

"You've slept for a long time, Arnobius. It's time to go to the church now."

"What hour is it?"

"Nearly the third hour."

I sat up. I could see the others were all ready to go.

"I'll catch up to you," I suggested.

Athanasius agreed to this and so they all departed to go to the church.

When I arrived some time later, Eusebius was already making the opening address as he had each morning. There he stood. He was proud I could see, gesturing for this and that, commanding his men to do his bidding.

"Whatever comes of this," he said, in reference to Athanasius, "we must go to Jerusalem to celebrate the building of the new basilica there."

As he said this, I took my seat behind Athanasius, Timotheos, and Philip. There was some discussion about the journey to Jerusalem, what would happen, and who would be responsible for what. Finally, Eusebius shifted course. "Now that we have dispensed with that, we must turn our attention once again to Athanasius. Although so far he has been able to slip away from justice—by what dark means, I cannot say—today we must investigate one last series of charges."

What more would there be? I wondered.

Following the pattern of the past few days, Eusebius left the substance of the work to Demetrius the priest. The latter stood to do his job while the other sat down, clean of all.

"Thank you, Lord Bishop," Demetrius said. "Today, my brothers, I must speak of a series of incidents which have transpired over the past few years."

As he said this, I noticed Athanasius motion to Philip. "Not yet," he gestured.

Demetrius continued. "As with before, these incidents establish a pattern of behavior on the part of Athanasius, a modus operandi and corresponding character that is quite below the just and holy behavior of any noble man, let alone a bishop. Let me explain.

"The first among them happened many years ago—yet he was never called to justice. The council charges Athanasius with sacrilege in ordering his man Macarius to harass the priest Ischyras."

Now, I noticed. Athanasius motioned to Philip that it was now time. The latter rose to his feet and cried out, "I protest the charge!"

"Speak," ordered the *comes* Dionysius, who had determined to take a more commanding role after the previous day's fiasco.

"This accusation was laid to rest years ago by the authority of the emperor Constantine. Why bring it up once again when both Athanasius and Macarius have been exonerated?"

"Indeed," replied Demetrius, looking first at the *comes* Dionysius before glancing at Philip and the rest of the councilmen. "And yet, we must reopen the incident if Athanasius is to be *fully* exonerated. For there still remains the shadow of guilt."

Philip balked.

Comes Dionysius nevertheless ordered the prosecution to proceed.

Therefore, Demetrius went on. "A full inquiry must be made, and so, for the sake of truth, we must reopen the investigation."

"Agreed," said Athanasius standing. "But first I must ask a question."

"If you must," allowed Demetrius, turning to him.

"What proof do you have to offer that Ischyras was or indeed *is* a priest of the Christ?"

"Proof?" asked Demetrius. "I'm not quite sure that it matters."

"But it *does* matter," asserted Athanasius.

"Why?"

"Because if he is not a priest, then two things follow. He can neither possess an altar on the one hand nor a chalice to hold the sacred blood of the Christ on the other. And if he claims both, then they are necessarily false."

Demetrius, however, disagreed. "No. There's where you are wrong. It actually makes no difference. The question is not about Ischyras and his status as a priest or layman, but whether or not *you*, the shepherd, have utilized violence against the flock under your care. And besides," asserted Demetrius, "we do have proof that Ischyras is a priest. He was ordained by the bishop Colluthus."

"But Colluthus is no bishop," countered Athanasius.

"However that may be, he was ordained by him, and now, rather than diverting the course of questioning in this errant direction as I see you prefer to do, we shall get back to the point. Here it is: you are charged with abuse, with ordering violence. You had your men, led by Macarius the priest, harass Ischyras in his own home."

Then, without allowing another word to Athanasius, Demetrius pointed to the back of the basilica and all heads turned to see what it was. There, standing in the dark—for the great doors were closed—was Macarius in chains.

"Come forward!" cried Demetrius.

He did. Escorted by four guards, his chains clanking along the smooth stone of the floor, Macarius came trudging along as a man weighed down with the full weight of the world. But he was not defeated. He was more like Prometheus who was unjustly chained by a despotic Zeus. Now his work was simply to bear up under the weight of his fate, to defy injustice. Athanasius' destiny was up to him and he knew it. So too was the future of the Alexandrian church and perhaps even that of the whole Church if Eusebius, Arius, the Meletians, and their men were able to wrest control of it from the homoousians.

Now, Macarius stood before Demetrius. I looked over and saw that Eusebius was grinning. Slightly, but there it was. This was his contest to win and Athanasius' to lose.

"Macarius," Demetrius began, "tell us why you went to see Ischyras."

Although the chains pulled him downwards, Macarius bravely stood straight to answer. "By command of Athanasius," he confessed, "in order to ascertain whether or not a rumor was true."

"And what was the rumor?"

"It had come to the bishop's attention that Ischyras was wrongly celebrating the mysteries."

"Do you mean incorrectly?"

"No—or that was not the question. The problem was that he was not properly ordained."

It was then that Demetrius veered from what might have been expected. Instead of suggesting that Ischyras had been ordained by Colluthus as he had done just moments before, he pursued another line of questioning.

"And who ordained you, Macarius?"

"Athanasius, of course."

"And who ordained him?"

Ah, I thought. Demetrius had cleverly brought the inquest around to the issue of Athanasius' own ordination as bishop—the very question that had split the Meletians from him in the first place.

"That is well known," Macarius replied.

"Perhaps that's so," admitted Demetrius, "but so too is it well known that you, on orders given by the same dubiously ordained Athanasius, went to Ischyras' house and molested him and his family before overturning his altar and smashing the sacred chalice."

"Well known," Macarius conceded, "but is it true?"

"That's precisely the substance of the present inquiry. And I must say I find it interesting that you yourself are in doubt. Maybe it was so long ago that you forget what happened."

"Not so!" shouted Macarius, defiantly.

"Do not grow angry," Demetrius chided, "it's not becoming of a priest."

For a moment, there was silence in the basilica. I could see Macarius was irate, and Demetrius thinly smiled to spite him.

Finally, the latter said, "That's enough. You may," he motioned with a flip of his hand, "go away now."

"But I haven't had my say!" Macarius shouted. "It's all a lie!"

"Still," said Demetrius. "You'll have plenty of time later."

The four guards, each brandishing a short sword, turned, and with them, they forcibly ushered Macarius down the nave and out of the basilica. The great center door opened wide and light flooded in before closing once again. Where they took him, we did not know. Or I did not. Athanasius, however, had already planned for this. He had stationed a friend outside in order to follow them so that we might discover and know where they held Macarius.

Inside, I was met with a sudden shock.

"Arnobius of Carthage, rise."

It was Demetrius.

Athanasius and Philip turned to me motioning that I must.

I stood.

"Yes?" I said.

"Come forward, Arnobius, so that all may hear you."

It was the *comes* Dionysius.

I stepped out next to Demetrius who was grinning at my evident surprise.

"Arnobius," he began, "I understand you are a man of considerable affairs and wealth from the city of Carthage. Is that so?"

"It is," I allowed.

"Then are you familiar with the business of the Church?"

"To some extent," I answered, "though I wouldn't say—"

Demetrius cut in. "And how long have you known Athanasius?"

I thought about it. It had been ten years since the great council at Nicaea. I declared so.

"And have you found him to be of consistent character?"

"Yes," I stated.

Demetrius held his tongue for a moment before inquiring, "Would you say that Athanasius is a passionate man?"

"He is," I agreed. But I should have asked for clarification; I should have asked what he meant by "passionate." Rather, I quite foolishly assumed Demetrius referred to Athanasius' desire for the Christ.

"That is all," he finished.

He dismissed me, and I sat once again behind Athanasius, Timotheos, and Philip.

Demetrius sighed. It was not heartfelt, however. Rather, like so much of what had occurred over the previous few days, it was the sighing of a man on stage. "Indeed," he said, "Athanasius *is* a passionate man. He rages with fiery anger, blown by the winds of ire, by the impassioned desire to control others."

I stood. "That's not what I meant!"

But Demetrius ignored me.

Then:

From the shadows of the back of the church, someone screamed. "He deposed me against the rules of our holy communion!"

We all turned to see what it was.

Demetrius cried, "What is it man?" He ordered him forward. When the man reached the altar, he queried, "Who are you?"

"I am Callinicus of Pelusium," the man responded.

Demetrius paced away from him. Then facing him again, he asked, "Callinicus the bishop?"

"According to rights, yes," he replied.

"What is your complaint?"

Callinicus began his long tale, accusing Athanasius of all manner of crimes, including several that were suspiciously similar to those allegedly committed against Ischyras. That is, he charged Athanasius and his henchmen with overturning his episcopal chair and breaking his so-called mystical chalice.

"Mystical?" queried Demetrius.

"Yes," affirmed Callinicus. "It is the precious cup which holds the consecrated blood of our Lord."

"And what else, then?" Demetrius asked after allowing Callinicus' remark to have its proper affect.

"I wish I could say no more, but I'm unable. It seems this evil against me was only a beginning. After he destroyed my chair and destroyed the cup, he placed me under the guard of several brutes who tortured me and forced me to admit to truths as untrue as a light that is darkness."

"What happened then?"

"He judged I was no longer the bishop of Pelusium. And in my place, he installed the deposed priest Mark whom I myself had justly removed for sleeping with another man!"

Among the councilmen, a murmur grew like a slow-moving fire in a field of grass. Now the fire exploded.

"He consecrated such a man bishop?" clarified Demetrius. "He installed one who had given himself over to lusting for—"

"A male." Callinicus shook his head disapprovingly. "Yes, he did."

Demetrius groaned. He groaned like a man on stage—an actor who wasn't, I must say, very talented at his profession. Still, it worked its affect.

"It's horrible," he judged, "because it's the same with all the other charges."

"Others?" demanded Philip, standing.

Demetrius shook his head. "Others," he confirmed. Then, motioning behind him, a whole line of men stepped forward from the dark behind Eusebius and the *comes* Dionysius. Gesturing toward them, he asserted, "Each of these in turn has been abused by Athanasius."

They testified accordingly. But I'll not give you the details, Theophilus, as all the charges were the same. In fact, it seemed we had heard them before. Athanasius ordered violence. His men carried out his orders. The conclusion? Athanasius was no better than the boss of a gang of thugs.

Philip impatiently objected. "Yet again," he argued, "the so-called evidence is circumstantial! As with Ischyras and the others, there is no direct tie between Athanasius and these acts of violence! Their testimony merely shows that among Athanasius' supporters there are some who are ill-intentioned and ill-behaved!"

"To say the least!" exclaimed Demetrius, grinning.

The room erupted with laughter.

Then gravely, Demetrius judged, "However that may be, it is clear that more work is required to ascertain the truth."

"Must we drag this on?" asked Philip. "It seems obvious he's innocent of all the charges!"

"Possibly," allowed Demetrius. "But justice to all parties involved cries out for full rather than partial disclosure of what happened. If he's innocent, then we are all better off in knowing and being certain of it; if not, then Athanasius has no business continuing on in the office of the bishop of Alexandria."

Philip cried out, "Absurd!"

But Athanasius silenced him. Standing, he queried, "What do you propose?"

"For now," Demetrius said, "a brief recess."

"For how long?"

"No more than a few hours," directed the *comes* Dionysius from behind.

Therefore, we recessed for a time.

When we were well away, Philip asked Athanasius, "Why in the name of the one God did you allow him that?"

"Quite simple," said Athanasius in reply. "If ever I'm to be cleared of these allegations, they must do their investigation and there must be a final acquittal in the court of the Church. Otherwise, they'll hound me forever."

The specific allegation was the one regarding Ischyras.

"I see," Philip unhappily conceded.

"But they'll stack the investigation against you," Timotheos cautioned.

"My exact point," Philip agreed.

"That's just it," Athanasius proposed. "We must make sure that doesn't happen. We must demand the right people, impartial men, who are loyal neither to Eusebius nor to me. Otherwise …"

"Otherwise they'll contrive something," I suggested.

And that, Theophilus, is precisely what occurred.

In just over a few hours, Athanasius stood to object. "Your procedure is both treacherous and fraudulent!" he exclaimed. "How can you send *your* men, men allied with Eusebius and Arius, when Macarius is kept here in chains, and I too am prevented from coming along to ensure a fair investigation?"

Demetrius ignored him.

Eusebius had decided, and the *comes* Dionysius had agreed, that six bishops, among others, would form the investigative party: Theognis, Maris, Theodorus, Macedonius, Valens, and Ursacius. They were all Eusebians. Not a one favored Athanasius or the creed of Nicaea.

"It's against all judicial regularity!" Athanasius went on, despite Demetrius' silence. "Your procedure is *ex parte*—it is plainly partial to Ischyras and to your side!"

No one was no listening. Rather by majority vote—as if there were another side, Theophilus!—and the approval of the *comes*, Eusebius put a hold on the council proceedings against Athanasius until they had finished both at Jerusalem, with the inauguration of the new basilica, and with their investigation of the Ischyras incident near Lake Mareotis in Egypt. Then, they asserted, they'd know whether Athanasius was guilty.

Athanasius, however, was not about to wait around for their decision. It was already quite evident what it would be. They'd go investigate getting whatever it was they required, whatever testimonies and material evidence, and then they'd come back and count him guilty before deposing him. Consequently, the ancient church of Alexandria, the one founded by the holy apostle Mark, would pass from the homoousion party to the Arians, who hold that the Son is not truly God.

No, Athanasius would not wait. As soon as we returned to our apartment, he began to discuss our escape to the New Rome in order to make a direct appeal to the emperor.

"*Our* escape?" I asked, incredulous.

Athanasius smiled.

The following conversation was similar to the one we had conducted before coming to Tyre. I had engaged in many such conversations in my life, Theophilus. Somehow, some other man had always led me to a place I hadn't considered going to before. Buteo. Constantine. Now, Athanasius—*again*. It was all too familiar.

I went on. "I'm quite attached to you, Athanasius, but I see no need for me to go along. You'll do perfectly well without me."

"I imagine so, Arnobius, but you *would* be of assistance."

"How so?" I asked, determined not to go.

"Because you've been to the New Rome, you know the city and can serve as our guide."

"True," I allowed, "but that's hardly significant."

"In itself, no. But what *is* significant are your contacts there."

Contacts, I thought. Hadn't it always come down to that—my contacts and what they could do for others?

Athanasius went on. "You know members of the court, and most importantly, you are Constantine's friend."

"Am I?" I countered. "I once was, but—"

"Still, if you come along, Arnobius, you'll be able to give witness to what and who I really am. You've seen this trial's mockery of justice. It's been more like a bad comedy written by a juvenile playwright. The emperor will listen to you."

Will he? I wondered. "I can't say if he will or not, Athanasius. I haven't seen him nor have I really communicated with him for nearly ten years."

"But you must admit it would be worth a try, and it would make our case all the stronger."

That it would, I thought. But I was not persuaded.

The truth is I did not want to see Constantine. No, not true, Theophilus. I wished to see him, but I was afraid. I feared how he would behave toward me. Would he see me as a traitor of sorts? A friend who had turned enemy? It had been so long, and the last time we'd seen each other had been under the dark cloud of intrigue, of murder and reprisal. No, our friendship was dead. It had perished ten long years before. Now there was a kind of comfortable, if sad, status quo. I had my memories and that was enough.

"Please consider it," Athanasius begged.

"I will," I promised. "But don't expect me to change my mind."

Later in the evening, I walked in on Athanasius and the rest making final plans for their escape the following night.

"We'll leave soon after the guards have fallen asleep," Athanasius said.

They too had noticed that every night the guards drank to the point of inebriation and slept soundly until the cock crowed.

"Eusebius and his party going to Jerusalem and on to make the investigation at Lake Mareotis will have already made their departure. If we can escape the watch of the guard, which shouldn't be difficult,"—everyone laughed—"then we should be able to make it to the boat and away in the morning before they awake." The reference was to a lumber boat for which he had earlier arranged passage by means of another man.

I then spoke up. "I'll go," I declared.

Everyone looked at me. "You will?" Athanasius said.

"I will," I confirmed."

Athanasius smiled and hugged me. "Thank you—you'll be a help to us."

"I hope so," I agreed. But I felt unsure. While I felt I owed it to Athanasius, I feared seeing Constantine again.

However that may be, we went on planning late into the night. As we did, I grew more excited while simultaneously growing more apprehensive. It was hard to know exactly where the buzzing excitement left off and the gnawing apprehension began. Over and over I couldn't help but wondering why in the name of the gods I was mixing myself up in all of this at my advanced age.

Thirty-five: Escape

Summer 335 A.D.

THE FOLLOWING DAY PASSED as a snail might over the length of a fallen tree. Although I myself was free to move in and out of the apartment, the others were not. Consequently, we waited there through each hour of the long day, apprehensively standing by to make our escape later on that night.

Athanasius himself had secured a number of men to prepare for our coming nighttime departure. One made final payment for our passage on the lumber boat leaving early the following morning. Another obtained food. A third confirmed that the Eusebians had made their departure for Jerusalem. One last man—it was I—visited Macarius.

"What shall I give him?" I asked Athanasius when he asked me to do this one favor for him.

"Just this." He gave me a papyrus note written in Coptic.

"What does it say?"

"It gives him the details of our exodus."

It was the one hour of that day that passed by quickly, Theophilus. I walked through the narrow streets of Tyre to where they had Macarius hidden away, bound in chains and guarded by two men.

"May I speak with the priest Macarius?" I asked upon arrival.

The two guards warily studied me. The Eusebians had instructed them to keep an even closer eye on their charge while the others were away in Jerusalem. I noticed both carried swords, and one had a set of keys tied to his belt.

Finally, the one with the keys replied, "On what business?" He fingered his sword's hilt.

"I'm leaving Tyre," I explained. It was what Athanasius had instructed me to say. "I wish to say farewell."

Finally, after glancing at the other man who snorted at me, the man with the keys gave in and let me pass into Macarius' room telling me I only had a few moments.

I consented and passed through the door.

When Macarius saw me, he smiled.

"How goes it, Arnobius?"

"Well," I responded, "and perhaps even better tonight."

"*Tonight*," Macarius confirmed.

Athanasius said he had already warned him of our plans. The note in my possession gave the details. I gave it to Macarius and bade him farewell. As I left, the guards told me not to come back. Smiling, I promised I wouldn't.

That night, we slept as usual—or at least, we lay down to sleep as usual. The difference, of course, was that we lay down fully dressed, ready to slip out of the apartment and out of Tyre. Outside our two guards were drinking as they always did and speaking rather loudly. Occasionally, someone in another apartment would shout at them, telling them to be quiet. One of the guards would return with one expletive or another. "We have a job to do, for the gods' sake!" he cried. "Then do it without being so cursed loud!" returned the neighbor. Eventually, the night grew quiet and still.

"They've passed out," observed Athanasius.

"Right," I replied.

Still, we waited in accord with our plan.

I counted. I counted goats as I had when I was a small boy on our estate outside Carthage. I counted, however, to stay awake rather than to fall asleep.

Then a noise. There was a quiet knock at the door.

"There they are," whispered Athanasius. I could hear excitement in his voice.

He rose and quickly went to unlock the door.

"Come in!" he offered in hushed tones.

They did, all three—Timotheos, Philip, and Macarius.

"Was there any difficulty?" Athanasius asked Macarius.

"No," he said. "Like your men, mine are drunk and asleep. Philip was able to get the keys and undo the chains without a problem. But we'd better be off before there *is* difficulty."

It was just after midnight. Above, the moon dimly shone as it had a few nights before when I had seen it among the thousands of stars, allowing for just enough light. We slipped out of the apartment and through the courtyard and past the two guards huddled on the ground. Then we passed into the narrow streets of the city.

"Follow me," Philip ordered.

We did. One by one, we trailed him making our way toward the harbor.

The plan was to board the lumber ship, one that sailed back and forth from Syria supplying wood to the Empire. We'd stow ourselves away and leave just as the captain had promised at the earliest rising of the sun. Unfortunately, Theophilus, plans don't always work out as hoped for.

Presently, however, all was going according to expectation. We followed Philip through the narrow and mazelike streets of Tyre before emerging into the forum and out into the temple precinct and into the markets along the quay. There was our boat, tied up.

A gangplank led from a small stone wall to its deck. On board, there was little movement. Indeed, I could only see one man, a guard of sorts no doubt, who seemed more agitated by sleep than by any fear of theft. His name was Quintus—or so I learned the following day.

"Wait here," Philip said.

We waited as he descended below deck. I glanced about the harbor and noticed a rare quiet. Soon, I thought, men would be waking to prepare for a new day and for the beginning of journeys abroad.

Finally, Philip appeared accompanied by an older man who was grizzled with silver stubble and wore a gnarled cotton tunic and worn-down, salt-encrusted leather sandals. When Athanasius greeted the man, he hardly made a reply. It was more a grunt of recognition that more cargo had arrived.

"Thank you," Philip said to him.

The man, our captain as it happened, called Malus for his seemingly disagreeable disposition, turned again and disappeared below. As for us, we stayed above, reclining the best we could along the deck. Tomorrow, Philip assured us, the captain would make room for us below.

Tomorrow, I thought. It could not come soon enough. I shivered at the thought of waiting there for the rest of the night until the sun rose to relieve our suspense and to grant us the peace of departure. Even so, we soon fell asleep, each of us covered with a cloak to keep us warm.

When I awoke, the sun was above the horizon by several degrees. As I came to full consciousness out of a deep sleep, I noticed that someone was negotiating with someone else rather impatiently and emphatically. It was Philip speaking to Malus, the captain of the boat.

"But we *must* leave!" he said, his voice full of urgency.

"We cannot yet," Malus assured him. "We have yet to load a last bit of cargo."

"But you guaranteed us we would leave at sunrise! No later, you promised!"

"Yes," admitted Malus. "And yet promises are never final."

With that, Malus walked away to one task or another and Philip returned to our little party. The others were standing not far from me.

"Did you hear him?"

"I did," Athanasius calmly confirmed. "All we can do is wait."

Macarius nodded.

"And pray," Timotheos suggested.

Around this time, the guards originally set over Macarius began to awake from their drunken slumber. I don't know this with certainty, of course, Theophilus, but given what ours did every morning, it is likely. They awoke and discovered, quite frightened and angry I can imagine, that Macarius was gone. "He's escaped!" one of them must have exclaimed. "Escaped?" returned the other, rubbing away the pain in his temples. "Yes! He's gone to the others!"

I can see them running the distance from the building where they held their charge to the other building where we—Athanasius, Timotheos, Philip, and I—were supposed to be.

"Wake up you fools!" they cried upon arriving. They must have kicked at our two guards who were wrapped in their cloaks to ward off the morning chill. "Are they still here?" they demanded. "Who?" one asked, still a bit drunk. "Your men, you idiots!" Then both of our guards must have quickly sprung to their feet. "Of course they are!" "Check—because our man has escaped!"

They checked. They unlocked our door and hesitantly entered the apartment to see if we were still there.

"They're gone!" cried one of the guards. "Run upstairs to see if the others are gone too!"

The other dashed up the stairs by twos.

"Gone!" he shouted when he returned a moment later. "What should we do?"

"We must search for them!"

"Where?"

"The obvious," declared one of Macarius' guards, attempting confidence. Then he ordered, "You two run to the harbor. They're sure to have gone there in order to sail back to Egypt."

"And you?" one of ours asked.

"I'll go to the city gate that leads south in case they plan to travel afoot." Turning to his own partner, he ordered, "You stay here—in case they return for something."

"Aye, sir," he nodded.

Off the three of them went. Our two rushed our way still feeling the effects of wine from the night before, and the other ran off to the southern city gate.

Meanwhile, our captain Malus was ordering the conduct of a great wooden crane that was loading some twenty-five logs onto our boat. "Easy!" he cried. "Don't jar the damn thing! Let it down easy!"

The crane lowered a great log four feet wide in diameter into the hold. It swung precariously above, then it came down steadily as one of Malus' men, a man called Hector, had it by the end as did another man on the other side. I noticed the many rings of the fallen tree, hundreds, and wondered at the beautiful if irregular pattern they made in orange, cream, and dark brown.

"Good," shouted Malus, "that's how to do it!"

Malus was not truly an evil man, Theophilus. He was simply short and to the point. He was all about business, or duty, which always trumped all other matters as with us then.

Again, Philip approached him. "When do we leave, captain?"

"Soon," answered the latter. "Can't you see we're working?"

Philip looked and counted five more logs. Each took about five minutes to load. Thus, at the very earliest we'd disembark in a half hour.

"Damn it!" cursed Philip to himself.

Athanasius heard him and counseled Philip to be more patient and trusting. All would happen according to the divine will.

As for me, I was unsure, and as the sun climbed ever higher into the sky, I feared for our situation more and more. Any moment, the guard would awake, and eventually they'd notice our absence as they were in the habit of checking up on us each morning. What I didn't know, of course, was they had already discovered this and were already making their way to the harbor in order to search for us. They must have been less than two miles away.

"Perhaps we should go below," suggested Philip. "That way, if anyone comes to search, they won't find us."

"You can't do that," opposed Malus.

"Why not?" asked Philip.

"Not during a load," he said flatly.

"But there's plenty of room!"

Philip looked to Athanasius. The latter motioned to him to be quiet and trust.

"But they'll be coming!" cried Philip, agitated.

"Trust."

"Fine," agreed Philip, "but at least I'll go and watch out for them!"

Athanasius let him go and I watched him walk the gangplank to the stone wall and some distance away in order to keep watch. Just about that time, they loaded another log into the hold. Now there were four to go.

Athanasius turned to me. "It's unlikely they'll find us—don't you think, Arnobius?"

"I'm sure," I answered, though I was anything but. Instead, I imagined the men, dirty as they were, hardly sober, stumbling up to where we were at any moment and demanding our return to the apartment under drawn sword. My heart raced.

As for our guards, they made their way through the narrow streets of Tyre at a slow pace thanks to their swollen state, awake but hardly sober. They ran or stumbled or walked along as best as they could, having to stop along the way to relieve themselves in a public latrine and drink water at a public fountain. Finally, they came out to the forum where men had already begun to gather for the day and then to the market along the quay where stalls of all kinds were set up to sell just as many kinds of goods.

I can hear them fighting as they often did. "Faster!" one cried, the larger one, a Goth who'd come to fight the Persians some years ago before settling for the relatively easy life of private security. "I'm going!" the other returned.

They ran along now in view of the harbor and the many ships that awaited departure times. Ours, thank God, was toward the outer edge. Consequently, after having searched the others, they would come to ours last.

One last log.

"Let's go now!" cried Malus. "We haven't got all day!"

I was glad to hear him put a little fire under the operator of the large wooden crane. The latter, I saw, mumbled something under his breath before lowering the last log into the hold.

"There," ordered Malus, "lower the damn thing there!"

The operator did, and the log came to rest with the others.

Finally, Malus walked over to Athanasius and said, "Where's that prig of yours?"

"Prig?" asked Athanasius, raising his eyebrows.

"Yes. Philip—I think that's what he calls himself."

"Oh," said Athanasius, "he's off the ship for a moment."

"Well, he'd better get his anxious self aboard. We're ready to shove off."

"I'll get him," Athanasius assured him.

Malus turned to go order his men to prepare for departure.

Just then, before Athanasius went to retrieve Philip, Philip came racing up the gangplank quite visibly unsettled.

"They're here!" he shouted.

"Where?" I asked, startled.

"Over there!" he motioned.

We all looked, and sure enough, our two guards were walking along the quay searching for us.

"Go below!" ordered Athanasius.

"Will he allow it?" asked Timotheos in reference to Malus.

"He must!"

But it was too late.

Just as we moved to go below, and just as I looked one last time at our guards, they spotted us.

"There they are!" cried one, the smaller of the two.

"By the gods, let's go!" shouted the other.

The two came running toward us—not very quickly, but here they came our way, and a shiver of fear flew up my spine like wind along the top of a field of wheat.

"Malus!" I cried, "We must go!" Then to the others, I shouted, "Here! Help me with the gangplank."

As I demanded this, Malus gruffly declared, "I'm the one to give the orders around here! What's your problem?"

Athanasius spoke up. "It's those two!" he shouted.

Malus looked. Then, with a wry grin that suggested many prior adventures—of previous scrapes with similar guards and narrow escapes—he loudly ordered, "Up with the plank, men! And quickly!"

Five men rushed to pull up the gangplank.

As they did, our two guards were nearing. They were now perhaps fifty yards away and running along. They'd arrive in moments …

"They're still drunk!" I exclaimed, observing a stumbling accent to their running, however slight.

"Thank God!" said Timotheos.

Still, they were nearing our ship. They were now some twenty-five yards away.

"Stop!" they cried. "Those are our men!"

But Malus' crew didn't listen. Rather, some heaved the gangplank aboard while others pushed off with long wooden poles.

Fifteen yards.

"Push!" cried Malus. "Push or be damned to the fire of Hades!"

They pushed and we watched our two guards approach the ship. By the time they reached the wall, there was only five feet or so that separated us from them. But it was much too far to step aboard.

"You can't go!" they announced to us, their chests heaving out of breath. "It's against the emperor's orders!"

Athanasius smiled. *We were going to the emperor.*

Turning to the larger guard, the smaller one asked, "What should we do?"

"What should we do?" retorted the other, angrily. "Let's jump aboard!"

They ran back some twenty feet in order to get a running start.

"They can't possibly make it," I asserted.

"I hope not," agreed Timotheos. "And yet, it *is* possible."

By then, the crewmembers had slowly poled the boat a few more feet away from the wall.

Now, the two made a run for it.

"Here they come!"

"Push!" cried Malus.

His men pushed and still another few feet appeared between the ship and the wall. Now the boat was perhaps ten or fifteen feet distant.

"Jump!" they cried in unison.

The two guards leapt into the air. They hurled themselves forward, swords to their side, with outstretched arms and hands pointing our way in order to get a hold of the side of the boat.

"Fools," declared Malus now standing next to us.

As for me, I was now actually quite frightened. They had succeeded and were pulling themselves aboard.

In concert, they grunted, "Up!"

Malus laughed and drew a sword as he walked to where the guards heroically clutched to the side of the boat. When Malus reached them, he lifted the sword as if poised to bring it down on the two men.

They looked up.

He lowered it to his side. "Do you wish to die?" he asked. "You're boarding my ship without my permission."

"But we represent the emperor," they countered, out of breath.

Malus repeated his question.

The two guards glanced at each other. Then:

"There they go," Philip announced, smiling.

They dropped into the water making quite a splash.

"I hope they can swim," Athanasius offered.

"I don't care much if they can," Malus declared.

Either way, Theophilus, we sailed off, leaving the two to sink or swim. We had a long journey ahead of us.

Thirty-six: Voyage by Sea

Summer and fall 335 A.D.

BY ALL ACCOUNTS, the first part of our voyage by sea should have been the most precarious. It was not, however. Rather, like a cloudless sky void of movement, the sea was calm by day and by night, and so we sailed from Tyre to Cyprus with very little incident. After running the length of the island, we cruised for a few more days before encountering the shores of Cilicia, Pamphylia, and Lycia. There we crawled along the coast, skirting by Caria and weaving our way through a plethora of tiny islands that dot the coast. Then Rhodes appeared.

On our stern, the great island came into view early one morning. I had already awakened and was slowly pacing back and forth along the lower deck of the ship when the night guard Quintus cried, "There it is!" He was up on the prow.

"There *what* is?" I asked, somewhat startled. I had walked as close as I could to him.

"The Great Colossus!" he answered.

The Great Colossus, I echoed, mentally.

As I remembered it from my pedagogue Tyrannio, Chares of Lindos erected the Great Colossus some six hundred years before in order to celebrate his stunning victory over Demetrius Poliorcertes, the so-called besieger of cities. Demetrius was son of Antigonus, ally of Alexander of Macedon. The Great Colossus was a statue of Helios, the sun god, and it straddled the bay as though a guard on watch. When he first raised it, the statue was the tallest the world had ever seen. But it had fallen years before—nay, centuries—and the Rhodians had left it that way, fearing they had somehow offended Helios.

I informed Quintus of this and he told me he could see its remains, prone along the ground. "They sparkle in the light of the rising sun," he said. "If I had to guess, the god isn't all that upset."

I smiled. Maybe not. I thought of Constantine and his own change in alliance years before—from Apollo the Unconquered Sun to the Christ, the light of God. Constantine had experienced nothing but success since then.

Finally, we came near enough so that all of us on deck could easily see the Great Colossus. Sadly, it lay like a fallen soldier awaiting burial. The closer we came the larger it grew. Pliny the Elder had written that a grown man could hardly wrap his arms around the thumb of the fallen god. *At the very least*, I judged. It was the largest statue I had ever seen.

"Don't you see?" observed Athanasius as we drifted by. He had joined us shortly after Quintus had announced the god's appearance. "It demonstrates the old order is passing away. It has been for hundreds of years. In its place comes the reign of the Christ."

I nodded, thinking it just may be so. At the very least, those with the power to rule seemed to believe it.

In the days ahead, we sailed by many other islands. Most of them rise precipitously from the sea, though some, the fortunate ones, have harbors and sandy beaches that allow for trade. These have many whitewashed houses clustered together near small markets. As we sailed by, I wondered what sort of life people lived on these minor islands. Aside from tending diminutive olive groves and vineyards, some pursue a craft passed down generation by generation, while some travel back and forth between the islands selling their wares. I judged their life was probably better than mine had been because simpler. I thought that if I had to do it all over again, I would choose something like their life—knowing, of course that it's not really up to us to choose our portion.

One day, Athanasius approached me excited.

"What is it?" I asked.

"It's Patmos," he responded.

I shrugged, not getting the reference.

"Don't you recall?" he prodded. "Patmos is the island where John, beloved of Jesus, was forced to stay in exile toward the end of his life."

It dawned on me. I had read about it years before in Alexandria when Athanasius had let me read from his collection of sacred scrolls.

"Ah yes," I said, "he's the one who wrote the *Apocalypse*."

"But more!" Athanasius announced. "It was John who first declared by inspiration that the Word of God, the *Logos*, had become flesh."

I listened to him as he quoted the Evangelist. "In the beginning was the Word, and the Word was with the one God, and the Word *was* God."

"The Homoousion," I remarked.

"That's the one," he confirmed. "The Word *is* God. And a few lines down the Evangelist joined the most elegant string of words together in any language. He wrote, 'The Word became flesh and dwelt among us.' Arnobius, what this signifies for us! It means God became one of us and dwelled with us—he pitched his tent among ours, so that we might dwell with him."

I considered this as Athanasius spoke. If true, it was indeed beautiful. Then I asked him how he could be sure the island was actually that of Patmos, for nearly all the islands appeared the same to me.

"I can't be sure," he admitted, "but Hector is, and he told me."

"How does he know?"

"He said it's the shape. He's sailed this way many times before. And look, Arnobius, somewhere up on that precipice is the cave where John dwelled when he lived on the island in exile."

I searched for a cave but didn't see one.

"That's where he must have had the divine visions of the world to come."

"Frightening," I said, recalling the nature of those revelations.

"Not if seen in the right manner."

I shrugged.

Athanasius muttered a prayer thanking God, and we voyaged on.

We sailed north and passed by Psora on our starboard side and Chios on our portside. Eventually we came to green Lesbos, the island home of Sappho, the Greek poetess who wrote about love and her pretty young daughter who wanted a decorative hair ribbon from Sardis in Lydia. I recalled her mother's response. She couldn't have a Sardinian ribbon, she said. She'd have to settle for something less. She'd have to settle for one locally made.

We journeyed on. The plan was to keep pushing forward, sailing into the Hellespont and up into the Sea of Marmara and finally to the New Rome. But plans, as Malus warned us so many times, are never certain.

It was several days after we passed by Lesbos when disaster struck. Up to that point the sea had been calm, or relatively so. But then, perhaps a day or so beyond Lesbos, and a day or so before we were poised to reach the Hellespont, the waters began to grow rough and an especially warm wind began to blow from the south.

"What's going on?" I asked Timotheos, as if he would know.

As his dark curls tossed up in the wind, he said he didn't know. Nor did Macarius when I asked him. Just then, however, Philip joined us, and he did.

"Malus says a storm is coming."

I could hardly believe it. There were no clouds in the sky. In fact, it was a warm day, gustier than usual, true, but the sky hovered blue above the green sea.

"He says it'll be here by afternoon."

"What'll we do?" I queried, assuming he must know.

"He's taking us further out to sea. He says we must be careful not to veer too close to land, as this coast is as treacherous as a ..."

He didn't finish.

"As a what?" I asked.

"I can't say," he assured me.

I conveyed my understanding, waiting in disbelief for this storm to come along. It was then I recalled the words of Hesiod circumscribing the sailing season on the Aegean. *Men can sail with safety for fifty days past the summer solstice and past the end of summer's toilsome part. Then the winds have clear directions, the sea is safe, and free of anxiety a man may trust. But beware once these days have passed; for then the sea will toss, and ships will be broken against the rocks.* I realized we were past those carefree days. We *had been* for some time now. I shuddered. Still, the clear blue sky gave me some small measure of hope.

Meanwhile, as the sun traveled its usual course, Malus and Hector ordered the men to prepare for the coming storm. Part of their preparation was a sacrifice to Poseidon the Earth Shaker. They poured libations over the side of the ship and slaughtered a rooster kept aboard for this very purpose. They did this because they did not have the preferred horse or bull. At any rate, it seemed the Earth Shaker, brother to both Zeus and Hades, and ruler of Our Sea, did not hear. Why? Toward the end of the day with just a few hours remaining, new winds gusted, growing cold, falling now from the north.

"The Bora winds," reported Quintus, "blown seaward by the god."

"The god?" I asked him, not placing the reference.

Afraid, he nodded, "Yes, the god of the North Wind, Boreas. Malus says the storm should rise very soon."

It did. Just like that, a bank of clouds appeared over the horizon. At first, they were white and friendly, but soon they darkened as they enveloped the whole of our view and passed swiftly overhead like an army of thundering chariots riding into war. Now, just above us, they were black and hostile.

As they came on to us, the sea, which had already begun to swell fitfully as though frightened by the coming storm, grew even more frenzied. Our boat heaved up, then down again—slowly up and quickly down.

"Shall we go below?" I suggested to Athanasius.

"Not yet," he returned. "Let's wait for the rain."

As we waited, the air grew colder and the winds picked up dangerously.

"It's the gods!" cried Quintus. "They're angry!"

I heard Athanasius praying. "The Lord gives, the Lord takes away, blessed be the name of the Lord."

Night came on. Now, it was dark not only because of the storm but also because the sun had finally fallen behind the earth. Then it began to pour down rain.

"Now?" I said to Athanasius, who covered himself with his cloak.

"Soon," he replied, "but you may go ahead if you wish."

I did wish. The rain was cold and the wind nearly unbearable. Nevertheless, I didn't want to go because I knew that below I'd feel the up and down heaving of the ship upon the swell of the sea with very little relief. Further, it would be hot, the air stuffy. No, I wouldn't go until the others went.

Then, gods, I swore aloud!

"To the fore!" cried one of the sailors.

We all looked as Malus and Quintus came rushing forward. It was an enormous wave poised to crash over us.

"Steady men!" cried Malus.

Up we went, ascending to the heights.

Quintus cursed his luck. "Zeus!" he bellowed. "Poseidon! Where are the gods!"

"Quiet!" Malus ordered.

But he was not. As the wave crested and water sprayed all about in torrents, Quintus screamed like a man unused to the sea. In fact he was. He was hardly seventeen.

We fell down the backside of the wave. As we did so, my stomach heaved through my throat, and we all shouted with terror at another swell just beyond.

Of all of us, Quintus shouted the loudest. Malus, on the other hand, was perfectly quiet. Indeed, as I looked at him as the next wave came on, he appeared to enjoy the storm. Quintus, by contrast, was terrified.

The wave drew closer. I saw it in a flash of lightning. It was as tall as a towering tree, a northern oak, perhaps, rising from the dark soil to the sky above.

Quintus screamed. "O Poseidon! The gods have abandoned us! We're doomed to Hades!"

I saw Malus calmly turn to Quintus, and cursing him, he said, "If you don't silence yourself, I'll do it for you without the help of a wave. I'll heave you over the side myself and you can sleep with all the sea monsters! Now be a man and be quiet!"

Quintus, however, wouldn't give over his fear. And the storm and waves seemed only to grow worse. We rode that wave, another, and several thereafter. We soared up high and dropped down low. It rained harder and grew colder and we all feared for our lives.

Suddenly Malus ordered, "All men below!"

I didn't hesitate. I turned to go down and Athanasius, Macarius, Philip, and Timotheos followed, seeking the shelter of the hold.

Below, the wood of the ship creaked with every passing swell. We all felt sick. I felt like I had when crossing the Fretum Gallium with Constantine and his father some thirty years before on our way to fight the Picts. Only worse.

After some time, I attempted to sleep, as there was little else to do. But sweet sleep, that comfort in times of trouble, hardly came to me. Instead, I compulsively counted the many times the ship went up and the many times it fell down. I imagined the waves were growing larger and larger. Meanwhile, Athanasius and the others prayed. I listened and hoped. *God*, I thought, *please bring us to safety.*

Eventually, Athanasius and the others grew tired. Finally, I could tell they were asleep because I could hear the slow heaving of their breathing. It was peaceful. They rested at last, and I envied them since I could not fall asleep no matter how hard I tried. It was like my lack of faith, I dejectedly supposed.

Then quite suddenly, all went dark.

I must have fallen asleep.

Or—

It was cold and wet.

Where was I?

I was floating.

No.

I realized my body was sinking.

I opened my eyes, which stung with salt, and realized I could see nothing. There was only darkness.

I'm drowning, I passively judged. Was I asleep?

But then I panicked for air, thrusting upwards.

I *hoped* it was upwards. My breath was nearly at end.

Upwards!

I saw a dim light.

I was terrified.

What if I never make it to the light?

I had never believed. Not fully. Nor had I been baptized. Nor confessed. And God! I begged. *The gods!*

I might die.

I might never—

I panicked. I thrashed in the water.

I was sinking. Going down. Lost to time.

Lost.

But I kept …

Then I was up.

I burst into the cold air above.

Air! I breathed it deeply.

And light! I saw it intensely.

I was treading water. I was all alone, but at least I was alive.

No, not alone!

I wasn't far from Athanasius and the others.

It was then I realized what had happened.

Somehow, we'd been thrown from the boat into the sea. And there they were, near to me, bobbing up and down in the water.

I tried to swim but found it hard going. Finally, I just let myself float. I *did* float. I looked up and there behind a patchwork of gray clouds that remained after the storm, the sky was growing lighter. It wasn't bright yet, but the sun had risen and was beginning its daily run.

"Over here!" Athanasius cried.

Macarius, Timotheos, and Philip had already reached him. By what miracle, I cannot say, but they had reached him and were all clutching desperately to a splintered piece of the old ship.

Finally, although my water-laden tunic impeded my going, I made it to them.

"Look," said Athanasius, pointing, "land."

I glanced to my side and saw that it was not more than several stone throws away. Along the shore, I could see and hear the crashing rows of waves, falling as they did world without end.

Then from behind someone shouted, "Climb aboard!"

We all swiveled around and Philip hollered with glee when he saw Malus astride one of those huge logs they'd loaded weeks before. He paddled with a broken board toward us.

After he approached us, we all managed to climb onto the log even though it rolled back and forth. Then, paddling together, we made it ashore with Malus' direction. He was able to steer us around the main break and along a channel that took us safely beyond the sharp rocks to a small sandy beach where we all disembarked.

When we had done so, I asked Malus what had happened to Quintus.

"I can't say," he admitted. "But we'll search. If the gods will it, he might yet turn up somewhere else, the bugger."

Later, when we made our search, we found that many of the men had survived the storm and subsequent shipwreck. Malus explained that we had drifted in toward the shore instead of moving out toward the sea as he had planned. Sometimes, he said, the gods take you where you don't want to go. I emphatically agreed.

"So that's why the ship burst apart?"

He nodded. "We must have hit one of those jutting rocks over there. Damn things'll tear up a ship like it's a child's toy."

I noticed he wasn't too upset. I wondered why, but I didn't ask him. He was a private man. I merely assumed he had insurance to cover the damage as sailing men often do supported by one another in associations for just such a disaster. But now that I think about it, Theophilus, I guess it was more.

"What's to be done?" asked Philip.

"Easy," replied Malus. After we gather, we'll head on foot for Abydos and then we'll cross over to Sestos.

This is what we did.

After recovering the rest of the men, those who survived—happily including Quintus who washed ashore sincerely thanking Leukothea, the white sea nymph—and locating water to drink, for we were all dreadfully thirsty, we slowly began marching toward Abydos where we arrived after nearly a week.

By then we were beyond tired and hungry. I looked out onto the Hellespont and felt a measure of relief knowing that our journey was near to its
end. I had never experienced such hardship, Theophilus.

"We'll cross tomorrow," Malus said, as if giving an order.

We all agreed, as we knew of no other way to proceed. Then we found
shelter for the night in a wooden shack along the shore. We were nearly
penniless and could afford nothing better.

In the morning, with the red sun rising over the horizon, we stood ready
to cross the Hellespont from Abydos to Sestos. Though it was not the same
place, Theophilus, I could not help thinking of that time thirty years before
when I anxiously stood with Constantine waiting to be ferried across to
Byzantium. He had piously poured out a libation to the god and I had
watched him in silence. Then we were racing to freedom, hoping eventually
to meet his father in Gaul. Now, what a difference it was. Although our quest
was similar—a flight from injustice to justice—the destination had become
my old partner in the escape, as we fled to *his* capital, to Constantine's city.

We crossed over to Sestos, and after saying farewell to Malus, Quintus,
and the other men who'd survived, we managed to make our way up to the
New Rome. We traveled along the coast of the Hellespont from one small
town and village to the next, and after a week, we were poised to make our
entry.

By this time, our party was well beyond exhaustion. Our feet ached and
our legs burned with dreariness. We longed for rest, for food, for water
aplenty. As for our appearance, we looked haggard in every way. Our faces
were unshaven, our beards full, and our skin chapped. As for our clothes, our
tunics were in tatters, sodden with everything encountered along the way. I
daresay we were hardly recognizable.

It was in this manner that we approached the New Rome and so Constantine's newly constructed wall along the main road leading into the city. It was
then that we heard and saw the emperor's entourage, Theophilus.

"What's that?" asked Athanasius.

"It's the emperor," said a gruff looking man, who was pulling his cart and
donkey to the side of the road.

"The emperor Constantine?" he requested, hoping for confirmation. But
the man didn't hear.

Nearby, a group of boys was playing ball. As soon as they heard the pounding of the horses' hooves in the distance, they fell to the side of the way and stood by for the imperial entourage. Everyone else also moved aside.

Everyone but for us.

"Athanasius," I warned, "we must move!"

He didn't budge.

"If it's the emperor," he countered, "I must speak to him, for his presence is a gift of God."

Whether it was or not, I judged, it wasn't wise to stay in the road.

As I saw Constantine and his group of men from afar, it looked as though they were returning from a hunt, high in spirits.

"Clear the way!" the guard cried. "Make way for the emperor!"

We were now the only ones in the road. I saw Constantine lean over to ask one of his guard who we were and what we wanted. As he did, I noticed he had aged far more than I imagined possible. His hair was a silvery gray and he seemed even thinner than he had been ten years before.

"Move out of the way!" commanded one of the guards, "or I'll bloody you with the end of my sword!"

They all laughed, doubtlessly lusting for blood.

Rather than move, however, Athanasius stood and called out, "I demand justice!"

Constantine inquired, "What's that poor man asking for?"

They were now trotting slowly.

"Death!" replied one of the soldiers.

They drew nearer.

As they did, I grew afraid. It can't go well, I thought. Athanasius, however, was beyond such calculations. He gave himself to the care of God alone.

"I demand justice from the emperor of Rome!"

My eyes followed his plea to the emperor. There he was, tall and exalted. He rode upon a great white steed surrounded by the candidati, swords drawn, ready to strike. He was a man of great power, of tremendous glory. His word was life or death like that of a god.

Down below was Athanasius. He was short. He stood anchored to the earth, standing weakly in the road, worn out, surrounded by us—two deacons, a priest, and me, a moneymaker. There he was, all tattered after weeks at sea and after the shipwreck and after days and days of walking to Constantine's city. Yes, he was a man of power. But his was power of a different kind. He was a man of heaven. The other, my old friend, was the opposite, a man of the earth.

Again, Athanasius boldly called out, "I demand justice from the emperor of Rome, from Constantine Augustus!"

One of the candidati turned and asked, "What should we do? Shall we make minced meat of him and his stubborn comrades?"

"No!" ordered Constantine. "They're no danger! They're unarmed! We must see what they want!"

He looked at us.

It was then that he noticed me. For a moment, Constantine stared at me, his eyes fixed as if searching for recognition.

I grew stiff.

Then I could tell. He *knew* me. Despite the matted hair on my face, my dirty tunic, and my tattered cape, he recognized and stared at me. Although I hoped for a smile, none came. His was a cold recognition.

Then, to my side, Athanasius shouted, "They're taking over the Church! You must hear me, Lord!"

Constantine's eyes turned from mine to Athanasius. It was then that he understood who it was.

"Athanasius," he queried, "the bishop of Alexandria?"

"Yes, Lord Emperor," he replied. "It is I, the patriarch of Egypt, Libya, and the Thebaid."

Constantine and his men came to a full stop.

Athanasius pressed on. "I must have your judgment!" he demanded. "The Eusebians wish to unjustly remove me from the episcopal throne. Their desire, Lord, is for power alone!"

Constantine glanced at me and back to Athanasius. Finally, with determination he answered, "Then I must hear what you have to say."

With that, he called some of his men to ride ahead to fetch horses and refreshment for us. Then after bidding us farewell for the moment, he trotted off with the rest of his men toward the Imperial Palace.

Soon, once the horses had arrived along with bread and wine, we trailed the emperor into the New Rome.

For now, we were safe. Eusebius and his thugs were far away. And now, my simple hope was that Constantine would recognize the truth and Athanasius would be free to rule the ancient See of Mark as a shepherd freely guides his own sheep. Then I could go home.

Book Six

Constantine the Judge

335 to 337 A.D.

Thirty-seven: Judgment

Fall 335 A.D.

MY HOPE DIED ONCE WE came to the Imperial Palace.

As it happened, Theophilus, by some fantastic twist of fate that I myself would not have believed had I not experienced it, several Eusebians, including that wily man Eusebius himself, had rushed to the New Rome once it was discovered that Athanasius and the rest had escaped Tyre. And because they had made haste, and because of our own long scrape with misfortune, they happened to arrive on the very same day as we did.

Their desire was to charge Athanasius with contempt of court, both imperial and ecclesial. With Constantine's cooperation, they expected to secure his deposition and exile. This plan, of course, required rapid revision as soon as they realized that Athanasius himself had come to the New Rome with precisely the opposite expectation—that *he* should be exonerated and that *they* should somehow be punished for their own mockery of justice.

When we arrived in the great hall of the Imperial Palace, the Eusebians were comfortably sitting near a roaring fire alongside the emperor's sister Constantia, a few courtiers, and none other than Pila, my old friend from Nicomedia and longtime resident of the New Rome. Caught in the middle of conversation, Eusebius blanched upon seeing us and nearly dropped the cup of wine held aloft in his well-manicured hand. Our presence hadn't been part of his calculation. Pila, on the other hand, flushed with rosy-cheeked joy. When he saw and recognized me by some mysterious power, he chirped, "My good man Arnobius! Wherever have you been?" It'd been ten years. Still, he was the same old Pila, I observed, at least in voice. His appearance, however, had significantly altered. It was evident that the passing of time and the many hours spent in eating delicacies, drinking fine wines, and reclining rather than moving had caught up to him. He was silver haired—a reflection, I must say, of my own hair—and now quite plump, his jowls hanging aside his face with a hedonist rotundity about the middle.

"Do you know him?" asked Eusebius, dismayed.

"I do," Pila avowed with evident cheer. "From better days long ago."

Poor Eusebius. He didn't like this fact. *Or just possibly.* I could see an idea stirring behind his conniving eyes. Perhaps he could win me over to his side. Little did he know!

Whatever the case, there they were, Eusebius and the other men we had hoped to escape in Tyre. The bishop of Nicomedia was arrayed in full ecclesial regalia, waiting for the emperor and astutely courting the others around him. What did this mean for us? Well, we didn't really know how matters would unfold, but presently things seemed grim. His presence appeared to negate ours, making the shipwreck and the troubles we had endured seem worthless. Indeed, his presence was almost worse than the rocks that had dashed Malus' ship to pieces.

Upon recognizing us, and once he had regained composure, Eusebius asked, "Where is the emperor?"

As if *we* knew. He had gone ahead of us and had long disappeared into some back room of the palace. Athanasius, however, ever mindful of charity, greeted Eusebius and his men. The other bishop in turn reluctantly acknowledged his presence.

Then Philip, joining us from a chamber off the great hall, revealed that Constantine was refreshing himself after the long hunt and hard ride, and that he'd be out within an hour.

Eusebius declared that's what he had expected, and without another word we passed by them to the far side of the hall.

As we did so, Pila called out, "Arnobius! We simply have to dine together, and soon! Who knows, maybe it'll be the last time granted by the gods!"

I happily turned to him and agreed, for he reminded me of a much simpler and sweeter time—or so it now seemed looking back through the haze of thirty years. "I'd like that," I returned earnestly.

I would have too, but it never happened. As so often occurs in life, Theophilus, events unfolded far too rapidly over the next few days for any human reckoning or control. As Pila may have said, the gods had their way in opposition to anything we men might have desired.

An hour later, clad in Tyrean purple embroidered with gold, Constantine entered the great hall and took his seat at one end upon a chair gilded in still more precious metal.

"Come!" he shouted imperiously.

We did—both Athanasius and his party, and Eusebius and his.

As we approached him, I thought Constantine was staring at me. Whether he was or not, however, he neither smiled nor frowned in recognition. Instead, he looked at me as though he didn't know me. *Did he anymore?*

When we had all finally gathered around him, the Athanasians to one side and the Eusebians to the other, Constantine held up his hand in order to speak. "My good men," he said, looking back and forth to both sides, "you know well what is dear to my heart."

I for one knew it. And I smiled slightly as a shiver of recognition suddenly fell upon me. Here was Constantine himself, my old friend, right in front of me. I could have reached out and touched him. The emotion of the encounter unexpectedly struck me. But what, exactly, did I feel? I felt I loved him. I felt I always had.

To be sure, it was unity that was dear to his heart. It was all he ever wanted. And the peace and prosperity that would follow therefrom. Constantine went on to give a brief speech, as he had increasingly liked to do. He spoke of the need for one empire and—this was new to me—for one world united beneath the one sky. He let us know that he was already considering a massive military campaign to the east beyond the province of the Oriens. He had written to the Persian king Shapur, he explained, wanting to persuade him of the truth of God in the Christ and the need to join as one. But the king refused to listen. Rather, he conveyed his wariness of the now Christian Roman emperor and of all Christians who were entering into his own empire like termites invading a house made of wood. Constantine, therefore, was planning a campaign of conquest. He had to do it, he insisted with great sincerity, for the greater glory of God. Eventually his speech came around to his own role. There must be one ruler, he assured us, one ruler to reflect the one God and ruler of all. He clarified. The one ruler would be him. Finishing, he said, "There must be one Church, dear brothers, mediating the one salvation of the one God. We can settle for nothing less. To do so, would be to give room to the enemy, to Satan."

Satan, I reflected. This was also new to me—at least compared with what the Constantine I had known would have said.

After this brief speech, the emperor went on to deal with Eusebius and Athanasius as he had with all the bishops at Nicaea.

"It is my understanding," he judged, "that all the charges against Athanasius have been disproved."

How he had come to understand this, I was not certain. But there it was. The *comes* Dionysius must have sent word of it.

Eusebius objected. "But Lord," he countered, "they have not *all* been dropped. Indeed, some are still pending—"

Athanasius interjected, "True, Eusebius—and yet you well know that all you have said is false. Even now you have a party of men searching for evidence in a way that is far beyond the norms of justice."

Eusebius began to argue, but was silenced by Constantine who abruptly ended the discussion.

"However that may be," declared the emperor, "we shall have to take it up tomorrow. For now, you all must be settled into apartments and gain nourishment."

Most of our party sighed. We sighed with relief on the one hand—for we were all still tired and hungry, and with anxiety on the other—for we wished to know how the emperor would judge. With his last remark, however, Constantine waved his massive hand indicating our dismissal. We turned away to plan the following day, our hopes for justice dashed for the moment.

Then loudly: "Arnobius!"

As we strolled down the length of the great hall, now half the distance away from where Constantine was enthroned, I heard my name called out from behind.

"Arnobius of Carthage!"

My heart raced. It was *his* voice; it was Constantine's, the emperor's voice.

Still, I kept walking. Slowly. But there it was again.

"Arnobius of Carthage, son of the Buzzard!"

I smiled and stopped.

Athanasius urged me to turn to the emperor. Philip told me I must. Timotheos and Macarius, I imagine, prayed for me.

Finally, I did. I turned in order to see him.

"Stay!" he commanded.

I looked at him. *What did he want?*

"I want you to dine with me," he said.

To dine with him, I repeated to myself. I nearly collapsed. How similar it was to those many years ago after Iamblichus' jettisoned lecture. Yet how different, too. Then a request; now a command.

Needless to say, I remained behind, and after a bath and change of clothes, I entered Constantine's own apartment somewhere in the depths of the palace.

It had nearly been ten years. As we sat across from each other in the imperial apartment, he on one couch and I on another, there was silence at first. I confess, Theophilus, that it was awkward. Doubtlessly, if I had been a woman and he the man, it would have been easier. We would have embraced and reconciled physically in the mutual bond of pleasure. But our love was not of that sort; therefore, our reconciliation would be different than that of bodies. Our love was one of words, of minds, of souls. And yet the silence which stretched from one end of those many years to the other was dreadfully powerful—so much so that I feared the tension would prove too much. He would snap; I would cringe; and away we'd go, the strangers we had become. I wished to tell him that it could be different, that the problems we had known in the past were irrelevant to our future, and that we could begin anew. But I couldn't find the nerve. I judged that he was the one who had to act. He was the prime mover in our friendship as he had always been. He was the one with power. I could only wait.

When Constantine finally broke the silence after what seemed like several minutes of gazing at each another, his words and expression were disappointing to me. The past, it seemed was dead to him.

"What do you think of Athanasius?" he asked, stiffly.

Of Athanasius? I thought. *Nothing*. At least nothing right now. Instead of admitting as much, however, I said, "In what way?"

He waved his hands. "This whole business—Eusebius and the rest."

"There's nothing to it," I responded, simply.

"I know," he conceded, "and yet ..."

"Yet what?" I asked.

"*Something* must be done."

Ah. It was always the case with Constantine. He always had to make one difficult judgment or another, always pitting the life and interests of one man against those of another.

"What will you do?" I queried.

He didn't say. Rather, he altered the course of conversation somewhat.

"Are you with him?" he asked.

"Do you mean, allied with him?"

"No," he said, "I mean are you now a believer in the Christ?"

I shook my head and looked down. "I can't really say," I disclosed.

I couldn't. On the one hand I was. Intellectually I had more or less come to believe in a set of ideas. On the other hand, however—on that hand were the many fingers of doubt, hesitation, and despair. Finally, I conceded a middle ground. "If anything," I explained, "I suppose I'm Athanasian."

"Uh-huh," he acknowledged, dryly, as if that were meaningless.

Then, once again, quite suddenly he changed course. His manner shifted warmly, and now he gazed at me with full recognition.

"What is it?" I asked.

"I've missed you," he admitted.

They were words that ignited a fire of joy in my heart. Yet caution.

Smiling he went on, "I've missed our friendship—our discussions, your questions, your mulishness."

I too smiled and looked at him full of affection. Still, however much I wanted to return his sentiments, I could not. Thus, he fell silent and his face grew stiff again.

As for me, I just sat there in silent consideration. I suppose I froze with a kind of irrational dread. I couldn't trust him. *That* was it. I didn't know if he spoke as the emperor or as my old friend. *Still*, I thought. *I must tell him my feelings.*

"What is it?" he asked, mirroring my own question moments before—he had always been able to read me like that, Theophilus.

I looked at him. Why couldn't I command my tongue to speak?

"I know," he read me. "Too much has happened. But I've tried, Arnobius. I've only done my best, however much I've missed the mark. I hope you'll forgive me."

I wanted to cry. I felt the emotion welling up, concentrating like a storm behind my eyes. It was true. He *had* tried. He had succeeded as well. And perhaps now I could forgive him.

"Arnobius ..." he went on.

But I didn't let him. Instead, the dread breaking, and leaving caution aside, I whispered, "I've missed you too. And I *do* forgive you."

The storm broke and we both wept.

Suddenly, he leaned across to me and embraced me. We held each other as brothers, reconciled.

And so, Theophilus, we dined together that night, recalling the past with a sense of melancholy and delight. I hesitate to say more.

"I'm glad you're here," he said at the end of our evening together.

"I'm glad too," I said before getting up to leave.

It was the last time I ever privately spoke with him.

The following day, I stood next to Athanasius once again, who stood alongside Philip, Timotheos, and Macarius before the emperor Constantine. On the opposing side were Eusebius and his men, bathed and anointed, wearing fresh white tunics.

With little delay, Constantine began the proceedings. "As I judged yesterday, all previous charges against the bishop have been disproved."

I glanced over at Eusebius and noticed he was grinning. But at what? I wondered.

"If there is nothing else, I command each of you to return to your own diocese in order to rule according to your own best judgment—Athanasius to Alexandria and Eusebius to Nicomedia."

"But Lord Constantine," countered Eusebius, "I must respectfully object." He stood forward.

Constantine turned to Eusebius. "What is it?"

"We agree to let all the other charges fall," he said. "Not that they are untrue, strictly speaking, but to show our willingness to reconcile, we agree to overlook them."

"Then what?" insisted Constantine.

"Still," Eusebius went on, "there is one matter that cannot simply be overlooked. Indeed, to do so would be to betray the Empire."

Constantine raised his thick brows. Then, assuming a look of skepticism, he leaned forward threateningly as if to suggest punishment for another frivolous, indemonstrable charge. "What is it?" he demanded.

Eusebius remained unperturbed. "Well, it's not that I'm happy to bring this before you, Lord Emperor, but I must. Out of duty, I must." Eusebius looked askance before revealing, "It's reported that when in Alexandria, Athanasius brags about how he could easily cut off grain shipments from Egypt to the New Rome. He boasts that he consequently has your manhood, as it were, in his hands."

The emperor twitched. Then he sat back and all eyes studied him as doubtlessly he thought about what a disaster it would be if Athanasius did such a thing. It *was* conceivable. Egypt is the Empire's greatest source of grain. If it happened, where would he get his bread? He had lured thousands to the New Rome, to *his* city, Constantinople, with promises of bread. But would Athanasius do such a thing? He might. And he *could*, he thought. Yes, he could, because he had appointed churchmen to the chief positions in the distribution of Egyptian grain, and Athanasius held reign over these. But had he make such a threat?

His eyes narrowed as he sat back in the throne. I could see the emperor was lost in deliberation.

If so, it was treasonous—highly treasonous. But *had* he?

Constantine finally turned to Athanasius and asked, "Have you ever uttered such a threat?"

Athanasius categorically denied it. "My authority as bishop has no concern for worldly affairs," he explained. "My business is not that of the Empire's. Although I pray for the Empire and for you, as does the whole Church, my concern is for my flock and the souls with whom I've been charged."

"But I have worthy witnesses," Eusebius interjected.

"Who are they?" Constantine asked.

"They're in Alexandria."

"But who?"

Eusebius walked forward and whispered their names into the emperor's ear.

"Can *we* not hear?" Athanasius objected.

"Is it necessary?" asked Constantine.

Then, without another word, the emperor dismissed everyone. He ordered all to leave, all but for Athanasius, whom he commanded to stay.

Later on in the day, Athanasius told me what Constantine had said to him.

"Athanasius," he began, "you know well what it means to have charge over the lives of men."

Athanasius shook his head. He did.

"I too have such a charge, though mine, strictly speaking, falls outside the walls of the Church. One might expect the traditional enemies of Rome—the barbarians who reside above the Rhine and Danube and the Persians who dwell to the east beyond the two rivers—to be my greatest enemies, the chief of all challenges to the peace of Rome."

Athanasius affirmed this expectation.

The emperor, though, countered it. "Contrary to this expectation, however, neither the barbarians nor the Persians are—as I can assure you. Rather, the Church, it seems, has taken their place."

"I'm sorry," said Athanasius. "But it shouldn't be the case. The affairs of the Church lay outside the immediate interests of the Empire."

"One would think. But I swear to you, it is not so. Already, the citizens of the Empire have lined up behind one faction or another in the Church, whether behind Donatus in Africa, you in Egypt, or Eusebius in Syria and Asia."

"But I have no such faction, Lord."

"I know you see it that way; still, the truth is you do. People are willing to bully others and lay down their lives for you."

"Not for me!" Athanasius protested. "But for the truth, for the Christ, for the Homoousion!"

"However that may be, this fanaticism threatens the integrity of the Empire."

"Don't you think I want peace, too? That's all I've ever really wanted," Athanasius avowed. I imagine he thought of his former life with Anthony in the desert. "Still, one cannot surrender to falsehood. Truth is always worthy of a fight."

"True. And yet one must make concessions. Not so much to falsehood," Constantine explained, "but to the men who hold to falsehoods—to pagans and Jews, and yes, even to the Eusebians who follow Arius."

"Impossible!" cried Athanasius.

"I understand your passion. But you must know that your obstinacy is harmful to the peace of the Empire. Because of this, you are my chief obstacle in this matter. I've asked you to simply restore Arius—that's all— and stubbornly you've refused."

"I cannot!"

"But you *must*. We must have unity of religion in order to strengthen the unity and peace of the Empire."

Athanasius heaved his hands upwards in disagreement. "But unity cannot be bought at any price! Only the saving truth of the Christ is true peace!"

Until then, Constantine had maintained an even manner, calm as befitting a wise ruler. Then he lost his temper. "*Any* price!" he shouted. "*Your* price amounts to petty, philosophical squabbling! How can you possibly defend yourself against *that* charge?"

"How? Simple!" Athanasius firmly declared. "The incarnation is not a matter of mere squabbling!" Athanasius paused for a moment, growing calm. He felt he must make the emperor see his point. "The Homoousion concerns the salvation given by the one God; it is about the provision of the One for the salvation of the many; it is God becoming man so that man might become God. Only with that will we have rest; only then, eternal peace."

Constantine grew flustered. While he believed Athanasius spoke the truth—at least as well as the truth could be spoken—he also knew he could not let the situation stand as it was. Thus, he said, "However that may be, Athanasius, you have become a serious obstacle to my peace—to the Empire's *temporal* peace."

"Do you then believe Eusebius' charge?"

Constantine sighed. "It doesn't matter—though if I truly did, know you would have already met your end."

"Death doesn't frighten me," Athanasius said in retort.

"Still," spoke Constantine, as if groaning, "I must be rid of you."

"So then, I'll be put to death?" asked Athanasius fearlessly. "For what? The truth?"

"No," Constantine shook his head, glancing downwards.

"For what, then?"

"I mean the Empire will not take your life."

"Then what?"

The emperor stood and paced back and forth. The bishop watched him. Then, turning to Athanasius, Constantine declared, "You'll be exiled."

The bishop considered this for a moment. *Exiled? For what?* Finally, he queried, "Because of my stance on the Homoousion?"

"No—of course not."

"For what, then?"

"For disturbing the peace of Rome."

The emperor and bishop faced each other in silence. Then:

"I'm sorry."

It was Constantine. "I'm sorry," he offered, "but it *must* be done. It's you or Eusebius. And since he seems to stir up trouble wherever he is, I'm hoping you'll be less of a cause of tumult than he would be."

Athanasius nodded his understanding, before asking, "Where will I go?"

"Treveris of Gaul," Constantine answered, as if speaking a necessary evil.

Athanasius conveyed his consent. Then he asked if the rest of his party could go with him.

"If they wish," said Constantine.

Again, Athanasius nodded.

With that and one final apology, Constantine dismissed him, ordering him to leave by noon the following day.

"Treveris of Gaul!" I exclaimed, as Athanasius' account ended. "*Tomorrow?*—but we've just finished our journey. I don't know if I can do it, if I *want* to do it."

"You don't have to, but think about it. Certainly you cannot stay here," Athanasius suggested.

"No, I suppose I cannot."

Yet I wanted to, Theophilus. I wanted to stay with Constantine at least for a while. Nevertheless, upon hearing the unjust judgment against Athanasius, I felt I could not. Constantine would always be this way, I thought. Despite his love for me—and *that*, I could hardly explain—he was a monster. Or so he had become. But what else could he be? Really, Theophilus? He was the one emperor of Rome. His was power, judgment, and will. No, I had to go. It was either that or I could remain to face disappointment even as I had before.

Athanasius went on. "Think nothing more of it, Arnobius. You'll merely be traveling home to Carthage by a different route."

"Yes," I said drolly, "and by the end of it, I will have practically rounded the whole of Our Sea."

I thought of it. It had only been a half year before that I had set out from Carthage on family business. I had planned on going as far as Pelusium. And now? How in the name of the gods had I ended up in Constantine's city again? Yet there *was* a purpose to it all, Theophilus, there was.

"Surely you don't want to go home by boat again?" Athanasius argued, enticing me to come along.

I considered that for a moment. The image of a stormy sea came to mind. Fear. Sickness. Shipwreck. Quickly I replied. "No, you're right. I'd much rather do as you say and go by land."

"Then you'll come with us?"

"Perhaps I will," I agreed.

"It's settled then," he confirmed. "We leave tomorrow."

Tomorrow? I echoed. *I know*, I thought. *Why resist?*

There it was again. *It's the flow of life that cannot be stilled, Theophilus.* *Why not?* I speculated. *Why can't it be stilled for just a moment? For a simple rest? For a tired old soul like mine?*

Further, I wondered why it was my fate to attach myself to men such as these. Whatever the reason, I'd be leaving with Athanasius and the others the following day. And tomorrow would come far too soon.

Thirty-eight: Journeying to Treveris

Late 335 A.D.

THE FOLLOWING DAY ARRIVED with a storm. Much as the one we had experienced a month before at sea, dark clouds rolled in as a womb carrying whole rivers of rain. Nevertheless, by order of the emperor, we were forced to ride, making our way out of the capital city around the noon hour. By then, the emperor's men had gathered all that was required for the journey that would last nearly two months. Each of us rode a young horse provided by the imperial post. A few pack animals followed carrying our provisions, including our papers, which gave us safe passage and at the same time guaranteed our arrival in Treveris instead of some other destination. To this end, we were accompanied by five guards who were charged with conveying us safely to Gaul and finally to Treveris, the city of wool, wood, and wine.

As for me, Theophilus, as I have indicated, I was free to stay or go. But as we made our way out of the New Rome through the wide avenues that had been constructed a half decade before and past the colossal statue of Constantine in the Forum holding the world aloft in his great hands, I more and more felt myself bound by fate to the destinies of Athanasius, Macarius, Timotheos, and Philip. I was theirs, I thought. Even so, although my sentiments were then such that I would remain with Athanasius and the others in their departure from the New Rome, I had not yet resolved to go all the way to Treveris in Gaul. Instead, I intended to go only as far as Italy and then turn southward toward Sicily and a ferry that would take me home to Mother, my brother and sisters, and to the life I had known on and off again ever since the day I was born some fifty and more years before.

When we departed from the city that day, no one came to bid us farewell, none but Pila—and this was incidental, as he happened to be on his way to one place or another.

"Pila!" I exclaimed, happy to see him.

Strangely, he was in no mood to talk. "Arnobius," he observed, without his usual charm, "you've shaved!"

And that was it. With those last words, he scurried off to wherever his own fate led him, leaving me amid my own thoughts and with my own saddened feelings that Constantine had failed to come. In this, I was disappointed. I had hoped to say a final goodbye to him, imagining it might be the very last time I set eyes upon him. But he didn't come.

And so, with a certain sense of melancholy, I mounted my horse and prepared with the others to ride out. We rode into the cold falling rain and began a journey that would last far longer than I cared to consider.

A week passed.

It was still cold, but the rain had finally stopped. Even so, clouds menacingly hovered above as they do in that part of the Empire at that time of the year. They do so not so much as to threaten rain but to reflect a kind of dreariness and dread. Their cold movement, darkly blanketing the sky, is like a disheartening speech—that life is meaningless, a mere spinning of the wheels; that we all are fated to the same end as Sisyphus, the everlasting toil of rolling a great stone up a towering hill only to see it fall down again and again.

As we neared to Serdica amid hills that serve as footstools to the soaring mountains above, I observed that all the leaves were gone from the hundreds and thousands of trees that spine the earth. Along with the gray clouds, the lack of color saddened me. I felt like I was lumbering along through Hades' realm, the realm of death.

As we rode on, meandering along rather than racing as I had done with Constantine thirty years before, we visited the many churches that had sprouted with new life since the emperor had defeated Maxentius at the battle of Milvian Bridge and since he had given legal life to the Christian religion. Along the way, Athanasius and the others came to know and talk to the many priests and deacons that served the Church, and occasionally we supped with an allied bishop—one friendly to the creed of Nicaea.

I could not help but smile as we rode through Moesia. For one, the clouds lifted as they had not in days, and the sun shone. But more, this is where the emperor Galerius' mother had dwelled those many years before, making sacrifice to dark spirits in the morning, evening, and late into the darkness of night. I couldn't help but smile because now, next to makeshift shrines propitiating the many gods, there were Christian churches as well.

As we travelled westward, I wondered where his mother was now. And where Galerius? Gone, I thought; they were dust. Even so, I wished them well, Theophilus, just as God wishes us well. Their own wickedness was their own reward, their punishment, as Socrates might have said. The drunkenness. The jealousy. The anger, rage, and violence. Now I hoped that somehow they had met the healing hand of God in the movements of the World Soul, which moves all things toward the Good. I hoped they had finally come to see the one everlasting light.

We trotted along. From early morning to late evening, we rode accompanied by Tedium who, if not a god, if not enshrined in some pantheon in some far off corner of the world, then he should be. So I felt—for his power is devastating.

Finally, when the sun disappeared behind darkened skies once again and gray clouds hovered above, that sense of melancholy returned. The feeling I had was similar to what Plotinus' student Porphyry must have felt if the reports are true. He wanted to kill himself. I felt depressed again for no other reason than the darkness above.

We trudged forward. *Clip-clop, clip-clop.* We came to Naissus on the Danube, the town of Constantine's birth. Glumly, I remembered when Constantine had explained to me how he was born along the great river because his father's military career had brought him there. Born to Helena, I recalled. I felt disgust for her. She was the one who had shed light on Constantine's crime. She had been the one to point out that Fausta had lied. She had made her own son realize he had put Crispus to death, that he had murdered him for no reason at all. And that's when he had changed. No, it was earlier, Theophilus. Some said that his mother had gone to Jerusalem to search for artifacts of the Christ. Others suggested the mission had been meant to bring healing to her son. I suppose it was a bit of both. Anyway, it wasn't really her fault.

Athanasius could see I was heavy with thought. Kindly, he asked what was on my mind.

"I was thinking of Constantine," I said in reply. "He was born here."

"Do you miss him?" he asked.

"I do," I admitted. "But it's the man of long ago that I miss, not the one who has commanded your exile."

"I understand," he remarked. "Either way, don't feel too bad for me."

"Why?" I asked. "You're far away from home and far away from your people. You've drawn a bitter lot."

He shook his head and patted his horse behind its ears.

After a moment of quiet, I tacked on, "Such is the whole of life a bitter lot."

Thoughtfully, Athanasius responded, "It is. As the psalmist declares, it is the valley of the shadow of death. Because of that, I know no home. I thank God for this, though—for this one fact drives me to Christ the Lord and his Church, my only real home until, God willing, I will come to rest in his everlasting kingdom."

As I often had done, I despondently wondered about my own home and whether or not this Christ and this Church were for me as they were for him.

Athanasius finished by declaring, "I'm a pilgrim, Arnobius."

"A pilgrim?" I echoed. *And me?* I wondered.

As if he had heard my silent question, he answered, "And you too. Don't feel too dejected. Trust and your life will unfold as it's meant to."

Trust? Ha! I couldn't do that. For then, Theophilus, on *that day*, I felt I was *not* a pilgrim. It was one of those cold and dreary days, and I felt as though the light of God had abandoned me. All happy thoughts of providence—those about Galerius and his mother, and me, I admit—had vanished. Instead, I believed fate and the gods merely rushed us downriver by the events of life, by men, by whatsoever happened to happen. It was all luck. No, I could hardly trust. I could hardly call myself a pilgrim led on to some better land, somewhere, wherever that was.

We rode on. While Athanasius intoned a song in praise of God, I brooded over my past. Where had I rushed down the river of life? Where had fate taken me? *Everywhere*, I surmised, and then some. Carthage. Alexandria. Nicomedia. Gesoriacum. Treveris. Rome. The New Rome. Nicaea. Tyre. And now? When does everywhere become nowhere? Why had this all happened to me? It's not what I had wanted. Where was the truth I had longed for? The steady and good life—the love? Was there anything that would last? Any person? Where had everyone gone? Where was this great river taking me next?

To Carthage, I supposed. But is that what I wanted? Yes, I thought. I desired my own home and family. I longed for my own bed where I could rest my weary head. And perhaps I would marry.

Yet there was more to what I desired, Theophilus. It seemed to me that Athanasius was proof of that. What more? you ask. This. If possible, I wanted to know where I was going. Not so much how the river would flow, but *where*. In that certainty, I wished to make my home.

It was for this I yearned. Nevertheless, because of all that had happened, and perhaps just the length and nature of life, I couldn't bring myself to believe. I was unsure, uncommitted.

Why? you ask. It's hard to explain. I *can't* explain. Still, I'll try. Though I had more or less come to believe as a matter of reason according to a certain logic, I still held back. Why? Because faith in the Christ did not match the beating of my heart. It didn't take hold of me as it seemed to do with other men; it didn't conquer my whole being, my whole way of life. This, it seemed, was the unhinged hinge. Though I half believed, I did not possess conviction.

Yet what is that? What is conviction? Right: it's an idea, a belief. But it's more. Conviction seems to rest more in a man's heart than in his head. If so, then this explained my own position. It was as though I intellectually knew the need to fight, to go into battle, but I had neither the heart nor the courage to go. I believed without believing.

How hollow my life seemed as a result. There was a hurt, an ache in both my heart and head. Something, I knew, was off. But what could I do? Nothing, I surmised. As a result, I hurried down the ever-turning, ever-surging, ever-rushing river of life, drowning half the time, my life shaped more by other men and the events of life rather than my own convictions.

It was later, perhaps a week later. We neared Mursa where I should have turned south toward Italy. It was then that I first truly thought about going all the way to Treveris.

I began to think of Katrina once more, the youth she had possessed, the beauty, and the family which had surrounded her, now all gone but for one. What, I wondered, would have happened if I had been lucky enough to marry her? How many children would we have had? I thought of the many nights of love we would have known and the offspring we would have produced as a result, and the many days I would have spent working with Belanus and Gaius Publius on the docks or in the field.

As I thought about this, I wondered how Katrina's family, what remained of it, had fared in those many years that had passed since I had last been in Treveris. I wondered if Luxilla was still alive. If so, I calculated she would be nearing her fifth decade of life. I thought of her as she had been. Those many years ago, she had been so young, so full of innocent life, so charming.

My heart beat with sudden desire. Unexpectedly I felt excited that I could meet her once again, speak with her, and somehow tie up everything that had become unraveled over the past decades. And yes, I confess it, Theophilus, I thought that perhaps she was unmarried, a widow. And just possibly ...

But I knew better. I did. I knew it was foolish. I knew it was unlikely. Still, as I reminisced and dreamt of what might be, however foolishly, I thought I must at the very least go to see what would come of it. Consequently, I determined to make the journey with Athanasius and the others to Treveris.

When I told Athanasius, he smiled as if he already knew. Of course, I would.

Thirty-nine: Luxilla

336 A.D.

WE RODE INTO GAUL just after the New Year celebration and entered Treveris several weeks later. The city had prospered since I had last been there due to a constant peace in the Empire that caused the various barbarian tribes to think long and hard before invading across the Rhine. Even before entering the city proper, I noted markets that earlier had not been present. There, old men hawked chickens, old women sold chestnuts, and others of varying age sold everything from candles and incense to leather shoes and felt hats. Children ran about from stall to stall, quite happy beneath the white winter sky, playing with one another and admiring all the different goods for sale.

Just outside the Porta Nigra, we stopped for one last time. The men who had served as guards—moderately amiable fellows for men of that particular occupation—dismounted and told us to do so as well.

"What's the need?" asked Philip.

"We must inform the head of guard on duty of our arrival," one of them said.

Soon afterwards, they came and bade us to follow them. We dismounted and walked after them through the rounded archway of the Porta Nigra and into a dark room that led to a flight of stone stairs that ascended round and round to one of the upper floors.

As we climbed, the guard turned and said, "The emperor's son wishes to speak with Bishop Athanasius."

"The emperor's son?" asked Philip.

"Yes, his son Constantine."

Constantine, I thought. I considered how long it had been since I had last seen him. Then, when in Rome and when the older Constantine had put Crispus and Fausta to death, he was only a small boy of maybe ten years.

Now, as we climbed the stairs to meet him, he was a young man nearing twenty.

When he met us, he expressed pleasure in coming to know the chief protagonist of the Homoousion. Indeed, the younger Constantine proclaimed he was a faithful follower of the Nicene religion, and from the start, he wished to let Athanasius know that he was fully at his disposal. Athanasius expressed gratitude but held his own in reserve. He had seen how emperors could behave, and therefore he knew the potential of the sons of emperors.

After speaking with the younger Constantine at length and receiving the nourishment of bread and wine, we departed, descending the stairs to the ground floor of the Porta Nigra. Then we made our way into Treveris and on to the part of the city where the elder Constantine had built a new basilica and where we hoped to find the bishop's residence.

The bishop, Maximus, was expecting us. When we arrived, he warmly welcomed us with every comfort. That night, and nearly every night for the next few days, Athanasius and the others met with him discussing what could be done to defeat the Eusebians and the Arian heresy—for Maximus was devoted even as they were to the cause of the Word made flesh.

As for me, I didn't sit in and listen to those conversations. I was done with all the controversy. Instead, I brooded upon whether Luxilla was still alive, and if she was alive, whether or not she was married. The more I thought about it, the more anxiety took hold of me and the more I grew afraid. *What if she had married?* It was likely. *What if her husband refused my presence?* Again, it was likely. And *what if she had moved away with him?* But there was more to my fear than that. More than anything, I dreaded she was dead.

Finally, I concluded I would bravely ride out to discover the truth for myself. So, Theophilus, I did. One morning, though afraid of losing the last I had known and loved of Gaul and Treveris, I rode out to Gaius Publius' estate to see what of it remained, and who, if anyone, was still there. Sadly, the terrain I traversed that day was hardly recognizable to me. As I trotted along, I wondered if this was because the land itself had changed or if my memory of it had grown so dim as to no longer match it.

Since it was winter, there was hardly any life about except for the occasional rabbit darting from the side of a wood to gather something before darting back again and the occasional peasant tending to an animal or gathering wood for the warmth of a fire.

When at last I arrived stoically braced against what I might discover, it was much as expected. With this, I sighed in relief. Indeed, the road leading through the estate and up to the house was the same as it had been before, as was the house's facade, though it seemed to have crumbled some over the years and to have taken on the dark color of the soil. Outside I spotted several children playing a game to the side of the house in the not too far distance. I could see they were young, possibly not yet in their second decade. There were a girl and two boys and a black and white dog that barked and dodged in and out of their play.

It was then that I saw her. It was the slave woman Ulfila. I knew her because she had always had a certain manner about her, a one of contentment, as though the lines of her face and the movement of her body somehow conveyed the expression of fulfillment.

I sauntered up the road and was now quite near to the house, no more than a stone's throw distant. As I rode forward, Ulfila saw me too and studied me, surely wondering who I was and what it was that I wanted. Then she recognized me, though it was a recognition that was still uncertain, I noticed, and doubtlessly surprised. Finally, as I drew near to her, she hesitantly queried, "Is that you, lord Arnobius?"

How she knew it, I cannot say. My face had grown long, my hair gray. Still, she knew it despite the passing of so many years.

"It is," I disclosed, bringing my horse to a standstill next to her.

She laughed. "It *is* you!"

I smiled, for I had grown quite fond of her those many years before.

"I'll go fetch Luxilla!" she cried, happily.

With those few words of revelation, she turned to run into the house, leaving me straddling my horse with the most satisfying of conclusions. *She's alive!* I thought, merrily. *Luxilla is alive!*

Even so, I soberly imagined the man who must now be the master of the estate. Because there were children, there surely must be the man who had sired them.

Not long after, a woman came to the wooden door of the house. She was middle aged but attractive, having long brown hair that was tied modestly behind and a face that lightly wore the passing of time. Her dress was simple, a plain woolen white embroidered with brown, yellow, and blue flowers at the end of its sleeves and hem.

"*Arnobius?*" she queried, tentatively.

It was Luxilla. And I saw she was as beautiful as ever. I recognized her in all her features and in her voice—with that one word, my name—the very voice I recalled from those many nights of playing War or Odds and Evens, or studying Latin grammar, or telling stories of nymphs and fauns.

"Luxilla?" I responded, equally tentative.

We silently stood there for a moment before she wiped away a single tear that had fallen down her cheek. Then she invited me into the same house I once had known as a second home.

As I walked through the door, I was surprised to see several Christian images painted upon the walls of the entryway into the house. There on my left was the good shepherd, on my right an image of the prophet Jonah rescued from the sea and the belly of the sea dragon, and above were images of peacocks and anchors, among other signs of the Christ, including a long, trailing vine. There were more as we went inside painted upon rectangular wooden supports. They reminded me of the portrait that had been made of me by Lake Faiyum. Some I recognized, some I did not.

With hardly a word, Luxilla disappeared for a moment. When she returned, it was with Ulfila and a jug of wine, a pot of stew, and a loaf of bread.

"Please," she offered after we had reclined, "have some."

We did, the three of us, Luxilla, Ulfila, and me. We sat there eating bread and a chickpea stew steaming from earthenware bowls, and drinking wine.

In silence, I was left wondering what had happened to all the household gods, the Lares, for they were gone. The house felt different. And Luxilla, I could tell, had changed.

Then, quite beyond the control of my own thoughts and more at the beckoning of a simple urge to know, I asked, "Have you come to believe?"

At first Luxilla said nothing. Then tilting her head, she clarified, "In the Christ?"

"Yes," I replied.

She nodded.

"How?" I queried.

She sat for a moment reflecting on my odd question. But if she only knew how difficult it was for me, Theophilus. How does one come to believe? How does one come to give that full assent of the mind and heart?

At last, she said, "By the grace of the Lord, I have come to believe."

But what is grace? I wondered. Sure, I understood on some level. Yet the idea or reality had always escaped me.

I pushed. "Would you mind telling me more?"

She shook her head. "I came to believe some time ago shortly after the death of my husband. Ulfila, the Lord bless her, shared with me the life of God in Christ Jesus, introducing comfort into my time of mourning."

We both glanced at Ulfila who shone with joy and Luxilla touched her hand to hers.

"She's my God-sent companion," she went on, the corners of her mouth turned upwards, "no longer my slave. Now she's like a sister."

When Luxilla shared this, I thought of Katrina and imagined the pain she must have felt upon losing her whole family in the short period of a few months.

Eventually I asked Luxilla about her marriage and children, her new family.

"I was married," she explained, "just long enough for the blessing of three children." She grinned widely. "Did you see them playing outside? Aside from the Lord, they're my life. Nothing would make me happier than to give them to God as living stones to build up the one body of the Christ."

I was happy for her.

Then Luxilla asked me if I had married and if I had been blessed with offspring. I said I hadn't. Again, I thought of Katrina.

"I'm sorry," she offered. "I know it must have been hard."

I shook my head. It had been.

Then, to my surprise, she asked, "Do *you* believe, Arnobius?"

Did I?

I looked at her. I gazed into her deep brown eyes and wished to disclose everything. But I couldn't answer. How could I explain that I wanted to believe but did not? She wouldn't understand.

In any event, she graciously didn't press; rather, she spoke of what was common to us, the past. It was then I finally learned all the details of Katrina's death, how she had contracted the plague and had fallen prey to it in three short days. Ulfila had nursed her, but it was useless. Rapidly, her body hardened with fetid, oozing bulbs, and finally, burning with fever, she faded into the darkness.

"She died," Luxilla explained, "on the third night."

"What did she last say?" I asked. "Do you remember?"

She did. "Her last words were a prayer to the gods, to Apollo and his son Asclepius, asking for healing, for everlasting health, and for the grace of eternal life with you in the celestial realm of the stars."

I smiled and chuckled as she revealed this. Then, like a small boy, I shook and nearly cried.

When I had gathered myself again, I asked, "Did she mention me by name?"

Luxilla nodded and her eyes swelled with tears.

Quietly we both remembered her.

At last, I asked, "What about your father?"

"He died a fortnight later."

"In the same way?"

Again, she nodded. "There was nothing we could do."

Luxilla asked me to tell her about Belanus' last moments. I did. I told her how he had bravely fought against Maxentius before meeting an honorable death on the battlefield. She didn't ask me for the details, and thankful she had not, I didn't supply them. I thought it unnecessary. All she required was to know of his virtue. That alone would prove immortal.

There was silence again. I stared at her with a warmness of heart, and she at me. Yet the whole of our conversation left me feeling sad. She as well—I could see it.

But Luxilla was not one to let it rest at that. She told me about her life since then. She told me of her children and her husband, a man from southern Gaul.

"How long has he been gone?" I asked.

"Eight years," she answered.

She told me more about the man she had married, the man she had loved, and how she had fared since he had died and since she had become a believer in the Christ.

Again, I was glad for her. I was happy that she had known love with her husband, and with Ulfila, faith and hope.

Yet at the end of it all, at the end of her story and at the end of my own telling, of explaining what had happened since departing over twenty years before, there formed a cloud of discomfort between the two of us. What more was there to say? The feeling was one that grew from our remembering a shared past, but then realizing that the present left a vast gulf of unknowing between us. Indeed, although we had once spent so much time together, now we were little more than strangers, the ghosts of our past fading as the words which gave them life fell from our mouths.

For a while, we sat there sipping at the wine, gnawing on the bread, and making small talk. How was the wine production? The wool? The supply of wood? The children's education? And so on.

A few hours passed.

Finally, when it was clear we had little more to say, I thanked Luxilla and wished her well, and soon I stood to go. She and Ulfila also stood to see me off.

"Perhaps we'll see each other again," I said, hoping we could become present to each other once more.

I wanted to embrace her. I wanted to take her into my arms in order to show her my affection. But I couldn't. She was not mine to embrace. And whether or not she felt the same, I couldn't say.

At last she offered, "Perhaps we will, Arnobius, and yet it's possible all is better left to the past."

I nodded my understanding, thanked her and Ulfila, and turned to mount my horse that had been drawn in from a surrounding field. Then, I rode to Treveris, sad.

Weeks passed.

Athanasius and the others continued their meetings with Bishop Maximus, discussing how best to deal with the Arian plague that had infected the Church in the East. It would be best, they thought, simply to wait and trust. They spent the better part of their time in prayer, attending to the liturgy, and otherwise in serving the poor and the sick of Treveris.

As it happened, the younger Constantine truly turned out to be an ally of the Homoousion, offering assistance in any manner necessary. For this, Athanasius and Maximus were sincerely grateful.

As for me, though I helped the others in whatever they were doing, I found I could concentrate on little else but Luxilla. Day and night, she haunted my thoughts. The very idea that she was a half morning's ride away taunted me with longing.

I could go, I thought, as I used to. I could ride out to the estate, unannounced, as I had done repeatedly. I wanted to. I wanted to be with her. But I was undecided. *Would she want me to?*

Finally, when I had resolved to go, fate intervened.

On the day before I planned to ride out to the estate, I saw her in the marketplace just inside the city walls. She was walking next to Ulfila. They were just then passing the place in the market where the pig butchers hang the carcasses to drain.

"Luxilla!" I shouted without reflection.

She turned along with Ulfila and saw me. For a moment, there was a kind of embarrassment when she recognized me.

Even so, I walked toward them. When I got close enough to her, I spilled myself.

"Luxilla," I divulged, "I need to speak with you."

She looked to Ulfila.

I asked if I could visit her once more.

She didn't respond. Then, as if stumbling upon a brilliant idea, she replied, "I'd like you to, Arnobius."

Happily, I declared I would.

But she wasn't finished. Rather, she explained, "Why don't we meet at the basilica?"

"The church?" I said, surprised at the suggestion.

"Yes," she answered, "for the feast marking the beginning of Lent. The whole of Treveris will be there."

Of course, I thought, and realizing it was just a few weeks away, I agreed.

When the feast came, Luxilla and Ulfila arrived to the basilica built by the elder Constantine in order to celebrate the sacred liturgy. Athanasius and Maximus presided, and Athanasius, as was the custom in Alexandria though not as much in Gaul, spoke to those of us standing along the nave of the church. He spoke of the sacrifice of the Christ, about his death upon the wooden cross. It was like the crossbeams above us, he suggested, spanning the width of the basilica. He explained the need for man's mind and heart to be reformed and restored by that one sacrifice into the new man God had foreordained from the beginning of time.

As Athanasius spoke, I attempted to listen. I tried, Theophilus. My heart and mind, however, were set upon Luxilla. She and Ulfila stood in the distance somewhere to the fore of the church in contrast to where I stood in the back, having taken my place there with the uninitiated. She was there and I here. It wasn't far, but it was far too far.

Afterwards, after the liturgy had been prayed and after the initiated had received the bread and wine, Bishop Maximus and the younger Constantine offered a feast to the whole of Treveris, to the well off and to the poor alike. It was then that Luxilla and I met under the attentive eye of Ulfila. We spoke at length, and happily on this occasion, Theophilus, we moved beyond that initial discomfort which had first separated us, and the gap between the past and present seemed to close somewhat. Nay, it closed significantly, for by the feast's end, she invited me to come to the estate once more. She told me she had missed me those many years and I told her the same.

Some weeks later, after we had celebrated the beginning of Lent, Luxilla told me of her admiration for Athanasius, whom she had met and listened to on several occasions.

"He's right," she remarked.

"About what?" I asked.

"It was God the Word who became man."

I nodded, completing the formula I had by now heard so often, "So that we men might become God, partaking in the divine life."

We dined together meagerly on that occasion just a few weeks after Lent had begun. As I said, Luxilla had invited me to come visit her on the estate, and happily, I had accepted the invitation. That day, we ate from a loaf of coarse bread and sipped a thin soup and spoke of the Christ—or she spoke, and I listened.

However it was, Theophilus, this is the point. There was a way about her—her manner, her speech, her way of being—that was authentic, and so, attractive. I cannot exactly say what it was, but her comportment was similar to what I had first observed in Ulfila long before. It was that of contentment, as though she had studied with the Stoics, though without all the pride one senses among the men of their school. She seemed satisfied, happy—fulfilled.

Over the next few weeks, as Lent passed by and the many in Treveris celebrated Easter with Maximus and Athanasius, I visited Luxilla at the estate and occasionally saw her in town when she and Ulfila came to do the shopping or on some other errand.

I was happy during this time as we came to know each other again with the same facility we had possessed before. The only difficulty, as I saw it, was that I could do nothing but think about her when we were apart. Consequently, as time passed by, I thought I must do something to secure her to my constant possession until the end of my days. To be plain, Theophilus, I came to love her and wanted her to be my wife. One day, therefore, perhaps a few weeks after Easter, I told her so.

Once again, we sat near to each other as we had many times over the previous months. By this point, Ulfila had taken to leaving us to ourselves, although she would oftentimes work or sit in a nearby room for the sake of propriety. We sat by a roaring fire as the day drew to a close, a day that was just beyond the dying of winter and the birth of spring.

"Luxilla," I announced, after making small talk, "I must tell you something."

"What is it, Arnobius?"

She looked at me with eyes of love. Yet I hesitated.

"When I'm not with you," I explained, "when I'm in town and you're here, I can do nothing but think about you. I wonder what you're doing and how you are—if you're awake or asleep or eating or what, and if you're happy or sad. But most of all, I think about when I'll see you next. I'm hardly functional." I chuckled. "It's like I'm a young man again, a fool, dumbstruck with—"

Luxilla didn't let me finish.

"I too," she admitted, "struggle with the same." She glanced at me, searching for the right words. "I think of you, as you do of me."

With her words, I grew happy. I knew they meant she had come to love me even as I had come to love her.

So I moved.

With a heart nearly bursting with delight, I leaned forward to embrace Luxilla. *Finally*, I thought. I had desired to hold her for months, to feel her body next to mine, the warmth of her breath, her mouth. To *know* her. But more. I had finally found my home, my love; I had arrived.

I edged close to her.

She drew close to me.

Yet then, as I leaned forward, my mouth drawing near to hers, her scent enveloping me like the intoxicating mist in a goddess's grove, Luxilla pulled back, her eyes dropping to the tile of the floor.

"What?" I asked.

"I cannot," she declared. A flood of tears washed over her eyes.

"What is it?" I beseeched, baffled. "What's wrong?"

For a moment, she said nothing. She couldn't. Rather she wept quietly, attempting to get a hold of herself.

Finally, she spoke. "Arnobius, there's something I haven't told you."

"What is it?" I begged.

"I've given myself to someone else."

From feeling sure of myself a moment before, I suddenly felt disoriented. She hesitated.

"To … whom?" I inquired.

She looked up at me. "I've followed the advice of the apostle."

The apostle, I thought. *Who?* "Do you mean Paul?"

She nodded.

"In doing what?" I demanded. *What could have he wanted with her?*

"I've given myself to the Lord."

It was gibberish. "What can that possibly mean?" I begged.

With her brief confession, Luxilla gained resolve. She dabbed at her eyes with the sleeve of her woolen dress.

Still, I objected. "We love each other, Luxilla."

Gently, she disagreed. "I'm not sure we do."

"But *I* am," I protested. "I'm sure. And you just said so yourself. You said you can't help but think of me, that—"

She cut me off. "No, Arnobius. I didn't."

"But you did," I countered, insisting like a foolish schoolboy in love.

She sighed. "If I did, I didn't mean it."

"So you don't?"

Again, a sigh. She didn't answer. Instead, she clarified, "Listen, Arnobius, it seems we are more in love with the past than with each other."

"What does *that* mean?" I asked.

"It means we long for the past. It means that you love Katrina in me, and I love my father and Belanus in you."

I said nothing. For how could I? I could say nothing now that she was taking away from me what I had most desired. My happiness, the joy I had felt just moments before, was now a wasteland. I *did* love her, I wanted to declare, and she loved me. And yes, I loved those memories in her of Katrina, those memories of the past, of who I was when young, and I loved the whole of her family and all we had shared together. But I said nothing.

Then, Theophilus, for a long moment, my life appeared to me as one immeasurable suffering. There was pain near my heart, a tightening, constricting pain. I feared I would die. It was as though I had been born whole, of one piece, and slowly, agonizingly, the whole had been torn down the middle. And that torn again. And again. *Why*, I wondered, *why did life have to be this way? Nothings lasts.*

After a while, Luxilla whispered my name. I didn't answer; instead, full of self-pity, I stared downwards.

"Arnobius," she whispered, "perhaps there is a greater love, greater than the one you and I feel for each other."

I didn't hear her. Or I heard her in part. I heard what I wished to hear. And looking up, I foolishly said, "So you *do* love me."

"Yes," she admitted, "but there's more."

I couldn't imagine it. What more could there be? What is greater than human love?

"I love you, Arnobius," she confessed, "but I've given myself wholly to *him*."

"To *whom?*" I asked.

"To the Lord," she said.

Again, it was gibberish, as though the speech of a barbarian.

"Then what are we?" I implored.

She considered the question before quietly answering, "We are siblings."

I glanced at her.

She smiled. "It's like we always were when Katrina was still alive and you spent half of your days here in this house. You're my brother, Arnobius, my dear brother."

I felt crushed as she said this, near to tears, helpless as though one in love with another man's wife. Lady Fortune had tricked me and was now laughing.

"Don't feel too bad," she offered, attempting to comfort me.

I felt only bad.

"It's for the best," she went on.

"How?" I begged.

"Because someday you will die or I will die, and then we must inevitably lose this human love."

True, I reflected. Still. I loved her *now*. I wanted her *now*. Wasn't that something?

"It's all so horrible," I declared.

"What is?" she asked.

"Life," I answered. "Nothing is permanent. All is a great river of passing, of suffering, flowing into a sea of darkness."

"You're right," Luxilla agreed. "That's our world."

"And love doesn't exist."

"No," she countered, "God is love. And God loves."

"God?" I laughed, as if *that* would comfort me.

"Yes, God. Think of it, Arnobius. God's love is different. It alone is everlasting."

"That may be," I said, "but what's the good of God's everlasting love if men don't love?"

"God helps us to love the little bit we do love."

"Do *you* love?"

"I try," she said.

I sighed. "Just not me, right?"

"Please, Arnobius. Don't say that."

Luxilla was crying again.

"I'm sorry," I said.

I got up and walked over to the arched doorway and stood there looking into another room where Ulfila was sewing at the other end.

She looked up. "What is it, Arnobius? Are the two of you okay?"

I shook my head.

Ulfila got up and joined me in the doorway.

"It's nothing," I said.

She took my chin in her hand and raised my face so that I was looking at her.

"Tell me."

I looked at Ulfila. What did I see in her deep brown eyes?

"Ulfila," I said, "do you love others as you should?"

She looked away. "No," she admitted. "I try, but mostly I fail."

"Do you believe that other followers of the Christ love as they should?"

"Some," she said. "Most don't."

"Why, then, do you believe in the love of God?"

I thought of Athanasius' argument from years ago when I sailed with him up the Nile. He had claimed that the many were changing, that the Christ was actually changing lives, whereas philosophers like Socrates, Plato, and Epictetus had only influenced the few.

His argument didn't work. Christians were no better. Since then, I had experienced very little of this promised love. If anything, I'd seen even greater rancor and competition among Christians. The truth was an excuse to fight and hate. The only place I'd witnessed men love was in the monastery in Tabennisi and perhaps among a few such as Ulfila and Luxilla. Despite their humble disavowals to the contrary, they seemed to love.

"Let's go sit down with Luxilla," Ulfila suggested, pointing to her.

I followed her.

When we were seated, she declared, "I don't believe in the love of God, Arnobius, I know it—I experience it."

I looked at Luxilla who was drying her tears.

"I do too," she said. Then she added, "What else is there? Where else would I go?"

I thought about that. It was true. I had never found a home. All my denials had never gotten me anywhere.

Ulfila reached over, touched my back with the flat of her hand, and gently stroked me as my own nurse had done when I was a boy and sick. Again, I looked into her dark eyes.

"Why not let God love you?" she implored. "What can it hurt to try? Let God worry about all the others. Let him worry about your own imperfections. His love is great enough for that."

I saw love in her eyes. I saw compassion. It was human. But more.

"Why not—?" I repeated.

I shrugged and nodded at the same time.

Was it assent?

Could I?

Luxilla touched my knee. "My dear Arnobius, God's love alone is what I desire. I've given myself to him. It's what I've resolved until the day I die, whether today or tomorrow or many years from now. I was born for him. God has made me happier and God will be my happiness forevermore— however much I now fail to love others."

Now I was thinking furiously. *Could I? And what of the distance? Did the One really love? How was that possible? Was it real? Why the silence? Why all the suffering? Why all the ...?*

Luxilla noticed me thinking, and so, gently, she suggested, "It's not only a matter of the head, Arnobius, but of the heart too. You rely too much on your own logic. Although it may be a beginning, you'll never reach God that way. What you need is grace; you require faith. Perhaps you have not yet given yourself to him in order to gain that freedom, that joy, which is beyond all comparison and understanding. To experience that, you have to die to yourself."

"It's possible," I allowed.

Yet, despite my tentative response, I knew it. I had not. And doubtlessly, I didn't know if I could. How could I take the step of committing myself in such a manner? Where could I find the conviction?—the grace she had spoken of? I didn't know. None of it made sense to me.

Ulfila added, "Just try it. Fall into his loving care. Like a seed, fall into the earth and die. He'll take care of you like a gentle gardener. Soon you'll find yourself growing into new life."

I felt helpless.

I couldn't do it.

I wouldn't.

After some time, nothing remained between us but for a feeling of discomfort. Ulfila and Luxilla sat there quietly, not knowing what to say, and I too failed to find words that might shift the conversation in a pleasant manner away from the terrible mistake I had made in revealing to Luxilla my true feelings.

Finally, after affirming the love of God once more, Ulfila went into another room to prepare the evening meal.

When she did, I realized I could no longer be with Luxilla. There would be no more ease between us, no more comfort, no more relationship. What we had possessed was now gone.

Now it seemed the pain of loss was too much to bear. I could tell Luxilla felt the same, though she was kind enough not to give voice to her thoughts.

"I must go," I declared at last.

"I know," she agreed.

Toward the end of that day, therefore, after coming near to possessing her only to lose her again, we parted as the sun began its evening descent. After a long, awkward embrace, and after I had said farewell to Ulfila, I rode toward Treveris in the dusk and at long last in the dark. I was alone.

As it happened, Theophilus, when I said farewell to her that day shortly after Easter, taking my eyes from her beautiful form as if looking away from the past, which is always ideal, and looking forward to some unknown, unformed, and thus, unattractive future, it was to say goodbye for the last time. Still, in some mysterious way, she remained with me—they both did.

Over the next few months, I sensed something shift in me due to the seed Ulfila and Luxilla had planted deep within my soul, their suggestions spoken in kindhearted affection.

Just try it. Fall into his loving care. Let God love you. Let God worry about all the others. What can it hurt? What else is there? Where else will you go?

Nowhere. That's what I had thought. But that's not what I wanted. Oh God, Theophilus, I wanted more!

I saw Ulfila's deep brown eyes. I saw Luxilla's tears and commitment.

Why not try it?

Why not? I thought.

Finally, after many weeks I did try it, Theophilus.

Throwing my hands up in exasperation, I surrendered. *What could it hurt?* I allowed God to dwell in the emptiness of my heart that had been vacant for so long. Into that place of nothingness, the nothingness of desire, of loneliness, of longing—for wisdom, for love, for meaning—the One came, and quietly something happened to me.

Over the days and weeks, Theophilus, something occurred that if pressed to put it into words I don't know if I'd be able to do it. And perhaps it's better left unsaid as it doesn't really matter and—as always—I still have my doubts.

But one thing I will say. I realized that to create is to suffer. To create is to die. Artists and poets have always said as much. I suppose that's why they're oftentimes so erratic and sad. It takes everything to make something. You must pour yourself into what you're creating. You must live it and love it. And in doing so, you become what you're creating, its limitations and all, so that it might become something beautiful. I thought that maybe, just maybe, that was like God.

In the end, I decided to ask for initiation. When I did, Athanasius was happy. So too were Macarius and Bishop Maximus. Philip said it was about time. I saw Timotheos look into the sky and thank God.

And so, in a quiet, private manner—unlike the usual initiations accomplished during the darkness of Easter's eve, with candles ablaze inside the basilica and white banners flapping in the wind outside—I was baptized and received into the holy, imperfect communion of the Church.

How glorious it felt when Athanasius prayed over me. Submerging me in living water in order to achieve my death and resurrection in the Christ, he solemnly spoke the words of initiation.

"I baptize you, Arnobius, in the name of the Father, and in the name of the Son, and in the name of the Holy Spirit."

I rose from the water a new man—the water dripping from my silver hair and eyebrows. I declared, "Amen," and quietly gave thanks. Grinning widely, my heart full of life, of joy, I knew I had finally found where I belonged. Was it perfect? Not at all. But it was better than what I had and where I had been.

Holding me by the shoulders Athanasius smiled and welcomed me home. Then he pulled me to him and embraced me.

Forty: Letters

336 to 337 A.D.

IT WAS ABOUT THAT TIME that a letter from the East surprised us in Treveris. In this letter from Alexander, the aged bishop of the New Rome, we received word of Arius' death.

The Eusebians had not ceased in their efforts to rid the world of the doctrines of Nicaea and those bishops who tenaciously held to them. Rather, not long after Athanasius had been exiled to Treveris, they plotted to hold another council—one that would cleverly, if not deviously, overturn the rulings of the former council. Eusebius of Nicomedia led the effort, supported by Theognis, Maris, Valens, and Ursacius, among others. Alexander of Constantinople vigorously fought against their conspiracy.

It was around that time that Arius returned from Alexandria to the New Rome, either of his own volition in order to join in the conciliar proceedings, as some say, or because Constantine recalled him for causing factional disputes in Alexandria. More than likely, his return was due to a combination of both. His arrival in Alexandria had indeed been the cause of an uproar.

Either way, Arius did return, and as the weeks of Eusebian plotting passed by he fell into line forming an essential part of the conspiracy against the Nicene Church and against Alexander, the Nicene bishop of the New Rome.

Alexander, for his part, resorted to every weapon in his fight against the Eusebians. First, he attempted to argue with them by means of dialectic, showing them from both the sacred oracles and logic how the Christ had to be truly one in nature with God the Father. The Eusebians, of course, refused to listen to his arguments. Therefore, reaching the point of exasperation, Alexander surrendered all hope in human persuasiveness and threw himself upon the mercy of the Divinity alone.

It was then that Arius gave false witness to Constantine. The emperor, sometimes gracious in matters of justice despite a countervailing tendency to suspicion and harshness, had agreed to an audience with Arius and his ever-present cohort, the priest Euzoius. In part, Constantine wished to hear his grievances, his side of the story regarding what had occurred in Alexandria. Otherwise, he wished to ascertain Arius' own beliefs. Thus, once he had patiently listened to the former, he had him explain the latter.

Arius affirmed that he held to the teachings of Nicaea. How he did this, I cannot say, for he brazenly continued to promote all the old formulas: that there was a time when the Christ was not, that he was a creature, and that he was not one in being with God the Father. Some say he couched his beliefs in terms of the divine scriptures. I cannot say. Nevertheless, Arius swore an oath, and generously, Constantine accepted his word as genuine.

Meanwhile, rioting that had originated in the great Hippodrome, tore the New Rome asunder. Two factions—one supporting Alexander and Nicaea and the other supporting Arius and the Eusebians—threw the whole city into confusion. Constantine was understandably frightened by where this factional fervor would end. He decisively moved to terminate it. As was so often the case in the past, his solution was simple and direct. He ordered the frail and aged Alexander to admit Arius into communion. Indeed, said Constantine, he *must* allow Arius to participate in the sacred rite on the following Sunday. This one move, he concluded, would lead to peace within the city, the Church, and the Empire.

Bishop Alexander, needless to say, was devastated. How could he possibly allow such a man to commune with the holy Church in receiving the sacred bread and wine? He could not. And so he would not.

Instead of announcing his resolution to the emperor, however, he quietly resolved to leave the matter to God. Accordingly, Alexander soberly turned to the One as his only refuge. He devoted himself piously to severe fasting and to a continuous regime of prayer. Shutting himself up in the church of Sacred Peace, that of Irene, he prostrated himself before the altar where the Creator becomes creation and wept his prayers for several days and several nights. There he begged that the true faith might be known. If Arius was right, he prayed, he asked that he himself might be taken to rest in the Lord. But if he held the truth, as he fervently believed, then he asked that Arius might suffer the punishment due to his wrongheaded, impious doctrine and stubborn refusal to change course.

Finally Saturday came. The following day Arius would be admitted to communion by force of the emperor. Arius, confident all would be well, made his usual rounds that day to all the women who supported him in swarms like flies gathered around a pile of animal refuse. It was then, when he was on his way to visit the matriarch of a family that had been recently elevated to the senatorial class, that something happened to put an end to all his plans.

Arius was crossing the Forum of Constantine. He had just passed through the massive southern gate and was heading northward in the direction of the new Senate House. As he walked along passing by the purple Column of Constantine, he encountered many of his supporters going about their own business. Like a gladiator famous for his courageous and clever moves or a champion chariot racer in the Hippodrome, he waved hello to this side and that, a fantastic grin stretched across his narrow face and along the length of his well-sculpted chin. Then, according to Alexander's letter, something quite inexplicable occurred.

What was it? Some say it was a spasm of conscience; some a nasty word from the rival faction; some an attack of the heart; and some declared that it was magic, pronouncing that it happened by means of another severed limb, this time the charred, withered foot of an Arabian man. I cannot say, Theophilus. Nonetheless, what followed was real enough.

Desperately, Arius asked pardon of the matron with whom he was engaged, and embarrassingly he begged of her directions to the nearest public toilet.

"There!" she said, pointing, noticing his quite sudden and evident distress.

Arius dashed off without another word, entered, and sat down to relieve himself.

It was the last anyone saw of him alive. The poor man never emerged from the latrine. Rather, sometime later, after a horrendous stench arose to cloud over the immediate vicinity, someone discovered him dead.

What happened? You inquire as though the fame of this did not spread from one mouth to another throughout the length and width of the Empire. It appears Arius fainted right on the spot. After he had emptied his bowels, he blacked out, fell over, and somehow his insides hemorrhaged. It was as though his intestines had liquefied. When Athanasius read the letter aloud to us, I nearly wretched with disgust for it all. *Portions of his spleen and liver were brought off in the effusion of blood that followed, so that he died immediately.*

So it was. Arius was dead. The one man who had caused so much anguish to Constantine and the Empire and to Athanasius and the Church was gone.

At letter's end, Athanasius lowered the scroll and quietly bowed his head. One might have expected otherwise from another man. But not from him, Theophilus. No, he didn't gloat over Arius' demise. Instead, he prayed for the man, begging that God would forgive him his blasphemy and bring him, like all men, to final restoration.

I too hoped the best for Arius, thinking that God surely must have prepared a way for him who had denied the one, divinely revealed way in the Homoousion.

Some, Theophilus, have compared Arius to Judas. They have suggested that both men came to a common end for betraying their Lord, one hanging in the Field of Blood outside Jerusalem and one dissolving in a public latrine in the New Rome. For my part, I cannot agree—for *merciful is the Lord,* declare the oracles.

In relation to more practical matters, that is, what Arius' death would mean for Athanasius and the rest of the Church, it was the subject of much conversation over the following weeks and months. On many occasions, Athanasius met with Bishop Maximus and with the younger Constantine in order to discuss how best to proceed in ensuring the council of Nicaea's place in the teaching of the Church now that Arius was gone.

As for me, I was not privy to those meetings. And honestly, Theophilus, I'm happy I was not, for during that time, I wanted nothing more of controversy. For me, all the battling had long been too much. Rather, I simply wished to know and follow the one God I had come to trust.

Life moved forward as it usually does over the next months and along the course of the year following Arius' death, until finally, nearly a year later, I received correspondence that may have once again shifted the direction of my own life. Sometime around Easter, I received a letter from the emperor Constantine. It began, *Constantine Maximus Augustus to Arnobius of Carthage,* and continued as follows:

> *I write at the commencement of a new campaign against Rome's ever-lasting foe, Persia. You may wonder, as I know you must, given your proclivity to skepticism, why I have lunged out against this eastern neighbor when relations have been relatively quiet ever since Galerius routed them so many years ago. I'll tell you.*

First, know that it distresses me to wage war at my old age when I should be enjoying the fruit of the labors achieved over the past thirty years, the victories wrought by the Divinity. I would not do so but for King Sarpon's treachery.

Treachery, you may wonder. Indeed. For in Persia, there are a great number of believers in the Christ. Instead of treating them well as he ought, as a fair and just ruler whose power comes from God, the tyrant has persecuted our brothers in the name of their unholy god, that deity of fire, that demon who doubtlessly rules through Sarpon from the fiery pit of Hell.

Therefore, as with all those who fought against God in the past, from the Pharaoh of old, to Goliath, the champion of the Philistines, to Galerius and others more recently, the strong arm of God must work to chastise and correct and bring justice in the place of wrong. Thus, Arnobius, the war I wage.

I write to you from within the most splendid tent I've ever possessed, and, dare I say, the most sacred tent made for me by the best of tent makers. It's my new field tent cut in the form of a magnificent church. When the bishops riding to war with me perform the holy rites, they do so in my tent on an altar consecrated for that very purpose made of the finest olive wood and encrusted with jewels.

I tell you this, Arnobius, not to impress you—for I am not foolish enough to think that such would move you—but so that you may know the underlying motivation for this campaign. In earnest, it is to unify the whole world stretching east and west under the one God.

Whereas I once held out my hand in brotherhood to the king of Persia, I'm no longer able to do so. Consequently, in the name of the one God, I ride against him. Like the others, he will fall as the One provides. When he does, there will at last be peace and unity; there will be one government in the service of man, and one religion in the service of God. So be it.

That was it. As my eyes drew to the bottom of the missive and to the day appended there, I came quite suddenly to the end of Constantine's letter. And though for a moment I felt let down—for there was no query as to my own well-being or any personal greeting—it was only for a moment. Soon I found that a smile enveloped my mouth quite beyond my control as I thought about

Constantine, my old friend, in great spirits pursuing the one mission which had captivated him so long ago and which still drove him onwards like one of the Furies.

As I rolled the scroll, I laughed. How absurd, I thought, a tent in the form of a church! Yet the more I reflected on it, the more I believed the tent suited his mission and the man himself. After all, he was a churchman—albeit one of a special kind. As he himself had asserted so many times, he was the bishop of external affairs. Now he was off to bring a greater portion of the world into the Church. Though perhaps he was wrong in the manner of his proceeding—of that, I couldn't say, Theophilus—it was nevertheless his own unique way.

A few days later, I received another letter from Constantine. *Arnobius*, this one began in an entirely different manner and tone:

> *You can't possibly enjoy life in Treveris. I know you! And when I first heard of it, I was surprised. But knowing what a man Athanasius is and how you might prefer the company of such a one to the savage tradesmanship of Carthage, I relented in my disbelief.*

True, I thought. How well Constantine knew me. Going on, he wrote:

> *Still, my friend, there are more men in the world, and certainly you have more than one friend. Let me be plain with you. I want you to return to the East and join me in our campaign against the Persians. Come help me complete the divine mission!*
>
> *You may wonder what you might do for me at this late stage in your life and during my own even later stage, no doubt! But remember, we are Roman. Therefore, whether young or old, in health or not, when duty calls, we respond. This is what I wish: as of old, I'd like you to be my procurer. And, I might add, it would be pleasant to speak of philosophy once again. Thus, aside from procuring goods for the army, you'll be my chief philosopher.*
>
> *If you please—and understand I ask as your friend and do not bid you as emperor—join us here in Nicomedia. Soon we ride eastward toward the great Euphrates and Tigris rivers where Sarpon will pay for his insolence and blasphemy against the One.*
>
> *Consider it and respond with all dispatch so that I may soon know.*

I must not lie, Theophilus. When I finished reading the letter, I longed to be by Constantine's side. In an instant, everything negative was gone. What memories I possessed—of our friendship and of our love for one another—came to the fore of my mind. All those disagreements we had had along with his monstrous behavior diminished in importance as I recalled the good of our friendship. I wanted to go. I would, I thought. I'd travel east and join him, and in time to come, I'd grow old and die near to him.

But the sentiment didn't last. Although I missed him, I soon realized my feeling was as Luxilla had suggested of our love. My longing was more for the past than it was for the present.

The truth is I hardly knew him any longer. Perhaps I knew the form of his soul, his urges, his desires, and the needs that propelled him forward, but I didn't know him as he was now. The man I yearned for was the one I had known before the mission had overtaken him, the *daemon* that drove him to a kind of mania, a manic obsession. I desired the old Constantine, son of Constantius Chlorus, soldier by the side of Diocletian thundering along the road into Alexandria in order to squash Lucius Domitius Domitianus. I desired the Constantine I had met at the lecture of Iamblichus, the one who searched for the true name of the One until, years later, it was revealed to him on a field outside Treveris of Gaul. I desired my old friend. But that one, Theophilus, was dead. And truth be told, I was too, however much the ghosts remained.

Therefore, after reflecting on this, I responded briefly. No, I wrote, I would not ride east to join him. I was too old to be chasing around in such a manner, too old to race into war—as if I'd *ever* been up for that. No dear friend, all I want is to live and die quietly in the service of God.

Still, I told him, I desired to know how things fared. I presumed he would meet with great success, I said. I wished him well.

The days passed by until it was Easter. Fifty days later, it was Pentecost, that day of all days when we celebrate the descent of the Holy Spirit upon the apostles. In all that time, I received no other communication from Constantine, and consequently I grew anxious to hear from him again. Yet as the days passed by, I came to recognize that he might not write at all. I had rejected him, I realized. I could imagine him interpreting my refusal to join him as an unequivocal personal betrayal. That's the way he was. Or that's the way he had come to be.

Still—this was my hope—I assumed the absence of any communication was merely due to the reality of his campaign against the Persians. Now, I judged, he was far from any Roman city. He was deep within Persia chasing Sarpon to his end. I wondered whether he would he string him up as the Persians had done to Valerian decades before, or grant him mercy. I prayed the latter. I wondered how long it would take to win. Would he have to chase Sarpon to the end of the world as Alexander had done with Darius?

Soon, given the lack of any correspondence, my thoughts of victory turned to anxiety about defeat. What if Sarpon instead conquered him and the Roman legions? What if Constantine in his old age and after all he had accomplished was strung up and drained of blood? My thoughts grew dim. I imagined Persian men mocking him, abusing his corpse, and skinning him in order display his flesh in the temple of their god, where his skin would slowly dry before the altar of fire.

I prayed. Fervently I beseeched God for his safety, for victory, that the nightmare scenario I had imagined would prove false.

A month or so after Pentecost there was finally another letter. This time, however, it was from Constantine's master of horse rather than the emperor himself.

Desperately, I unrolled it.

I read.

As I did, as I flew down the script of the letter word by word, tears welled up in my eyes.

The news was bad. It was final.

Constantine was dead.

I felt shocked. I should not have been, but I was. Despite his years, I had come to believe he would prove victorious. He was Constantine; he had always won. Yet this time, he had not.

I wept.

There he lay, far away from me, never to open his eyes, never to speak, never to fight again for the one goal for which he had heroically given his life.

What happened? I will tell you. In short, Constantine never fought Sarpon. Instead, soon after his prior letter in which he had invited me to join him in the East, Constantine fell ill. At first, it was a simple and harmless body ache. Quite soon, however, the ache morphed into disease. At the time, he was in Helenopolis in Asia. Although he wished nothing more than to move on toward Persia in order to pursue the campaign against Sarpon, his advisors vehemently disagreed and insisted he return to Nicomedia in order to receive the best of care from the best of the Empire's physicians. He finally capitulated to their advice, and giving into their demands, he made his way back to Nicomedia. But the move didn't help.

As the feast of Pentecost approached, the emperor continued to deteriorate, so much so, indeed, that finally he asked for the sacrament of initiation. You seem surprised, Theophilus, at this fact—that Constantine had never been baptized. I understand. But it's true. Upon his request, Eusebius obliged—*the* Eusebius, partisan of Arius against Athanasius and bishop of the city where Constantine lay dying. Eusebius baptized the emperor, and so Constantine was happily enrolled into the ranks of those who will never die.

Yet then he died.

On Pentecost, shortly after the noon hour, my friend breathed his last while the Spirit of God came to rest upon thousands and thousands of Christians throughout the Empire and the whole world.

As I read of it in Treveris of Gaul that day, I cried. Mixed with sorrow, however, were tears of joy. True, his corpse lay dead, I thought, yet his soul was alive. My friend, the immortal Constantine, had ascended unto the realm of the immortal God.

I see his ascent now just as it's depicted on recent imperial coins struck to commemorate his death. I suppose you've seen them, Theophilus. There is Constantine, the holy emperor, rising upon the wings of a chariot pulled by four white stallions into the light of the everlasting sun.

The Cell in Tabennisi

Night

Theophilus: IT HAD NOW GROWN DARK outside.

Inside and between us was a single lamp lit hours before, the sole light driving away the darkness. Light and shadows flickered upon the walls.

Now that Arnobius had come to the end of his story, I noticed that a certain peace had descended upon the features of his face. Still, the story was not yet complete, Abba. Therefore, I pressed on, though both of us were exhausted at the end of this very long day.

"Arnobius," I queried, "what happened to you and Athanasius after Constantine died?"

Quite to the point, he disclosed, "We were free to leave Treveris."

"Just like that?"

He nodded. "The younger Constantine signed a letter giving him safe passage and official reentry into Alexandria."

"But what of his brother Constantius?" I asked. "Wasn't Constantine interfering in his jurisdiction?"

"Strictly speaking he was. But the younger Constantine didn't see it that way. Rather, as he always had, he viewed Athanasius' exile as void of all legal force. Therefore, relying upon his imperial ally, a one that was willing to use force against his younger brother, Athanasius traveled eastward."

"Did you travel with him?"

"No," said Arnobius. "For once I said no."

"What, then, did you do?"

"I did what I had originally planned to do. When we reached Augusta Praetoria, I bade Athanasius and the others farewell and turned south toward Sicily. From there, I sailed on to Africa and came at last to Carthage."

"Were you there for long?"

"For just a few years," he answered.

"What happened?"

Arnobius considered the question. "Ultimately I realized I'd become inured to family affairs. I'd lost all appetite for trading and making money. But more, Mother died."

"I'm sorry," I offered. "How old was she?"

"Seventy-five." Arnobius smiled. "She died in peace, secure."

"A believer?"

"No, but a good and decent woman."

At that, silence fell between the two of us. I could see that Arnobius had tired of our conversation and wished to go off to pray and sleep. It was late. Still, we were not quite finished.

"What did you do next?" I asked.

"I sailed to Alexandria to be with Athanasius. My hope was to study at the Catechetical School, and, if providence so led, I wished to end up here in the monastery."

"So it has happened."

"It has," he allowed, "but in a way I would have never desired."

"How so?"

"I mean the violence."

"Ah," I acknowledged, "the Lenten Disturbance."

He stretched forward. "One night last year, during the holy season of Lent, Constantius' men burst into the church of Theonas as we were singing the evening prayers. They galloped in on horseback, wielding weapons against men and women who had nothing more than empty hands extended in prayer to God."

"What happened next?"

"The prefect Philagrius ordered his men from behind. 'Forward!' he cried. 'After the bishop, men!' We at the front soon knew how serious it was. Athanasius' life was in peril. And so without delay, a group of monks surrounded the bishop and spirited him away through a door behind the great altar."

"What did you do?"

"We ran. And as we fled, leaving the violence behind, the imposter Gregory of Cappadocia was cowering in some dark corner of the church, afraid to show himself in the light. We passed through several dark streets and came to the house of a wealthy man who had remained faithful to Athanasius during his first exile."

"And afterwards?"

"We went into hiding for a month."

"Why didn't you leave Alexandria?"

"Athanasius refused."

"Why?"

"He believed it was his duty to remain."

"But eventually you departed from the city?"

"Yes. We fled just after Easter."

"To Rome?" I asked.

"No."

"But isn't that where he is now?"

"What I meant to say is that I didn't go."

"Why not?"

"I didn't care to. I'd had enough of running, enough of conflict."

I nodded.

"Consequently," he explained, "when they sailed to Sicily, I begged off. I told Athanasius that I was far too old, that I could take no more. I told him I wished to head south."

"Did he understand?"

"He did and he blessed me."

With that, Abba, and with a few more words, I understood how Arnobius had come to Tabennisi. At first, he visited Anthony's community in the Nitrian desert. He lived there for a few weeks, praying and working with them. But, he said, he had always had it in mind to go on, to sail up the Nile to Tabennisi where he had first known the love of God. So he did.

"Are you happy now that you're here?" I asked him, but it was more for me.

He didn't answer.

"I mean have you found what you were looking for?"

He smiled. "Is there ever a final answer to that question, Theophilus?"

I couldn't say, Abba.

"Let's go pray and sleep," he suggested, yawning.

I consented.

Finally, at the end of that long day and the end of his long tale about the emperor and the bishop, Arnobius grew quiet as he got up to go to his own cell. I knew at once that the silence would not be broken again. Arnobius had come to the end of his story, and now he wanted nothing more than to rest in the quiet of the desert.

As he left, I stared at the lamp sitting on the small wooden table beside me. When he was gone, I followed its light to the mud brick wall next to where he had been sitting only moments before. The dancing shadows and flickering light mesmerized me. The rest of my cell was darkness.

ADDENDUM OF THEOPHILUS
For Abba Pachomius

Abba—I must leave the narrative at that, and still, to be faithful to your initial commission, I must tell you what has happened since then, though I bequeath the rest of the story to some other author whom, I trust, will be sponsored by some other patron, even as you have sponsored me.

I wish I could report that all has ended well. But as you know, Abba, matters are still uncertain, even as they were when the Eusebians wickedly conspired to banish Athanasius from Alexandria by means of the false council of Tyre and their lies afterwards in the New Rome.

Following Constantius' attack in the church of Theonas by means of his henchman Philagrius, Gregory of Cappadocia was installed as an imposter bishop in the ancient See of Mark. Fortunately, the people of Alexandria are convinced of this, that is, that he is a fake, a usurper. Of this I can assure you, Abba, for while I was there researching into these matters, many told me as much.

As for Athanasius, he has discovered a solid ally in the bishop of Rome. He—Julius is his name—strongly favors the Homoousion.

Perhaps in the future, some man will tell the remainder of the story of this struggle against the Eusebians and their pernicious doctrines. However that may be, I trust all will turn out in favor of the truth. If not, I believe it will only be a temporary crisis as it was when the pagan emperors persecuted the Church—for our Lord promised to be with us until the end of the age.

May God be with you, Abba Pachomius, and the rest at the monastery, and may God bless Arnobius of Carthage until that final day.

Sources and Gratitude

Thanks so much for reading *The One, the Many*!

This work of historical fiction rests upon the labor of many authors who wrote from the days of Constantine and Athanasius to our own time.

The earliest of the authors are the anonymous chroniclers who wrote the *Festal Index* and the *Historia Acephala*. Gelasius of Caesarea (although none of his work is extant), Lactantius, Eusebius of Caesarea, Rufinus of Aquileia, and Athanasius of Alexandria himself who composed many accounts of what happened, all wrote in the fourth century and influenced later histories. As for the various letters and speeches such as those of Constantine, some are from contemporary documents and some from later histories. A few sources were discovered only recently, such as the letter of the monk Callistus to Apa Paieou and Apa Patabeit (London Papyrus 1914). Other minor though contemporary authors are Lucifer of Caralis, Hilary of Poitiers, Gregory of Nazianzus, Jerome, Cyril of Alexandria, and Epiphanius of Salamis.

Aside from the earlier Rufinus and Gelasius, ecclesiastical histories include those of the fifth century historians Sulpicius Severus, Socrates Scholasticus, Theodoret, and Sozomen, as well as a summary of Philostorgius (also fifth century) found in the work of Photius, the ninth century patriarch of Constantinople (perhaps based on a lost Homoian historian). Later there is Severus Al' Ashmunein's tenth century history of the patriarchs of the Coptic Church.

Although these chroniclers have been gone now for ages, I give them my profound gratitude, for without their work we'd be in the dark about this most pivotal event and period in history. For better or worse, both Constantine and Athanasius irrevocably changed their world. Next to Jesus and Paul, they are the two most responsible for the *fact* of Christianity, its contents, form, and practice—whatever good and whatever ill it has caused through time and however much it is in decline in many corners of the world today.

I also thank the many scholars who have worked to distill all the primary sources into a more reliable account of what likely happened. There are the obvious ones such as the academics Timothy Barnes, Richard Hanson, A.H.M Jones, Duane W.H. Arnold, Rowan Williams, and Archibald Robertson (of Nicene and Post-Nicene Fathers fame). I should also mention the more popular and exciting Richard Rubenstein—although I disagree with many of his more sensationalist conclusions. Aside from these, there are less obvious writers, such as Iris Habib el Masri who wrote *The Story of the Copts* (1978). This is a book I received from the kind hands of Bishop Antonius Markos when I was in Nairobi, Kenya, many years ago and happened to attend the divine liturgy at St. Marks Orthodox Church on Ngong Road (a road made famous by Isak Denison's *Out of Africa*). Otherwise, there are many devotional books from the life-of-the-saints genre that are mostly pious and pro-Athanasius.

Please go to www.timjyoung.com to see a full listing of both primary and secondary authors and titles. While I cannot promise they all make for exiting reads (especially some of the modern academic accounts through which I had to slog aided by cup after white porcelain cup of double espresso), each one is essential to a full understanding of the period in terms of influential characters, ideas, and happenings.

I have attempted to remain faithful to a plausible and fair account of what occurred given the sources we have, though doubtlessly there will be some who dislike or disagree with my presentation. Aside from the professed author Theophilus, the only major fictional character is Arnobius of Carthage (including, of course, his family and various loves). That said, even he is based upon a nameless man who, according to the *Ecclesiastical History* of Sozomen, interpreted for Constantine at the Council of Nicaea. There Sozomen tells us, "The emperor pronounced his this discourse [at Nicaea] in Latin, and the interpretation [in Greek] was supplied by one at his side."

There's much more on my website, www.timjyoung.com.

Presently I am working on a history of the origins, nature, and practice of ancient Greek (and Roman) happiness and human flourishing and a companion guidebook should one wish to get his or her hands dirty with the very messy business of happiness. Please check my website for more information. Both should be out in late spring to early summer 2014.

On a more commercial note, I truly appreciate every tweet, Facebook like, and review on your own blog, on Amazon.com, and otherwise (what new app or site is there now?!), and of course your kind recommendations of my novel and other works to all your friends, family, and acquaintances.

Thanks to Gayle and my family and all who read manuscripts along the way. And thanks again for reading *The One, the Many*!

Tim J. Young
January 2014—Sugar Land, Texas

About the Author

After studying undergraduate history and theology for a master's degree in graduate school, Tim J. Young taught for many years and just as many subjects before turning to writing full-time. He now lives in Sugar Land, Texas, with his wife and four children. Although they've considered adding a dog and a cat to the mix, they've never managed more than a hamster, a few zebra finches, a wild lizard, a Venus flytrap, and several versions of a red beta fish (all named Tomato).

Tim is presently working on a history of the origins, nature, and practice of ancient Greek (and Roman) happiness and human flourishing. The history will have a companion guidebook exploring the ways Greek (and Roman) thinking about happiness can help us today.

Please visit Tim's website, www.timjyoung.com, in order to see what he's working on or just to drop him a note.

www.ingramcontent.com/pod-product-compliance
Lightning Source LLC
Chambersburg PA
CBHW020249030726
47499CB00001B/119